ONCE THE CLOUDS HAVE GONE

What Reviewers Say About KE Payne's Work

Because of Her
"A must-read."—*Lesbian Fiction Reviews*

365 Days
"*One of the most real books I've ever read. It frequently made me giggle out loud to myself while muttering, 'OMG, RIGHT?'*"
—AfterEllen.com

"Payne captures Clemmie's voice—an engaging blend of teenage angst and saucy self-assurance—with full-throated style."—Richard Labonte, *Book Marks*

me@you.com
"*A fast-paced read [that] I found hard to put down.*"—C-Spot Reviews

"*A wonderful, thought-provoking novel of a teenager discovering who she truly is.*"—Fresh Fiction

Another 365 Days
"Funny, engaging, and accessible."—*Kirkus Reviews*

The Road to Her
"A wonderful, heart-warming story of love, unrequited love, betrayal, self discovery and coming out."—*Terry's Lesfic Reviews*

Visit us at www.boldstrokesbooks.com

By the Author

365 Days

me@you.com

Another 365 Days

The Road to Her

Because of Her

Once the Clouds Have Gone

ONCE THE CLOUDS HAVE GONE

by

KE Payne

2014

ISBN 13: 978-1-62639-202-1

This Trade Paperback Original Is Published By
Bold Strokes Books, Inc.
P.O. Box 249
Valley Falls, NY 12185

First Edition: October 2014

CREDITS
Editor: Ruth Sternglantz
Production Design: Susan Ramundo
Cover Design By Sheri (graphicartist2020@hotmail.com)

Acknowledgments

My sincere thanks to Ruth Sternglantz, Stacia Seaman, and Cindy Cresap for their continued help and advice. To Sheri for another fantastic and beautiful cover, and to each and every other member of the Bold Strokes Books team who make publishing my books such a pain-free journey. Thank you all.

Thanks, as always, to Sarah Martin for her beta-reading skills, and to Mrs D for always being just an e-mail away if I need someone to lean on.

BJ—you're the best. Thanks for always being there, and for putting up with all the grumbling when it comes around to grumbling time. Without your love and support, none of this would ever be possible.

Finally, a massive thank you to all the readers who continue to buy my books, and who take the time to contact me. I truly appreciate every e-mail, Facebook comment, and Tweet that you send me. Your continued support is immensely important to me—thank you all so much.

CHAPTER ONE

The paint on the door was olive green. That was different. The last time she'd stood in front of it, just as she was now, it had been dark brown. Russet, her father had called it, rather than just plain brown. Tag Grainger lightly ran her fingers over the bobbled wood of the cafe's door frame and smiled wistfully. Her father had always been a stickler for those finer details. Her eye fell to a small crack in the bottom corner of one of the door's windows and she gave a quick blink, remembering in an instant that she had caused the crack so many years before. A cup thrown. Or had it been a plate? Tag couldn't bring *those* finer details to her mind at that moment, but did it really matter now? It wasn't important any more, even if it must have been important to her at the time.

"Excuse me."

Tag swivelled round.

"Are you arriving or just leaving?" The elderly man standing behind her lifted his chin to the door.

"Arriving." Tag swallowed. "Sorry. Please. After you." She pulled the door open and stood to one side, allowing the man to pass, acknowledging his thanks with a brief nod.

Her gaze was drawn back to the broken window frame. So they could repaint the door but not replace a broken piece of glass after all this time? Sounded about right. With a final longing glance out over the car park, towards the sanctuary of her car, Tag followed the man into the cafe and closed the door behind her.

Her past rushed to greet her as the door clicked shut, trapping her inside. Her childhood, locked away for the last nine years, clambered about her, vying for her attention, pulling her by the hand to revisit past sights and smells. Tag looked about her. Although the cafe looked slightly different now, it smelled the same as it always had done: an unmistakable odour of fresh coffee and baking, mixed in with the faint whiff of cleaning fluids and the heady smell of musty age that still clung stubbornly to the walls.

"What can I get you?" A girl from behind the counter called over to Tag.

Tag looked up. The elderly man was already seated, his newspaper spread out on the table in front of him. Tag approached the counter. Tiredness dragged at her eyes, thanks to a combination of the nightmare drive up from Glasgow that morning, following a sleepless night in her charm-free motel in the heart of the city, tossing and turning over her thoughts until the small hours. The endless traffic passing by her window the entire night had done little to help her insomnia either.

"Cappuccino." Tag paused. "Can you make it decaffeinated, please?"

The girl pulled a mug down from a stack behind her. "We don't do decaffeinated, I'm afraid."

"No decaffeinated coffees?"

"'Fraid not."

"Every cafe offers decaf, don't they?" Tiredness inflamed Tag's irritability. Perhaps an espresso might be a better option…

"In the city, maybe." The girl smiled. "In a small town like Balfour?" She lifted her arms out. "You're kind of lucky your only options aren't just teabags and Nescafe instant." She laughed.

Tag stared at her. The girl was a comedian.

"Then I'll have a cappuccino," Tag said. "Make it a large one."

"With pleasure." The girl placed the mug into the coffee machine. "Anything else?"

Right on cue, Tag's stomach rumbled, reminding her that it had been too long since she'd had breakfast.

An hour ago she'd been on the familiar road that wound its way all the way up to Balfour, and even though Tag hadn't driven along it in nearly a decade, she'd remembered every bend, every landmark, and every viewpoint as she'd slammed her rented car into fifth and floored the accelerator, enjoying the freedom of the road and the lack of other cars which she'd left far behind her in Glasgow. That was what driving in Scotland was all about, she'd thought. Freedom, space. No one else around to hold her up as the scenery had scudded past her, the road hugging the lochside, a dense forest of pine trees running alongside it. The occasional tantalizing glimpse of a murky-green loch, its surface foaming in the strong wind that was relentlessly battering it, reminding Tag of past journeys.

Journeys she'd thought she'd probably never see again.

Finally the trees had cleared and then to her left had been water as far as the eye could see. Tag had turned her head slightly, appreciating the beauty of it as she drove on. She'd forgotten how much she'd missed the bleakness of the loch in winter and the arresting sight of the snow-capped mountains dotted around them. Her home in Liverpool was okay, but for sheer exhilaration there was nothing quite like being in amongst such imposing and majestic scenery.

"Sandwich? Shortbread?" The girl's voice filtered through to Tag. "All freshly made here on-site."

Just as her mother used to do.

Tag snapped her head up, expecting to see her mother. Instead, a stranger stared back at her.

"Shortbread. Thanks." Tag's stomach gave her another nudge of hunger, but this time mixed in with the nausea caused by finally being back in the very same cafe she'd stormed from nine years before, vowing never to return.

This was really happening. Tag was back in her childhood town, and now it was really starting to freak her out. All the while she'd been stuck in traffic, and when she'd been so wrapped up in the novelty of seeing the lochs again, she'd managed to stem the fear. But now, standing in the cafe that her parents used to own, her palms were starting to sweat and an irrational feeling of panic threatened to engulf her. The demons of her past nipped at her, blinding her.

"You okay?" The girl dipped her head. "You want to grab a seat and I'll bring these over when they're ready?"

Tag had been staring blankly. The girl must think she was crazy.

"Cheers." Tag walked numbly to a seat by the window, a low hum of conversation from the other customers washing around her. She sank into her chair and stared out. Her father was dead. Tag bunched her fists, watching as her knuckles whitened slightly, then slowly released her grip. She hadn't cried since she heard the news. She'd cried for days when her mother had died thirteen years before, but then she'd just been a teenager. Now? In adulthood, was she really that detached from her emotions that she found it impossible to grieve for him? Even when her father's solicitor had tracked her down and called her to tell her, she'd hung up, picked up the remote control from where she'd left it, flicked the TV channel over, and carried on watching as if nothing had changed.

"One cappuccino, one shortbread."

A shadow fell across the table. Tag glanced up, then sat back further in her chair as the girl placed them both on the table, smiled and retreated. Tag followed her progress back to the counter. Cafe servers, she figured, didn't have to have any conversation in them. Neither did their customers. She spooned sugar into her coffee, then wetted her finger, dabbed some loose sugar from the top of her shortbread, then licked it off.

Thinking about her father had clicked her anxiety up a notch again. As a distraction, Tag focused her attention on the girl. She was about the same age as Tag, possibly slightly younger, but not much. Slimmer, too, but again, not much. Tag looked down at her shortbread, smiled, then back up to the girl. She was singing softly to herself, and although Tag couldn't hear her over the hubbub in the cafe, she could see her lips moving as she busied herself behind the counter. Her face, now that she was singing, was more animated and showed, Tag thought as she sipped at her coffee, more of her character than she had seen just before. Tag's mood mellowed again.

The girl had a nice face. Expressive and open. It was little wonder, Tag reflected, that her father had employed someone like that. The friendly face of the cafe.

Dad.

The low hum of conversation returned to her ears as she turned away from the girl and stared, unblinking, out of the window. Images of her parents danced on the edge of her subconscious as snapshots from her childhood played out in her head, intermingled with more recent images of just her father. They lasted only seconds before they drifted from her mind again.

Tag fixed her eyes on the table, panic rising in her throat again. Her mother returned to her, this time standing in a park in summer. Which park? The one in Balfour? Or somewhere else? Tag couldn't tell. Her mother was wearing a blue dress—the one she'd always said was her favourite. Tag shook her head, chasing the image away. Remembering her parents now wasn't going to change a thing.

Tag pulled her phone out from her jacket pocket. A distraction. That's what she needed. Anything to quell the next panic attack that was just one more thought away. She peered at her contacts, needing to talk to someone. Anyone who'd tell her everything was going to be okay. But who? Anna? She was nothing to Anna now. Why would she want Tag calling her up, pouring her heart out? Tag scrolled down the list in her phone. There was no one else she felt she could ring. They were acquaintances, not friends. The result, Tag thought as she put her phone back into her pocket, of spending your life acting like you don't need anyone's help.

She was alone, she knew that. Just like always. And, like always, she'd deal with this on her own. Tag gazed down into her coffee, and then, unthinking, pulled out her wallet and the familiar battered photo from inside it. She looked down at the photo, cracked and dog-eared from years of being stuffed in and out of her wallet, and studied the faces staring back at her.

Yep. Alone.

Drinking back her coffee, Tag pushed her shortbread away, uneaten, and stood. She placed the photo back in her wallet and walked to the counter.

"All okay?" The girl's eyes flitted to Tag's table, to the uneaten shortbread, then back to Tag.

"Fine." Tag checked herself. Her server didn't deserve rudeness. "Thanks." She opened her wallet again, tucking the photo further inside as she did so, and thumbed a note out.

"So, one cappuccino, one shortbread." The girl ran her finger down her menu. "That's four eighty-five, please."

"How much?" Tag had misheard, surely.

"Four pounds and eighty-five pence. Thanks." The girl held out her hand.

"For a coffee and a biscuit? How did you get that?" Tag frowned up at the drinks menu on a board behind the counter.

"Two eighty-five for the cappuccino. Large. And two pounds for the home-made shortbread." She emphasized the *home-made* part, as if to drive her point home.

Tag lifted a brow. "Wow. Okay. Bit steep"—she glanced at the name badge on the girl's polo shirt—"uh…Freddie." Tag placed a five-pound note on the counter.

Freddie's eyes flicked down to her name badge then immediately back to Tag. "Our regular customers would disagree." Freddie swept the note from the counter. "They appreciate good quality home-baking."

Tag's eyes met hers. Freddie's slow blink and continued stare made Tag's neck go hot, even though she was determined not to break the stare first.

"Fifteen pence." Tag held out her hand.

"I'm sorry?"

"My change."

Finally, to Tag's relief, Freddie turned away. She opened the till, scooped the change from it, and dropped it into Tag's still outstretched palm.

"Thank you." Tag stuffed the two coins into her trouser pocket.

"Pleasure."

Tag strode from the counter without another word, pulled the door open, and stepped outside. Four eighty-five! Was that her father's doing? Hiking up prices in what was, frankly, just a two-bit cafe in the middle of nowhere?

Tag dragged in a lungful of air. The thought of her father brought her reason for being back in Balfour crashing back to her. She pulled her car keys from her pocket, then looked at her watch. Tag swallowed down the coffee that was threatening to rise as hot acid back into her throat. Nearly midday. Time was creeping on, which meant that in just under three hours she would be at her father's funeral.

Then the demons really would come back out to play.

CHAPTER TWO

It was like time had stood still when Tag drove down from the cafe and along the high street of her old town. Okay, the shops had changed, but the basis of Balfour was still there. She named the old shops as she passed them: Gordon's the Butchers, now a haberdashery; Wendy McKay's hair salon, now a bike-hire shop; the sweet shop that she and Blair used to visit each Saturday morning, now a violin repair workshop.

"A violin repair shop?" she said aloud as she slowly drove past it. "Why the fuck does Balfour need a violin repair shop?" She glowered at it as she drove past, as if to reinforce her point.

Turning left off the main street, Tag glanced down at the address of the B & B she'd booked into. Even that was new to her. She counted down the houses, past the small fountain set into a wall, until she reached the fifth house, a large Edwardian granite-stoned property set back from the road. Tag pulled up outside and looked up. Four Winds Bed and Breakfast.

She got out of the car and retrieved her suitcase from the boot, then walked up the two small steps to the front door and rang the bell. After a few moments a short woman with salt-and-pepper hair opened the door.

"Ms. Grainger?" she asked pleasantly.

Tag nodded her response. The woman opened the door wider and ushered her in.

Tag automatically wiped her feet on a mat in a footwell just inside the door.

"I'm Connie Booth." Connie closed the door behind them. "Welcome to Balfour. Did you have a good journey up here?"

"Once I'd shaken off Glasgow, yes." Tag stood in the hallway and looked around. Twee pictures of Balfour looked back at her. Yes, there was even some tartan too. She smiled inwardly. Such a cliché.

"You've come straight from Glasgow?"

"Mm." A smile. Tag was tired. It was the best she could come up with right then.

Signalling her to follow, Connie took Tag to her room, tucked away towards the back of the house.

"Here we are." Connie swept into the room. She straightened the blanket on the small single bed and turned to face Tag.

Tag scanned around her. Nice. Small, but nice. It'd do.

"You here for the walking?" Connie nodded towards Tag's walking trousers and boots. "Planning on tackling our big brute?"

Tag dipped her head and looked out of the window. The sun was just disappearing round the side of Ben Crathie, the mountain that stood guard over the town. "No, no walking," she said vaguely.

"Just having a few days R & R, then?" Connie returned to the door.

"Something like that," Tag replied. Nope, she still didn't want to engage Connie in conversation.

"If there's anything you need," Connie said, opening the door, "just come and find me or my husband."

"I will," Tag said, adding, "thanks."

"I've laid out a tray for you." Connie looked at something just over Tag's shoulder. Tag turned and looked too. Well, it seemed polite to. "Tea, coffee, snack. The usual."

"Thank you," Tag said again. *Take the hint, Connie.*

"Well I'll leave you in peace," Connie said "Breakfast is at eight tomorrow, but just shout if you need anything in the meantime."

She left. With Connie gone, Tag felt like she could finally relax. She pulled her suit from her suitcase and hung it on the back of the door. She smoothed it down, picking a few pieces of fluff from it. Feeling thirsty, she filled the small kettle from the tray with water and started making herself tea, adding two packets of sugar to it—a luxury Anna had frequently frowned upon when they'd been together.

It's bad for you. Anna's voice filled Tag's ears. *And it'll pile on the pounds.*

"Good," Tag said aloud, patting her flat, toned stomach. Her eye caught a packet: a fruit scone, laid out next to the teapot, along with a small pat of butter and jar of strawberry jam. Picking the scone up up and turning it over in her hands, she read the packaging: *Graingers' Watermill and Bakery. A family business since 1856.*

"Apt." She opened the packet and sniffed inside. It smelt awesome. Suddenly hungry, Tag pulled it out, tore it in half, and slapped a healthy dollop of butter onto it. She lifted it into the air and saluted Anna. "Bite me, Deveraux." Tag bit into the scone. Awesome didn't even come close. Light as a feather, the slightly salty flavour of the butter perfectly complemented the yeasty taste of the flour. Tag chewed, her brow furrowed. "Nice flour, Dad." She lifted her eyes to the ceiling and nodded, then looked down again quickly, suddenly feeling foolish.

After a cup of tea and a shower, Tag felt ready to take on anything that might get thrown at her later. She put on the clothes she'd chosen, a simple, exquisitely tailored suit she'd picked up in Selfridges, knowing that she couldn't go to her own father's funeral looking as scruffy as she normally did. She looked at herself in the mirror and felt distinctly uncomfortable at the starchiness of the stiff material. Uncomfortable and stupid. She pulled irritably on the collar of the cream blouse she'd put on underneath and unbuttoned the suit jacket. She put her hands into her trouser pockets and wiggled them about. She sighed. Whilst Tag knew she had to wear smart-casual clothes at work to impress clients, she felt far more at home in combat trousers and long-sleeved T-shirts, and jeans and vests. Sweatpants, even. What was wrong with sweatpants, anyway? She glanced at her recently removed clothes, chucked into a heap on her bed. Comfortable clothes. Clothes that didn't fucking suffocate her. Tag yanked at the collar on her blouse and untucked it from her trousers. Better. She looked at herself in the mirror once more, blouse tugged open untidily at the neck, jacket wide open, hands plunged deep into her pockets.

Like father, like daughter.

She looked at her watch. Time to go. Tag brushed her hair one more time, reluctantly buttoned up her jacket again, tidied up her collar, smoothed her suit down, and nodded. That'd do.

Grabbing her keys and leaving her room, Tag had hoped to get out of the B & B and into her car without Connie seeing her. The second she started to walk down the stairs, however, the door to Connie's private quarters opened and she appeared, looking up the stairs towards her.

"Hello again," Connie said pleasantly.

Tag stared at her. Like her meeting Tag was a coincidence?

"Off out?"

"Mm." Tag stopped mid-stair and jangled her car keys in her trouser pocket.

Connie looked her up and down. At the black suit and the look on Tag's face, shadowed with nerves. "I didn't realize you were here for a…"

"Funeral?" Tag finished her sentence for her. "Yes. Well, solicitor *then* funeral at three if you want all the gory details. I'm in for a fun day, aren't I?" Tag carried on down the stairs, smiling pleasantly. She really didn't need this right now.

"I'm so sorry." Connie reached out and touched Tag's arm. "And there was me babbling on earlier about climbing mountains."

"It's fine." Babbling. Good way to describe it. "You weren't to know." Tag made for the door, eager to leave.

Connie glanced up at a clock on the wall. "Three p.m., you say?" She frowned. "Adam Grainger's funeral?"

Tag stopped, her hand on the front door. "Yes. Adam Grainger's." Even to her own ears, her voice sounded strange. Had Connie noticed? She quickly cleared her throat.

"Of course!" Connie raised her eyes heavenwards. "Grainger! You're a Grainger. I didn't put two and two together when you booked your room over the phone, but now…"

Genius. The woman was a genius.

Connie studied Tag carefully. "What relation are you to Adam? Such a lovely man. I didn't know him that well, only to pass the time of day with, but he supplies—*supplied*—all our breadstuffs for the B & B, you know," Connie said. "A stalwart in the town, he was. People will miss him."

Tag inhaled slowly.

"What relation did you say you were again?"

I didn't, Tag thought. She pulled her car keys from her pocket and studied them. *Stay polite. Rudeness doesn't suit you, Tag.* "I'm his daughter," she finally said. She watched in amusement as Connie's mouth opened slightly. Cogs whirled.

"So *you're* the daughter?" Connie asked. She didn't make any effort to hide the look of surprise on her face.

"That's me." Tag opened out her hands.

"I've heard about you," Connie started. Paused. "I mean, I heard that Adam had a daughter called Taggie that lived away." Awkward.

Her father's favourite name for her. Taggie. Sometimes Taggie Tiptoes because Tag was always trying to make herself taller so she could get up into the tractor cabin when her father was using it, so she could be with him. A coldness swept over her. "It's Tag now," she said, chasing the chill away.

"Your father always used to refer to you as Taggie when he talked about you. Right up until the end." Connie laughed self-consciously. "I always imagined a wee girl with plaits." She glanced at Tag's long, slender frame. "Silly, really."

Her father had spoken about her even after she'd gone? Tag squeezed the keys in her hand, almost as a distraction.

"You must have left in the spring as I arrived here in the autumn the same year," Connie said. "We missed each other by about six months."

"I left in the April, yes," Tag said. "April fifth."

"So I believe—" Connie stopped herself.

Tag tried to read her thoughts. Possibly something along the lines of: *and gossip was still rife around the town about how you'd just upped and left, leaving your father heartbroken.*

"Mm." Tag chewed on her lip. "I really must go." She pulled the door open. "I won't tell you how the funeral went later because I'm sure someone will get here first and tell you before I get back."

"I don't want you to think…"

Tag stopped her. "I'm joking with you," she said, amused by the panicked look on Connie's face. "I remember how this town just *loves* to talk, that's all." A wry smile played on her lips. "And by three o'clock this afternoon, they're going to have a helluva lot more to talk about."

CHAPTER THREE

Freddie Metcalfe locked the door, turning the key once, then twice, just as she always did, then rattled the door handle once, then twice. Just as she always did. She let her fingers drag over the brass numbers on the bright red wooden door one last time. Snapshots of past encounters, filled with both laughter and sorrow, marched through her mind. Life in rewind.

"Okay?" Pete's voice rumbled with concern just behind her.

Freddie turned away and fought the tears which she knew were just one more retrieved memory away. She was being ridiculous, she knew. It had been over six months since she'd shared this house with Charlotte, six months since she'd last been happy. But there was something about locking the door for the last time and dropping the key back through the letter box for the letting agent to find in the morning that was heartbreaking. Even after all this time, the hurt refused to leave her.

"It's so final." Freddie lifted the letter box flap and poked her fingers through the slot, not quite able to make herself let go. Charlotte had crushed her. No, more than crushed her. She'd torn out her heart and stamped on it for good measure. Wasn't it bad enough that Freddie had lost her sister, Laura, just months before? She was still grieving for her only sibling when Charlotte had come home one night, to this very cottage, and told her that she couldn't cope any more. The next day, she was gone. Five years of their life together scooped up and blown to dust. Just like that.

"You have a whole new life waiting for you," Pete said. "New house, new town. A new start."

"You're right, I know." Freddie finally released the keys and relinquished her past along with them. She listened as they clattered to the floor inside, then pulled her hand back swiftly, removing her fingers as the flap snapped closed.

"The new cottage is awesome," Pete said, finally going to her. He pulled her into a bear hug. "Lyster is a fabulous village too, and it's way closer to work. Win-win all round. Think of it that way."

"Yeah, work." Freddie gave a small laugh into Pete's shoulder. "That'll be my next thing to worry about, now that Adam's died."

"You love work." Pete eased his hug. "You love running that cafe, you love the customers…what's there to stress about?"

Freddie stepped away. She shook snow from a small conifer outside the front door, watching as it showered to the ground. "Everything," she finally said. "Everything will change now Adam's gone."

"Doesn't have to."

"But it will." Freddie looked at Pete. "Blair's taking over everything his father used to do, so I guess he'll be my new boss."

"And the problem with that is?" Pete asked. "You like Blair."

"Adam's daughter's coming back this afternoon, too."

"For the funeral?"

"Mm. From England, according to Blair."

"Fair enough."

"And coming back to claim her inheritance, I guess," Freddie said. "She's getting half of Graingers'. Blair's furious."

"But that doesn't necessarily have to affect you," Pete reasoned.

"Unless when she comes back she doesn't like the way we've been running things at the cafe," Freddie said, her niggling thoughts coming to the fore "People do that, don't they?"

"Not like how cafes are run?" Pete widened his eyes.

"No, come back with a bloody great broom and decide to sweep everything clean." Freddie frowned. "Change things. This daughter, what's to say she won't do that? What's to say she might decide to shut the cafe and the gift shop down? Concentrate on just the milling side of the business?"

"Graingers' is so more than just about the mill, as well you know," Pete said. "It's a way of life round here. It's Graingers' Bakery and Cafe. Always has been, always will be. Besides, there'd be a riot down in Balfour if anyone swanned up here and started tinkering with anything."

Freddie smiled. It was true. The mill, bakery, and cafe had been a part of Balfour for as long as anyone could remember. Growing up in a town more than twenty miles from Balfour, she'd only visited the mill a handful of times as a child but had always known about its existence and had always been made aware of its importance to the local community by her parents. Because that's what Graingers' meant to people: Community. Security. Loyalty.

Then, when the opportunity to run the cafe had arisen four years ago, Freddie had jumped at the chance. What could have been better? A chance to run her own cafe, for a business with strong family ethics, in a town steeped with a strong sense of belonging and consistency. It had been just what Freddie had always wanted.

But now? The death of Adam Grainger was putting everything that Freddie held dear into jeopardy. Her four years of sanctuary could finally be coming to an end—and the thought terrified her.

"I wish I had your optimism." Freddie picked at the conifer.

"You don't need to be worrying."

"I can't help it. I was very happy with the way things were. Work was the one thing I could rely on to keep me on an even keel, and now I feel as though I'm wobbling again," Freddie said. "I just don't want anything to change around here, that's all." She sighed. "You know how much I have to have consistency in my life. For both me and Skye."

Freddie's thoughts wandered to Skye. At school right now, Skye would in all probability be giving Mrs. Murray, or Mr. Dench, or whichever poor teacher was trying to instil some education into her, a hard time because Skye had lost her pencil case the previous evening. It had taken all of Freddie's energy and resolve to hustle Skye out the door that morning, insisting that the school day didn't have to be cancelled just because somewhere, in amongst the move, her Winnie the Pooh pencil case had been lost.

"Skye's doing all right," Pete said. "You can't spend the rest of your life worrying about her, about work, about long-lost Graingers turning up out of the blue to claim inheritances…"

"I know, I know." Freddie raised her hands in submission.

"Anyway, you, me, and Sarah can easily deal with any kick-ass daughter that thinks she can just rock up here and try and change things," Pete said. "Just like we all dealt with Charlotte." Pete dipped his head to catch Freddie's eye. "Yeah?"

"Your fiancée doesn't need to be worrying about fighting my—"

"Sarah will take out anyone that stresses you," Pete said. "You know that." He paused. "I know you miss Charlotte, Freddie," he said, "and a lot of your stress still stems from what happened with her." He playfully punched her shoulder. "But she's *so* not worth all this anguish."

"You're right, I know."

"And the right girl is out there for you," Pete continued. "Just waiting to have a family life with you and Skye." He smiled. "Everything one day will click into place. Home, work, love, life. Then you'll look back and laugh at all this."

"Can I just start with looking for now?" Freddie laughed. "There was a girl this morning, actually…"

"Serious?" Pete rested a shoulder against the front door. "Spill."

"Nothing to spill." Freddie looked at the ground. "A girl came into the cafe this morning. Was fairly obnoxious, complained that I didn't do decaf, then grumbled about the bill."

"And yet, a few hours later you're still thinking about her?" Pete raised his eyebrows.

"Yeah. Whaddya know?" Freddie grinned, her mind falling back to that morning. It had been the briefest of moments—the girl had only stayed for ten minutes after all—but something about her had stuck. "First time I've felt *anything* since Charlotte."

"So?" Pete pressed. "Did you talk? Swap numbers?"

"Don't be silly." Freddie pulled her car keys from her pocket. "She paid her bill—reluctantly—then left. Drove off in her car down towards Balfour."

"You watched?"

"Of course." Freddie jiggled her keys. "Probably halfway to Aberdeen by now." The jiggling stopped. "Still, it was a nice feeling while it lasted." She started to walk. "Shall we go? I've got a funeral to get to."

"Sure." Pete hastened after her.

Freddie waited for Pete to fall into step with her before continuing down the path. "Thanks for giving up your lunch hour to come back here with me today, by the way."

"Anytime." Pete walked to the passenger side of Freddie's car. "It wasn't so bad after all, was it?"

"No." Freddie looked back at the cottage. "Just...ugh. All so final."

"As all break-ups have to be, sometimes." Pete smiled.

"Mm." Freddie gave one final, fleeting look towards her old front door, then opened her car. "Tell you what," she said, "after the funeral and the wake, and only if we get the unpacking finished by seven over at the new place, I'll treat us all to a Chinese. How's that?"

"You got yourself a deal."

The thin shaft of watery February sunshine cutting through the window of the small, stuffy offices of Parker, Flynn, and McKinlay Solicitors did little to lighten the gloom inside. It was eerily quiet. Only the muffled whirring of John Flynn's computer as he studied the screen in front of him punctured the almost suffocating atmosphere inside the room.

Tag rolled up the sleeves of her shirt, thinking that she wouldn't be able to bear the heat in the room a minute longer. To compensate against the bitter wind swirling around in the courtyard outside, the staff inside had chosen to crank the heating up to an almost unbearable level. Tag sank back into her chair and squeezed her eyes tight shut, lifting her hair away from her forehead in the vain hope that it might cool her down. She couldn't bear to be holed up inside this stuffy, claustrophobic office when it was so bright outside. Breezy and fresh. The perfect day to pull on a fleece and go walking by a loch. Or go snowboarding. Or take a hike up into the mountains. All the things that a perfect, fresh day like today demanded.

Tag opened her eyes again, allowing them to rest briefly on the piece of paper on the table in front of her, then stared at the face of her father's solicitor sitting opposite her. Surely this meeting couldn't go on much longer, could it? All she had to do was sign a few official documents. How long did that have to take?

Much to Tag's dismay, John started talking again.

"I trust your flight up to Scotland was okay?"

"Apart from a small child kicking the back of my seat throughout the entire flight, you mean?" Tag smiled. "It was okay, yes."

"You caught the early morning shuttle up from Liverpool, is that right?"

Tag nodded. The move to Liverpool two years earlier had been the longest she'd stayed in one place since leaving her childhood home of Balfour nine years before. It wasn't perfect, but the area in the city centre where she'd finally settled had afforded her what she'd desperately needed: a job, and with it, financial security. Add to that an apartment owned by her ex-girlfriend at a vastly reduced rent, and Tag was, for the first time in years, more than financially comfortable. Now, if what John had told her in their numerous phone conversations over the past few days was correct, both her financial security and her future were cemented.

Financially, Tag was content. Her future? That was a whole different ball game.

"So," he said, as if reading her mind, "how do you feel about it? Now you've had time to think about it, I mean."

"Honestly?"

"Honestly."

"Freaked." Tag put one hand in her trouser pocket and rested the other, palm down, on the piece of paper, as if by doing so she might somehow make it magically disappear. "Totally and utterly freaked."

If she didn't know any better, Tag would have sworn her father had left her half of his business on purpose. Just to punish her for her past wrongdoings.

"There can't be many young women of your age around who can say they've been given an opportunity such as this, Ms. Grainger—"

"Tag, please," she said hastily. "Everyone calls me Tag. Ms. Grainger makes me sound like I'm a schoolteacher." She looked down at her hand, still resting on the paper. "I understand what you're saying," she said, "but is there really no way I can wriggle out of this?"

"These are your father's wishes—that the Balfour Watermill and Bakery remain in the Grainger name." John picked up his piece of paper, identical to Tag's. "That's what he wanted. What you do with your share now it's yours is up to you, but…"

"But if I sell it, he'll come back and haunt me, is that what you mean?" Tag's eyes rested on the words in front of her. *The Last Will and Testament of Adam George Grainger.* Her father's will. And in it, a whole heap of trouble that she neither wanted nor needed.

Tag stared down at the table and said, half to herself, "I wonder what my brother thinks of this." Finally she looked up.

"Blair's signed for his inheritance."

Just the sound of his name after so many years sounded weird to Tag. "You've seen him already?"

"His appointment was yesterday." John shifted uncomfortably in his chair. "He requested an individual appointment, rather than—"

"Rather than having to be in the same room as me?" Tag finished John's sentence. "Fair play to him." She shrugged. "It's not like I've been busting a gut to see him either. Even after nine years."

Her words hung uneasily between them.

Nine years. A lifetime ago now.

Balfour Watermill and Bakery had been in the Grainger family since Queen Victoria's reign. A thriving flour mill which had been passed down through the generations, it had grown from being a small, rural mill on the banks of a large, freshwater loch in Balfour, to being a tourist hotspot throughout the 1980s and 90s. Throughout Tag's childhood, all she knew was a life up at the mill. It was all that four generations of Graingers had ever known in their lives too—until Tag grew up and realized that wasn't what she wanted any more, that was.

"So now what?" Tag scribbled her signature across the paper in front of her and pushed it back to John. How hot did this room need to be, really? She reached down and picked up her bag, then stood up, desperate to get outside and fill her lungs with fresh air.

"I'll get everything sent to you." John looked at his screen.

"Send it to the mill." Tag strung her bag across her shoulders. "You recommended a few weeks to get everything completely sorted, so I'll be sticking around here for a bit."

Tag had taken five weeks off in the end. She was due holiday—okay perhaps not five weeks—but she figured Anna owed her that at least. Especially when she took into account all the overtime she'd worked for her. Plus all the other favours over the years. And if Blair didn't want to have anything to do with her once their father's funeral was over, then she'd just take herself off. A tour of the Highlands would do her just fine; it had been too long since she'd just kicked back and rediscovered her homeland.

"You'll meet your staff at the funeral, I'm sure." John followed her to the door. "Then you'll have suppliers, contractors—"

Tag stopped dead. "I have staff?" Her eyes went heavenward. This had to be a joke, right? "How many, uh, *staff* do I have?"

"Not many." John couldn't help but smile at the look on Tag's face. "Most in the bakery. Then a couple in the mill, a few in the gift shop. Oh, and two in the cafe." He opened the door for her. "They'll be worried about their futures," he said slowly. "It's important you meet them sooner rather than later so you can put their minds at rest."

His staff had always been so important to Adam. *Treat your staff well, Tag,* he used to say, *and they'll stick with you for life.* Unlike parents do. They'd been a tight family unit for the first eight years of Tag's life, the Graingers. Until one stormy night when her mother had gone out in the truck to the cash-and-carry for supplies and had never come home. It had all changed then. In the blink of an eye, the Graingers weren't the close-knit family they'd always prided themselves on being. Adam had changed overnight. A widower at forty-three, he'd retreated into himself, shutting Tag away when she needed him the most. That's how it had seemed to a fourteen-year-old Tag, anyway.

"Once again, my condolences on the loss of your father." An undertaker's handshake. Clammy. "I hope the funeral goes well later."

"Thank you." Tag dropped John's hand, resisting the urge to dry her palm down the leg of her trousers. "So do I." She made to leave. "Although somehow I think my past is going to come hurtling back to me with a vengeance this afternoon."

CHAPTER FOUR

Freddie grimaced as Skye arced higher and higher on the swing. Her heart was in her mouth as Skye kicked out her legs, straight as rods, and urged Freddie to push her higher still. She was fearless, a chip off the old block. Laura would be proud, Freddie thought sadly.

"Last push, okay?" Freddie said, ignoring the grumbles cascading down. "You're quite high enough now."

She came round to the front of the swing to watch Skye.

"Afterwards, can we watch TV?" Skye called down from her lofty height.

"I have to go out, remember?"

"Uncle Adam's funeral?"

"Then when I get back, we said we'd make cookies, didn't we," Freddie called back. "Then finish unpacking the boxes from the old house."

"Cookies!" Skye's eyes widened. "I'd forgotten about them." Freddie took a sharp intake of breath as Skye gripped the chain of the swing tighter and lunged over closer to her, grinning and tucking her legs up under the swing's seat as she did so, to go faster again. "With chocolate chips like last time?"

"If you want."

Skye leaned over further and beamed. Freddie knew that as far as Skye was concerned, chocolate-chip cookies were the best things ever. Especially because Freddie always let her lick out the bowl afterwards. She watched as Skye stretched her legs straight again, pointing her toes and tilting her head back to gaze up at the fusion of blue sky and white clouds as she swung back and forth. Freddie always put extra chocolate chips in too, always making sure Skye saw her do it. It was their little routine.

Freddie reached out slightly as Skye soared higher, her eyes closed. Her mind, Freddie knew, would still be full of the prospect of their home-made cookies. Sometimes they had white-chocolate chips, sometimes milk-chocolate chips, which was Skye's preferred choice.

"Be careful!" Freddie sensed Skye's concentration, now thoroughly distracted by thoughts of chocolate, wavering. She'd seen that look before: away in her own little world, unaware of everything and anyone else. Freddie grimaced as Skye teetered on her seat, flipping it up and tipping her out. When she landed in a heap on the grass, Skye let out a howl. Freddie was by her side in an instant.

"What happened?" She knelt beside Skye.

"Fell off." Skye rubbed her arm and frowned at the swing as if, Freddie thought as she kept her eye on her, she held it personally responsible for her fall. "I hurt my arm." She lifted her arm to Freddie.

"Let's take a look, shall we?" Freddie kissed her hair.

Skye nodded and wiped away a tear, smearing mud across her cheek as she did so. Freddie gazed at her. Yes, just like her mother. Freddie's chest tightened. It was times like this that the memory of Laura came back to her with such ferocity, it knocked the breath from her. Her sister had been just twenty-five when she'd died. The cancer diagnosis had been a shock to them all; no one in the immediate Metcalfe family had ever had so much as a cancer scare before, let alone anything worse. So when Laura found the lump, not one member of the family believed that it would take her from them less than two years later.

"Is it bleeding?" Skye twisted her arm round and tried to see her elbow.

"A bit. You've skinned it, that's all." Freddie pulled a hanky from her pocket. "Let me clean it."

Everyone's lives had changed when Laura died. Named as Skye's legal guardian in Laura's will, Freddie suddenly found her own life turned upside down, instantly being thrust into the role of mother whilst at the same time grieving for her sister. There was no one else to help her other than Charlotte. Skye's father, a fellow student from Laura's university course, hadn't wanted to know when Laura fell pregnant. Last heard of backpacking around Thailand, never to be seen again. Freddie's own parents owned a vineyard in Portugal, and while they begged Freddie to let them take responsibility for their granddaughter, Freddie wouldn't hear of it. Laura, she told them, had entrusted her daughter to her, and she owed it to her sister's memory to carry out her wishes. So her parents stayed in Portugal and visited Freddie and Skye every two months initially. Now that Freddie was settled into motherhood, their visits had tapered to a handful per year.

Not that Freddie minded. Once she'd got over the initial shock of being plunged head first into being a parent, she'd settled into the role as if she'd been doing it all her life. A guinea pig and hamster had been bought, so that Skye could concentrate her mind on something other than the loss of her mother. Paddington and Fudge had been so much more than a pair of hastily bought pets, though. They'd been a distraction, not only to Skye, but to Freddie as well. They were two living, breathing creatures that needed care, so that both Freddie and Skye could carry on living and breathing too. It had worked. Skye had blossomed into a thoughtful, caring child, and now Freddie couldn't imagine her life without her. Skye was everything to her— daughter, companion, best friend—and Freddie loved her with a fierce protectiveness that she never thought she could ever be capable of.

"Ow." Skye screwed up her face. "It's stinging." She drew her arm away from Freddie and cradled it protectively against her.

"I need to get the grass out, Skye." Freddie held her hand out. "This is what happens if you insist on rolling your sleeves up all the time."

Skye, chastised, offered a wary arm to her. Freddie dabbed at the red skin on her elbow, occasionally picking a blade of grass from it, sensing Skye watching her intently, sometimes frowning.

"Be careful."

"I'm always careful." Freddie wiped slowly.

"Do you remember when I fell off the wall and had to go to hospital?" Skye asked.

Freddie's wiping slowed. The hospital story again. "Mm-hmm. I remember."

"Charlotte's hanky was pink," Skye said. "Yours is white." She pointed determinedly to Freddie's hanky, in case Freddie wasn't sure which hanky she was talking about. "Charlotte always had a pink hanky."

"She did." Freddie concentrated on Skye's arm.

"Do you remember when she took me to hospital?"

"I do, yes." Freddie remembered the phone call at the cafe. The blind initial panic at hearing Skye was in hospital until Charlotte had laughed and told her Skye was busy chattering to all the nurses and eating sweets.

"And afterwards she took me to McDonald's," Skye said. "And I had nuggets. I liked that." She thought for a moment. "We *never* go to McDonald's now. Not since Charlotte left."

"No, we don't." Freddie studied Skye's arm. Zone in. Don't let Charlotte come back to you. Not again.

"Freddie?"

"Skye?"

"Why did Charlotte go?" Skye turned her arm over and inspected her injury. "Didn't she love me?"

Freddie sat back on the grass. She drew her knees up and looped her arms round her legs. They had been through this so many times before, but still the same questions were asked. "She loved you very much," she said. "I've told you that before."

"I wish she hadn't gone."

"I wish she hadn't either," Freddie said. "But she went a long time ago now, and we just have to accept that she's never coming back, don't we?"

Freddie carried on wiping Skye's elbow. With every wipe, Charlotte's face returned to her, as clear in Freddie's mind's eye as the day she'd left. She could still hear her voice. Her laughter. Her last words to her as she walked out of the door, never to return. *I'm sorry.* Freddie's stomach curdled at the memory. Sorry? Was that it? Such an insipid word that couldn't even begin to make up for all the hurt she'd caused.

They'd been together five years. Shared a house together for four of those. They would have married, too, Freddie was sure of that, if Sam hadn't come on the scene and taken Charlotte away. Freddie's jaw tightened. Sam should have stayed the fuck away from Charlotte and her family. But Charlotte should have been stronger too. She was as much to blame for their affair as Sam had been. Knowing that Charlotte shared parental responsibilities for a vulnerable child who'd not long lost her mother should have been enough for both of them to ignore their feelings for one another. Sam should have walked away. But she didn't. The only time she *did* walk away, Charlotte walked with her, out of Freddie's life, out of Skye's life. And Freddie would never, ever forgive her for that.

"It's better." Skye's voice pulled her back. "You can stop wiping now." Skye carefully rolled her sleeve back down. "Can I go back on it?" She lifted her head backwards and motioned to the swing.

"I have to go get ready." Freddie hauled herself to her feet. Charlotte slunk to the back of her mind once more.

"'K." Skye clambered up too. "The swing was rubbish anyway."

"Silly swing." Freddie laughed and batted away a tear she hadn't even known was there.

"Silly swing," Skye echoed. "Can I watch TV while you get ready?"

"Under the blanket?" Freddie offered. "I think a girl with a poorly arm deserves a blanket at the very least, don't you?"

Skye nodded sombrely.

They walked from the small play park, swaying their entwined hands backwards and forwards. Skye had been Freddie's salvation after Charlotte had left. She'd clarified so many things for Freddie— the first being that Charlotte wasn't worth all the tears she'd shed for her. After she'd recovered from Charlotte's deception, Freddie had decided her own needs were less important than Skye's and had made up her mind that from that day on, it would just be the two of them living a life entrenched in routine, stability, and more love than it was possible to give one child. Skye didn't need anything else, and Freddie could give her all these things.

That, and plenty of chocolate-chip cookies too.

❖

The church was finely dusted with the first of the day's snow by the time Tag arrived. She was on time, but as she gazed around at the number of people milling around in the churchyard, she felt as though she must have been one of the last to arrive. The churchyard was packed. Her father, Tag remembered soberly, had been a popular figure in the town.

She looked about her, searching amongst faces she didn't recognize. Searching for Blair. Faces came and went, voices caught and then left her ears again. Finally, Blair appeared in her line of vision, standing in the church doorway, talking with a tall, robust-looking boy with a mop of thick, curly hair and a suit that looked too big for him. Tag studied Blair, ducking her head to examine the ground each time he looked around in case he spotted her. She wasn't ready to see him again. Not yet.

Blair.

The last time she'd seen him he'd been twenty-three, recently married to Ellen and with a five-year-old child who had only just started school. Now he was stockier, thicker of neck. She watched as he tugged on his shirt collar, knowing he'd be just as uncomfortable in his suit as she was in hers. He looked a lot older than she'd remembered him, the few flecks of grey in his curly black hair catching her eye. He stepped back as the undertakers removed her father's coffin from the back of the hearse and went to stand next to a woman. Ellen. Tag hung back, keen not to be spotted. Her eyes, though, were constantly fixed on them.

Tag was nervous. No, terrified. Her scalp pricked and her palms were curiously cold yet sweaty as she watched Blair say something to one of the pallbearers, nod, then step back further as the procession made its way slowly and silently into the church. Tag waited until the last of the other mourners had started to file in. She fell in behind them, painfully aware of the prying eyes cast her way and the few nudges and nods of heads directed towards her by people who evidently had just recognized her. Balfour folk, she reasoned, had never been known for their discretion.

St. Mary's was a small medieval church, able to accommodate no more than sixty or so worshippers, which was apt as most Sundays it barely manage to top a dozen. But today, for her father's funeral, the church was packed. Each local, it seemed, wanted to pay their respects to a man who was, as Connie Booth had told Tag earlier, highly regarded in Balfour. As the last mourner entered through the heavy oak doors of the church, Tag slipped quietly in and sat herself down in a pew at the very back. She craned her neck so she could see exactly where Blair had seated himself. Where was he?

He was sitting, head bowed, at the front of the church. Ellen was to one side of him, while the boy Blair had been speaking to outside was on his other side. Past and present collided. Tag realized with a jolt that he must be Magnus, the wide-eyed, giggly child she'd last seen the night before she'd left Balfour. For years after she'd left, seeing kids had broken Tag's heart because she knew that in some quiet corner of the Highlands, Magnus would be growing up without her there to see it. She'd learned to toughen up, though. Blot it out. Or at least, she'd tried to. Over the years she became adept at shaking the sadness from her—but the hurt had always remained.

Tag leaned her head to one side and studied the back of Magnus's head. His hair was thick and curly, just like Blair's. Tag liked that. While Tag had inherited her mother's auburn hair, it seemed both Blair and Magnus had been blessed with the Grainger dark curls. It made Magnus look exactly how Blair had at that age, Tag realized with a jolt. She wondered if Magnus's hair was unruly now and refused to be tidy for him, like it always used to be when she would brush it for him when he was a child.

"Did you know him well?" A voice beside Tag made her flinch.

"I'm sorry?"

"Adam?" the voice said. An older man was smiling at her. "Did you know him well?"

"Yes." Of course she knew him well. "A long time ago now, though."

"We only knew him for around four years," the man said, "when we first moved here."

"Right." What else could she say? Tag looked to the front pew again. When were they going to start?

"Thought we'd pay our respects, you know?"

Why was this man still talking?

"That's kind of you." Tag checked herself and looked ahead again. It wasn't her place to be thanking people for coming to pay their respects. Not any more.

The arrival of the vicar at the front of the church saved Tag's blushes. She picked up the order-of-service sheet that was on her pew and opened it. A photograph of her father immediately looked back at her, and Tag swallowed as she stared down at it, astounded by just how much he'd aged. She frowned. So stupid. Of course he'd aged. Did she really think he'd look like the same man she'd known all those years ago?

"Adam Grainger was a father, a grandfather, a friend." The vicar, another face Tag no longer recognized, spoke. While his voice droned on, Tag sat transfixed by the photo of her father. She studied his face: his eyes and his hair, so much greyer than it had ever been, the wrinkles she didn't remember. Surely he'd had wrinkles nine years ago? She stared at it again. The picture was taken up at the mill—that much Tag did recognize—and although the sun was shining down on him and he was smiling, his eyes were sad.

"People remember the first day they ever met Adam." The vicar again. "Once you met him, you knew you had a friend for life…"

His words became white noise to Tag. Instead, she gazed down the aisle towards Blair. His arm was around Ellen, who had her head resting on his shoulder. How ironic, Tag thought, that Ellen was probably mourning her father more than she was. Despite the picture of Adam in front of her and the sight of his coffin at the front of the church, and with the sound of weeping around her, Tag still couldn't cry.

She stiffened as Blair unlooped his arm from Ellen's shoulder and stood. He tugged at the hem of his jacket and smoothed his hands down each arm. Had the vicar finished talking? Tag had had no idea. As if in slow motion, Tag watched as Ellen reached up and placed a hand on Blair's arm. He stepped from his pew and walked up to the front of the church. He pulled a pair of glasses from his top pocket and put them on.

Blair wore glasses?

Tag shook her head slightly. Something else that was new around here.

Blair paused. He retrieved a sheet of paper from his trouser pocket, unfolded it with slightly shaking hands, and placed it on the lectern in front of him.

"My father once told me a story of when he was a little boy," he began, reading from his crumpled sheet of paper, "and how he used to like to go to the mountains to watch the eagles…"

Tag sat mesmerized by the sight of her brother.

"…and then many years later he'd take me with him up to the mountains," Blair continued, "so that we could watch them together."

And me, Tag thought.

"We'd take a picnic with us and just sit," Blair said, "looking down onto Balfour. My father would point out landmarks that he'd known all his life. We'd be able to see the mill from there. The land that surrounded it. My father would show me all the wheat fields he owned. The tractors harvesting *his* wheat that he would then use in *his* mill to make *his* bread to sell in *his* bakery." Blair punched out every word. "I loved it. I loved his enthusiasm. I loved the sense of heritage my father had, and most of all, I loved his passion."

Heritage. That was the perfect word to attribute to their father, Tag thought. Adam was immensely proud of all he'd achieved since he'd inherited the mill from his own father in the late 1970s. The renovations, the growth, the sheer hard graft to keep everything moving. Then, once Tag's mother had died, the hard work he'd endured to sustain everything they'd built together—a testament to his wife. Tag had had to grow up fast without her mother, even faster once Adam retreated, wounded by the loss of his wife, into himself—just when Tag had really needed him.

Self-pity anchored itself to Tag. She remembered the long days without her father, the feeling of abandonment and isolation as a child, to be replaced, at sixteen, by the startling realization of expectation from him. He had her future mapped out for her, and there was nothing she could do about it. With Blair already established as an integral part of the mill, Adam had then turned his focus onto Tag, rapidly railroading her into a life she didn't want. Tag blinked and dredged with a stark clarity from her memory the moment she'd decided she'd seek a more exciting life for herself, far away from Balfour.

"…and then, once Magnus came along," Blair now said, looking down towards his son, "he'd take *both* of us up there." He pulled his glasses off and looked around him. Tag wanted him to spot her; she needed him to know she was there. His eyes briefly roamed around the church, apparently seeing a sea of faces, but there was no moment of recognition to suggest that he'd seen Tag. But she desperately wanted him to see her. "That was the sort of thing he loved to do," Blair continued. "He loved to share his knowledge of Scotland, of Balfour, of the environment, of nature, of the land around us," he said. "And knowing that one day Magnus and I would inherit it made Dad very happy indeed. Knowing that Balfour Watermill would be safe in our hands one day was all he ever wanted."

This time, Blair's eyes flickered to hers and held them. He looked away again. If he'd seen her—and Tag was fairly sure he had—he didn't let it show in his face. Instead he calmly placed his glasses back on and finished his eulogy without missing a beat. It was only when he was walking back down the aisle to his pew that he finally fixed his stare on Tag.

That's when she knew for sure.

He *had* seen her. The barely disguised look of disdain on his face as he held her gaze told her everything she needed to know.

CHAPTER FIVE

"Tag." Blair's voice rumbled, low and quiet, behind her. Tag felt a hand on her arm and stiffened. "I would hate to think you'd just up and leave, you know."

Tag stepped back from the queue streaming from the church, allowing two or three people to pass her, then spoke. "I wasn't just going to leave," she said feebly. She looked up at Blair, instantly transported back to her teenage years.

"I'm surprised you came." Blair lowered his voice. "I didn't think you'd bother."

"To my own father's funeral? What do you think I am?"

"You need me to answer that?" Blair asked. He turned to acknowledge a hand on his arm from an elderly woman passing down through the line of people, then looked back at Tag. "No word from you in years?" That stung. "Hardly a letter or phone call? Nothing?" He lowered his voice again. Now was neither the time nor place to cause a scene. "How do you think I felt, not even knowing where you were to tell you that Dad had died? How do you think that made me feel?"

"Good job John Flynn used some investigation to find me, then." Tag shrugged. "Or his common sense." But faint guilt tumbled over Tag. Blair was right. The last time she'd contacted him, she'd been in Newcastle. Or was it Manchester? She couldn't quite recall.

"Hello, stranger." Ellen arrived at Blair's side. She looked at Tag, an easy smile on her face. At least one of them was pleased to see her. "Long time, no see."

"Understatement of the century." Blair strode away to speak to a couple who were waiting for him in the church entrance.

Tag's heart sank as she watched him go. That went well then. She swung round to face Ellen, the friendly look she hoped she wore on her face contradicting the ache inside at Blair's rebuff. To Tag's surprise, Ellen reached over and pulled her into a hug. "I'm so sorry about your dad," she said quietly, holding onto her for a few more seconds before releasing her. "It was a shock to us all."

"John said it was a heart attack. Up at the mill."

Ellen nodded.

"Ironic that it happened at the mill," Tag said. "I always thought that place would be the death of him, the hours he used to put in." The words jarred.

"We'd booked him a surprise for his birthday this week too." Ellen gazed away. "Blair thought he was looking tired. We thought a weekend away would do him the world of good."

"But instead of celebrating his fifty-sixth, we're saying goodbye to him." Tag could no longer maintain her cheerful facade.

"You've lost your accent a little since I last saw you." As if sensing Tag's anguish, Ellen changed tack. She ducked her head to catch Tag's eye. "You don't sound so Scottish now. Well, not as Scottish as I sound, anyway."

"Ah, but you know what they say," Tag said, looking around her, "you can take the girl out of Scotland, but you can't take Scotland out of the girl." She spoke with an exaggerated accent, making Ellen laugh. Tag turned her attention to Blair, still talking to the couple. "He really hates me, doesn't he?"

Ellen followed Tag's gaze. "Hate's a strong word, Tag." Diplomatic. "He's…disappointed in you more than anything." Not what Tag wanted to hear. "He adored you, you know that?" Ellen said. "You taking off without a word hit him hard. He couldn't understand why you'd done it. He thought it was something he'd done."

"Is that what he thinks?" Tag asked. "I never had a problem with Blair. Okay, I regret walking out on him too, but I just had to go." She tossed a look over to him. To his back. Apparently he couldn't even bear to face her. "Surely he realizes that?"

"I don't think he does." Ellen started to move away. "So maybe today might be a very good time to tell him."

Balfour Watermill was set in the shadow of Carr's Rock, a small peak that sat next to its much bigger brother, Ben Crathie. The River Dynne ran alongside the mill, powering the huge watermill that dominated the building and everything surrounding it. It was, in short, a magnificent feat of Victorian architecture and industry. A truly imposing sight. And to Tag, it was so embedded in her memory, she'd thought for years she'd never be able to escape the image of it.

And she never had.

As Tag pulled up again in the car park to the cafe immediately after the funeral, it struck her as ironic that the place where her father had died, and the place that caused his death, would now be the very place where they would all celebrate his life.

Tag killed the engine of her car and sat, staring at the front of the mill. Only the sound of the beating of her own heart filled her ears. It was time to be brave. Returning to the cafe earlier had been hard enough; this time it would be a hundred times worse, because this time she'd have to try and ignore the looks she knew she was about to face inside from her fellow mourners. She got out and strode in through the cafe doors with far more confidence than her shaking legs were feeling. A wave of gratitude hit her when, just like in the church before, Ellen came to her rescue by intercepting her on her way in. Pathetic gratitude. But it was all she had right now.

"I thought if I got you this now it would save you having to run the gauntlet of stares at the counter." Ellen handed Tag a glass of orange juice. "You look tired."

Tag took her drink. "My night sucked," she said. Voices ebbed and flowed around her, whispered comments. Were they talking about her? Pointing her out to those who hadn't yet heard the stories? Tag cradled her drink, standing close to Ellen as if by doing so she'd remain unseen to the rest of the room. "I can thank the worry about today for that."

"Understandable that you'd be apprehensive about coming back here," Ellen said. She took a sip of her drink. "So, dare I ask where you've been hiding yourself all these years?" she asked. "Last time we heard from you, you were in England." She studied Tag carefully. "But that was over four years ago now."

"I ended up in Liverpool," Tag replied, "via Edinburgh, Newcastle, Manchester. Oh, and London. Briefly."

"You've been busy."

"Took a while to settle."

"And now?"

"I rent an apartment overlooking the Mersey." Tag stepped aside to allow someone to pass her. She met his eye as he brushed past and waited for a sign of recognition from him that never came. Tag hastily took another drink; she was being stupid. Not everyone automatically knew who she was—did they?

"I mean, are you settled?"

"Oh. I guess."

Ellen raised an eyebrow. "You live alone? With someone?"

"Alone," Tag said. "Although I'm sure the local gossips would prefer it if I was shacked up in a lesbian commune. Much more titillating."

"Are you working?" Ellen asked. "Don't tell me you're some high-flying hotshot there."

"Nothing so exciting," Tag replied. "I do freelance work for my ex." Her eyes sought out Blair. "I suppose my brother *is* going to come and speak to me at some point, is he?" she asked, her eyes still on him.

"You know there's not a day gone by when he and your dad—all of us—haven't thought about you," Ellen said. She beckoned Blair over to her. "Your dad particularly."

"Don't set me off." Tag swallowed back the lump in her throat.

"Where are you staying while you're here?" Ellen asked. "Pub? B & B?"

"Four Winds." Tag sipped at her orange juice. Damn lump was still there. "I've booked a room there. I figured I'd have a lot of things to get sorted while I'm here."

"Connie Booth's place?" Ellen mock-shuddered. "She talks so much, she'll make your ears bleed."

"Maybe I'll take a trip down to Martins' Pharmacy and buy myself some earplugs."

"You'll have a job." Ellen looked away. "It's a pet store now."

"Does nothing ever stay the same?" Tag followed Ellen's gaze. Trepidation pinched at the base of her stomach as Blair sauntered over to them. Would he cause a scene? Would he even speak to her?

"Apparently not." Ellen moved away. "Right. Time for me to mingle."

Ellen shot Blair a look as she passed him, as if to say *over to you now*, then wandered off to talk to a small group of people by a window.

"Tag," Blair said. He stood, glass of water in one hand, the other hand in his trouser pocket. He glared at his sister. Tag glared back.

"Blair." Tag took a drink from her glass, if only for something to do. "I thought your eulogy was nice," she said, "you know, before. At the church."

"Well we couldn't really ask you to say something, could we?" Blair said. "Bit difficult to talk about someone you no longer know, isn't it?"

"Blair, don't," Tag said softly. "I don't want to argue with you. Not today of all days."

"Why not?" Blair shot back. "I've had years to think about what I'd say to you if I ever saw you again." He glared at her. "Your eighteenth, Tag! For fuck's sake. The day after your eighteenth!"

Seemed Blair wanted to argue after all.

"And was he there for me, then? Did he even *know* it was my eighteenth?"

"Of course he knew!" Blair spat. "He talked of nothing else in the weeks and months afterwards, when he was still clinging to the hope you might come back or, heaven forbid, even contact him to let him know you weren't dead." His eyes blazed. "All he could think about was how guilty he felt that you'd just upped and gone without a word or an explanation."

"We've been over this *so* many times before." Tag stared down into her glass.

"Yes, in one of those five-minute phone calls you deigned to give me over the years," Blair responded savagely. "Shame you never found time to ring your own father, isn't it?"

"Okay, perhaps I should have been more thoughtful—"

"Understatement of the century, Tag," Blair said. "You left me to deal with everything and I've been dealing with it all ever since. Even now Dad's dead, it's all been left to me. The funeral arrangements, the business…" He took another drink. His hand, Tag noticed, shook slightly. "And now you rock up here as if nothing happened and expect everyone to welcome you back with open arms?"

"I don't expect anyone to do anything for me," Tag said. She lowered her voice. People were looking; of course people were looking. After all, what was better than a family tiff at a funeral? "I learned a long time ago that I was on my own in everything I ever did."

"Your selfish attitude will get you far." Blair gripped his glass. "That'll endear you to the guys up here."

"Like I'm staying?" Tag retorted. "Where I'm not welcome?" Where her own brother could hardly bear to be in the same room as her?

Blair looked slowly at her. "You have responsibilities now." A smile twisted. "We have to work as a team, me and you." He signalled to the other side of the room. "See those people over there?"

Tag followed his gaze to a small cluster of people in the corner of the cafe.

"They're your staff now," Blair said. "They'll be looking to you and me for reassurance that their futures are safe." He sipped at his drink. "Or are you going to do what you did to me and Dad and run away from it all again?"

"I didn't run away." Tag glared at him. "Running away would indicate—"

"Semantics." Blair looked away. "You don't have any choice in the matter now, though." Tag sensed he was almost enjoying this. Making her squirm. Filling her head with yet more worries—if that were even possible. "You're their boss. I'm their boss. They need us."

Tag was no one's boss. She'd never been responsible for anyone in her life, and she wasn't about to start now. What did she know about being in charge of a bunch of people? No, as far as Tag was concerned, the sooner she worked out the best way to offload her share of the business back onto Blair and get away from Balfour again, the better.

"You can have my share." Tag gripped her glass so hard she thought it might shatter. "I don't want it."

"You don't want the hassle of it, you mean?" Blair replied dismissively. "Same old Tag. Nothing changes."

Tag was aware of the whispers again. The ill-disguised looks. "Think what you like." Fury burned in her chest. Fuck these jerks. Fuck everyone in the room. Especially Blair. "So I've got to be a boss to a handful of people for five minutes. Fine. You know what, Blair? I'll deal with that in the time I'm up here. I'm a survivor. It's what I do." Tag slammed her drink back. "And I'll make damn sure I survive the short time I have to be back here before I can get the hell away from you all again."

CHAPTER SIX

Freddie felt sorry for the girl sitting alone in the corner of the cafe, her back to the room, her head cradled in her hands as though she was trying to make herself as small as she could so she could be as inconspicuous as possible. Although quite why she'd want to do that now that the cafe had finally emptied of mourners, Freddie wondered, only she would be able to answer. Freddie studied the back of the girl's head as she repeatedly looked to the window, then sank her head back into her hands, evidently waiting for someone that never came.

"You look all done in." Freddie, still dressed in her black funeral clothes, approached the girl.

Their mutual surprise at seeing one another again was tangible as the girl pulled her hands from her face and stared up at Freddie. "Long day," she finally said. She kicked her legs out in front of her and rubbed the tiredness from her eyes. "Stressful. As funerals tend to be, of course."

"Of course," Freddie replied guardedly, her caginess stemming more from her own reaction at seeing this intriguing girl again now.

"I didn't know you were here," the girl stuttered. "I mean, I didn't see you in here. During the wake."

"It was pretty packed." Freddie nodded. "I'm sure I was lost in amongst the throng." Freddie stood awkwardly by the table, a tray of dirty glasses in her hands. So she was in Balfour for the funeral? This girl who had so annoyed her, yet stirred something inside her, wasn't, as Freddie had assumed, halfway to Aberdeen but sitting back in her cafe, staring straight back at her. And causing the exact same reaction as she had four hours earlier.

"You don't have to clear all this up," Tag said, lifting a chin to the tray of dirty glasses in Freddie's hands, "I'm sure my brother's got someone in to do it."

"Your brother?"

"Blair."

"He's your brother?" Freddie put the tray down on the table. *She* was the dreaded daughter? Fascination, accompanied by a shimmer of worry, crept over her.

"Mm."

"So you're the famous Tag, are you?" She snagged the seat opposite Tag. Just wait until she told Pete about this one.

"Infamous, don't you mean?"

"Only if it's all true." Freddie laughed.

"Trust me," Tag said, "everyone around here would like it to be."

"I'm Freddie." Freddie reached over and enthusiastically shook Tag's hand.

"I know." Tag caught her eye. "I saw your name badge earlier, remember?"

"When you complained about the price of your coffee." Freddie wasn't about to let *that* one pass.

"Commented," Tag corrected, "not complained. I paid up, didn't I?"

"Reluctantly." Freddie studied her carefully.

Tag didn't reply.

"I'm sorry about your father," Freddie said. Time to change the subject; playing a game of one-upmanship with a stranger after her father's funeral wasn't kind.

"Thanks."

"I'd heard about you…" Freddie stumbled. "I mean, I'd heard you were coming back today."

"You'd heard about me?" Tag sat back. "Let me guess. The locals—my father and brother included—made me out to be some sort of first-class bitch."

"The locals, maybe," Freddie said, "but never your family."

"Well, I can tell you that none of it is true," Tag said. "Despite what the locals would have you believe," she added.

"Your father was a nice man." Now that she was sitting opposite her, Freddie could evaluate Tag properly. Same age; pretty much the same auburn hair too. Different colour eyes, though. Tag's were blue, not green like her own. A nice blue, Freddie thought. Almost azure. "I had a lot of time for him. He was a good boss."

"That means a lot." Tag nodded. "So you liked working for my father, then?"

"I sort of worked for him," Freddie corrected. "I run the cafe." She spread her arms out. "My own little empire." So Tag was the new boss that had her so worried? The niggling intensified as Freddie continued her survey. Up from England, no doubt with a headful of fresh ideas. One of which was probably revamping Freddie's entire menu, no doubt to introduce bloody decaffeinated drinks to it. And then reduce the prices, just to add insult to injury.

"The cafe's changed a lot since I was last here." Tag's words pulled Freddie back from her thoughts. "Much more modern than when I last saw it."

"I decided a few years ago that it needed dragging into the twenty-first century," Freddie said. "After the bypass was built and took some passing trade away. Your dad wasn't keen at first, but I persuaded him to invest some money into it to try and modernize it, encourage people back."

"Even though your range of drinks is limited?" Tag arched a brow.

"The regulars don't seem to mind…"

"Chill." Tag raised a hand. "I'm kidding with you. It's nice here."

"And half of it's yours now," Freddie said. She faltered when she saw the look on Tag's face. "Sorry. Blair told us your dad had left you fifty-fifty each."

"Mm."

"I suppose this means you're my new boss," Freddie said casually, watching carefully for Tag's response.

"I wouldn't worry about that too much. I won't be here long enough to be anyone's boss," Tag said. "As soon as I've sorted Dad's finances out, I'm handing my share to Blair and then I'll be off again."

"Just a flying visit, then?" Freddie wiped at the table with the towel that was in her hands. So no sweeping changes? No throwing her weight around? The tension in Freddie's shoulders eased a little.

"Enough time to try and reconnect with my nephew, sort out Dad's stuff," Tag said, "try and make amends with my brother, and then I'll be off again."

A blast of cold air from the opening door stalled the conversation.

Blair stepped in. He stamped the snow from his boots and, spying Tag, marched straight to the cafe counter.

"You're still here?" He pitched her a disdainful look. "Thought you'd be halfway back to England by now."

"Mature, Blair." Tag inspected a menu that was on her table. "Give me time, though. I'll soon be out of your hair again."

"I see you've met my sister." He addressed Freddie then threw his gloves onto the counter, completely ignoring Tag's comment. "Is the coffee still hot?"

Freddie rose to embrace him. "It was a lovely service and wake, Blair," she said. "Adam would have been proud."

"I hope so." Finally he drew his attention to Tag. "It was done as he would have wanted."

Freddie shot a look to Tag. Just as before, she thought Tag looked small. Insecure and small. Her brother blanking her and shooting her daggers didn't help, Freddie was sure.

"You have your paperwork?" Blair asked. "For this place?"

Tag snapped her head up. "It's at the B & B."

Blair slung his coat on the back of a chair and sat. "We'll have to talk," he said. He pulled an organizer from his coat pocket and opened it up. "At some point."

"That'll mean you'll have to say more than three words to me," Tag shot back.

Freddie wondered whether the temperature was rising in the cafe, or if that was just her imagination.

Blair glowered at Tag. "You still have staff to meet, remember?" he said. "You didn't mingle at the wake. That would have been the perfect time."

"I'll meet everyone in time," Tag threw back. "John's already briefed me about them." She glared at her brother, obviously tired of the continued animosity directed at her from him. "I'm not stupid, you know."

"No, you're very clever."

"What's that supposed to mean?"

Blair sat back in his chair and folded his arms across his chest, silently fuming. "Are you telling me it's pure coincidence that you come out of the woodwork now that Dad's gone?" he asked. "That you only decide to come back here once you knew you'd inherited half of his business?"

Freddie saw the hurt on Tag's face. "I came back to come to his funeral," Tag finally managed. "Of course I did! Do you think I'm that selfish that I'd have stayed away? What kind of daughter would that have made me?"

"Okay, so you came to the funeral. *Well done, you!*" Sarcasm. Classy. "The prodigal daughter returns a little later than expected. The same daughter her father doted on, even though she treated him like shit, and the same daughter that then falls straight into owning something that she didn't give a toss about ten years ago and probably doesn't give a toss about now but will still have it, thank you very much because it's worth a few quid?" His voice escalated.

"You think I want this place?" Tag stared open-mouthed at Blair. "You think I only came back so I could get my hands on my share?" She stood, shunting her chair back. "You really don't know me at all. I don't give *that* for this place." Tag clicked her fingers. "I told you at the funeral, I don't want it. Never have done. I hate the place, and the sooner I offload it back to you and get out of here, the better."

Freddie watched in silence. Tag's vitriol towards her father, Blair, and the business left her stunned. The same girl who'd been so pleasant, laughing and joking with her just moments before, was now pouring out her hatred through the cafe. *Her* cafe. Tag's reversion to how she'd acted when Freddie had first encountered her that morning—rude, stand-offish, and, yes, petulant—shocked Freddie; perhaps everything she'd heard about her over the years was true after all. Tag was trouble. A selfish little madam. That's what she'd heard. Had just upped and gone one day and had never been back. Had broken Adam's heart and had—

"Of course Dad loved you!" They were arguing about Adam now. "Why do you think he worked all the hours God sent? Because he wanted to?" Blair asked. "No, he did it for you and me, so we'd never want for anything growing up."

"Bullshit." Tag stopped. "He was too wrapped up in himself to see what we needed." She placed her palms flat on the table and leaned towards Blair. "It was so selfish! I mean, how did he think *I* was coping?"

"You think *he* was being selfish?" Blair snorted. "Just listen to yourself. It's not all about you, you know," he said. "And if you'd actually bothered to talk to him over the years, rather than just choosing to believe what you wanted to believe—"

Freddie caught Tag's eye. Now she looked devastated, and back to being every inch the lost little girl. Freddie didn't want to be hearing all this family hatred, dredged back up in front of her.

"We should talk about this later," Tag said to Blair, flicking a look her way. "Freddie doesn't need to get dragged into all our family shit."

Tag must have been recognized Freddie's own unease in spite of her own misery. Freddie was still standing by the coffee counter, trying not to watch as Blair stared Tag out. "Fair enough," he muttered. He slammed his organizer shut, then stood, pulling his coat from the back of his chair. "Can I leave you to lock up, Freddie? I've had more than enough for one day." Blair picked up his organizer. With a nod of his head to Freddie, he left the cafe again without another word to Tag.

❖

Mature. Real mature.

An uneasy silence hung in the air. Tag, still reeling from the strength of Blair's anger, stared down at the table in front of her. She chewed irritably on her bottom lip and picked up a menu, just for something to do, and stared down, too afraid to meet Freddie's eye. How could he have spoken to her like that? In front of Freddie, a total stranger too? It had cut deep, deeper than Tag had anticipated. Blair had loved her once. She knew he had. Despite their five-year difference, Blair and Tag had been as close as twins when they were growing up. Now? He could hardly bear to look at her. Tag brooded at the menu in her hands. Blair hated her. Her big brother hated her.

Tag tossed the menu down. Just why was she here again?

Finally, when the silence in the cafe was more than she could bear, she spoke. "I'm sorry about that." She lifted her eyes and looked straight at Freddie. "As I'm sure you've realized, there's a lot of bad blood still between me and my brother."

"Guess you could have done without that, hey?" Freddie said diplomatically.

"It would have happened at some point." Tag dropped her eyes. "Would have been nice if he'd not done it in front of you, though."

"Families, hey?" Freddie pulled herself away from the counter and walked to the table. "Can't live with them, can't live without them."

In spite of her neutral words, Tag could sense Freddie's shock. Understandable. She'd seen the growing horror on Freddie's face at the harsh words she and her Blair had flung at each other. "I'm a nice person really." Tag half laughed. She needed Freddie to know that. She didn't know this person at all, had only met her hours before, and yet? She didn't want her to think badly of her.

The look on Freddie's face was telling Tag otherwise.

"I think perhaps," Freddie said, sitting down opposite Tag, "you and your brother have a lot of talking to do." She paused. "Rather than shouting."

"If only you knew me," Tag said, laughing again, "you'd see I'm the most placid person ever." She met Freddie's eye. "Not the angry, argumentative idiot you just saw."

Freddie didn't answer. Instead she smiled, stood, and returned to the relative safety of her counter.

Tag sighed.

It was going to be a long few weeks.

CHAPTER SEVEN

Tag didn't believe in ghosts. Her father had once told her that he thought she'd been born cynical and he'd never met anyone in his life who was so contemptuous of myths, or so opposed to any ideologies that couldn't be proved without rock-solid photographic evidence. Growing up, there were never fairies at the bottom of the Grainger garden. The Easter Bunny was, to Tag, quite frankly a scary concept, and Father Christmas? By the age of four, Tag had decided he was just some big bloke in red who sat in the foyer of Balfour's one and only supermarket around Christmastime and who was really Frank Peterson, the town's milkman. Tag told her parents this with absolute conviction because, according to her, he "smelled of curdled milk and anyway I recognized him."

But for a girl who thought of ghosts as being just a figment of people's vivid imaginations, Tag nevertheless felt a sense of apprehension the second she stepped into the watermill, barely three hours after her father's funeral. Everything was exactly as she'd remembered it, and as she walked silently around, the ghosts that she knew didn't exist nevertheless continually caught her eye. There was her father, hoisting up heavy sacks of wheat and pouring them down a chute, while her mother, flour up to her elbows, watched the corns being shaken into the eye of the runner stone, occasionally glancing up to her husband with a reassuring smile. It was a scene Tag had seen so many times growing up, and now she was seeing it, clear as day, once more.

But, no. No ghosts here.

Tag shivered. She stood in the doorway to the watermill, listening to the deafening grinding of the millstones as they pounded down the wheat, and gazed around her. It was an ear-shattering sound that once upon a time irritated her beyond belief, and yet now it was one she found strangely comforting.

"Does it bring it all back?" A gruff male voice, raised to be heard over the noise, startled her.

Tag swung round. Someone was working? Today of all days?

"I know what you're thinking." Whoever he was, he was a mind reader. "Do you think your father would have had it any other way?"

Tag shook her head. "Guess not."

"Life goes on, even when you want it to pause for a while." Seemed this old guy was a philosopher as well as a mind reader. "We've got an order to get out by tomorrow," he explained, shaking a sack out and sending a plume of dust into the air. "Remember how you and Blair used to play in here?"

Tag looked at his rugged face, seeking familiarity. "You worked here when we were kids?"

The man gave a smoky chuckle. "Since before you were born." He folded the sack against his chest.

"I don't remember your name." Tag felt her face colour. "I'm sorry."

"It's Tom." He reached out a floury hand.

"Tom Brennan?" He was older. Craggier.

"As I live and breathe."

"You would always play hide-and-seek along with us." Tag pictured herself, scurrying between the machinery while Blair stood and counted up to ten by the enormous wooden doors that led out to the mill's courtyard outside. She always had a sneaky feeling he used to count to twenty. Give her a fighting chance. "Never giving away where I'd hidden myself." A memory of crouching behind the old thresher, her finger to her lips, eyes fixed on Tom, crashed over her like waves on a rock. "I remember now." Tag's mood brightened.

"You used to love it." Tom gave another wet laugh. "Health and safety would have had a field day these days, though."

"So who works in here with you now?" Tag roamed the floor, looking about her. "It used to be…Gordon something-or-other, didn't it?"

"Williams." Tom shook his head. "You *have* been gone a long time, haven't you? Gordon died eight years ago." He flicked a switch on a wall. The grist stones started to slow. "I have a lad, Alan, in here with me now."

"I still have to meet so many people." Tag frowned. Worry, simmering all day, surfaced again. "It all still feels a bit much."

"They're wary." Tom watched as Tag slowed her pace. "The staff."

"Of me?"

Tom cocked his head. "Of what you'll do." He assessed her. "Your plans."

"What do they think I'm going to do?" Tag rubbed at her face. She'd only come in to reacquaint herself with the mill. Not to have an impromptu staff meeting. "I'm relying on *them* to tell *me* what to do."

"They think you'll sell up." Tom sat back against the wooden railings that bordered the large bed wheel. He crossed thick, muscular arms across his chest. "Maybe to a foreign investor. Leave them all out of a job."

Is that what they thought? Tag hadn't even met them and they were second-guessing what she was going to do. Like she'd be sticking around long enough to even think about what she wanted to do. All she had been concerned with so far had been making a good impression. Letting them all see she wasn't as bad as she was sure they'd all been told. Seems they'd already all made their minds up about her, though. Had Freddie already made up her mind about what sort of person Tag was too? Her head automatically turned towards the door to the cafe. To Freddie. It wasn't as if they'd exactly met under the best circumstances, Tag acting like a total fusspot over something so trivial as a five-pound bill, then arguing with her brother in front of her. Did Freddie have her pegged? Decided for herself that Tag was to be avoided and to be suspicious of?

"How can you have all decided what I'm like without even talking to me?" Tag voiced her thoughts. "I've hardly spoken to any of you yet."

"We're just all a bit worried about the future," Tom said. "There's a lot of us rely on this place."

"Give me a chance." Tag's laugh masked her annoyance. "I've only been back five minutes."

"Why don't you use the ceilidh on Wednesday as the perfect way to say hi to everyone?"

"The ceilidh?" Tag asked wearily. Tiredness was creeping over her.

"For the anniversary," Tom said. "You're staying until then, aren't you?"

"Dad still used to do that?" Tag was amazed. Every year, without fail, her parents had held a traditional Gaelic gathering in the cafe, after hours, to celebrate their anniversary. Started as a bit of a gimmick for their first wedding anniversary, the party had become something of a tradition each year after that. It was a real Scottish affair: a hired band, lots of singing and dancing. And Scotch. Always plenty of Scotch, Tag recalled. Staff, their families, and friends would all be invited, and over the years, it had grown from being nothing more than a bit of fun, to being a yearly event which everyone looked forward to. Even after her mother had died, Adam had continued the tradition, although more out of loyalty to his wife's memory, Tag had often thought, than anything else.

"We always had one every year without fail," Tom said. "Now Blair's determined to keep it going, no matter the circumstances."

"I remember them well." Sitting on her mother's lap, clapping her hands along with the music was just one of many memories. Tag blinked the thought away.

"If I quiz you now on the intricate workings of a grist mill, you'll be able to tell me everything I need to know?" Freddie spoke from just inside the door. "Hi, Tom." Tom waved his greeting back.

Tag swung round, Freddie's appearance in the doorway to the mill a welcome sight. Freddie grinned across at her, prompting both surprise and relief. Freddie, Tag thought, looked genuinely pleased to see her, despite her concerns. "Ah, I can't guarantee that." Tag's melancholy dissolved the instant she saw Freddie again, just as it had in the cafe earlier. "We were just talking about the mill."

"Oh?" Freddie came further into the building.

"Apparently the guys up here are wary of me." Tag nodded her head to Tom. "Wondering about my intentions."

Freddie caught Tom's eye. "Understandable," she said tactfully.

"So I'm going to make it clear to everyone what my intentions are before I go," Tag said. "Blair already knows that I want to hand over my share to him." She dragged a sack across the floor to Tom. "Seriously, no one has anything to worry about," she said over her shoulder. "I'm not here to get rid of you all. Just to help Blair sort out the inheritance. Once that's done, I'll be on my way."

"You'll come to the ceilidh though, won't you?" Freddie came over to her and helped her pull the sack the last few feet.

"I told her she has to come." Tom took it from them and hauled it over to the corner of the mill.

"Yes, you absolutely must." Freddie's smile was genuine. Tag liked it.

"Then I will." Tag returned the look. "I'll be here for a good few weeks." She stretched her back and winced. "So you'll be seeing me around a lot."

"Well, I just came in to say I'm closing up." Freddie jammed her thumb over her shoulder. "It's gone five."

Tag looked at her watch. "I didn't realize the time." She zipped up her coat. "I'm sorry if I've kept you both here." She hastened to the door. Shame. Tag could have happily spent much more time in Freddie's company today. "I was hoping to hide in here for a bit longer as well." Tag held the door open for Freddie. "Kill a few hours before I head over to Blair and Ellen's for dinner rather than going back to that soulless B & B."

"Where are you staying?" Freddie followed Tag out.

"Wind-something or other," Tag replied, "down on Sheep Street."

"Connie Booth's place?" Freddie asked. "Four Winds?"

"That's the one."

"Yeah, you're better off hiding up here," Freddie said, "or you'll be quizzed to death for the next two hours." She pulled her phone from her pocket and looked at it. "I can stay for another hour. Come and sit in the cafe with me for a bit."

"It's fine." Tag smiled. "I appreciate the thought, though." She started to walk to her car.

"Seriously"—Freddie put her hand on Tag's arm and stopped her—"I'd like to."

❖

The look of relief on Tag's face when Freddie had offered to hang out for a few more hours had been cute, Freddie thought as she walked by Tag's side back across the car park. Freddie hadn't known what had compelled her to poke her head inside the watermill on her way home, when normally she wouldn't bother, but she was glad she had. Finding Tag still around the place had pleased her, and seeing her talking to Tom, her face etched with concern, had touched her. That had shown Freddie more of the girl she'd spoken to in the cafe before Blair had crashed in, hostility seeping from every pore, which had evidently upset Tag far more than she would ever let on. Tag's conversation with Tom, heard muffled by Freddie as she lurked in the doorway, offered Freddie a glimpse of who she thought—wanted, even—Tag to be.

She had felt sorry for Tag's sake over Blair's animosity; after all, hadn't Tag just said goodbye to her father too? She'd have been feeling raw, yet Blair hadn't seemed to take that into consideration. To Freddie it was understandable that Tag was going to fight back and stand her ground against his onslaught. Anyone would in those circumstances, surely.

And then Tag had felt the need to justify herself to Freddie, had urged her to believe she was really nice. That had comforted Freddie. That Tag was worried about what she and others in the mill—Tom included—thought about her went against any opinions Freddie might have had about her based on rumour and innuendo and gossip.

"Thank you for this." Tag's voice pulled Freddie from her daydream and brought her gaze to meet Tag's. Tag looked tired, Freddie thought. Tired and defeated. Her sympathy towards her increased.

"It's been a long day, huh?" Freddie asked.

"You've no idea."

"Then a chill-out in my cafe is just what you need." Freddie meant it too. Skye would be fine with Pete and Sarah for another hour. Suddenly the thought of a chill-out with Tag in her cafe seemed like a very good idea indeed.

For them both.

❖

Tag sat back in the cafe, her legs kicked out in front of her. She circled her head, allowing the stresses of the day to ease from her body, and felt herself start to relax properly for the first time that day. There was no need to speak, she figured. Silence was okay. As long as she didn't have to think about Blair, her father, or the mill for five minutes. Let alone ceilidhs and flour and staff and grists.

"So what was this place like when you were little?" Freddie was the first to speak.

"My mum used to run it back then," Tag replied.

"I heard," Freddie said

"It's nice in here. Mum would have liked it." Tag pulled a packet of sugar out from its small china holder in the middle of the table in front of her and held it between her fingers, studying it, deep in thought. If she listened very carefully, she could hear her mother's voice echo round her. Always a towel draped over her shoulder, her mother had been the lifeblood of the cafe. It was the only part of the mill where she had absolute control, where she could do what she wanted, run the place how she wanted, and serve what she wanted. She adored the cafe and treated each and every customer who came in through her doors as a personal friend. Halcyon days, thanks to her mother.

"It used to be fit to burst back then," Tag said. "Returning customers, regular new daily ones." She looked around her. "A hive of activity."

"If only I could say the same now," Freddie said.

"It's not like that?"

"The modernizing I told you about before?" Freddie waved an arm around. "We did it because we thought it might bring in a fresh wave of customers."

"Did it?"

"I wish." Freddie laughed. "But we manage."

"I didn't realize." Freddie's laugh seemed to mask deep discomfort. When had the cafe last been full? It was half Tag's for now. But perhaps this gave her more impetus to jump ship sooner rather than waiting a few weeks. "Is it very bad?"

"No, of course not."

Tag changed the subject. Now was not the time to talk business. "It's colourful in here, just how Mum liked it."

"You think she'd approve?" Freddie cast her a look.

"I do think she'd approve, yes." Tag nodded. "The sunshine went out of this place when mum died. Dad never bothered with it after that, but I think you persuading him to bother has brought some of the happiness back."

The day her mother had died, darkness gathered over the mill and never left. Tag always believed that by moving away and leaving her past behind, she could outrun the dark clouds and at last get some light back in her life. Over the years Tag thought that once the clouds had gone, the sunshine her mother had always offered her would return. But it never did. Always chasing happiness, she had spent years moving from city to city, always seeking the contentment she'd known as a child. The companionship. The laughter.

"I heard about your mum," Freddie asked carefully. "It must have been awful losing her in a car accident like that."

Tag now started to make small circles in her sugar pile. "It was," Tag said. "It was years ago now, but it still feels like it happened the other day."

"I'm sorry." Freddie's cheeks flushed and her voice rang with compassion.

"I've been thinking about her a lot all over again," Tag said. "I guess Dad dying as well has brought it all back to me. Everything suddenly becomes a reminder, you know?"

"It does," Freddie agreed. "I lost my sister a few years back and I still get reminders every day. It's hard."

"I'm sorry."

"Thanks" she said. "Losing a member of your family's awful at the best of times, but for you, I guess losing your second parent makes everything all so final, doesn't it?"

"Makes you realize you're really not a kid any more, that's for sure." Tag's voice sounded thin to her own ears. She cleared her throat. "You're no one's child. It's just you on your own from that day on."

Freddie nodded. She glanced at the clock on the cafe wall and her face fell. "Shit, I have to go." She scraped her chair back noisily and went to a tall, wooden coat stand by the door. She grabbed her coat and bag from it. All in the blink of an eye. "I'm sorry," she said. She yanked her coat on and looked at Tag.

"No, I'm sorry." Tag hastily brushed her sugar pile into her hand and hurried to the bin behind the counter. "I've kept you talking when I'm sure you had other things to do." Had they really been talking for nearly an hour? It had felt like just minutes, and now she didn't want Freddie to leave—not just yet.

"Not at all," Freddie said. She opened the door. "It's been really nice." Freddie held the door open wider for Tag, then followed her outside. Freddie wrapped her coat around herself against the cold. "Are you coming back up here again tomorrow?"

"Not sure." Tag pulled her car keys from her trouser pocket. "I have to phone work. I've taken time off, but I still have to check in with them, you know?"

"Of course." Freddie pulled out her own car keys. "Well, it's been great to meet you." She held out a hand to Tag, who shook it quickly. "Even if it wasn't in the happiest of circumstances." Freddie walked down to her car then looked back over her shoulder to Tag. "It'd be good if you could make it tomorrow though," she said with a smile. "I'm baking scones—you can be my guinea pig."

CHAPTER EIGHT

Glenside, Blair and Ellen's cottage, was an unassuming place, hidden halfway up a rough track around five minutes out of the centre of Balfour. Tag remembered the ancient crofter's cottage fondly as being old Mrs. Marshall's, the widow that used to run the newsagent's in the town square, and who used to let Tag pick apples from her tree each autumn.

Now, despite the apple trees all gone and replaced with roses, the cottage remained more or less as Tag had remembered it. Happy memories tailspinned around her mind as her car crunched up the track. Warm fires. Cocoa. Soft lighting. And apples. Always lots of apples. Tag rang the doorbell and stepped back. How long had Blair and Ellen lived there? A good while, if the lived-in look was anything to go by. A railway lamp dangled from the porch in front of the door, sending out just enough pools of light to allow Tag to see a few flecks of white paint peeling from the window frames and the remnants of last summer's clematis, which still clung messily but valiantly to the trellis that arched over the front door. Mrs. Marshall wouldn't have been pleased, Tag thought with a wry smile.

The tall boy who answered the door to her a few minutes later eyed her with a mixture of suspicion and shyness.

"You must be Magnus," she said. "Last time we knew each other, you were about this tall." She held her hand out above the ground. Lame. Didn't she just used to hate people saying that to her when she was Magnus's age? He didn't seem to mind, though. He stepped aside to allow her to come in and mumbled something incoherent which Tag took to be an offer to take her coat. No doubt prompted by his mother who was standing in the doorway to her kitchen, an amused look on her face. Tag took her coat off and handed it to him. She stood, awkwardly, in the hallway.

"Don't expect him to speak." Ellen came over to Tag and spoke in a lowered tone. "And don't take it personally. He's gone to the grunting stage now. We've had barely a word from him since before Christmas."

"He's grown." Tag immediately felt stupid. "I mean, of course he's *grown*. I guess I didn't expect him to be so tall already."

Magnus disappeared into the lounge and fell back onto the sofa.

"He'll be fourteen soon." Ellen signalled for Tag to follow her into the kitchen. "Scary, huh?"

Fourteen? So many years missed. Tag's heart sank.

"Thank you again for inviting me over." She followed Ellen into the kitchen. "I must admit, the thought of spending the evening alone in my room at the B & B didn't exactly fill me with much joy."

"I figured that," Ellen said. She opened a cupboard door and pulled out a bottle of red wine. "Let's face it, it's been a hell of a day for you. The journey up here, the funeral, and then having to face everyone at the wake, all in the space of a few hours. You must be exhausted."

"I am."

"It's been a horrible day for everyone, one way or another. But the last thing you needed was to be alone with your thoughts all night." Ellen held up the wine bottle and waggled it at Tag. "Not tonight of all nights."

"Don't suppose you have beer, do you?" Tag asked sheepishly. "If you don't, it doesn't matter." Never one to look a gift horse.

"Never did have you down as a wine sort of girl." Blair's voice sounded behind her. Tag swung round. He sauntered past her and went to the fridge and pulled out two bottles, then swiftly pulled the cap off one and handed the bottle to Tag. All without another word. Before she'd had a chance to thank him, Blair had walked from the kitchen again and joined Magnus on the sofa, playfully slapping his legs to make him move over so he could sit down.

Tag looked at both Blair and Magnus from the doorway. There had been a time when she'd been incredibly close to both of them, but now? Her nephew didn't even know who she was, and her brother could barely bring himself to say two words to her.

"He *will* come round." Ellen put her hand on Tag's arm, reading her mind. "You know Blair as well as I do. His pride won't let him tell you he's happy to see you. He needs to keep up this pretence of being angry with you, but it won't last forever, trust me."

"I want to make amends," Tag said. She took a drink from her bottle. "I want to get to know him again."

"He wants to get to know you as well," Ellen said. "But that can only happen if you stick around." She grabbed an oven glove from the kitchen table and went to the oven. "You are staying on, aren't you?"

"I already said." Tag took a piece of raw carrot from a saucepan and nibbled the end off it. "I'm not eighteen any more, Ellen."

"I'm just checking." Ellen held her oven-gloved hands up. She opened the oven door and pulled out a tray. The piece of beef in it, with potatoes nestled around it, sizzled and spat angrily. "I hope you haven't gone veggie since we last saw you." Ellen looked back over her shoulder, her face masked by the steam.

Tag shook her head. She rested her hip against the sink and took another drink from her beer. "After I left Balfour," she said slowly, "I thought of you all a lot, you know." She dwelt on her words. "Especially Magnus. I was always very fond of him."

"He adored you." Ellen closed the oven door. She uncorked the red wine she'd just taken from the cupboard and poured herself a glass. "And I'd be lying if I said you leaving like that didn't affect him." She sipped at her wine. "But kids can be resilient creatures. He asked about you for a while, then suddenly one day he didn't ask any more."

Tag's eyes misted. That hurt. But what did she expect? That he'd spend his entire childhood crying for her?

Ellen walked past Tag, pulling on her arm as she passed. "Come and talk to them both."

Tag followed Ellen into the lounge. She sat down in a chair next to the woodstove, sensing Blair glance at her from the sofa as she did so. He didn't speak. Instead he chose to bury himself in his newspaper while Magnus played on his phone. But after a well-aimed kick from Ellen hit its target, Blair finally put the newspaper down and looked at Tag properly.

"So," he said. He picked up his beer bottle from the floor by his feet and took a long drink from it. He looked at Tag again.

"So," Tag repeated. She mirrored Blair's action of drinking from her bottle. Anything to deflect from the clunky atmosphere.

Blair held his bottle in his hand and studied the label carefully. Tag sat in silence and watched him as he occasionally picked at it with his index finger, all the time avoiding eye contact with her.

"For goodness' sake, Blair!" Ellen exhaled loudly, breaking the silence that Tag didn't think she'd be able to bear a second longer. "Talk to her."

"And say what?" Blair's head snapped up. "What can I possibly say to her after all this time?"

Magnus shifted uncomfortably in his chair, his eyes fixed resolutely on his phone.

"You could start by asking her how she is," Ellen replied. "She did just bury her father today, you know. You weren't the only one."

"The father she didn't care about when—"

"I did care about him." Tag wasn't having that. "Of course I did!"

"Yeah, felt like it."

"I don't want to argue with you, Blair." Tag sat forward in her chair. She rested her elbows on her legs, beer bottle clasped in both hands, and stared down at the rug by her feet. "I came here tonight to catch up with you, to talk about the mill, and perhaps to start making amends for the past." She glanced at Magnus. "And to try and get to know Magnus all over again."

Magnus lifted his eyes at the mention of his name. He stared straight back at Tag, then back at his phone again.

Tag swallowed and entreated Magnus to look her way again. He didn't.

"I'm here for a few weeks," she continued. This time she looked at Blair. "I thought it would be neat if you, me, and Magnus could hang out together one day while I'm here. Just for old time's sake?"

She sensed a flicker of something pass across Blair's face. Regret? Hope?

"Hang out, huh?" Finally Blair spoke. "We're honoured. Don't you have another life somewhere else that you need to get back to though?" Tag leaned away from her brother as she sensed his resentment seeping from him.

"I do, actually." Tag ignored his sullenness. "Along with a mountain of paperwork to sift through."

"Beats having to get up at four every morning, I guess," Blair said bitterly.

"You still do that?" Tag raised her eyebrows. "You still get up and light the ovens every morning?" That had been his job all those years ago, when he'd just been a teenager. The same job her father insisted she take over when Blair turned twenty. Surely he wasn't still doing it after all these years?

Blair shook his head. "The head baker took that on a handful of years ago." He chewed on his lip, his brow furrowing. "It's his responsibility now. I just stick to what I know best."

"Which is?"

"Growing the crops and managing them," Blair said. "Crop rotation and harvesting. That sort of stuff." He glanced at Tag. "All the things I always loved doing."

"So you get to drive that fabulous John Deere now?" Tag asked. "I'm jealous."

She saw the hint of a smile play on Blair's lips, even though he hadn't answered her. Instead, he drained his drink and stood. He held his hand out for her bottle and waited while she too drained it, then took it from her and went back to the kitchen. Bonus.

Ellen caught her glance and nodded in encouragement at the question in Tag's eyes. Steadying herself, Tag got up and followed Blair into the kitchen. He retrieved two fresh bottles from the fridge and handed her one.

"Was it quick?" Eventually Tag spoke. She needed to know. "Dad? Was it quick?"

Blair pulled the cap off his bottle. He nodded and drank back some beer. Tag waited for him to speak.

"The only good thing about a heart attack like that," he said, wiping his mouth, "is that it's a blessing that it's over fast. Paramedics reckon he was gone before he hit the floor."

Tag's breath hitched. Needles pricked at her eyes. She pulled the cap from her bottle and chugged her beer back. She hoped Blair hadn't sensed either her tears or the flush that she knew was rapidly spreading across her neck as she fought the tears back. She thought about saying something more. What more could she say? Nothing that would sound right or proper. Not yet. Instead, she and Blair stood at opposite sides of the kitchen, quietly sipping at their beers and avoiding eye contact with one another.

"Dinner," Ellen said, marching into the kitchen and breaking the silence, "is the usual Ellen Grainger feast of *I plonk it on the table and you all help yourselves*." She handed her empty wine glass to Blair for him to refill for her as she passed him on her way to the oven. "Otherwise known as a free-for-all."

Tag had finally managed to have something resembling a conversation with her brother. She was relieved. No, grateful. It had been a start. She busied herself laying the enormous scrubbed wooden kitchen table. He'd spoken to her at least, and had told her about Dad. Anything after this would be a plus. Tag took the place mats and cutlery that were now being passed to her by Blair and set them in some sort of order around the table. And who knew with Blair? Two words today. Three tomorrow? Tag nodded to herself. Slow and sure. That's all she could hope for right now.

She looked around her, to Ellen, busy with the food, her wine duly replenished. To Blair, helping her, occasionally running a hand down her arm. They were so in love, Tag thought. Even after so many years. A twinge of jealousy snapped at her. She'd never had what they had, the companionship and love that Blair and Ellen still had. The jealousy intensified. She had made it to the age of twenty-seven without ever knowing what true love felt like; now, seeing Blair and Ellen, so in love with one another, so tactile and caring towards each other, made her desperately miss something she didn't even realize she'd missed until now.

Tag sensed Magnus behind her. He was hanging around by the kitchen door, so Tag sauntered over to him. The kid was shy. She got that. Talking games always helped combat shyness, she figured. "So what games have you got on your phone?"

Magnus shrugged. "Basic stuff," he said. He looked down at his phone still in his hand. "But then it's a basic phone, isn't it?"

"You seen this game?" Tag reached into her jeans pocket and pulled out her iPhone. Magnus's eyes widened. She ran her thumb over the screen until she found the game she was looking for and handed it to him. "Now, this is addictive."

"You've got an iPhone?" Magnus accepted her phone and held it as though it was a piece of china. "Respect."

"It's supposed to be for work." She bumped his arm. "But if you look at my awesome high score, you'll see that I use it for other things as well."

"No way." Exaggerated surprise. *Way* exaggerated surprise. It was cute, Tag thought. "Seventy-eight thousand? For real? Best I could get was about forty thousand when I played it on my friend's iPhone." Magnus jabbed his finger on the screen and narrowed his eyes. "You've got this game too? That's mental." He held the phone to Tag. Approval from near-fourteen-year-old obtained. Result.

"You got Perdition on here?" He frowned down at her phone.

"Yes, I've got Perdition," Tag said. "I like it. It's good."

"Mm, it's good, except…"

"Except?"

"Well, every time I get as far as the watchtower on it, I get shot." Magnus screwed up his nose. "You got past that stage yet?"

"Past stage eighteen?" Tag asked. "I passed that stage ages ago. I'm on at least stage thirty now."

"Nah, you're messing with me." Magnus made big eyes. "How?" He glanced down as the phone rang, and handed it immediately back to Tag. "It says *Anna* on there." He shrugged.

"Cheers." Tag clamped the phone to her ear. She mouthed an apology to Ellen, who was stirring something in a saucepan, and walked into the lounge. "Hey." She spoke quietly and glanced over her shoulder.

"How was it?" Anna's voice sounded at the other end of the phone. Tag could hear loud voices and music in the background, followed by a woman's voice nearby.

"Where are you?"

"The Loft. So…how was it? The funeral, I mean."

The Loft? So Anna wasn't bothered about taking her new girlfriend there, after everything? The same place she and Tag used to go? Their own private hideaway? Tag tried to feel something— anything—at the thought of Anna being there with someone else. But there was nothing.

"Okay," Tag said. "Glad it's all over, though."

"Cool," Anna said. A pause. "I was thinking about you today."

"Were you?" Tag felt a coldness. "Cheers. But no need." She swivelled round. No one was waiting for her so they could start eating.

"I still care," Anna said. "I know you don't believe me, but—"

"You cared so much you left me for…what was her name again?" Tag knew damn well what her name was. "Caroline? Was that it?" It still pained her to say her name, even though it had been months. Betrayal did that to a person, even if you thought you had no more pain left in you. Tag shivered, remembering.

"Don't." Anna's voice hardened.

"No, let's." The beer in her empty stomach had emboldened Tag.

"I also rang to tell you there's some e-mails coming your way tomorrow," Anna said. "I didn't ring for us to have an argument."

Tag pinched her eyes shut. Anna wanted to talk work? Today of all days?

"Sure." Tag sighed.

"Stills for the Milton project for you to choose," Anna continued. "A decision by next Monday would be good."

"I'm on it." She so wasn't.

"Right, I have to go," Anna said curtly. "He's waiting."

"Stefan, huh?"

"Yeah," Anna said. "Sorry."

"Don't be," Tag said. "I didn't care about Stefan when we were together. Even less so now." She looked back over her shoulder. "Anyway, I've got my brother and everyone waiting for me in the kitchen so I better go."

"Happy families? Quaint."

"Not quite."

"Well, I'm glad the funeral went all right," Anna repeated. "Look, I've really got to go."

"Sure."

Anna cut the call without replying. Tag tried to ignore the return of her loneliness. She put the phone back in her pocket, painted a smile on her face, and went back into the kitchen.

Yes, she had family waiting. So why did she still feel so alone?

❖

"Everything okay?" Ellen placed a steaming tray in the middle of the table and pulled her oven gloves off.

"Yeah. All good." Tag lifted her phone to Magnus. "You have to take out the Black Goblin first," she said. "He's the War Lord's sniper. Take him out before you do anything else and you stand a better chance of getting to the top of the watchtower."

"The Black Goblin?" Magnus sat back in his chair and threw his arms out. "I thought he was his servant, that's all."

"Nuh-uh. He pays him to take out intruders." Tag approached the table and sat opposite Magnus. "That's why his money level goes down during fights if he doesn't make enough hits."

"For sure?"

"Trust me."

"I have no idea what you two are talking about." Ellen placed a large spoon in the tray and held her hand out for Tag's plate. "But if it involves any blood and gore, then I don't want to know."

Magnus caught Tag's eye, a *she never understands* expression on his face.

"Can I go eat in my room?" He passed his plate to his mother.

"You have homework?" Ellen filled his plate and handed it back to him.

"Yuh-huh."

"Okay, scram."

Blair was quiet. Tag's eyes flickered over her brother's face, noticing properly for the first time the worry lines carved into it, the shadows under his eyes.

"You look done in," she said to him.

"I feel it."

"It's been hard," Ellen interjected. "Since your father—"

"Since before," Blair countered. "Since long before." He tossed a look to Tag, then hunkered over his meal, his shoulders heavy. He began to eat, each mouthful more wearied than the last.

"We need to talk," Tag said, "about the future." Blair didn't reply. Tag started to eat, if only to relieve the oppressive silence. For a short while, the only sound came from the scraping of cutlery on plates, or the occasional clearing of a throat. Finally Tag put her knife and fork down.

"I'm not here long, Blair," she said. "Once we've sorted out Dad's finances I *would* like to get something sorted about the mill before I go home again."

"Before you run out on us again, you mean?"

"Before I have to go back to work."

"Hang on." Blair put his fork down too. "I thought you said you were freelance down there? Worked for yourself?"

"I am, kinda. I'm on Anna's payroll, though."

"So you're not actually your own boss, then? Only…*kinda*?" Blair air-quoted. "Another lie. There's a surprise."

"Don't split hairs," Tag protested, wondering why she had to justify herself.

"But I thought this Anna person used to be your girlfriend," Blair argued. "You're telling me she'd mind if you stayed here longer? Do me a favour." He glared at her.

"It's complicated," Tag said.

"Isn't it always with you?" Blair said darkly.

"She's not my only boss." Tag skimmed Blair's and Ellen's faces. "Her husband is too."

"Her husband?" Ellen sounded shocked.

"Priceless," Blair sneered. "You had an affair with a married woman?"

"No." Tag's face darkened. "A married woman had an affair with me."

"There's a difference, is there?"

"When it comes to Anna Deveraux, then, yes," Tag replied. Anna had pursued her. Relentlessly. Showered her with gifts, said all the things Tag had needed to hear when she'd been at her most vulnerable. Tag had fallen for it—fallen for Anna. Then it had all started to unravel. "I took far more time off than I should have," Tag continued. "As it is, I came up here having not been paid for the last three jobs I've done for them."

"The sacrifices we make for family, hey?" Blair replied caustically.

"Don't." Tag fired a warning shot at him. "You have no idea about my life."

"And whose fault is that?"

Another silence glided briefly across the kitchen table.

"The mill." Tag cleared her throat. Change the subject. Fast. "You know as well as I do that I have no right to my share of it."

"At last she talks some sense." Blair picked his plate up and took it to the sink.

"So, like I keep telling you, I want you to have my half," Tag said. "The sooner you accept, the sooner I can go."

Blair cast a look to Ellen.

"It's your entitlement, not mine," Tag continued. "John Flynn made it clear that it was Dad's wish for it to stay in the Grainger name. So it's only right that you have one hundred percent of it."

"I see." Blair hung back by the sink. "You still don't want anything to do with it? Not even after all these years?"

"I wouldn't even know where to start with it, Blair," Tag said. "I work in advertising in a large city. Everything I ever learned around this place has long been forgotten."

"It's in your blood, Tag." Blair picked up a towel and wiped his hands on it. "Even if you don't think you know anything about it, you do. It's instinct."

"I don't." Tag shook her head firmly. "And I don't want any part in it. I want you to have it."

"I need to think about it."

Not the reaction she wanted. Why hadn't Blair jumped at the chance to have control of the whole place? Isn't that what he'd wanted all these years?

"But we can come up with something reasonable between us, surely?" Tag asked. *Just let me get shot of the place. And soon.*

"And once it's all signed over to me? Then what?" Blair asked. "You'll go straight back to Liverpool, I suppose?"

"I guess." She met his eyes. "There'll be nothing keeping me here then, will there?"

"No." Blair hurled his towel down and brushed past her. "I don't suppose there will be."

CHAPTER NINE

Freddie could tell that Skye felt very special right now. Even though her little girl had had to stand on her small stool to see her reflection better in her bedroom mirror, Freddie knew the pinafore dress she'd chosen for Skye to wear to the party was perfect for her. With a patchwork of light and dark blue squares, a sprinkling of pink splatters, and an accompanying cream polo neck underneath, the dress was perfect. Teamed with a pair of woollen navy tights and sturdy brown boots, Freddie was confident Skye would be the best-dressed five-year-old in the entire room.

It was Wednesday evening. The ceilidh. The cafe at the Mill was in a mixed mood, and the staff and their families that were now mingling inside were a combination of those who were determined to celebrate, regardless of the circumstances, and those who thought mourning Adam was still more appropriate, rather than drinking and dancing.

Freddie clutched her drink. Her cafe, cleaned from top to bottom just that afternoon, was always a source of pride to her, and seeing it filled to near capacity pleased her. If only it could be this busy all the time, though. Tag's words to her two days before returned. What had she meant, she'd have to have a think about things? Regardless of what Freddie had told Tag, the lick of fresh paint and a few new paintings flung up on the walls had done little to encourage customers in. Thanks to the new bypass, now taking much needed passing trade away from the cafe, there were days—increasingly just lately—when all Freddie had to do was sit at her favourite table by the window and wait for the next customer to arrive, watching as the cakes went stale.

And Freddie so desperately wanted Tag to think she was capable, and not just from a business point of view either. The truth was—and Freddie had had plenty of time to think about it over the last few days—that she cared increasingly as the days drifted past, about not only what Tag thought of the cafe, but what she thought of her too.

"You okay?" Pete spoke loudly to be heard over the band. "You look a million miles away."

"Just thinking how nice this is." Freddie lifted her glass to the room. "Seeing it full of life and voices." She glanced around her. "Skye okay?"

"She's showing Magnus Colonel Sam." Pete nodded his head to the corner of the room.

"She brought her plastic soldiers?"

"Just the colonel."

"Well I suppose he is head of her platoon." Freddie laughed.

"So, I met Tag just now," Pete said. "And guess what? She's not the snooty bitch everyone in this village made her out to be. You were right."

Freddie's stomach twinged at the mention of Tag's name.

"Fancy that." Freddie rolled her eyes. "Village gossip gets it wrong again."

"I thought she was very nice, actually." Pete took a drink from his glass.

"Seems to be," Freddie said, her face giving nothing away. Her eyes immediately fell onto Tag. Of course they did; she had barely been out of her line of vision for the last ten minutes.

"And what do you think?"

"Oh, she's nice enough," Freddie said, choosing her words cautiously. More than nice. Attractive; funny; attentive. Trouble and unobtainable. Freddie frowned down into her glass. Definitely trouble.

"I'm sensing a but." Pete leaned his head to one side.

"But, well, it's like I told you before—she's one of my new bosses, isn't she. Blair I can cope with. But what if she goes ahead and does what I've been thinking she'll do and recommends a load of changes before she goes again?" She stole another look towards

Tag. "I'll be on my guard with her for a while, I think. Just until I know what she's planning on doing while she's here." On her guard professionally and emotionally.

"I guess she's not here long enough to make an impact," Pete said pragmatically.

"What I'm worried about," Freddie said, steering Pete into a corner, "is that she'll do something when she finds out the mill's not ever going to make her a millionaire."

"Sell, you mean?"

Freddie shrugged. "Or close parts of the mill. The cafe in particular. Whatever she says, whether she sticks around or not, she *does* own half of it."

"She's a Grainger," Pete said. "If she has even a quarter of Adam's kindness, you'll be okay, though."

"I did think that too," Freddie said. Her line of vision drifted across the room and settled on Tag again. Memories of their afternoon spent together in the cafe after the funeral came to her, swiftly accompanied by the now familiar feelings of sympathy and attraction. "I wonder exactly why she left all those years ago." Tag was alone, sitting at the counter. "The rumour mill came up with so many things. I reckon she'll have a few skeletons in her cupboard."

"Interested?" Pete sized Tag up. "She's kind of cute."

"Don't even go there." Freddie patted his stomach. "But yes, she's *very* cute." She widened her eyes to Pete, making him laugh. Humour, she figured, was always a good distraction to deflect someone's true feelings. "Still, one to be avoided, I think."

"You haven't had a date since Charlotte."

"Even so"—Freddie drained her glass—"it's not about me any more, is it?" she said. "My focus is Skye. I have to think about her."

"Even though you've just told me you think Tag's cute?" Pete nudged her.

"Cute, but way too much hassle." Freddie meant it too. For as much as Tag intrigued her and crept into her thoughts more and more frequently the more she saw her or heard her name mentioned, Freddie knew her life needed simplicity. And Tag didn't suggest simplicity to her.

As Freddie watched Tag from across the room, she saw Magnus attract Tag's attention. Tag's expression changed in a heartbeat from melancholy to delight, pricking at Freddie's insides. Tag hopped down from her stool and made her way across the cafe floor towards him, saying something that Freddie couldn't quite pick up, despite her full attention now being on her.

"You think she's trouble?" Pete's voice cut through the hubbub in the room. "The black sheep of the family?"

"I think she has a story to tell, for sure," Freddie said. Magnus was talking excitedly to Tag. She had, Freddie noticed, her entire focus on him alone, as if no one else in the room mattered. "I think it'll be an interesting one too." Tag, Freddie figured, didn't strike her as boring. A frisson of curiosity spread across her chest again. Freddie took a gulp from her drink, swallowing the feeling down before Pete could notice. Her eyes, though, returned to Tag.

She was sitting on the floor, her knees pulled up to her chest. Skye was to one side of her, Magnus to the other. Colonel Sam in front. Tag was talking animatedly to Skye. Arms were lifted, eyes widened. Skye was transfixed, so was Magnus, even though he was pretending not to be. Although his head was bent over a phone, he repeatedly grinned into his fleece and lifted his head as he listened to Tag talking. Freddie was entranced at the ease and friendliness with which Tag spoke with both children.

Pete set his empty glass on a nearby table. "I think I better go save her." Pete nodded towards Tag and her fan club. "Skye has one of those looks on her face that says, *You're not leaving here until I've told you my entire life history.*"

"I'll go." Freddie drained her drink. There was no way Pete was getting to Tag first. "Could do with a refill anyway."

She wandered from him before he could stop her. Grabbing another wine for herself, and a bottle of beer for Tag, she weaved her way around others in the room and approached them. Tag's voice filtered through the closer she got.

"…it was this big, and this wide…the biggest I'd ever seen…fell into the water and *splash!*"

Skye's stream of giggles drew a smile from Freddie, who continued to watch, fascinated, as Tag told her tale, Skye's eyes fixed firmly on her, as if there was no other person in the room at that moment. Tag, Freddie thought with a small flutter of excitement, had the same effect on her. It was as though the second Tag was within Freddie's vision, nothing and nobody else mattered to Freddie. Tag's effect on her, Freddie thought as she gripped her wine glass tighter, was enthralling.

She was a natural with Skye too, Freddie noted, as she continued to both entertain and delight her, treating her with both gentleness and kindness. That warmed Freddie. Rarely—certainly not since Charlotte, anyway—had Freddie seen Skye so wrapped up in one person. Tag, for her part, seemed to be perfectly enjoying her storytelling too. Freddie studied her face and her body language as her tale reached its conclusion and saw no hint of anything other than genuine pleasure at the reaction she was getting from both Skye and Magnus.

As Freddie approached the trio, Skye finally pulled her eyes from Tag and gazed up at Freddie. "Tag caught a fish," she managed to say through her laughter. "And fell in the water." Her eyes immediately went back to Tag, fascinated.

"The fish fell in the water?" Freddie peered down at them.

"No!" A chorus of voices.

"Tag did," Skye corrected. "She fell in the water." More giggles. Then a hiccup. More laughter, even from Magnus as well this time.

Tag, her cheeks suffused with warmth from the heat of the room and from her spirited storytelling, glanced up at Freddie, pleased that Freddie's eyes were already on her. At last she'd come over to her; all the while Tag had been storytelling she'd been acutely aware of Freddie and Pete watching her from across the room. She had willed Freddie to come over and talk some more with her, rather than hanging back with Pete. Now, with their eyes firmly on one another's, Tag knew if she didn't cut her storytelling and take the opportunity to talk to Freddie again before she left, she'd regret it. Talking to Freddie—no, *being* with Freddie—was all she could think about just lately. Tag spied the bottle of beer in Freddie's hand and, hoping desperately Freddie had brought it over for her, immediately saluted

Skye. "It's been lovely to meet you, Skye," she said. "And Colonel Sam." Another salute. "Keep up the good work, Colonel."

"Are you going?" Skye's face fell.

"Just for five minutes." Tag scrambled to her feet. "And when I get back, I'll tell you the story of how I saved a fox from the River Dynne when I was smaller."

Skye's mouth widened. "You saved a fox?"

"I certainly did." Tag took the bottle of beer that was handed to her. "So you wait there and I'll tell you all about it later."

"Okay." The word was drawn out.

Tag high-fived Magnus, who didn't look up, and moved away from them. She waited for Freddie to finish giving Skye whatever instructions she was giving her and return to her.

"Thank you for the beer." She chinked the base of her bottle lightly against Freddie's wine glass.

"You looked like you needed a top up," Freddie said. "And saving from Skye."

"She's lovely." Tag looked back over to her, a smile automatically returning to her lips.

"So I think you've met everyone now?" Freddie asked. "Vernon, just before the music started up again, was the last one."

"I think so, yes," Tag replied. She was alone with Freddie, tucked away in the corner of the room. Tag allowed her eyes to linger on Freddie, to her slightly flushed cheeks, to her hair that tumbled around her face, and felt her own skin flush even more. It was astonishing, Tag thought as she drank her beer, that a girl whom she'd barely known for seventy-two hours could have already started to infiltrate her thoughts; that her very existence made Tag wake up each morning excited about what the day might bring with her.

"Well that's the worst bit over," Freddie said, and Tag realized she'd been staring. She couldn't help it. There was just something about Freddie Metcalfe that made Tag want to look at her, again and again, to study every detail of her face, to envelop herself in her. Tag took another hasty drink.

It was more than just Freddie's beauty and personality which had hooked her, though. Freddie's kindness had knocked her for six too, and her compassion, Tag thought as she gazed out around the room, had really touched her. A sea of faces had greeted Tag when she'd arrived at the ceilidh earlier. Some she recognized vaguely from her past, others she remembered seeing at the funeral. Others she didn't have a clue who they were. A sense of dread had washed over her as she'd seen the expectation and worry on their faces, and the realization that they were—albeit temporarily—her responsibility had hit her like a train.

Each person had introduced themselves to her over the course of the evening, their names barely filtering in to Tag's panicked brain: Alan, George, Tim. How had this happened? Steven, Sally. How, in the blink of an eye, had she inherited all this when she neither needed it, wanted it, or felt able to cope with it? Graham, Vernon.

Tag had sought reassurance from her brother but had found none. Blair, it seemed, was deliberately allowing Tag to shoulder everything on her own. Rather than being with her when each member of staff had approached her, bombarded her with their questions and worries, Blair had chosen instead to secret himself away with his Scotch in the corner of the cafe and let Tag just get on with it. She knew Blair was teaching her a lesson. She wasn't so naive that she didn't know what he was doing. So he'd taught her a lesson and Tag had handled it with maturity. Perhaps now Blair had got it out of his system, he'd finally start to come round.

The only reassurance the entire night, she thought, had been from the eyes that now met hers. Freddie. She had been a rock when Tag felt as though she was floundering. Freddie'd told her more about who each person was after they'd left; she'd stood by her side as new faces and names came to her, time and again. It was only when Vernon had finished his small talk with her that Freddie had finally left her side. Tag had appreciated that. Freddie was kind and funny, a refreshing change from the curtness she'd been used to from Anna. She stole another look at her. Kind, funny, *and* beautiful; some people had it all. Freddie certainly did. Tag looked away, embarrassed, as Freddie caught her looking again.

"It's nice that we've still done this, isn't it?" Freddie's words drew Tag back to her.

"I can't believe my father carried it on for so many years," Tag said. "It started as a bit of fun really. An excuse to have a party when Blair and I were children."

"The other guys like it," Freddie said. "It's a chance for everyone and their families to get together." She drank back some wine. "Adam always said it was important for families to do at least one thing all together during the year." She stopped. "Sorry, I didn't mean…"

"It's okay." Tag's gaze roved around the room. "It's just ironic that this party was pretty much the only time of the year we still all used to get together after mum died."

Her eyes settled on various faces. Husbands and wives. Fathers and sons. Mothers and daughters. Families. There was laughter and happy chattering. Unity. Just as it used to be for her as a child. As she looked around her, the sense of her own isolation hit her with a force she'd never experienced before. She was an outsider. An intruder. This was a gathering for families. What did Tag know about family? She'd been on her own for such a long time it had become second nature. Tears she didn't even feel coming pooled in the corners of her eyes.

"I need some air." Tag slammed back her drink and shouldered past a startled Freddie. She headed for the exit before anyone could see her tears. If there was one thing Tag didn't do in front of other people, it was tears.

❖

The cold night air slapped Tag as she stepped out into the car park. Winter had blown in hard over the course of the day and now icy fingers wrapped round her. Tag shivered, wishing she had something warmer on other than the lambswool sweater that was doing little to keep the cold off her bones.

She tilted her head back, listening to the muffled music still playing inside the cafe, and took in a gulp of air. The night sky was the colour of ink, stars dotted like silver beads. She'd forgotten the intensity of the sky in the countryside. Stars loomed down at her, appearing so close that she felt as though they were in reach.

Tag closed one eye. She reached up and scooped a handful of stars, stuffing them into her trouser pocket, then reached for some more.

"You okay?"

Tag spun round at Freddie's voice. She wiped at her eyes with the inside of her sleeve.

"Just needed some air."

"It's hot in there, isn't it?" Freddie came and stood beside her.

"Very." Tag wavered. "And I got sad. Back in there, I mean."

"I guessed that." Freddie allowed her hand to rest on Tag's for the briefest of moments.

"Seeing everyone with their families," Tag said, "made me miss something I know I had a long time ago."

"Who's to say you can't have that again?"

"Maybe." Tag wrapped her arms around herself. "But I know I'll never have that in Liverpool."

The brief conversation ended. Both stood in silence side by side, watching the stars. Tag's phone vibrated somewhere in her pocket and she retrieved it to look at it before putting it back again.

"Problem?" Freddie asked.

"Nah." Tag turned her phone over in her pocket. "Just work."

Anna, to be more precise. Another text about the photographic stills for the Milton contract. The same photographic stills Tag was supposed to have be working on since Monday.

Tag inhaled slowly, choosing not to reply to it. Anna could go to hell. She wasn't here to be thinking about work. It was bad enough Anna constantly e-mailing her work without bugging her now with texts about the fucking Milton deal. Why couldn't she see that? Tag stared ahead into the endless darkness. A nerve thrummed in her jaw. Irritation always made her do that. She breathed back out again, even slower.

"You look pissed off about it." Freddie spoke quietly.

"Wouldn't you? Getting a text from work when you're supposed to be grieving?"

"I would, yes."

"The fact it was from my married ex-girlfriend as well didn't exactly help." Tag laughed through her nose.

"You work with your ex?"

"Nah. Work *for* her."

"And she's married?"

"Yup." Tag shunted a look to her, expecting to see judgement in her eyes. She saw only empathy.

"That's gotta make things awkward, hasn't it?"

"Yeah, especially when she was the one that did the dirty on me," Tag said. "So. What about you? Any significant other?"

Freddie pulled a face. "Oh, I'm very dull in comparison," she said. "Single, and definitely no married lovers hiding anywhere, that's for sure."

"What brought you and Skye to Balfour?" Tag asked.

"The mill," Freddie said firmly. "I used to help out in a cafe about twenty miles from here. Then a few years ago the chance came up to run the cafe here. I applied for it and got it." She squinted into the darkness. "We don't live in Balfour, though."

"You live just over in Lyster, is that right?" Stalker alert. "I heard," Tag added hurriedly.

"Yep, that's right," Freddie replied. "Actually, Pete and I only just moved there," she said. "It's closer to both our workplaces, and it's a really nice village."

"Pete who I met earlier?" Tag asked.

"My housemate," Freddie said. "His fiancée lives in the next village along, so it's convenient for him too."

"Blair and I used to go fishing in the river by the church in Lyster when we were kids," Tag said. "And then when we were a lot older, we'd sometimes go to The Bull pub, down by the bridge. Is it still there?"

"It is." Freddie's face lit up. "Nice place. Skye and I go there when we can. She loves the swings in the gardens there."

"How old is she?" Tag asked. "Skye?"

"Five," Freddie said, "going on twenty-one."

"You're very lucky to have such an awesome kid."

"Sometimes, especially during her tantrums, I do wonder." Freddie laughed, then shivered.

"Cold?"

"Frozen."

"You want to go back inside?" Tag resisted the urge to fold Freddie into her arms, to rub her skin until she was warm again. "It *is* kind of cold out here."

"How do you feel about it?" Freddie asked. "We can stay out here a bit longer if you need time to yourself." Her teeth chattered and she pulled her arms tighter round herself. "Let's stay. It's a bit of a lion's den in there."

Tag studied Freddie, touched by the sincerity and concern on her face. Despite her obvious cold, she'd be prepared to stay outside with Tag, if it meant saving Tag from the demons that waited for her inside the cafe.

"It's okay." Tag started to walk. Easing Freddie's discomfort was more important to her than not wanting to return. How hard could it be? She thought of Skye and Magnus, waiting for her inside. Her angst dissolved in an instant. "I could use another beer anyway," she lied.

"If you're sure?" Freddie's concern was moving.

"Sure." Tag held her hand out for Freddie. It was frozen. "After all, there's a little girl waiting to hear the tale of the fox in the river," she said, squeezing Freddie's hand and pulling her inside.

CHAPTER TEN

Freddie grabbed an armful of hay and shuffled in through the back door of her cottage, kicking a pair of small shoes out of the way as she did so. The shoes scudded across the linoleum of the utility room, out of her way, only to be replaced by another pair. This time, directly in Freddie's path.

"Skye." Freddie stopped walking. She waited and called again. "Skye!"

So Tag thought Skye was awesome, did she? Freddie smiled as snippets of their conversation returned to her, as they had done the entire night after they'd parted at the ceilidh. It wasn't just their conversation that constantly dripped back into Freddie's mind, delaying sleep and now demanding that she stop what she was doing and give it her full attention. The looks that had passed between them frequently returned to Freddie, sometimes at the strangest moments, taking her quite by surprise. Over breakfast that morning, even just the memory of Tag wiping her tears away when she thought she was alone, then looking to Freddie with eyes so full of sorrow Freddie had thought her heart would crack, had caught her so off guard that even Pete had asked her if she was okay.

"Skye!" Freddie called again, louder this time. Tag had the ability to do that, Freddie thought as she waited patiently for Skye to appear. Catch her off guard. Throw her. And she liked it.

"Yes?" A small voice called from the front room.

"Come here."

"Why?"

"Because I want you to."

"But why?"

"Now."

Freddie never knew five-years-olds could sigh quite as much as Skye could. But her summons to the utility room had elicited a long, impatient puffing of the cheeks from Skye who now stood, hair sticking up at the back, in the hallway. The spitting image of her mother at the same age. Freddie's annoyance dissolved.

"Do you deliberately leave your shoes where I can trip over them?" Freddie asked her over the top of the hay.

"Sorry."

"Come and help me clean out Paddington." Freddie dropped the hay onto the floor. She pulled the door of a hutch open and reached inside, scrabbling with her hands until she made contact. She drew the wriggling, squeaking guinea pig to her chest, then shushed him soothingly and smoothed down his fur. The guinea pig quietened.

"So, how was school today?" Freddie gently handed Paddington to Skye. She waited as Skye repeated Freddie's action of stroking and soothing him, then turned back to the hutch.

"It was okay."

"What did you do?"

"Music and movement." Skye bit at her bottom lip and rolled her eyes. "And spelling." Paddington wriggled.

"Keep a tight hold, please." Freddie nodded to him. She busied herself pulling old bedding from the hutch. "Anything else?"

"Nope." Skye frowned. "Wait. Yes. We did sums too." She pulled Paddington closer to her. "But they were boring."

"Sums are always boring." Freddie screwed up her nose.

"Boring." Skye drew the word out and then giggled. "Did you see the lady at work again today?"

"The lady?"

"The lady that fell in the water," Skye said. "She told me at the party last night."

"Tag?" Freddie liked how her name sounded when she spoke it. "No, not today." She stuffed soiled straw and hay into a bin liner.

"I've never been fishing." Skye spoke as if it was the worst thing in the world. Ever.

"I can't say I have either," Freddie said.

Skye tutted. Freddie resisted the urge to laugh.

"Who is she?"

Freddie fluffed the hay up. "Well, you know Blair? From where I work?"

"Yuh-huh."

"She's his sister."

"She's funny." Skye gripped Paddington tighter.

"Is she?" Freddie smoothed Skye's curls down. She was. Funny and beautiful and…"She make you laugh?"

"Yeah." Skye thought for a moment. "Freddie?"

"Yuh-huh?"

"Is she your new friend?"

"Well, she's sort of my new boss," Freddie said. But did bosses make you lose all rational thought, as Tag was making Freddie do? "But I suppose you could call her a new friend too," she added. That, Freddie thought, was possibly the first understatement of her day.

"What's she called again?" Skye handed Paddington back to Freddie.

"Tag." Freddie pulled the guinea pig to her.

"Tag?" Skye looked perplexed. "Funny name."

"Not to her." Freddie placed Paddington back in his hutch and closed the door.

"To me it is."

"Wash your hands, please." Freddie put a guiding hand on Skye's shoulder and steered her to the sink.

"Did she like it?" Skye rolled her sleeves up with the care and precision of a surgeon. She held her hands under the tap and waited for Freddie to turn the water on. "The party?"

"Tag?"

"Mm."

"I think so, yes." Freddie handed Skye a towel.

"Freddie?" Skye gave her hands a cursory wipe and handed the towel straight back to Freddie.

"Yes?"

"If you and Tag ever go fishing," she asked, "can I come too?"

"Well I don't think we'd ever—"

"Freddie?"

"Yes, Skye?" A patient sigh.

"Can I go and watch TV now?"

❖

"We must stop meeting like this." Freddie spun round at the voice. Tag's smile was genuine and sincere, and drew, Tag noticed with pleasure, a spontaneous smile back from Freddie.

It was late Thursday afternoon, the day after the ceilidh and just three days since the funeral. And even though Tag was well aware Balfour was only a small town, the number of times she'd encountered Freddie in the time she'd been home had been astonishing. Not that she was complaining. She'd thought about Freddie a lot in those three days and bumping into her never failed to cheer her up. Or, curiously, from making her heart beat just that little bit faster. It was as though Freddie had the ability to make even the most miserable person break into the biggest smile. Such was her sunny nature and the way she was never anything other than cheerful. It was infectious.

"Are you feeding the five thousand?" Tag signalled to the bulging bags of groceries that Freddie was holding. "Hello, Skye."

"Hi." Skye fell shyly against Freddie's leg, the short time since the ceilidh making all her bravado go again.

"Sometimes it feels like I'm feeding a small army." Freddie groaned.

A silence settled between them.

"I'm glad to see you, actually." Tag spoke first.

"Yeah?" Freddie placed the bags at her feet. She wiggled her fingers where the handles had dug in. "You're not going to quiz me over customer numbers for the cafe are you?"

"No, of course not." Shyness washed over Tag. Freddie was all that was on her mind right now, not the mill, and certainly not customer numbers. She looked at a point in the distance and hoped the shyness would pass. After all, she didn't actually *do* shyness. Ever.

Freddie looked at her expectantly. "You were glad to see me…?"

"Oh, yeah." Way to feel stupid. "I just wanted to say, well, thanks for the chat at the ceilidh last night. You know, outside. After I…" Her face flamed. "I appreciated it."

"Any time," Freddie said.

"It's been years since I've felt like I could just talk to someone like that." A point behind Freddie suddenly became very interesting to

Tag. Make eye contact. Look at her. "It would be great to do it again sometime." Tag flicked a glance Freddie's way, then away again. "Coffee and a chat, you know?"

"I'd like that, yeah," Freddie said. "Perhaps again before you go?"

Skye's grip on Freddie's leg loosened.

"And I just wanted to say…yeah, before I go again, perhaps." Tag stuttered. She swallowed. Since when was talking to a girl so fucking difficult? Get a grip. "No, I just wanted to say, I hope I didn't go on about stuff too much. When we were up there. I hope I didn't bore you."

"Stuff?"

"About Dad and the cafe and that."

"You didn't go on about anything." Freddie assured Tag. "And I wasn't bored, I promise."

"Okay, because it's been bugging me since," Tag said, "and I thought if I saw you, I'd mention it. Say sorry." Rambling. Quit rambling. Take a breath. Talk. "So, there you go." Lame. Totally lame. "Anyway, how are you, Skye?" The fire on her cheeks remained.

Skye nodded but didn't answer.

"It's fine. Honest." There was Freddie's smile again, impossible to ignore. Tag returned it. "And, you know, any time you feel like you want to spill. Just let me know."

"That'd be good. Thanks."

"Well, I'd better head off." Freddie bent to collect her bags.

"Head off. Yes." Tag plunged her hands into her pockets. If she didn't, she thought, she'd punch herself for acting like a complete tool. "Me too. Better go."

Nothing inside Tag wanted Freddie to go. Nothing. The eighteen or so hours since she'd last seen her had felt like days, and who was to say it wouldn't be ages until Tag could see her again after today?

Freddie hauled her bags up and grimaced. "I'll see you soon?"

She was leaving. Tag looked at the bags. Go with her. Another ten minutes with her is better than nothing. "Where are you parked?"

"Town square. By the memorial." Freddie looked over Tag's shoulder.

"Here, let me." Tag reached over for one of the bags. "I'll walk with you."

"You sure?"

"Yeah, 'course. I'm heading that way anyway." Liar. Freddie handed her a bag and stepped to one side.

"This way, yeah?" Tag signalled with her head.

"No, this way." Skye pointed towards the left.

"Are you sure you're going my way?" Freddie asked.

"Totally." Tag almost convinced herself too.

They all walked, side by side, across the street and made for the town square. Mostly they walked in silence, Freddie occasionally lifting her head to someone she knew. Tag followed. She switched her bag from hand to hand as it felt heavier the longer they walked. She mentally calculated that, by the time she'd walked Freddie to her car and had gone back over to her own car, in totally the opposite direction, she would be back at Glenside an hour later than she'd anticipated. Not that she cared. Her choice between escorting Freddie and Skye across Balfour, or spending the rest of the afternoon at Blair's talking accounts, was a no-brainer.

"It's just there."

Tag followed Skye's pointing finger to a slightly battered Ford, parked up in the square. Freddie's car, Tag reflected, suited her well. Colourful, spirited, full of character. No frills. Functional. Not in the least bit ostentatious. Somehow she could never envisage someone as unmaterialistic as Freddie ever having anything remotely expensive or fancy.

"Thank you." Freddie stopped walking and held out her hand for her bag. "I appreciate it."

"It's no trouble."

"So what have you got planned for the rest of the week?" Freddie hauled the boot of her car open.

Seeing you? Tag smiled inside. "For this afternoon, Dad's paperwork at Blair's." Tag screwed up her nose. "There's still so much to sort out. Insurance policies, Dad's bank accounts, stuff like that. Tomorrow? Same, probably. Saturday and Sunday? No idea. Blair, Ellen, and Magnus are going to see Ellen's parents down near Stirling on Saturday."

"We're off to the park." Skye stood up on tiptoes. "Saturday."

"The park?" Tag made big eyes. "Well I hope it doesn't rain for you at the park."

"Once we went there with Charlotte and it rained so hard we had to go under the slide." Skye giggled to herself at the memory.

"Charlotte's your friend?" Tag asked.

"Freddie's friend." Skye's face fell. "She doesn't live here any more."

"If it does rain, we'll revert to plan B." Freddie interrupted before the conversation turned into a post-mortem about Charlotte. "DVD," she mouthed.

"Well, I hope you have an amazing time at the park, Skye." Tag turned to leave. Her feet slowed. "Freddie?"

"Mm?"

"I'm talking with Blair tonight. About the mill."

"Okay."

"And"—Tag thought on her feet—"I just realized something. If I need to ask you anything about the cafe, well, I don't know how to get hold of you." Her insides screamed at her ineptitude. "So I was wondering if I could have your phone number?"

"Sure." Freddie's phone was instantly brought out. "You ready?"

Tag nodded. She tapped in the number Freddie gave her.

"Awesome. Thanks." Tag took a step back. "I doubt I'll need it, but…"

Yeah, right.

"Freddie?" Skye's quiet voice floated up. "Freddie?" Louder, with a tug on Freddie's sleeve.

"Skye?" Freddie looked down.

"Can we invite Tag?" Skye flitted shy eyes towards Tag. "To the park? Can we?"

"I'm sure Tag's too busy for parks, Skye." Freddie flashed an apologetic look at Tag. "Don't bother her."

"It's fine." Tag looked down, her heart thumping. Of course she wanted to go! Ask me yourself, Freddie. Just ask. I'll jump at the chance. "She's not bothering me." She poked her tongue out at Skye.

Skye hunched her shoulders up and melted into a fit of giggles. "Please can she come?" She beseeched when the giggles had passed. "Tag can tell me the story about the fox again."

"Again?" Tag widened her eyes. "I told it to you twice last night."

"It was funny."

"We're going to Dover's Park. Over by the swimming pool," Freddie said. "Around two on Saturday. If you've had enough of your paperwork and fancy a bit of company, Skye would love it if you came along." She caught herself. "And I would too."

Tag opened her mouth to answer. The park. With a beautiful girl you like, and her kid that you think is the cutest thing ever. Then, infuriatingly, Tag's brain decided to wrestle with her emotions: yes, she wanted nothing more than to go, but was there any point in hanging out with a couple of people she wouldn't even be seeing again after a month? She glanced at Freddie. Any point in getting herself close to them, even though she knew she secretly wanted to?

But Freddie *did* say she'd like her to go.

"Are you sure?" Tag asked. She met Freddie's eyes, searching, entreating.

"More than sure." Freddie held her gaze. "But"—she faltered—"we'll understand if you don't want to come. Or you can't come. Won't we?" She nudged Skye.

"No, I'd like to." Tag nodded. Fuck it. Where was the harm? "I'd like to very much. Parks beat paperwork every time."

A hissed *yes* and a fist pump filtered up from Skye. A glimmer of pleasure from Freddie.

"Until Saturday, then." Tag turned and traipsed away, head bowed over her phone. She heard the beep behind her as her text arrived in Freddie's phone. "That's me, in case you hadn't guessed." She called back over her shoulder. "Don't delete it now, will you?" Tag twisted away, smiled into her scarf at Freddie's response, and headed back to her car.

"The business has got more holes than a sieve." Tag dropped an armful of files onto the table. "Why did he never tell you?"

"You know your father." Ellen picked one up and opened the cover. She frowned. "If he ignored it, it would go away."

"You see, *this*," Blair said, pacing the room, "*this* is what you get when your stubborn bastard of a father won't hand any control over." He rubbed his arm irritably. "This is what you get for trying to deal with everything on your own."

"How bad is it?" Tag asked.

"How bad?" Blair swung round. "It's even worse than I thought." He sank down into a chair. "You know the worse thing of all? Dad worked himself into an early grave to keep this place going. And for what? Nothing."

"But we had our suspicions," Ellen offered.

"We both did." Blair dropped his head into his hands. "I kept asking to see the books but he wouldn't let me. I knew this would happen. Just knew it." He spoke through his fingers. "It's all such a mess."

"So the mill's having a rough time of it right now," Tag said. "It'll pick up, won't it?" She looked at the spreadsheet in front of her, at the sea of red that loomed out. The business had always done so well, hadn't it? Tag frowned. During the years she was away, as her mind would drift back to Balfour—as it frequently had—she had always imagined the mill being as she'd left it. A hive of industry, a success. Not the limping, sickly business she was now rapidly realizing it had become.

"According to these accounts," Blair said, jabbing his finger on one of the files, "it's been having a rough time for years." He scratched irritably at his cheek. "I *told* him. I told him we needed to change things up a bit, especially after the bypass opened and took trade away, but would he listen? No. Just kept saying people relied on him and the mill had worked fine for hundreds of years and—"

"He never listened because to him that would mean defeat," Ellen, ever the realist, said. "And your father would never admit defeat."

"Well I wish he would've, rather than just ploughing on regardless." Blair clenched a fist and released it again. "Then I wouldn't be having to pick up the pieces now."

Tag watched him slump back in his chair, staring in defiance at the files on the table in front of him. They both knew what their father was like; never one for communicating at the best of times, it was obvious to Tag now that he had told Blair nothing of the troubles the mill was in. Nothing about their debts, the red reminders, the cancelled orders. Why? Did Adam really think he could deal with it all on his own? Hide his head in the sand and hope it would go away? Tag looked at the files. Nope, those files were going nowhere.

She hadn't wanted to scrutinize the damn accounts in the first place. Leaving Freddie at her car to return to Glenside, when all Tag had wanted to do was hop in her car with her and spend the rest of the day with her and Skye, had been agony.

Where were they now? Back at home? Tag's mind took itself over to Lyster and tried to imagine the set-up there. What sort of cottage did they live in? Large? Small? Cosy? She smiled. Definitely cosy.

"Have you told Freddie?" Tag plonked herself down opposite Blair. "She needs to know." Her name was out before she'd even realized.

"Why just Freddie?" Blair frowned, irritated. "They all need to know. Tom, Vernon. All of them."

"Because…" Because Freddie is always the one person at the front of my mind. Because Freddie matters. And Skye, and…

"Freddie *does* need to know before anyone else." Ellen voiced Tag's concerns. "She's the thread that keeps this place together."

Freddie was the thread. Butterflies released themselves from some invisible net deep inside Tag. Freddie mattered to them all.

"She needs to—?" Blair glared at Ellen, then checked himself.

Tag read his expression. It was unfair of him to be mad at Ellen. She saw his face soften. Without Ellen, Tag knew Blair would be lost. She was the one who held their family together; she was the one who got things done, made the decisions. Without her steadying influence? The mill would be closed within a month, Tag knew.

"She's like family to us, Blair." Ellen pulled a file towards her and flipped it open. "She's been with us through thick and thin. She needs to know if we have a problem. Which we do." She ran her finger down the page, then went to the next one, reading down a list of figures. "The gift shop, the cafe. Both running at losses."

"So there you go," Blair said, looking at Tag. "If you really have only come back for the money, you're going to be in for a nasty surprise."

"You're still banging that drum, are you?" Tag shook her head. Seriously? Still?

"If you've come back hoping for a nice fat inheritance," Blair said, shrugging, "then you're going to be disappointed. That's all I'm saying."

"Why do you have to be so bitter all the time?" Memories of her chance meeting with Freddie, coupled with the anticipation of hanging out with her at the park in a few days' time, were dashed by Blair's cruel words.

"How can you think that's all she wants?" Ellen asked. At least *she* had Tag's back.

"Why else would she come back?" Blair lifted a childish shoulder, avoiding eye contact with them both.

"Because she loves you?" Ellen responded furiously. "Because her father dying has made her realize you're all she's got left?"

Tag watched in silence.

"Me and Dad were all she had left years ago," Blair argued. "But we weren't enough for you then, were we?" Finally he addressed Tag. He picked up a file and hurled it across the room. "And now you swan up here and—"

"Grow up, Blair." Tag walked to the file and retrieved it.

The colour drained from his face. "I'm a farmer, Tag. What do I know about running a business?" He entreated her. "My life's been spent in the fields, not sitting in front of files with figures I don't understand."

"Then let me help you," Tag said, returning to the table.

"I adored you."

"I'm sorry?" Tag looked up. Had she misheard?

"You were my little sister and I would have done anything for you," Blair said. He squeezed his eyes shut. "You never had to worry about bullies in the school playground, or boys pestering you for dates when you clearly weren't interested in them."

"I know, but—"

Blair held up a hand. "I defended you when you told Dad you were gay, and that you'd been dating a girl in the next town for the last four months."

"And squared up to him in the bakery when he'd not been able to accept it initially." Tag grinned. "I remember."

Blair had always had her back. He was her rock, her protector, and he'd promised her back then that he would always look out for her. Tag looked across at her brother, to the weary eyes, the slumped shoulders. If only she'd not forced him to break his promise.

"I've had nine years to get used to the idea you were never coming back." Her brother opened a file and peered down at it, unable to meet her eye. "I programmed my brain to forget I had a sister, but seeing you again has made me miss you all over again."

"But now I'm here." Tag reached over and closed the file.

"But for how long?" He stood up. "You'll sort out everything you need to here, then go back to England, and I'll lose you all over again."

Tag stared at him. Was that what he thought of her? Always running? England was so far from her thoughts right now. Her old life? Lost to her in amongst all her new and exciting feelings of being home and finding Freddie. Her mind scurried back to Freddie. Her mood darkened. Was that what Freddie thought of her too? Unreliable, unpredictable Tag who fled at the first sign of trouble?

"I'm not like that any more." She was saying it to Freddie as much as to Blair. Trying to make her understand how she felt about her, imploring her to feel the same way. "You have to trust me that I won't let you down. Just give me a chance?"

"Prove it." Blair shrugged. Freddie disappeared. "Prove to us all that you mean it."

To them all?

Tag's resolve hardened. She knew she was genuine. Reliable. Even if Blair and Freddie had their doubts, Tag knew that craving their respect and gaining their trust would be all the encouragement she needed to prove her sincerity to them.

"I will." Tag stood and faced Blair. Freddie needed her. Skye needed her. Blair and Magnus too. *They all did.* "I'll show you all I mean every word I say."

CHAPTER ELEVEN

The ceiling that Tag stared up at the next morning, once she'd shaken the fog of sleep from her eyes, wasn't immediately familiar. Her ceiling in Liverpool was taupe. This one was cream. And chipped. Who did she know with a chipped ceiling?

She'd just woken from the best night's sleep she'd had since she'd arrived back in Balfour. At least she'd managed to sleep the whole night through. That had been a first. Now, staring up at Connie Booth's chipped, cream ceiling, Tag felt better than she had done in a long time. She lay in her single bed, her mind pleasantly blank, then wondered fleetingly whether she ought to ring Anna to tell her she was working her way through the e-mails of work that Anna had been feeding her throughout the week. But the thought of getting out of her warm bed and fetching her phone, across the other side of her room, convinced her it would be better to turn over and pull the duvet up over her head instead. Work could wait. Anyway, if she told them she'd been working through her e-mails, that would have been a lie. She'd been doing everything but, because Blair had finally—after much persuasion from her and Ellen—allowed Tag to take the accounts back to the B & B with her. Any work for Anna seemed immaterial after that.

She could hear Connie moving around downstairs in the kitchen. The sounds of pans clattering against one another alerted Tag to the fact that she was, in all probability, now cooking breakfast. And cooking breakfast inevitably meant that Tag would soon have to give up the comfort of her bed, shower, and show her face down in the communal dining room. Just five more minutes. She closed her eyes again, hoping there were still few other guests staying at the B & B. The daily prospect of having to engage in polite, idle chit-chat over the bacon and eggs never filled her with glee.

Neither did the prospect of work, still waiting in her inbox. She knew she really ought to finish it. Tag pulled the duvet higher around her ears. Anna would be waiting. She wouldn't let a small detail like bereavement leave worry her. She'd be waiting for a reply to an e-mail, getting more irritated the longer Tag took to reply. Tag buried her head down and groaned into her pillow. Why should she always jump when Anna clapped her hands? She'd always been too keen on doing that. In the office and out of it, when they'd been an item. Even afterwards, if Tag was honest. Expecting Tag to be there at her beck and call all the time.

Tag closed her eyes, feeling sleepy again. Her mind tumbled over.

The mill was in a mess. Blair was up to his eyes with it and was still, despite Tag's speech the previous evening, showing distrust towards her intentions. His cynicism towards her evidently continued to run deep. Tag squeezed her eyes shut. She needed to gen up on the business if she was to start helping to make it a success again. But she still knew so little about the place. Her name was on all the official paperwork, but she didn't know vital details such as contracts, or even how much they paid the staff. And what about all the other, smaller details? How many pens did they sell in the shop? How many bags of flour? How many coffees and cakes in the cafe?

The cafe. Tag's subconscious tugged towards Freddie. How much did she know about what went on up there? Maybe she could supply her figures. Percentages. Sales details.

Tag's mind oscillated from Blair to Anna to the cafe and back again. Truth was, even though she knew she'd be seeing Freddie the next day at the park, she wanted to see her again sooner. Any excuse would do. The story of her life with Anna was always that Anna clapped and Tag jumped. Both professionally and emotionally. But Freddie? Freddie seemed like an oasis of calm in comparison. Tag doubted very much that she could make anyone jump to her demands, even if she tried.

She had Freddie's phone number, right? She could just call her up and say she wanted to talk to her and Tim, who worked with her, about the cafe and see some accounting details. Make up some crap about Blair asking her to. Or maybe she should just go up there. Visit the cafe and then the gift shop to talk to…who ran the gift shop again? Tag blinked. No idea. But here was an idea. Perhaps Tag could go and help them both in the cafe? Then look at the books. Perfect. Anything had to be better than spending a beautiful, sunny day stuck indoors at Four Winds sifting through endless sheets of official paper. Anyway, wasn't that's what bosses did? Help their staff out? Even temporary bosses helped out sometimes.

Freddie might even like to hang out after the cafe closed. Who knew?

"Only one way to find out, Grainger." Tag pulled the duvet back and swung her legs down. She padded to the shower room, her feet soft against the carpet. Freddie could guide her in the right direction over the mill. She was smart like that. As well as cool. Tag liked her. And Skye. So where was the harm now in just hanging out with the girl for a few hours?

"It's Tim, right?" Tag approached the teenager behind the counter at the mill cafe, her satisfaction when he nodded his head in response, that she'd actually managed to remember the kid's name, contrasting with her disappointment that Freddie wasn't the face that now greeted her.

"Blair's around somewhere." Tim wiped his hands on his apron and came out from behind the counter. "Out back, I think."

"Okay, cool." Tag picked up a slightly frayed menu from the counter and looked at it. She put it back down. Where was Freddie? Her anticipation at seeing her again had amplified on the drive up to the cafe. Now all Tag felt was flat. "Although I didn't really come up here to see him, to be honest." She looked around her. "Is Freddie working today?"

"Emergency at home or something," Tim said. "Not coming in this morning." He went back behind the counter. "Good job. It's dead in here." He opened his arms out to an empty cafe. "Coffee?"

"Make it a cappuccino?" she asked hopefully.

"Is this my test?"

"I'm sorry?"

"See what kind of coffee I make for the boss? Mess up and I'm out on my ear?"

"Shit, no." Who did he think she was? Mafia?

"Chill," Tim said. "I was just teasing." He switched the coffee machine on and came to join Tag at her table. "If you're anything like your dad and your brother, then you'll be a fair and decent person to work for. That's all any of us ask."

"Hey, it's nothing to do with me," Tag said. "Seriously, I have *no* experience of being in charge of people, so I won't be telling you lot what to do." He didn't need to know right now she wouldn't even be hanging around long enough to be shown how a coffee machine worked.

"Us lot?" Tim queried. "It's just me, Freddie, and Vernon in here. No need for any more."

"Ah, but who's in charge of who?" Tag joked.

"Freddie keeps us both in order." Tim grinned.

"She a good boss?"

"The best." Tim got up from the table again as the coffee machine finished steaming. "I'd have to say, Freddie Metcalfe is the nicest, fairest, and best boss I've ever had."

"I'll tell her that," Tag said. She knew she would too. "You like working here?"

"Are you compiling a profile on us?" Tim laughed. He handed her the cappuccino.

"I just wondered what it's like," Tag said. She took a long drink from her mug and licked froth from her top lip. "What customer numbers are like, what sort of menu you offer. That kind of thing."

"Well, the food's great, but we don't get much passing traffic through here since the bypass opened three years ago," Tim said. "That's what the others told me, anyway. It's a shame. Freddie's cakes are awesome." He nodded his head towards the counter. "But let's just say, we never run out of them."

Somehow Tag knew Freddie's cakes would be awesome. She was an awesome kind of girl. Tag gazed round. A total of three customers sat at tables. "So it's this quiet every day?" Her mother would be sad at the thought of her cafe being so empty.

"Sundays are okay. Ish. But..."

"What?"

"The rest of the week tends to be like this, if I'm honest." Tim's face flickered. "I feel as though I'm being a sneak."

"It's better that I know as much as possible early on." Tag stirred her coffee, staring deep in thought as ripples circled inside the cup with every move of her spoon. The cafe had always been the heart of the mill when she was growing up, so she'd assumed it would be the same now. Perhaps it really was time to man up and take a long, hard, look at those accounts. Her disappointment at Freddie's absence had peaked. Pointless hanging around the cafe if she wasn't there. The place was empty enough as it was; without Freddie there, it was even more soulless.

"Everything okay?" Tim asked.

"Mm?" She lifted her eyes from her cup.

"You were miles away for a second there."

"Just thinking that I'd better go." Tag drained her coffee and then stood. She held her hand out for Tim's cup. "I have a heap of paperwork to sift through." Not Anna's, though. She could wait some more. Right now she needed to have some thinking time. Maybe jot down a few calculations. Think some more about Freddie, as if that were even possible. Tag took Tim's cup from him then walked behind the counter and placed both cups in the sink. "Although"—she faced Tim—"if you're a person short here today I guess I should stay and help. In case you get an afternoon rush?"

Way to go being a boss, Grainger.

"Nah, you're good." Tim stood up and came to the counter. "And to be honest I'd rather be here today being paid than stuck at home doing nothing." He flicked the towel over his shoulder and started filling the sink with hot water.

"If you're sure?" Tag buttoned up her jacket and made for the door.

"Sure." Tim nodded back over to her then turned his attention back to the sink. "If we get a sudden rush, I'll call for you." He smiled at his own joke.

"Deal." With a nod of her head, Tag left the cafe and made for her car. Head bowed over her phone as she walked, she did a neat sidestep without looking up as a blue Ford came past her and pulled into the space next to hers.

"Can't stay away, huh?"

Tag's head snapped up. Freddie peered out from her wound-down window as she pulled on the brake and cut the engine. She grabbed her bag from the passenger seat and got out of the car, slamming her door shut behind her.

Disappointment to happiness in a nanosecond. The Freddie effect. It had *so* been worth dropping by the cafe after all.

"Your window?" Tag lifted her chin towards Freddie's still-open driver's window.

"You think anyone's going to nick anything from this heap of junk?"

"No, I don't." Tag loved the look on Freddie's face—amused and playful. Sexy. Tag sat back against her own car, so they were now facing one another, and held her look. "But I do think your car will be full of snow by the time you get back to it if you don't shut the window." She put her hands in her jacket pockets. "Bearing in mind the revolting weather forecast I've just seen for later this afternoon." She pulled one hand out of her pocket and lifted her phone in the air.

"You," Freddie said, waggling a finger at her, "are definitely a Grainger." She shoved herself away from her car door and opened it, winding up the window. "I could just hear your dad saying something like that."

A vision of her father came crashing around Tag. His voice and his laugh. It had been too long, Tag thought, since she'd heard it.

"So, I just met Tim," Tag said. Adam disappeared once more. "Nice guy."

"Very nice guy, yeah. Good kid to work with."

"He said you weren't coming in today. An emergency at home or something?" Prying. Whatever.

"All sorted." Freddie waved her hand. "Skye's hamster managed to wriggle its way out of its cage. I found it behind the wood burner, eating a piece of chocolate."

"She has a hamster? That's cute."

"She nearly *didn't* have a hamster, though." Freddie shuddered. "Were you just heading off?" She motioned towards Tag's car.

"Mm." Tag delved into her jeans pocket and pulled her car keys out. "I did come to talk to you about the cafe's weekly turnover," she said, "but it can wait."

"We could go talk now." Freddie signalled to the cafe.

And talk shop? Tag knew she'd rather talk about *her.* "I think Tim's told me enough already."

"You've been here five minutes and you're asking my guy questions behind my back already?" Freddie laughed, but there was no humour in it.

Tag stopped dead. "I said I came to see you," she said. "And I haven't been asking questions behind your back, thank you." Why had Freddie taken it the wrong way?

"So why focus on the cafe alone?" Freddie looked irritated. "You should look at the other parts of the mill too. Not just the cafe. That's not fair."

"I will do." Tag was exasperated. "Another time." Freddie had her all wrong. She'd had gone up to see her, not snoop. What had started off as being a pleasant opportunity to see Freddie on the off chance she was working had rapidly turned into a discussion Tag hadn't anticipated and wasn't prepared for. "Let's just say the sooner I go back, look at some paperwork, and have a chat to Blair, the better." Tag rested a shoulder against her car. She saw the worry that floated across Freddie's face.

"So can I ask what you're looking for in amongst all this paperwork?"

"No." Tag smiled pleasantly. "You don't have to worry about it."

"But I do," Freddie said firmly. She jerked her head to the cafe. "This is my cafe. If there's something bothering you about it, then I want to know."

"It might be your cafe, but it's my family's responsibility," Tag corrected. Seriously? They were seriously having this conversation? "I don't want you to have to shoulder any of the worry."

"Please don't patronize me," Freddie said. "I thought your family had enough respect to not hide the truth from me. And I *am* still in charge up here. At least that's what it says on my job description."

An unexpected atmosphere shimmered.

"The mill." Tag sighed. She so didn't want to do this right now. "The mill's having a tougher time than we first thought." Tactful. "I need to try and work out what we can do to get it going again."

"Financially?"

Tag nodded. "You know the cafe's not been doing so well," she said. "Truth is, the rest of the place isn't so good either."

"How bad is it?" Freddie asked. "I know about the cafe, but—"

"It's more than just about the cafe's profits." Should Tag sugar-coat it? Or just tell her the truth? The truth won. "We owe money all over the place."

"Lots?"

"Enough."

"So what does that mean for all of us?" Freddie tried to keep the wobble from her voice.

"Unless things start to pick up again," Tag said, "we might have to reduce staff."

"And if that doesn't help?"

"Then I guess Blair and I will have to sell the mill to an investor."

"That can't happen."

"What choice would we have?" Tag threw out her arms. "We can't keep the place going if it's leaking money faster than a dripping tap." She was disappointed. Flirtation with Freddie had dropped to serious conversation about the mill, and Tag resented it. "Which is what it's doing now."

"Hang on," Freddie shot back. "I need this job." She stared at Tag as she gathered her thoughts. "You don't seem to get that. I have responsibilities."

"Don't we all?" Tag shrugged.

The shrug seemed to elicit an instant change in Freddie. "It's all right for you. You're not exactly laden with ties and responsibilities." Freddie swept a look to her. "But some of us have people relying on us."

"Oh yeah?" Tag was hurt by Freddie's anger. Confused by her change in attitude, like Tag had said or done something wrong, when all she was doing was trying to help. Okay, two could play at attitude. "Well, right now I've got Blair relying on me, haven't I?" Her voice rose slightly. "You think I need all this too?"

"And I have a child relying on me." Freddie retorted. "So do *you* think that *I* need all this?"

Tag didn't respond.

"The mill is my life," Freddie said slowly. "If I don't have that, then I'm screwed and so is Skye."

"Which is why I'm going to do my damnedest to make sure it stays open," Tag said. "And I *do* understand that my situation's probably different from yours." Resentment tore through her—for the mill, for her situation. For this stupid argument she was having with Freddie.

"Not probably." Freddie brushed her off. "*Is*. It's totally different from mine."

"But you have to understand," Tag stressed her point, "if the place is leaking money, then I have to do something."

Freddie stared at Tag. Suddenly she understood. "You have no idea about me, or my life," she said. "You have no idea how much I need the mill. How much I rely on it." How could she have been so naive? Tag didn't care about the mill or about her or Skye. All she cared about was profit margins and how much money her new business was going to make her. "It's all about the money for you, isn't it?" Freddie was furious with herself for being sucked in by Tag. For believing her. For lending an ear so many times in the cafe when Tag was upset, when all Tag was interested in was whether she could feather her own nest. Blair had been right all along. She *was* unreliable. Selfish.

"It's not about the money," Tag argued. "You're sounding just like Blair did when I first came here. I don't give a shit about the money. What I *do* give a shit about, though, is trying to support a dying business if it's clear it should have been put out of its misery years ago."

"That dying business," Freddie said, "is my life. Is everyone's life. Has been for years. Without it, we have nothing. Without it, Skye has nothing. What part of that don't you understand?"

"I *do* understand," Tag replied. "I know you need to work for Skye." To Freddie's dismay, Tag reached for her. "Why are you angry with me? It's not like it's my fault, any of this."

Freddie wrenched her arm away. "You're my employer." She hitched her bag over her shoulders. "Nothing more than that. I was stupid to ever think—" She stopped herself. Time to backtrack. "As an employer it's up to you to make sure your staff are all looked after."

"Which I will." Tag stood her ground. "I promise."

"Even though you're not sticking around?"

"Even though."

"I'm worried." Now it was Freddie who stood her ground.

"I know. I just need to take a look at the cafe's accounts, that's all," Tag said. "Figures. Profits," she said. "Perhaps we can talk about it tomorrow at the park?"

"You're still coming?"

"You still want me to come?" Tag asked. "I did kind of promise Skye."

Of course I want you to come. I've thought of nothing else since Skye asked you. "Skye's psyched that you're coming." Freddie knew that wasn't the answer Tag was looking for.

"Seriously? That's sweet."

"She forms attachments quickly." Freddie cut her glance away and focused on a point in the distance. "If I told her you weren't coming, well…" She pulled her attention back to Tag. "Just don't let her bug you too much tomorrow, okay? She can be a bit full-on."

"I won't." Tag seemed calmer again. "And we *will* talk about the cafe tomorrow, I promise."

"Yes." Freddie lifted her chin. "We definitely will."

CHAPTER TWELVE

The ringing of her phone the next morning woke Tag from a light sleep that had been punctuated by vivid dreams of Blair, her father, and the mill. Her conversations over the past few days with Blair about the mill's finances had weighed heavily on her, and her dreams that night had been racked with unease, as she wondered what else she'd find out. There had been arguments in her dreams. Accusations. Worries about how much money the mill was losing. Her father was refusing to accept anything she was saying. There had been a lot of shouting, too, and Tag worried as she fumbled for her mobile on the bedside cabinet, that she'd been shouting in her sleep. The last thing she needed was a question-and-answer session with Connie over her cornflakes.

"Tag Grainger," Tag sleepily answered her phone. She extended her legs out straight under the duvet and stretched her toes, enjoying the satisfying pull on her calf muscles.

"Hey." Anna's voice diffused through Tag's tired brain. "Just thought I'd touch base with you. See how you're doing."

"Oh. Right." Tag rolled onto her side, phone still clamped to her ear. It was Saturday. Why the fuck was Anna ringing her on a Saturday? She drew her knees up to her chest. "What time is it?" She looked up towards the curtains. A half-light poked through the gap.

"Eight," Anna said. "I'm playing golf at nine so I'm kicking my heels for a bit at home."

"Stefan's not there, I'm guessing?"

"He's just gone," Anna said. "So, how're you? I've not rung to talk about Stefan."

"I'm all right, yeah," Tag replied truthfully. "It's not been as bad as I thought it would be."

"Good," Anna replied. "I found the Milton stills, by the way."

"I'm sorry?"

"I texted you the other day about them."

"You did, yes. Sorry." The Milton files? Tag had already forgotten about them.

"You didn't reply."

"No. I was busy." Tag's thrumming nerve reappeared in her jaw. Anna had a habit of making it return. "Anna?"

"Mm?"

"It's difficult for me to be thinking about work right now." How could she put this politely? "I've taken time off to sort out my father's things. I could do without the distractions."

"I'm sorry I've been bugging you." Anna gave a small laugh. "But we *are* still paying you. I can get someone else in to do it if you can't cope."

"I just need headspace." From work. From Anna. "To concentrate on getting stuff sorted up here."

"Okay, I'll leave you to it."

"Sure." Tag could picture Anna's face. She'd be furious, she knew.

"Quick question before I go?"

"Yup?" Tag breathed in and fought the feeling of suffocation that always accompanied Anna.

"The blue file with the charts in it that I need for the Everson property portfolio," Anna said. "Can't find it anywhere."

"Right." Like she couldn't look for them herself? "It's in the cabinet to the left of the water cooler," Tag said, "I put it in there myself the day before I came up here. I did tell you that. You must have forgotten."

"Awesome." Anna puffed a sigh of relief. "Did you tell me that? I don't remember."

"I did." Tag reached up and pinched the bridge of her nose. She was suddenly weary. "Because I knew you'd need it today."

"You're the best," Anna said. "This is why I can't cope without you."

❖

"You're happy." Ellen came up behind Tag in the kitchen. She looped an arm round her shoulder. "You were singing. You never sing."

"Is that a crime?" Tag nudged her with her hip.

Saturday was looking as though it was going to have the best weather since Tag had arrived. Now bright and breezy, with no hint of rain in the air, a visit to the park would be a definite. Tag had arrived at Glenside in the morning full of intentions to talk to Blair, only to find he'd rather be ploughing the top field than talk to her about the mill. That, Tag figured, was his lookout. He wanted to delay talking about the accounts and would rather take himself off than confront their problems, even though he'd specifically asked to see her? Fine. Nothing was going to spoil Tag's day. An afternoon at the park with her two new best buddies loomed, and Tag couldn't be happier.

"The way you sing is, yeah." Ellen pulled a bottle of juice from the fridge. She opened it and sniffed it, then shrugged and drank some back. She wiped her mouth. "More to the point," Ellen continued, intrigued, "*why* are you singing?"

"I'm going out this afternoon." Tag liked to be mysterious. Especially with Ellen. It was fun. "Or, more specifically, I might have been asked out this afternoon." She plunged her hands into the soapy suds in the kitchen sink.

"With?"

"Someone." Tag held up a glass and inspected it.

"Spill."

"No."

"Now."

"Freddie," Tag said simply. "I'm seeing Freddie this afternoon."

"From the cafe?"

"You know any other Freddies in this town?"

Ellen put the juice bottle back in the fridge. "Please don't tell me you've been here five minutes and you're hitting on all the local girls already."

"Do you mind?" Tag rinsed a plate. "I'm not *hitting on her,* as you put it. I like her. She's good company."

"She knows you're gay?"

"She does." Tag bristled. "And hey, guess what? Her world didn't tip on its axis." She stacked the plate on the rack.

"So where are you going?" Ellen asked.

"Dover's Park," Tag replied. "With Skye."

"Cute."

"Not cute," Tag shot back. "Something for me to do while you're busy at your parents." She grabbed a tea towel. "Anyway, Skye asked me to go."

"Now that *is* cute."

"What can I say?" Tag did a comical shrug. "She likes me. Kid's got taste."

"And Freddie?"

"Two girls can totally go to the park together with a kid without anyone thinking something else is going on, can't they?" Tag flicked Ellen with the towel.

"Not when one's a screaming lesbian and the other is as hot as Freddie, no." Ellen lowered her voice.

"She is a bit, isn't she?" Tag lowered her voice too.

"Is what?"

"Hot."

"See? I knew it." Ellen fell against Tag, the pair of them giggling like a pair of schoolgirls.

"Seriously, though"—Tag pushed Ellen away—"I appreciate her asking me. At least someone's looking out for me while I'm back here."

"Meaning?"

"Blair." Tag came back to earth with a bump. "He's ignoring me, isn't he?"

"Blair's being Blair," Ellen said with diplomacy.

"He gave me the mill's accounts on Thursday," Tag said, "and then disappeared. I've been trying to collar him since yesterday afternoon."

Tag folded her towel. Blair hadn't so much as given her the files as flung them at her and told her to *take the damn things and we'll talk later.* Very professional. Although perhaps more professional than her. The files were now flung on her room floor up at Four Winds.

If Connie came in today to clean her room, Tag now thought dryly, she'd have some good reading matter to while away a few hours.

"Read them." Was Ellen reading her mind? "Take a good look at the accounts and then perhaps you'll understand exactly why Blair's being the way he's being."

❖

Skye was looking cutely shy all over again when Tag met them at the park later that afternoon. After Blair, Ellen, and Magnus had left for Stirling, Tag had returned to the B & B to find, much to her relief, her room untouched and the files still on her floor. The two hours that Tag had allotted herself to study them and get back over to Dover's Park had instead passed in a flurry of showering and dithering over which clothes to wear. The all-too-brief flick through the spreadsheets inside the files had confirmed what Tag had thought on the drive back from Glenside after her chat with Ellen: the mill was in a mess.

Despite knowing she ought to stay and study them further, the prospect of seeing Freddie and Skye again was just too tempting. Two o'clock creaked closer, and now, finally, Tag was at the park, as arranged, waiting for them. Accounts, she figured, could wait for later. After all, it wasn't as if Blair was busting a gut to discuss them with her, was it?

Tag spotted Freddie first, definitely dressed for a winter's afternoon at the park: hooded waterproof jacket, the collar flipped up high around her ears against the cold, thick walking trousers, and a pair of robust boots with a pleasing amount of mud smeared across them. Freddie was also wearing a bright red beanie—the sort that Tag would normally wear when she wasn't wearing her more favoured trapper hat—with matching gloves. Never one to be able to resist a girl in outdoor gear, to Tag, she looked awesome.

"Hey!" Freddie approached Tag. "Nice hat." She pulled back and cast an admiring eye over Tag's hat.

"You don't think I look daft in it?" Tag lifted the flaps on her trapper hat. She pulled a face, then let the flaps drop again, making both Freddie and Skye laugh.

"No dafter than usual."

"Hello, Tag." Skye looked up at Tag, all eyes and woolly hat.

"Hey, Skye."

"Tag?"

"Mm-hmm?"

"Why are you called Tag?"

"Because it's my name, sweetheart," Tag said.

"How spelled?"

"*T-A-D-G-H*."

Skye frowned. She cast an impish look to Freddie. "Tah-duh-guh?" She emphasized every syllable.

"No, Tah-guh," Tag said, laughing. "The *D* and *H* are quiet."

"The *D* is quiet?"

"Yuh-huh."

Skye thought for a moment. "As in dinosaur?" Her eyes twinkled.

"Dinosaur?"

"Well, they're quiet, aren't they?" A mischievous smile tugged at the side of her mouth.

"Dinosaurs are quiet?" Tag looked questioningly to Freddie, who just raised her eyebrows and shrugged.

"Yeah. Because they're all dead." Skye fell against Freddie, laughing.

"She's teasing you." Freddie pulled Skye upright again. "I remembered you telling me at the ceilidh how you spelled your name." She placed her hands on Skye's shoulders and swivelled her round to face the front. "And I made the mistake of telling this little monkey here."

"Oh." Tag was bemused.

"She's been thinking up a joke to tell you ever since yesterday," Freddie said. "Pete came up with that little gem last night."

"Oh," Tag repeated. "Okay."

"Don't worry. You'll get used to it," Freddie said, then immediately checked herself. Tag wouldn't be around to get used to anything. Her heart squeezed at the thought. So stupid. Freddie looked out to an unseen spot and tried to quell the disappointment her thoughts had just conjured.

"Well, for telling me such a good joke…" Tag put her hand in her coat pocket and pulled out a small brown piggy bank, hastily bought in the newsagents on the way to the park, with the words *Chocolate Fund* written on the side. "You get this." She handed the pig to Skye.

A whispered "thank you, Tag" accepted it.

"I put a few coins inside it just to start you off."

"It's very kind of you." Freddie watched as Skye carefully turned it over in her hands, listening to the coins rattling inside. "But you didn't have to—"

"Everyone needs to have a chocolate fund," Tag said. "Right, Skye?"

Skye nodded enthusiastically, her pig clutched tight against her chest.

They moved from their meeting spot and headed towards the park, Skye running on some way ahead, her pig held in both hands in front of her.

"I'm glad you came along," Freddie said. She cocked her head to Tag. "After yesterday."

"Yesterday?" Tag acted like she didn't remember. Of course she remembered.

"I thought I might have come across as a bit"—Freddie rolled a hand—"snooty. A bit, I don't know. High and mighty. About the cafe."

"Okay." Tag nodded. Snooty hadn't been the word. Pissed off, yes. But snooty? Tag had had the whole evening to replay their meeting up at the cafe, but despite analysing it to death, she still couldn't think of how or what she could have said that would have made things better. The fact that Freddie had met her today with a welcoming smile and a joke from Skye had been a pleasant surprise.

"I just worry, that's all." Freddie walked with Tag towards the swings.

"As do I." Tag was almost apologetic, but she wanted to stand her ground. If there was a problem with the cafe too, she needed to know. And fast. "Which is why I really need to know what's going on up there."

Freddie stopped walking. "But what if you don't like what you find?"

"Then I guess I'll cross that particular bridge when I come to it," Tag threw back over her shoulder as she strode on.

❖

The park was packed by the time they arrived at the swings. The first proper rays of sunshine they'd seen in days had encouraged everyone to spill from their houses, so it seemed, and descend on the one and only large park in Balfour.

The swings and slides glittered in the sunshine, just waiting for a small child such as Skye to fling themselves onto them. Freddie let Skye run further on in front once they neared the play area, grimacing as she tested out the robustness of three swings in quick succession and then hurled herself down one of the slides.

"Remember what it felt like to have no fear?" Freddie sighed, her heart in her mouth as she watched on.

"It's like she's desperate to test them all out as quickly as possible," Tag said, "as though she's worried they might take them away from her."

They stopped walking, as if by an assumed agreement, and stood, side by side, a short distance from the play area. Skye waved to them from the top of a slide.

"Can I go down backwards?" Skye's voice, normally so quiet, boomed out around the park. Her hands gripped the sides of the slide. She leaned back down it, her feet poking up in the air, her hair dangling downward, and grinned upside down at Freddie as she hurried over to her.

"No." Freddie stood against the side of the slide. "On your bum, feet first, like always."

"Aww." Skye carried on looking at Freddie upside down.

Freddie pulled her best *don't mess with me* face and helped her to right herself. She watched, shaking her head slightly, as Skye flung herself down the slide then ran across the grass to the next piece of equipment.

"Were you like that too?" Tag came and stood next to Freddie again. "A gung-ho little bundle of adventure?"

"No, she's like her mother." Freddie wrapped her arms around herself and gazed fondly at Skye. "Laura didn't have a frightened bone in her body."

"You're…?" Tag's brows creased.

"Skye's auntie," Freddie said. "Well, her legal guardian now."

"I didn't know."

"Let's sit." Freddie signalled to an empty bench. "I'll explain."

They sat on the bench, one eye still on Skye. An occasional wave from her slowed Freddie's story, only for her to start again.

"My sister, Laura," Freddie said, "died eighteen months ago."

"I'm so sorry."

"Cancer." Freddie looked at her gloved hands. "It was a shock to us all." She caught Skye's attention and waved again. "Of course I knew Laura had named me in her will as Skye's guardian, should ever anything happen," she said, "but you never think anything *is* going to happen, do you?"

"No," Tag reflected, "you never do."

"So," Freddie continued, "I have sole responsibility for her."

Freddie didn't take her eyes off Skye all the while she spoke, her thoughts a mixture of love and concern. Would Tag understand the sacrifice she'd made? Could she relate to just how difficult it had been—and still was—to play the role of mother, auntie, and protector all rolled into one? Freddie cast a look in Tag's direction and wondered, as she had done frequently over the days, whether someone like Tag would have done the same.

"Your parents?" Tag asked.

"Live in Portugal," Freddie said. Her eyes returned to Skye. "They offered to have Skye but, well, Laura's last wish was for me to raise her."

"Can I have some water?" Skye rushed up to Freddie and launched herself against her. She tilted her head back and panted in exaggeration. Despite the cool of the day, her cheeks were rosy from playing, making the smattering of freckles across her nose appear even more pronounced than normal.

"Come and sit down for a bit." Freddie took Skye's hand. "The park will still be there after you've had a rest," she added, as she met resistance.

They sat, the three of them, and gazed out across the park, Skye in between Freddie and Tag, occasionally commenting excitedly about a particular tricky manoeuvre on a swing, or the durability of the ropes she'd just been hanging from. In between gasping her tales of daring, she drank noisily from a bottle of water, the exertion from hard playing apparently giving her a thirst. When she'd had enough, she wiped her mouth with the back of her sleeve, then waggled the bottle at Tag, who politely declined.

The sun got warmer as the afternoon progressed. Now it brightened the whole of the park, its arms embracing each blade of grass and each slide and swing, warming both the cold metal and the children using them. Freddie threaded her arm across the back of the bench and tilted her face upward, contented. She could get used to this. Sitting in the sun, listening to the wonderful sound of an excited child explaining to Tag, in intricate detail, the finer points of a roundabout. Company, sunshine, and friendship. It had been a long time, Freddie thought, since she'd been as happy as she was right then.

"Can I go now?" Skye swivelled her whole body round on the bench to face Freddie. She pressed pleading hands together in front of her and made huge puppy-dog eyes. "Please?"

"Go on, then."

On Freddie's bob of approval, Skye propelled herself off the bench and headed for the first available swing she could find.

"So where's Skye's father?" Tag asked, when Skye was out of earshot.

"Michael?" Freddie grimaced. "He buggered off when Laura was pregnant. Last I heard, he was backpacking across Thailand."

"Does he know?" Tag lifted her head to Skye.

"*Father unknown*," Freddie said. "That's what Laura had put on the birth certificate."

A sudden gust of wind chased Michael away.

"So what about you?" Freddie finally asked. "How did the married girlfriend thing come about?"

"By my own stupidity, probably," Tag replied ruefully. "I was new to Liverpool. She gave me a job. We dated. I thought she was the real deal."

"You didn't know she was married?"

"Nope. Not a clue," Tag said. "Oh, I knew about this guy called Stefan who worked with us. Anna told me he was her ex, and they just worked together."

"But she was still with him?" Freddie could sense the hurt.

Tag nodded. "Married, four-bedroom detached house in the suburbs, one dog, two cats," she said. "I only found that little gem out six weeks after we started dating."

"But you stayed with her, even after you found out?"

"Do you think me bad for that?" Tag asked. "She wasn't a woman who was easy to say no to."

"Any kids?"

"No, they didn't have kids." Tag's face blackened. "Actually, the subject of kids was what brought about the end of us." She waved to Skye and nodded to her as Skye gestured that she was moving onto the next set of swings.

"She never wanted them?"

"No." Tag rested her elbows on her legs. "I thought I was in love with her." She pitched Freddie a look. "I saw my future as being with her. Thought she'd leave Stefan for me. Set up home with me. Two point four kids. The lot."

"Like me and Charlotte." Freddie's voice was quiet. "I was with a girl called Charlotte." She felt like she needed to explain. "Before Laura died."

"The Charlotte that Skye mentioned the other day?" Tag sat back.

"Mm." Freddie focused on a point across the park. "Skye adored her. *I* adored her."

"So what happened?"

"I thought we'd get married," Freddie said, "and have the cosy family life you thought you'd have with Anna."

"Yeah, except all Anna wanted from me was a bit of fun," Tag said. "When she'd had that, she got bored of me."

"Nah, Charlotte was different to that," Freddie said. "I'm sure she loved me in her own way, but she just couldn't hack being a mother to Skye. Said she was too young to be saddled with someone else's kid."

"Ouch."

"Quite," Freddie said. "Skye doted on her too. Charlotte left me with a shitload of trust issues, but, you know, life moved on and things slowly changed."

"Oh, trust." Tag groaned. "Don't talk to me about trust."

"You too, huh?"

"Yeah, big time," Tag said. "Anna started seeing someone while I was still with her."

"Why do they always do that?" Freddie sighed. Tag had been hurt too. A rush of protective feelings came from nowhere, and she impulsively smoothed a hand down Tag's forearm.

"Probably my fault," Tag said. "Looking back, I think I wanted a kid to fill the hole left by Magnus. That's all I ever wanted—a family of my own."

"Really?"

"I adored Magnus," Tag said. "He was my shadow. I think I felt more guilty about leaving him than I did anything else."

"But you still went?" Freddie asked. "Even though you knew it would hurt him?"

Tag stopped.

Freddie shifted on the bench, sensing Tag's unease. Had she said too much?

"I meant…" Freddie began.

"I was different back then." Tag chewed on her lip. "Selfish."

"So Anna never wanted kids?" Freddie changed the subject.

"No." Tag stared down at the grass. "I pushed her and pushed her, and eventually she freaked out. Left me for this Caroline woman."

"Like Charlotte did with me. Freaked out and left."

"Women are bitches sometimes, aren't they?" Tag laughed, but her laugh was hollow.

"Yup," Freddie mused. "And it's always us good guys that are left to pick up the pieces."

She turned and looked at Tag, noting the anguish in her eyes. Anna's deceit still hurt her, she could tell, just as Charlotte's did with her. As she continued to look, Tag turned and held her gaze. No more words were needed.

"Can we go?" The arrival of a panting Skye forced their gazes apart. "I'm hot."

Freddie stood, ambling away from the bench after Skye. She turned and smiled back over her shoulder to Tag, encouraging her to catch up.

CHAPTER THIRTEEN

Tag loped up to Freddie and Skye, falling into step beside them. Freddie started to talk as they walked further away from the park, joined at intervals by Skye. A story about something that had happened at their new cottage a few days before. It was peppered with humour, embellished with exaggerated arm movements from Skye, and laced with drama, again ably assisted by Freddie.

Tag was no longer listening to the story, though. Freddie's words were lost to her as she walked with her, enveloped by her presence. Freddie's eyes were wide and engaging as she carried on talking. Skye was repeatedly asked to confirm or deny a certain aspect of the story. Their faces were both animated and expressive, their laugher infectious. Freddie was adorable, Tag thought, as she repeatedly dissolved into fits of unguarded giggles at her story, making both her and Skye laugh too. She was wonderfully vibrant, and so alive. Quite unlike any other girl she had ever met. And the complete antithesis to Anna. Engaging, attentive, tactile.

But more importantly, she now thought with rocks in her stomach as she followed them up towards the duck pond, Freddie was the polar opposite to the soulless mess that was her life back in Liverpool.

The view across Balfour from the lake at the top of the hill which led from the park was spectacular. With Skye and Freddie busy feeding the ducks in the small lake behind them, Tag stood alone, gazing out in silence across the town, her eye picking out landmarks she'd long since forgotten.

She followed the road up through the town. A faint wisp of smoke spiralled into the sky. Cars passed one another on the streets. Cows hunched in corners of fields. Tag's eyes eventually pulled to a honey-coloured building lying adjacent to the River Dynne, snaking through the town. A smattering of cars were parked outside. Next to them was a similarly honey-coloured watermill, the type often seen in fairy-tale books. Its huge waterwheel, embedded in the dark river, sent white spray frothing as it turned slowly but surely. Behind it all lay a patchwork of fields, gradually returning to their original rich, dark peaty colour now the last hints of recent snow had gone. Parked up in the field in the distance and just visible to the naked eye was the familiar sight of Blair's green tractor, waiting for him. Ready to plough deep grooves into the earth. Ready for planting again in a few weeks. Ready for the whole cycle to begin again.

It was a hive of industry. The metaphorical wheel that never stopped turning. Blair, the staff inside. The tractor ploughing. The waterwheel supplying the power to the mill by driving the enormous Victorian millstones to grind the wheat to make the flour to bake the bread. Everything working in unison to make Balfour Watermill tick over so that it could bring essential trade to Balfour and offer a decent standard of living to the staff that worked there.

"What are you looking at?" Freddie was standing besides Tag.

"The mill."

Freddie didn't answer, as if sensing Tag needed to say more. She waited.

"Perhaps I never truly understood what this place meant," Tag said suddenly. "I think perhaps I've spent the last nine years trying to forget it ever existed, because the stubborn cow inside me chose to."

Nine years spent running, always seeking what she'd had as a child. Nine years pretending the mill wasn't still there, because to remember it was too painful.

"Now I'm older, I wonder if it's not so bad here after all." Tag rotated her hat round in her hands and studied the label inside. She frowned. She mustn't cry.

"Your dad would be pleased."

That didn't help.

"What was he like?" Tag asked. "All I can remember was a broken man who could barely look at me." She stared down at her hat. "I'm sure he couldn't really have been like that."

"He was lovely." Freddie was sincere. "Very fair. Very loyal. We all liked him a lot."

"If I could turn the clock back," Tag spoke softly, "I'd never have gone."

"So why did you?"

"I thought I was doing what was right for me at the time." Tag shook her head sadly. "But it was never meant to go on so long." She frowned. "I never meant to cut them off."

"So why did you?"

"When I first left, I told myself I was justified in going," Tag said. "I'd spent the first eighteen years of my life living in a small town where everyone knew everyone else's business." She gripped her hat. "I moved to the first large city I could think of, and suddenly I was like a kid in a sweet shop. No one knew me. No one wanted anything from me. I could reinvent myself."

"And go a little crazy?" Freddie offered.

"Perhaps. All at once I could be the person I thought I wanted to be," Tag said. "I figured a few phone calls home would be okay. I'd go back and see them when I'd had a chance to make Dad see I was serious about wanting to make a life for myself outside Balfour. Outside the mill."

"But you didn't?"

"Life was too much fun." Tag shrugged. "Months passed, years passed. Still having fun. If I returned home? The fun would stop and I'd find myself sucked back into mill life and being suffocated by my father again." Even to her own ears, it sounded horrendous. "Maybe I wanted to punish him."

"How?"

"He wasn't there for me when I needed him, so why should I be there for him when he needed me?"

"You were young…"

Tag waved Freddie away. "I was so stupid. So selfish." She cleared her throat. "But it wasn't about me, was it? It was never about me." Sorrow clawed at Tag's insides. "I miss him." Tag stared down at her hat. Microscopic concentration. Keep staring. Don't look up. Tears were just one more word or look away. "I miss him so much."

"And now the guilt's finally coming out," Freddie said softly. "Am I right?"

Tag nodded. No words would come.

"Have you cried for him yet?" Freddie asked.

"No."

Freddie didn't speak. She glanced round at Skye, still talking to the ducks, then put her arm around Tag and drew her to her. She waited, knowing what Tag needed to do.

Slowly, Tag rested her head against Freddie's shoulder.

"I miss him," she repeated.

"I know." Freddie spoke gently. "We all do."

"I've had all this time to miss him." Tag's tears were warm and damp down her cheeks, falling against Freddie's neck. "But I didn't. What sort of person does that make me?"

"The sort that probably deep down always knew you'd see him again one day," Freddie replied.

"And now I'm never going to see him again." Tag's voice was barely a whisper before it dissolved into a flood of tears.

Freddie didn't answer. While Tag's body shuddered with the tears she'd held in for weeks, Freddie wrapped her arms tighter around her, rocking her back and forth until she felt the tears subside. Finally, Tag was quieter.

They stood wrapped in one another's arms for a few minutes until Tag finally pulled away. She pulled down the sleeves of her coat over her fingers and wiped the dampness away from her cheeks. Freddie wandered to Skye, allowing Tag time to gather her thoughts before she turned back to face her.

"Now I feel *really* embarrassed." Tag joined Freddie. She crouched at the side of the pond and stared into its dark depths. "But I probably needed to do that a long time ago." Emotional exhaustion engulfed her. She stood and walked a little way off. No one in all her adult life had ever hugged her with as much empathy and compassion as Freddie had just done. Tag rubbed at her eyes. Because no one had ever cared. No one had ever just held her. Not like that. It had felt good.

"I think perhaps you needed to see just what the mill really means." Freddie joined her. "Not just to Balfour, but to you as well. Perhaps because you'd made up your mind as a teenager that you hated it, you thought you could never change your mind about it."

"Perhaps."

"Sometimes we need to look at something that we feel negative about from a different perspective. Like from a hill in a park," Freddie said. "And then we can finally see the positives in it."

"Are you a secret psychologist?" Tag stood.

"No, just a humble cafe manager." Freddie caught Tag's eye and smiled. The charm in her smile instantly warmed Tag.

"Well, whatever you are," Tag said, looking down and concentrating hard at a pebble at her feet, "you've helped. A lot." Finally she lifted her head. "So thank you."

Quite without warning, Ellen's words from earlier trampled through her mind. With very large boots on. A spontaneous smile twitched at Tag's lips. *If only she could see me now, too scared to even look at Freddie because, yes, she's hot and, yes, she's just hugged me in broad daylight in front of half of Balfour.*

"What's funny?" Freddie dug an elbow into Tag's side.

"I don't think I can tell you." Tag fiddled with the zip on her coat.

"I hope you're not laughing at me just because I've given you a load of psychological bull." Freddie's face fell.

Tag was horrified. "God, no." How could Freddie think that? The things she'd just said had warmed Tag more than anything anyone had ever said to her before. "I didn't mean to smile. I'm sorry." She paused. "I was just thinking about something Ellen said to me earlier, that's all."

"Which was?"

How to proceed? "My sister-in-law," Tag eventually said, "is many things. But diplomacy isn't her strong point."

"I don't understand."

"Ellen said people would talk because you and I have been hanging out together." Tag looked over to Skye, determinedly following three ducks up and down the path.

"Is it anything to do with anyone else?" Freddie asked. "I'd say not."

"She told me I shouldn't be hitting on you after only five minutes."
Tag faltered. She coughed. Why couldn't she speak properly? So
dumb. She rolled Freddie a fake, impatient *Isn't that so stupid?* look.

"And are you?" Freddie asked slowly.

"Hitting on you?"

"Mm." Freddie held her look.

"Well, let's say Ellen's right about two things," Tag said,
watching Freddie carefully. "One, I've only been here five minutes."

"And two?" Freddie slow blinked, throwing Tag. Why did she
have to do that?

"And two?"

"Bread's gone." A small voice at Tag's side made her words get
swallowed back down. "Got any more?"

"I…" Tag frowned. "No. No more bread. Sorry sweetheart."

"Then we should go." Skye started to move, decision made.

Tag's gaze returned to Freddie. She was still looking at her.

"And two?" Freddie pressed.

Tag felt a small pull of her hand from Skye. As she walked
from Freddie, still rooted to the spot, she turned and looked round,
capturing her eyes once again.

"Take a wild guess." She smiled back to her.

❖

The coat that was dropped in Freddie's hallway when she and
Skye returned still had sand from the park on it. As Skye ran to the
lounge and flung herself down onto the sofa, oblivious to the mess
she'd left behind, Freddie gathered up the trail of shoes and coat and
sand left in her wake. She opened her mouth to chastise Skye for her
untidiness then stopped when she heard low voices from the lounge:
Pete and Sarah. Freddie's shoulders sagged. For some reason, she
didn't feel able to cope with company right now. She knew she'd have
to walk into the lounge, force a smile on her face, and be sociable
when all she wanted to do was hide out in the conservatory with a cup
of tea and be alone with her thoughts. Thoughts of Tag.

She had just spent three hours in Tag's company and yet
missed her the second they parted. She hung back in the hallway,

remembering. Tag was telling her, wasn't she? Telling her she liked her, and if it hadn't been for her impatient daughter, Freddie was sure she might have eventually responded with the same.

Timing sometimes sucked.

She and Tag had parted at the park. Despite Skye's repeated begging for Tag to come back with them, Tag had, to Freddie's disappointment, turned the offer down. Freddie knew she'd have given anything to hang out longer with Tag: a stroll round the park, a visit to the bandstand, afternoon tea up at the pavilion. Any one of those would have been paradise. But any one of those would also mean another step closer to Tag, another stage of attachment. Another chance for Tag to look at her the way she'd looked at her when she'd walked away from her, her hand firmly in Skye's. Interest. Wanting and needing. A slow blink and a held gaze that had sent a shard of ice down Freddie's back. A look she hadn't seen since Charlotte, and one that Freddie hadn't been able to shake from her head all the way home. She knew she wanted Tag to look at her like that again. But what would that mean for her? Or Skye, for that matter? Freddie knew it couldn't happen again.

"Have you seen this?" Pete called from the lounge. "This guy's about to walk across a tightrope without a harness."

Freddie poked her head around the door. A scene of Saturday afternoon domestic bliss hit her: Pete and Sarah on the sofa, Skye wedged between them, spellbound by the TV. A family unit.

"How was the park?" Sarah tilted her head back on the sofa.

"Busy." Freddie sat down. "Half of Balfour was there."

"Tag went down the slide with me. Twice." Skye didn't move her eyes from the screen.

"Tag, huh?" Pete caught Freddie's eye.

"She got me this." Skye clambered from the sofa. She went back into the hall and came back with her piggy bank. She rattled it with a flourish and marched back up to Pete, holding it up an inch from his face. "It's a money box *and* she put…" She tilted her head to one side and looked over to Freddie. "How much did Tag put in it?"

"Two pounds sixty-five," Freddie answered. She looked at the pig. The gesture had added yet another lovely layer to Tag, as if in Freddie's eyes right now she even needed one.

"And she put two pounds sixty-five in it," Skye confirmed.

"It's lovely." Pete took it from her and studied it. "That was nice of her."

"She's nice." Skye took the pig back from him and carefully placed it on the mantelpiece.

"You like her?"

Skye landed back on the sofa and leaned her head against Pete's arm. "She's funny."

"Tea?" Sarah stood and looked pointedly to the kitchen. Freddie took her cue and followed her from the lounge. "So the park was awesome, huh?" Sarah opened one of the cupboards.

"Skye enjoyed it." Freddie knew what Sarah was angling at.

"And you?" Sarah dipped her head and caught Freddie's eye.

"It was good."

"So tell me about Tag." Sarah plopped teabags into a teapot. "The look on your face tells me you want to, but you don't want to."

"Right on both counts."

"Pete told me you've been seeing a lot of her lately."

"Maybe too much." Freddie sat down. She cradled her head in her hands. "That's what scares me." Tag loitered in the perimeters of her mind, waiting for Freddie to give her full attention. Waiting for Freddie to forget about anything and everything else. Just like she'd been doing for days. Their afternoon at the park, the look Tag had given her, the hints she'd offered, had merely accelerated Freddie's thoughts.

"Pete says she's nice." Sarah pulled herself up onto the kitchen counter. "He likes that you're seeing her."

Freddie caught Sarah's eye, finally understanding. Pete wanted Freddie to get attached to Tag because he knew that he wouldn't be there forever. Like a gust of wind, the realization blew at her, blowing sense and understanding in her face. Pete would be married soon. Gone, to another life with Sarah, and Freddie would be alone with Skye once more.

"Is he trying to push us together?" Freddie stood up, suddenly annoyed. "Because if he is, he's wrong. Tag's not a permanent fixture in Balfour. She's—"

"He just wants you to be happy, Freds," Sarah implored. "And who's to say Tag won't come back to visit once she's gone? She has to, doesn't she? For Blair and Magnus?"

Pete had been wonderful when he'd first come to live with Freddie. One of her oldest friends, he'd known both Freddie and Laura and had been at Freddie's side throughout Laura's illness. He'd known Charlotte too and hadn't hesitated in moving into their cottage to support Freddie when Charlotte had left. Sensing Freddie's dread at having to start over alone, he'd protected her, steered her through her haze of depression and panic attacks, and had been there for her when finally she'd come out the other end. He'd never left her, despite meeting Sarah a few months later, knowing Freddie still needed him. He'd been her knight in shining armour, her shoulder to cry on, and her best mate when Freddie had felt as though the whole world had let her down. Freddie, of course, knew one day Pete would go again, and she was ready for it. But Tag, she knew, couldn't and wouldn't ever be his replacement.

"I need someone permanent, Sarah," Freddie stressed. "Okay, Tag *might* occasionally come back, but it's not enough. Skye needs it too, not a temporary face in her life who comes and goes." Her eyes slid back to the lounge. Skye was nestled in the crook of Pete's arm. Tag's piggy bank, retrieved once more from the mantelpiece, was clasped tightly in her hands. "Anyway, one look at Tag's past record should be enough to tell me to steer clear of her."

"Because she left once before?" Sarah asked.

"Because she left even though she knew Magnus doted on her." Freddie reinforced her point. "What sort of person does that?"

"A naive eighteen-year-old?" Sarah offered. "Pete's told me all about her. I can sympathize with her, though. At eighteen all you can see is a big, wide world just waiting for you. You're not the same person when you're nearly thirty." She nudged her. "We should know. Are you telling me you didn't do things as a teenager that you regret?"

"I guess not." Freddie looked back to Skye. "But Magnus was about Skye's age when she left. It just makes it personal to me. How would I feel if I let Skye get close to her, only for her to go and never come back?"

She smiled as she watched Pete tickle Skye, Skye doubling over and nearly toppling from the sofa.

"I want a family. Like you guys will have one day." Freddie knew that with absolute conviction. She wanted what Pete and Sarah would eventually have together: a family unit. She wanted security and love. Someone to come home to every night. Someone to snuggle up with on the sofa, and to watch cartoons with Skye. Unity, unwavering love, and protection.

It was something, Freddie knew with a sinking heart, that she'd never have with someone as unreliable as Tag.

CHAPTER FOURTEEN

Accounts from the last five years." Blair placed a pile of files on the table in front of Tag. "Farming accounts, figures from flour production, mill accounts." Another pile. "Receipts, staff payroll documents, farm equipment servicing receipts." The mountain of files slowly slid into a muddle on the table.

"Great filing system." Tag groaned. "Half of these folders are falling apart, Blair."

"Blame Dad." Blair sat opposite her. "I always told him to get an accountant in."

It was now Tuesday. Tag had spent the entire morning hiding away in Blair's office at Glenside with the accounts while Blair had returned to finish ploughing the riverside fields. Now he was back, armed with yet more files. Despite still replaying her Saturday afternoon at the park with Freddie and Skye, Tag had known the sooner she knuckled down and made inroads into the mill's accounts, the better. After all, with work out of the way, she'd have more time to play with Freddie and Skye again. It was that thought that now sustained her through the second pile of files Blair had just tossed onto the table. Hours of scrutinizing facts and figures loomed.

Freddie loomed closer. Tag had hinted, hadn't she? Freddie had been testing the waters, Tag had been sure of it. She smiled as she flipped a file open and pulled out a tax return statement. And now Freddie knew. What had her reaction been? She ran her finger down the line of figures and tried to pull Freddie's expression to the front of her mind. She hadn't stalked off, that was for sure. So that had to mean she'd liked Tag's hint. Tag's smile deepened. "It's at times like this," she said, not lifting her head, "that I wish I'd concentrated harder in maths at school."

"How do you think I feel?" Blair sat back. "Ask me about wheat prices, I'm your man. Anything else? Forget it."

"It says here on your tax return that four years ago"—Tag turned the page—"outgoings were higher than incomings. But if you look at this figure here, it looks as though it was the same the next year too."

"Four years ago we had that terrible summer," Blair said. "Crops were wiped out. We had to play catch-up for a while."

"Where's last year's file?"

Blair lunged across the table and grabbed the largest file. "Here." He pushed it over to Tag.

She opened it, then flipped through the pages. "Who marked all the red in here?"

Blair pulled a face. "Dad?"

"You don't know?"

"Nope."

"Are you being deliberately awkward?" Tag slammed the file shut. "This is important." Important to them all. To their futures.

"Tag, I'm just as much in the dark about all this as you," Blair said. "This is the first time I've seen these files since Dad died."

"He never showed you?"

"What do you think?"

Tag inhaled slowly. "These files read like a horror story, Blair." She opened another file. "Losses. Bills paid late. Question marks written all over everything."

Blair looked steadily at her. "Now can you see why I don't want your share?" he said. "Why would anyone want one hundred percent of a failing business like this?"

"You never knew we were in a mess?"

"You know Dad." Blair sighed. "He just employed me to do the wheat stuff. Work the land. Do you think he ever mentioned we were in a pickle back then?"

"It's so much more than just being in a bit of a pickle, Blair." Tag pulled her hands through her hair. "I've just skimmed these files, and I can see how much of a mess we're in."

"I'm going." Ellen's head poked round the door. She surveyed the situation. "Just in time, by the looks of things."

"Ask Tom to call me, will you?" Blair looked back over his shoulder at her.

"You're going up to the mill?" Tag asked. She stretched, feeling the enjoyable crick in her neck as she did so. Four hours sitting on a hard chair had done nothing for her posture.

Ellen nodded. "Dropping off some recipe cards for Freddie."

Freddie? The sound of her name made any more thoughts of files disappear like dust to the wind.

Tag cast a cursory glance at the files, then thought of Freddie. The files could wait. Hadn't she spent enough time on them already this morning? "I'll take you." She rose. "I was going to go up there later anyway. Talk to Tom about stuff." The lies flowed. They sounded credible, though.

"Already?" Blair looked up at her. "But what about these?"

"I've been here since nine this morning, Blair." Tag straightened her arms above her head. "If I don't get out for five minutes I'm going to go stir-crazy." She needed a distraction, and what better distraction than Freddie?

"I'm not putting you out?" Ellen asked.

For the chance to see Freddie again?

"You're really not," Tag replied.

Freddie was hunched over the sink when they arrived. The cafe was empty, just two teacups left on a table the only evidence that anyone had been in. She turned at the click of the door and saw Ellen first, then Tag. It was Tag she addressed first, though.

"Hi, again." The easiest of smiles animated Freddie's face when she saw Tag.

"Hey." Tag manoeuvred her way round the tables towards her. "Just the person I'd come to see." Feigning surprise at seeing her. Very grown up.

"I thought you came to see Tom?" Ellen whispered beside her. Tag chose to ignore her.

"We brought recipe cards for you," Tag said. "Well, Ellen did."

"For the counter." Ellen slipped Tag a look. "The ones we talked about the other day?"

"Thanks." Freddie took them. She flicked through them and nodded. "They're perfect."

"Shall we go see Tom?" Ellen motioned towards the door leading into the gristmill. "After all, that was the other reason we came up here, wasn't it?"

"I'll catch you up." Tag focused on Ellen, urging her to leave. "Bye."

"Okay." Ellen flashed Tag a mischievous look. "Don't trip over your tongue while I'm gone. It's hanging out," she said as she walked away from them. "See you in a bit."

"What did she mean?" Freddie took a cake from its cooling rack and placed it onto a plate.

"The cakes," Tag said hastily. She gestured to the plate. "She knows I like cakes." Her eyes bored into Ellen's retreating back as she disappeared back out of the door. "She's so funny. Or at least she likes to think she is."

Tag took a step back as Freddie came out from behind the counter. Her eyes followed her as she grabbed a cake dish from across the other side of the cafe. Tag picked at a spot on the counter. Just talk to her. Ask her how she is.

"So, how are you?" she asked.

"Good. You?"

"Same."

"Good." Freddie went back to the counter.

"Skye okay?"

"She's good, yeah. Keeps asking when you're coming to the park with us again." Freddie laughed. "I think you're a hit with her."

Silence returned. Tag never thought the ticking of a clock could sound so loud.

"So." Tag raised her eyes upward. "I, uh, I finally got round to having a proper look at the mill's books earlier."

"Yeah?"

"Yeah. Be good to hear your thoughts on stuff sometime."

"You're going to tell me it's not as healthy as you thought it would be, aren't you?" Freddie offered. "I already know."

"Sounds like you know as much as Blair does." Tag laughed.

"Meaning?"

"That Dad kept things to himself." Tag backtracked.

"I did mention to Adam I was worried," Freddie started. "Quite a while ago, actually."

"Let me guess," Tag replied. "He told you not to worry?"

"He told me it didn't matter if the cafe was ever going through a rough patch," Freddie said, "because the rest of the mill was flourishing."

"I think my father used to embellish the truth sometimes."

"Should I be concerned now?" Freddie asked slowly.

"We should talk, for sure." It was a noncommittal answer, but what else could Tag say?

"Okay." Freddie stood behind the counter. "I'm free tomorrow, if that helps?" She wiped her hands on her apron. "I'd rather talk sooner than later, if I'm honest."

"You have a bit of flour," Tag said. "Tomorrow sounds good, yeah." She waggled her finger. "Flour in your hair, I mean. You don't need to be worried about the cafe." A lie, but what was the point of worrying her?

Freddie groaned. "Don't tell me I've been wandering around with flour in my hair all morning." She dusted her palm against her hair. "What time are you free to talk tomorrow?"

"More to the back." Tag pointed to the left-hand side of Freddie's head. "Anytime. You could come to Glenside," she offered. "Or we could go somewhere down in town. Away from here. Mull everything over a cup of coffee?"

"Sure. Foxy Brown's do an amazing mocha." Freddie grinned. "Although perhaps I shouldn't be saying that, considering you're probably going to tell me I need to be encouraging more customers in here." Freddie batted at her hair. "Gone?"

"Nearly."

Freddie rolled her eyes upward and round, trying to see.

"You'll not see it," Tag said. She stayed rooted to the spot. "Bit more to your left."

"Better?"

"Almost."

More batting. The flour remained steadfast.

"Did you actually manage to get any in the cakes?" Tag lounged against the counter, amused.

"Funny." Freddie tried to sound pissed off. She failed. The mischievousness on her face while she spoke didn't help.

"Hang on." Tag finally pulled herself away from the counter. She stepped round the side of it and approached Freddie.

Freddie took a step back. "It's okay, I got it." She yanked at a strand of hair.

"You haven't." Tag brought her hand to Freddie's hair. She flicked lightly at it and pulled a small crumb from her hair, then flicked at it some more. Their eyes were level. Tag stared at Freddie's hair with an acute concentration she didn't know she was even capable of. She tried desperately to halt the flow of thoughts cascading through her mind as her fingers caressed the soft strands. Erratic thoughts sparked, as if by magic, by their intimacy, thoughts of the look Freddie had given her at the park, the look on her face at Tag's unannounced arrival in the cafe just now.

Freddie's breath fluttered warm and light against Tag's skin, sending her thoughts and senses spiralling. Freddie knew Tag liked her. Their faces were inches apart. Freddie knew but she hadn't run from the park. Lips inches apart. All Tag had to do was lean a little closer still, then Freddie would know for sure how Tag felt. Tag wouldn't be able to stop herself from kissing her, she knew. Just another hint closer, another pull from Freddie's eyes, and any resolve she might have had would be gone.

Freddie focused on a point to her right. Tag was inches from her and if Freddie didn't centralize her entire attention on the picture hanging by the door, all her resolve and everything she'd told herself the day before would be for nothing. She slowed her breathing, as if the barest hint of warm breath against Tag's skin would tell her of her restiveness at Tag's touch. She couldn't allow herself to look at Tag. She *mustn't* allow herself. One look back at Tag's face, one tiny glimpse towards her, and she'd be lost in the blue depths of her eyes.

"All gone now." Tag, to Freddie's relief, finally stepped back from her and hastened to the other side of the counter again.

The atmosphere weighed thick as the silence ticked by between them. Freddie drew air slowly in, quietening her thudding heart. She must stop her heart from doing this each time she saw Tag or got close to her. No good would come of it. She must think of Skye each time her thoughts strayed to Tag and remember her responsibilities to her, rather than her own selfish emotions. That would be enough to quell her feelings, wouldn't it? It was simple: Skye needed her. She was her priority.

"Thanks." Freddie finally spoke. She automatically brought her hand to her hair and tidied it up. Her hand was rock steady. But she knew her cheeks were flushed. Had Tag felt it? The atmosphere? The chemistry? Freddie's hands were giving nothing away. Her face though…

"Anytime." Tag stared down hard at the counter top, her own hand trembling. "What time tomorrow, then?"

"Two?"

"Perfect." Tag moved from the counter. "I better go speak to Tom," she said.

"Sure." Freddie busied herself again at the sink. "See you tomorrow." She looked back over her shoulder to Tag.

"Of course." Tag strode to the exit, her breathing ragged. "See you then."

❖

Even Tag was impressed at the questions she asked Tom after she'd left the cafe. She hadn't planned them, had no idea what she'd ask him when she'd left Freddie, had only known she had to get away from the tension in the cafe. She'd managed to remember details from the files Blair had given her at Glenside earlier and now almost sounded as if she knew what she was talking about. Almost.

Her head was in turmoil, her wanting almost blinding her. They'd nearly kissed. The ache inside Tag told her just how close they'd come to it.

"I'll get the figures to you by the morning." Tom dusted floury hands down his overalls. "Distribution details, numbers, contacts. You name it."

"I appreciate it," Tag said. She shot a look to the door leading out towards the cafe. Freddie was just a few footsteps away. So close. Tag turned away, giving her full attention to Tom.

"Anything else you need, just shout."

"I will." Tag looked around the mill. Still weird. Still way too weird.

"Does it bring it back?" Tom noticed the look on her face. "I thought last week when you were in here you looked sad."

"Being in here?" Tag crossed her arms. "I'll say." She wandered away from Tom. "Amazing how nine years can feel so long, but so short at the same time." Her eye settled on a machine. "This thing still work?" she asked. A hefty 1800s giant thresher sat idiosyncratically next to a bright twenty-first century wheat-sorting machine.

"I reckon so." Tom came to stand next to her. "She hasn't been fired up in, oh, over twenty years." He ran his hands over the metal. "Bit of oil, I think she'd run no problem at all, though."

"But you don't use it any more?" Tag asked. The way Tom was looking at it with such affection strangely comforted her.

"Have you forgotten everything your father told you?" Tom chuckled. "Threshers like this aren't used any more. It's all this high-tech machinery now." He motioned with his head towards the corner of the mill. "Quicker. More efficient."

"So why keep it?" Tag asked. "Couldn't the space be used for something else?"

"No one wants stuff like this." Tom wrinkled his nose. "Maybe a collector. But it's the hassle of getting it to them."

"I guess."

"Besides, it's nice," he said. "Don't you think?"

"Having an old piece of machinery gathering dust?" Tag teased.

"Having *original* machinery gathering dust," Tom corrected. "There's only a few of us left now that have original stuff still on-site."

"Are there?" Should she have known that? More specifically, was that the type of fact she ought to know now she was a mill owner?

"Or that in 1900 there were ten thousand water and windmills in Britain?"

"Nope."

"How many do you think now?" Tom's eyes sparkled. At least he was having fun.

"Hit me."

"Barely thirty."

"Seriously?"

"I'd say that kind of makes us like a working museum, wouldn't you?" Tom said. "All right, so we don't use that thresher any more, but we still use the original runner and bedstones."

Tag looked down at them. They were stones. Okay, an impressive sight, but still stones nonetheless. "They're both old, I take it?"

"Victorian." Tom nodded. "Like the waterwheel."

"And they still work okay?" Tag followed Tom.

"Fine." Tom looked down at them. "Canny bunch, the Victorians. Built stuff to last. Unlike today."

"Well, I guess we have the technology now—"

"It's all modern hydropower technology." Tom dismissed her thought process with a wave of his hand. "It won't last as long as this will." He spun his arms out. "It's a living, breathing piece of history, this place." He eyes shone. "Want to try sometime? Fire the thresher up again one day?"

"Sure. Some other time." Tag gazed around her. Tom was right. It *was* like standing in a living museum. She blinked as she heard her mother's laughter echo around her. She listened again. She was being silly, she knew, but nevertheless a coldness enveloped her. Tag trembled. Enough with the history lesson. She looked round one last time, half expecting to see her parents watching her. "So I'll see those figures in the morning, yeah?" she asked, heading to the exit.

"You most certainly will."

"If you're not down here in five I'm going without you." Freddie stood at the bottom of the stairs, coat and bag in hand. "And four, and three, and—"

The staccato clatter of footsteps on the landing alerted her to Skye's arrival. At last.

A muddle of blond curls bobbed over the bannister.

"You can't go to school without me." A pair of blue eyes peeked out from under the curls. "They wouldn't let you in, anyway."

"Just come down, Skye." Freddie held up the coat and bag. "I don't have time for this."

"Okay." Skye drew the word out. She bunny-hopped down the stairs.

"Coat." Freddie handed it to her.

"Not the blue one." Skye handed it back. "The red one today."

Freddie sighed. "Skye, honey." She placed a hand on Skye's shoulder and swivelled her round. "You're five years old. When you reach double figures you can dictate which coat to wear. Until then"—the coat was hustled onto Skye in one swift, expert movement—"you wear the blue one."

"Can I wear the red one tomorrow?" A firm hand propelled Skye to the front door.

"If it's that important to you."

"What's for tea tonight?" Skye waited by the door while Freddie grabbed her coat.

"I don't know yet."

"Pasta?"

"I don't know." Freddie reached past her and opened the door. "Shoes?" She motioned to Skye's socked feet. "Where are your school shoes?"

"Outside."

"You left them outside again?" Freddie wearily wiped her eyes. "Skye, how many more times do I have to tell you?"

"So can we have pasta?"

"What?"

"Tonight. For tea. Can we have pasta?" Skye plonked herself down on the doorstep and lifted a leg. She leaned back and waggled a shoe on. "With cheese?" Skye fumbled with her laces, frowning.

"I'll get something in town later." Freddie stepped over her. "Hurry up."

"Laces." Skye lifted her leg again. A shoe hung perilously from her toes. "I can't do them."

"Have you got in a jumble with them again?" Freddie crouched in front of her.

"I've got in a jumble with them again," Skye mimicked.

"I'm going out this afternoon," Freddie said, tying Skye's laces, "but I'll stop by the supermarket on my way home and get the little shell-shaped pasta that you like. Sound okay?"

"Mm." Skye clamped her lips shut and nodded, too busy watching Freddie to answer properly.

"There." Freddie stood. "All done."

Skye jumped up. She bent over and pulled at her laces.

"Done to your satisfaction?" Freddie drew her into a hug.

"Yep. Where are you going?"

"This afternoon? Just having coffee with a friend." Freddie closed the front door and hastened Skye down the path.

"With Pete?" Skye waited by the car.

"No, not with Pete." Freddie opened the car. "Get in."

Skye scrambled into her car seat and waited as Freddie buckled her in. "With Tim?"

"Not Tim either. And don't be so nosy." Freddie closed the car door. She opened her driver's door and slotted herself into her seat.

"With Hazel, then?" Skye wound down her window a little.

"Who's Hazel?"

"Melissa Gordon's mummy."

"Why would I be spending the afternoon with Melissa Gordon's mummy?" Freddie looked at Skye in the rearview mirror. "I don't even know Melissa Gordon's mummy."

"Dunno." Skye shrugged. She looked out of the window. "First name I thought of."

"I'm having coffee with Tag." Freddie pulled out of her parking space. "Happy now?"

"Tag?" A gasp.

"Yes."

"Can I come?"

"No."

The sound of Skye's coat rustling as she folded her arms crossly drew Freddie's eyes to the mirror again. She resisted the urge to laugh. Laughing at an indignant Skye, she knew, was an absolute no-no.

"But I like her," Skye said.

"Good. But it's still a no." Freddie glanced at Skye's reflection. Her arms were still crossed, her frown still patently evident. "We're talking about work. You'd be terribly bored."

"Does she like pasta for tea?"

"I don't know."

"'K." Skye sank lower into her car seat. "Freddie?"

"Mm?"

"Do you think she's as nice as Charlotte was?"

Freddie's breath caught. Charlotte. She swallowed.

"She's not Charlotte, honey." Finally the words came. "There won't be another Charlotte."

"I liked Charlotte," Skye said. "But I think Tag's nicer than her."

"I liked Charlotte too." Freddie fumbled for the radio. "A lot." Her hands trembled.

"Do you like Tag?" Persistence.

"Yes."

"As much as Charlotte, or more?"

Freddie jabbed at a button on the radio. "Shall we listen to your CD for a bit?" Change the subject. "We can sing number five together."

"And seven?"

"And seven."

"'K."

CHAPTER FIFTEEN

"No school today?" Tag reached across the kitchen table and picked up the half-empty jar of jam next to Magnus. "You sure about that?" She looked out of the window. "Because I'm sure I heard on the radio everything was open as usual today."

"Had a text," Magnus said between mouthfuls of toast. "Heating's down or something. 'Cos of the snow."

The previous evening's rain had turned to snow. Tag had watched, from the safety of Glenside, as the wind whipped drifts up the drive to stick against the cottage, making any chance of getting back into Balfour and to Four Winds that night impossible.

Now, despite a break in the snow, Tag found she had no desire to head back to Connie Booth and her cooked breakfasts. Just as well too. Blair and Ellen had headed out early, leaving Magnus to make his own way to school, which he would have done if it had been open.

Tag was dubious. Was it a coincidence that Magnus's school's heating chose to break down on the very day Tag was hanging out at Glenside? Or was it a ruse so he could hang out with her? Did he even want to still hang out with her now, like he used to when he was younger? Tag looked at him, remembering how they used to be together. She was always the cool auntie of the family—way cooler than any of Ellen's sisters anyway. Young, funny, funky. Magnus would follow her everywhere. Her own little shadow. Did he even remember that now? Or did he just see her as some weird, old stranger who just parked up in Balfour out of the blue? Her heart grew heavy.

"Right." Tag studied him. "So school's closed?"

"It's on my phone." His voice rose slightly. "You wanna check it?"

Tag held her hands up. "I don't want to check it," she said, seeing him visibly calm down again. "I just want to make sure you're not pulling a fast one because your parents aren't here."

Her phone vibrated from inside her jacket pocket hanging by the door.

"Want me to get your phone for you?" Magnus signalled with his head to her coat. "It just buzzed. Might be Mum."

"Sure. Thanks." Tag feigned indifference, but her eyes followed Magnus's every move.

Magnus crammed the rest of his toast into his mouth and got up from the table, wiping his hands down his trousers. Tag watched him saunter over to her coat. It would be Freddie. It had to be. All the while, she was running options through her head about what her message might say. Can't wait to see you later? I just want to hang out with you all the time? But what if it was more like: Go away? Leave me alone? I'm in love with Sarah? Tag tapped her finger on the table, irritated with herself.

"What are PPI claims?" Magnus handed Tag her phone and sat back down.

"I'm sorry?"

"Your text was from a PPI claims company."

"You shouldn't read my texts." Tag replied. Too matronly. Way too matronly.

Magnus shrugged. "You want to do something today?" he asked, "Seeing as how school's closed?"

A prick of hope. So he did want to hang out?

"Like what?" Tag deleted her PPI text. The nagging disappointment pulling in her stomach that it hadn't been Freddie remained.

"Dunno." Magnus pushed back into his chair. He locked his arms above his head and yawned loudly.

"Well, what do you normally do when you're not at school?"

"Not much," he said. "Try and avoid having to help up at the mill, mostly." He grinned, eliciting a bigger one back from Tag.

"Do you snowboard?" she asked suddenly. "I figure the way the snow came down overnight, we could take a board up to the Ben. What do you think?"

"Do *you* snowboard?" Magnus's eyes widened. "I mean, *can* you?"

"It's been a while," Tag admitted, "but I'm sure it's like riding a bike, isn't it?"

"That's awesome." There were those cool points again. Yeah, she was still the young, funny, funky auntie. "I didn't think anyone older than me ever did it."

"I used to freeride until fairly recently, thank you very much," Tag said. "I used to hang out with a group a while back, and we'd go over to the Alps some weekends."

"But not now?"

"Well, then I met someone and…"

"They didn't like it?"

"Something like that." Tag bit into her toast. "I thought I was in love with her at the time, and I wanted to please her," she said, "so I quit." Thanks to Anna and her illogical loathing of everything to do with her snowboarding. That, plus the incessant sulking every time Tag disappeared for the weekend without her.

"No way?" Magnus stood up from the table, taking his plate with him.

"Way."

"You kept your board, though?"

"Nah." Tag looked away. She remembered the arguments. So many damn arguments. "I sold it. It was a Salomon, so I got a good price for it."

"A Salomon? That's sick."

"It was," Tag agreed. She threw him a sideways look. He wasn't shy or hesitant in her company. No weird, old strangers here, as far as Magnus was concerned. This had been the first proper conversation they'd had together since Tag had returned, and she couldn't be happier. He wanted to talk to her, to be with her. He wanted to know stuff about her, and that could mean only one thing—he wanted to get to know her all over again. Happiness tinged with sadness—she had so many years to make up to Magnus. Tag drained her coffee. Enough talking about Anna and her past; now it was time to get up onto the mountain and really start to reconnect with Magnus.

"Now you've made me want to start boarding all over again." Tag joined him at the kitchen sink. She bumped his side. "You so better have two boards now."

❖

Freddie sat in the late morning gloom of her front room. Daytime TV was proving to be a poor distraction on her day off, and the methodical ticking of the clock didn't help either. A shard of sunlight pooled across the mantelpiece, making fine dust particles dance in front of her eyes. She watched them, unblinking. She was alone in the house, the thoughts in her head her only companion. As she held her first cup of tea of the afternoon, fingers gripped tight around her mug, her mind roller-coasted.

Freddie sipped at her tea and stole a glance at her phone on the table next to her. She had three hours before she was due to meet Tag. Where would she be now? She'd surprised Freddie with her arrival the previous day with Ellen, but not unpleasantly so. Freddie smiled into her mug. Her impromptu visit had certainly caught her off guard, setting off fireworks inside her when she'd seen her coming in through the door.

Fireworks she hadn't felt since Charlotte.

And Tag had touched her hair. Had Tag noticed how much her face had coloured when she'd done it? Her proximity had made Freddie's heart beat faster than it had in a long time; that certainly hadn't happened since Charlotte either. Freddie hastily chugged back another mouthful of tea. Thinking about Charlotte again now *so* wasn't a good idea. But was it any better to be replacing thoughts about Charlotte with those about Tag?

"Watching daytime TV?" Pete's frame filled the lounge doorway. "Slippery slope, kid."

"Jeez, Pete." Freddie clasped her hand to her chest. "You scared the shit out of me."

"I called out."

"I didn't hear."

"No kidding." Pete threw himself down on the sofa next to Freddie. He unbuttoned his top shirt button and tugged at his tie, loosening it. "So why are you here?"

"I live here, remember?"

"I thought you were going out."

"That's later. Anyway. Change of plan." Freddie snatched up her phone. "Wait a sec." She opened up her recent text messages and found Tag's message to her from the previous night, then opened up a reply.

Hey Tag, she wrote. *Can't make it this afternoon after all. Really sorry. Will try and catch you up at the cafe tomorrow. F.*

Freddie watched her text disappear. Disappointment clung to her. She tucked her phone down the side of the sofa. Disappointment could go and cling. She'd done the right thing, she was sure of it. If she told herself that enough times, she figured, she might start believing herself. Besides, she needed to talk with Pete.

"Skye mentioned Charlotte today," Freddie told Pete without thinking.

"After all this time?" Pete's face fell. "What did she say?"

"Not much." Freddie studied her hands. "I told her I was going out this afternoon. With Tag."

"Blair's sister? Again?"

"Mm."

"Right." Pete arm-bumped Freddie.

"Don't." Freddie shrugged him off. "We're just having a coffee."

"Okay."

"Don't say it like that."

"Like what?" Pete raised his hands. "I'm saying nothing."

"Anyway, I'm not going now."

"Let me guess." Pete twisted round so he was facing Freddie. "You mentioned Tag's name to Skye and she asked if Tag was like Charlotte?"

"Yes."

"And after Skye said that, you texted Tag and cancelled?"

"Not immediately afterwards." Freddie avoided eye contact with Pete. "In fact, even about ten minutes ago I was still going to go."

"And then sitting here in the dark, thinking about what Skye said made you reconsider?"

"It shows she's still thinking about Charlotte, doesn't it?" Freddie frowned. "I thought she was okay about it all now."

"She loved Charlotte," Pete reasoned. "She thought she was going to be her second mummy."

"*I* loved Charlotte." Freddie bit at a finger. "We were both let down by her."

The bitterness still rose, even after all this time. Charlotte had known how vulnerable Skye was, but she never once stopped to think about how her actions would affect her. That's how much of a selfish bitch she'd been, just looking after number one and to hell with her and Skye. Well, no more. Selfishness wasn't just the privilege of others. It was time for Freddie to look after herself and her child.

"So where does Tag fit into all this?" Pete's voice stirred her.

"She doesn't," Freddie replied emphatically.

"But you like her?" Pete asked. "The look on your face tells me you do, despite all your protestations at the ceilidh last week."

"More than I should. We kind of clicked straight away."

"More than you should?" Pete rested his head against the sofa. "You're allowed to like someone, Freds."

"Yeah, but *Tag*?" Freddie groaned. "Of all the people for me to fall for." This couldn't happen. It would be like Charlotte all over again, Freddie just knew it. Before long she'd have slipped back into anticipating Tag's call, and feeling disappointed if she didn't call, just like she did with Charlotte when they first dated. She'd start to relish Tag's undivided attention as though Freddie was the most important thing in her world, and love Tag's increasing affection for Skye. Freddie felt nausea rising. How could she have been so weak as to let Skye get so close to someone again? Could Tag give herself emotionally to both Freddie and Skye, so they were both the focus of her whole life? Charlotte couldn't. Why should Tag be any different?

"Does she even know you like her?" Pete pressed.

"No." Freddie bent forward. She reached behind her and plumped her cushion up. "And I want it to stay like that."

"Does she like you?" Pete dug Freddie in the ribs.

Freddie squirmed and batted his hand away. "I've no idea."

"You must have an inkling."

"There's been hints."

"Go on." Pete sat up straighter.

ONCE THE CLOUDS HAVE GONE

"And there was an incident," Freddie said slowly. "Yesterday, at the cafe."

"An incident?"

"I had flour in my hair."

"As you do."

"And Tag got it out."

"Is that it?" Pete fell back.

"I couldn't look at her," Freddie said. "I thought she'd see my heart was going nuts and I'd gone bright red."

"Goes like that when you're hot for someone." Pete clutched dramatically at his heart.

"And that's just my problem." Freddie ran her hands through her hair. "I've been seeing too much of her lately."

And it was all her own fault, she knew. She'd been too soft, too friendly. She just had to say no to Tag in the future. Act like she didn't give a damn. Keep it professional and not let her emotions get in the way. That was her trouble, Freddie thought. She was too emotional, too needy. Tag would be gone in a matter of weeks. That's the thought Freddie had to keep telling herself over and again. Tag was temporary.

"You're only going for a coffee, Freds," Pete contested. "A social meeting. That's all."

"I do like her company." Freddie looked to the cushion as she heard her phone give a muffled buzz. "But I just can't allow myself to fall for someone who might not be here this time next week."

"That her?" Pete signalled to the cushion.

"Probably."

"You're not going to see?"

"Nah." Of course she wanted to read Tag's text. Maybe later. When Pete had gone.

"The next girl along isn't necessarily going to be another Charlotte," Pete said gently. "Charlotte was a bitch. Chased you and chased you until you gave in. Gave Skye a load of crap about how she wanted to be a mother to her and then what?"

"She fucked off."

"She fucked off," Pete repeated, "and you had to take happy pills for six weeks to get over it."

"Thanks for reminding me."

"And Skye cried herself to sleep every night for a month, refused to go to school, hated Charlotte—"

"Hated me—"

"—and all because that selfish cow couldn't cope with the idea of Skye."

"No," Freddie corrected, "all because I was stupid enough to fall for Charlotte in the first place."

"Everything that happened was because of her. Not you."

"Anyway." Freddie sat up straighter. "It's all water under the bridge now. I've cancelled Tag. I'm steering clear of her until she goes back to England, then no one gets hurt. Not me, not Skye."

It was easy. If only someone would tell her breaking heart, though.

"And Sonny—he's in my year at school—well, he's a total airdog." Magnus hugged his knees to his chest and gazed out in front of him. "But I prefer speed, not dumb tricks all the time."

"Sonny the airdog is your mate?" Tag asked. She shot him a look. Studied his profile, illuminated by the low morning sun. Her mind fell pleasantly blank. Her nephew, this kid that she'd adored as a baby, as a toddler, and still adored now he was a teenager, had chosen to hang out with her for the day. *Her.* He could have chosen to spend his day off with Sonny, or whatever other friends he had, but he'd chosen to spend it with her. He'd *chosen.* She hadn't asked him, he'd asked her. That made Tag feel special, and as she now gazed out around her, feeling Magnus's ski jacket occasionally brush hers as he spoke, she thought even if she and Magnus never spent another day together while she was in Balfour, she'd never forget this moment.

"I do have friends, you know." Magnus hugged himself tighter. "I'm not the saddo loner that Dad seems to think I am."

"He doesn't think—"

"He does." Magnus pulled his beanie off and ruffled his hair. "But I come up here with Sonny and another friend from school called Ryan most weekends when there's enough powder," he said. "But Sonny sometimes just wants to muck around. I like freeriding, not jumping about like a jerk."

He was sitting close, comfortable in her company. Tag stretched her legs out in the snow in front of her, her breathing finally slowing after the long climb back up the hill. They'd had a blast, she and Magnus. Tag nestled her chin down into her jacket and smiled, content. As Magnus spoke, her eyes lifted to seek out the road up to the cafe. She pictured Freddie behind the counter; Freddie chatting to customers; Freddie enthusing about whatever homemade cakes she might have to offer them today. Tag's smile deepened. She'd tell her that she'd spent the day snowboarding with Magnus. Freddie would like that, Tag was sure. Did Freddie like snowboarding? Tag narrowed her eyes and tried to focus on the cafe from so far away, knowing she wouldn't be able to see Freddie from where she was, but wanting to try anyway. Just in case.

"Aren't I?" Magnus's voice pulled Tag's eyes away from the cafe and back to him.

"Aren't you what?" she asked.

"Better at freeriding."

"You laid a few tricks down back there." She jabbed her finger over her shoulder. "I thought you were awesome."

"You were pretty sick too." He scratched at his cheek. "You sure you haven't done this for years?"

"So you think falling over twenty times in a row is awesome?" Tag groaned at the pain in her hip. "And, yeah. I'm sure I haven't done it in, like, forever. Seriously."

"Well," Magnus said, "you're good."

"Cheers."

They sat in amongst a small coppice of fir trees. Adrenaline had faded to tiredness. Magnus's face and her own too, she was sure, were crimson from a combination of the cold, exhilaration, and the effort of the repeated climb back up the hillside. As she sat and zoned out, Tag could feel beads of sweat trickling down the small of her back. The snowboarding had been amazing. Better than she'd remembered. Their boards had slashed through the soft, powdery snow, sending up sprays of white as they raced one another down the slopes over and over again. They'd laughed and shrieked. They'd supported one another, and they'd tried, of course, to knock one another over on every single descent.

She cast a look over to Magnus, feeling absurdly happy. The years fell back; she was eighteen, he was five. Back then, they'd always loved coming out together when it snowed. They'd sit, side by side, with their tongues hanging out, trying to catch the snowflakes as they fell, both betting the other that they could catch one hundred flakes before the other did. The first one to catch the treasured hundredth flake would have good luck for the rest of the day. Those were the rules back then.

They'd both loved and shared a lot of things then: packets of jelly babies, silly jokes, cartoon reruns in the afternoons that she would sit and watch with him for hours on end. Now, nine years later, it seemed they still shared a love of something: their snowboarding.

Magnus sat, deep in thought, as his eyes roamed the landscape. Without speaking, he shrugged off his rucksack from his shoulders, letting it fall softly into the snow behind him. He opened it up and rummaged around for a few seconds before he pulled out a bottle of water. After he'd drunk from it, he handed it to Tag, who took it and drank from it too. While Tag was drinking, Magnus delved back into his rucksack, this time pulling out a notepad and pencil. He flipped the notepad open, then flicked his eyes from the trees and back to the blank sheet of paper in front of him. Then he began to sketch.

"You like drawing?" Tag moved closer to see. The outline of a tree began to take shape on the page.

"Mm-hmm." Magnus peered up at a branch, then sketched what he'd seen. "I love it," he said. "I carry this thing with me pretty much everywhere I go." He tapped the end of his pencil on his notepad. "I can never resist scribbling down a quick sketch of something I've seen, or somewhere I've been."

Tag watched as his hand became a blur, drawing the view that was right in front of them. Occasionally he'd stop to put the end of his pencil in his mouth. Then he'd start again, even faster, it appeared to Tag, than before.

"This is amazing." The drawing came to life with every stroke of his pencil. "How long have you been drawing for?"

Magnus shrugged. "Since I was little." His brows bunched into a frown with concentration. "Mum gave me a box of pencils and a sketch pad when I was about six, and it all kinda went from there."

"She never told me how good you are at it." Tag rested back on her elbows.

"She doesn't know." Magnus flipped his pencil upside down and hastily erased something before starting again. "I just do them for myself. I never show them to anyone."

"Not your dad?"

"Nah. Not him."

"You should."

Magnus hunkered further over his pad, engrossed. "He thinks I'm weird enough as it is," he said.

Tag's heart pulled. So Magnus would never show his parents his work, but he'd had no hesitation in drawing in front of her? The invisible thread pulling her closer to him tightened. Would he tolerate a hug? Tag watched him from the corner of her eye as he carried on drawing, lost in his own little world. Perhaps not yet. Kid was nearly fourteen after all, way past the hugging stage, and Tag had racked up the cool points with him today. No point in losing a few just because Tag felt grateful to him for sharing one of his secrets.

"He wants me to be a farmer, not an artist." Magnus flicked her a look. "Dad."

"And what do you want?"

He slid the pencil behind his ear and held his pad up, blowing pencil residue from it.

"I just want to be allowed to draw in peace," he said simply.

"Your father," Tag began, "says what he says for a good reason, I guess." She held up her hand when Magnus tried to retaliate. "A long time ago your granddad used to think I was a daydreamer as well because all I ever wanted to do was draw, or muck about on mountains, or skateboard my arse off all day."

"You draw?" Magnus's eyes widened. "Unreal. What? Paints? Pastels? Sketches?"

"All of those." She sat up and drew her knees to her chest. "Don't you remember? I used to draw things for you when you were a kid. Silly cartoons, funny faces. Stuff that used to make you laugh."

"I don't remember." Magnus rolled a shy look to her. "I don't remember much from when you used to live here. I wish I did, though."

"I started drawing when I was about your age." The look on Magnus's face had near killed her. "I started off doing what you're doing now." She nodded at his picture. "Pencil sketches."

"Now?"

"Then I progressed to pastels and oils." Tag shrugged. "And I turned it into my job."

"You get paid to paint?" Magnus threw himself back onto the snow, mock-groaning. "Seriously? I'd love that one day."

"I take photographs when I'm out and about," Tag said, "then develop the pictures and sketch or paint what's on the photo." She looked down at him, still lying in the snow. "It's all to do with advertising. Clients wanting a more natural picture and all that."

"And you seriously get paid to do that?"

"I do. I get paid a lot to do that."

"That's insane."

"I know." She laughed. "But what I'm trying to tell you is that your granddad always thought it was a waste of my time drawing because he thought nothing would ever come of it," she said. "So don't let your dad be the same with you. He always supported me so much when I was your age."

"But if he supported you then, why doesn't he now?" Magnus asked. The kid was smart.

"Your dad still has a lot of forgiving to do where I'm concerned." That jarred. Tag jumped to her feet. Time to snowboard again. "And with everything with your dad, Magnus," she said, hauling him to his feet, "it'll take time for him to trust me again."

CHAPTER SIXTEEN

The pile of papers scattered across the floor of her room reminded Tag that her petulance hadn't faded with age. Paperwork with figures and calculations loomed up at her. Red pen marks. Scribbles and exclamation marks. Tag had even put a *WTF?* in a margin somewhere. Her dad would have been furious—assuming he'd known what it meant, of course.

Accounts, she figured, were never going to be her strong point.

Anyway, what was she even doing here? At breakfast she'd thought it was going to be the perfect day. A morning's snowboarding with Magnus, an afternoon with Freddie. Returning to her phone back at Glenside shortly after lunch had put paid to that. Freddie had bailed, so where was Tag now? Holed up in her room at Four Winds, trying to make sense of the mill's accounts when she should have been savouring Foxy Brown's apparently awesome mochas with Freddie, that's where.

Tag stepped over her papers and sat back on the floor. Invoices dating back, apparently to the Middle Ages, demanded that Tag think of them rather than mochas and Freddie. Service reminders for machinery she didn't know existed screamed up at her. But Freddie had blown her off. She stared down at the floor, bored with it all.

Her phone rang on the carpet next to her leg. Anna. Tag watched her name flash on and off the screen. She'd ignored three calls from her already today. Could she ignore a fourth?

She grabbed it up. "Anna."

"There you are." Anna sounded grumpy. Great. "I've been ringing you all morning."

"Been busy."

Hey Tag, Can't make it this afternoon after all…

Such a lame text. Why had Freddie cancelled? Had she had a better offer? Or didn't she want to hang out with her after all?

"When are you coming back to me?" Anna put on a girly voice. "I miss you."

"Don't."

"Don't what?" Anna gave a small laugh. "Tell you I miss you? I'm telling you because it's true."

When I don't give you a second thought? Tag bit down furiously on a nail. Why did Anna always have to do this? Be a head-fuck? She pulled at her nail with her teeth. Why did Anna like to play with her like this?

"I'm joking with you," Anna said when it was clear Tag wasn't going to answer. "I rang to talk to you about the Branson deal."

"What about it?" Tag moved some papers around on the floor.

"We got it."

"Cool." Tag should have cared. She'd worked damn hard while she was in Liverpool to help get that deal sealed. So why did she feel so flat? "Well done."

"So it'll mean all systems go next month." Tag could hear Anna was moving around. Where was she? The office? Tag heard phones ringing, computers beeping. Yes, the office. The place where once Tag had felt at home, where she'd spend hour after hour working closely with Anna. Where they'd stay on after everyone had left for the day and—

"Did you hear me?" Anna's voice was hard. Anxious. "It'll mean longer hours and—"

"I heard you."

Why hadn't Freddie explained more about why she'd cancelled? She was the one who'd suggested it in the first place. Tag frowned. Maybe Skye was ill. Maybe she ought to go up there and make sure everything was okay.

"It's a four-month deal," Anna said. "Double pay. Triple if we nail it. Oliver Branson has assured me."

"Well, congratulations."

"So, you're in." It was a declaration rather than a request. "You'll work exclusively on this contract until midsummer."

Tag sat up straighter. "Anna, wait." She paused. "I don't know if I can be back in time."

"You said you'd take five weeks off," Anna said. "And I complied, which I think was more than generous of me."

"Things are complicated here." Was Tag still talking about all the paperwork? Or Freddie?

"Seriously, how long does it take to wrap up details on your little mill?" Anna sounded bored. "Just grab your inheritance and get back here pronto. I'm surprised it's taken you this long already."

"I still have so much to do." How did Anna always manage to make her angry? Even after all this time? "Dad's bank details, transferring funds, changing names on all the paperwork." Why was she fuming like this? The fact that she wasted any emotion on Anna was galling. Anna, Tag figured, so wasn't worth the effort. "And, anyway, you haven't paid me for the Schofield contract yet. That was months ago. So before we start talking about a new contract—"

"Well I can pay you for Schofield when I see you." Anna almost purred. Tag shuddered. "Then you can take me out for dinner. How about that? We can have a catch-up." It was decided. If Anna said that was what was going to happen, then it was a certainty.

"I have to go." Anna's voice was clipped. That meant she was annoyed. "I just wanted to tell you about the Branson deal."

"Sure."

"We'll talk again later." The call was killed before Tag could respond. Nothing new there.

Tag tossed her phone over her shoulder and up onto the bed. She stared at the wall for a few seconds, digesting her conversation with Anna, then scrambled over on all fours to gather up some papers. This was more important right now. She clutched them to her chest and sat back against the bed. Why did they have to get the Branson deal now? It felt too soon to go back to Liverpool just yet. She knew she wasn't ready to stop doing what she was doing in Balfour. She mattered here; she was making a difference. She was helping.

Tag stared down at the patterned carpet. What was up with her? She hated Balfour, didn't she? Had spent all these years forgetting it existed, and yet now she was nauseous at the thought of leaving it again. Leaving Freddie.

Where was Freddie now, anyway? Not sitting opposite Tag in a warm cafe, that's for sure. A thought struck her. Maybe Freddie was trying to make a point. Telling Tag she wanted her to back off a bit. Tag pursed her lips. Boy, hadn't she been *there* before? Tag lost count the number of times over the years Anna had stood her up at the last minute.

This rankled more, though. And it ate into her specifically because it was Freddie that had done it, not Anna. Pure and simple. Tag drew her knees up. With Anna, she'd laughed it off with a resigned shrug. She'd brood for a few minutes, then find someone else to hang out with instead. But Freddie was different. Freddie wasn't like anyone else. Even before their awesome afternoon in the park she had burrowed under her skin quicker and deeper than any of the others. Freddie stayed with her more than any of the others had as well. She was there 24/7. Freddie was in her head when she woke and was still there at bedtime. Kind of hung around all day too.

"Shit." Tag rocked her head back against the mattress and groaned up at the ceiling.

The paperwork in her arms called to her. She bobbed her head back down and glared at the spreadsheets.

"Shit."

❖

Tag squeezed her eyes shut, then opened them again. The papers were still there. In black and white, with some red. And all of her scribbles. A lot of scribbles.

She looked over to Blair, sitting opposite her. He looked annoyed; not a great start to their meeting.

"You wrote *WTF* on this." Blair tapped a pencil on the paper.

"I was bored." Understatement of the century, Tag thought. Three hours locked up at Four Winds having numbers swimming in front of your face would make anyone bored, she figured.

"Text-speak on official accountancy paper. Mature."

"Whatever."

Blair slid his glasses back up the bridge of his nose. "So, in essence, all these scribbles tell us what?"

"Well, they tell us we're in trouble, for a start," Tag said.

"How much trouble?"

"I'm no accountant," Tag said. "But I've compared like-for-like figures for the last five years."

"And?"

"And we've lost a total of this"—she pointed to a spreadsheet—"over that time."

"Bloody hell." Blair moved closer. "So what are these figures here?"

"Salaries."

"And these?"

"Consumables."

"These?" Blair asked.

"Utilities. Gas, electric."

"As much as that?"

"You want them to freeze in the cafe? Sit in darkness?" Tag pulled out a sheaf of papers from a plastic file. "This is income from sales. See what it was back then?" She jabbed a finger at it. "And now present day."

"That was the year they built the bypass." Blair swept his hand across the page. "The rot really set in after that. The year after that, the summer was a washout. That, combined with less passing trade, did for us."

How had Freddie coped, that summer? Her wonderful cafe, recently modernized so they'd attract more customers, empty because some idiots in suits chose to build a bypass that very same year. Tag's mind swam to Freddie. Lovely, sweet Freddie who'd do anything for the business, who loved her cafe, loved being part of the Grainger family. Tag stared back down at the file, shame burning at her. She'd been bored reading the accounts yesterday. She'd scribbled on them because she was bored and frustrated at being blown off by Freddie, when she should have just accepted Freddie's decision, then knuckled down and got on with the work. How could she have been so blasé about the accounts when Freddie's future was at stake?

"So we've been playing catch-up since then?" Tag asked.

"Looks like it."

"And then there are the debts." Tag pulled a red file towards her. "At least Dad kept those in a separate file. Very organized."

"We owe money?" Blair sank back. "On top of everything else?"

"The garage in town." Tag read down a list. "Suppliers. Logistics companies."

"Great. Just great." Blair pulled his glasses off. "We keep this up, we'll have gone under this time next year."

"The only people we don't owe to are the staff," Tag said. "Whatever else has been happening, they've always been paid on time."

"But we owe money everywhere else?" Blair asked.

Tag nodded.

"I don't believe this." Blair rubbed at his face.

"You sound surprised." Was Blair for real? "Like this has come as a shock to you."

"Because it has."

"You didn't realize it was this bad?"

"Would I be looking like this if I did?" Blair pointed to his ashen face.

"How could you not have known?" Tag was incredulous. "What, you just jumped in your tractor each day? Ploughed merrily up and down? Got paid at the end of each month and never asked how things were going back here?" How could he have been so uninterested? So clueless?

"No, of course I didn't."

"Dad must have known, though." Tag paced the room. "Was he blind?"

"You think you're so superior, don't you?" Blair snapped. "Swanning back here and criticizing everything we've done?"

"Not superior." Tag stopped pacing. "Just realistic enough to know I needed to look at the books now I own part of this place."

"So I'm what?" Blair countered. "Some dumb farmer boy who doesn't know an ear of wheat from an ear of corn?"

"No," Tag said, "you're a son whose father never gave him the responsibilities he needed to run this place. A pig-headed father who thought he knew best. And look where it's got us."

"That's right." Blair stood up. He brushed past Tag. "Blame the father who's not here to defend himself any more."

"You think storming off is going to push profits back up?" Tag winced at the sound of the door slamming. "Way to go, Blair," she shouted at the door. "Way to go."

❖

"That went well, then." Tag rested a foot up on the small garden wall surrounding Ellen's vegetable patch.

"I take it the slamming of the kitchen door was my husband?" Ellen stood up and batted her gloved hands together to remove the earth that was caked on them. "Sounds about right."

"He stormed upstairs." Tag bent over and pulled a stray spindly weed from the patch. "Like he's going to find the answers to our problems up there."

"*Our* problems?" Ellen looked knowingly at Tag. "Not mine and Blair's problems?"

"Since I've been looking at the books and realized how bad things were," Tag said, "the problems became all of ours. Mine included." Since Freddie became her problem too.

"It's pretty bad, isn't it?"

"Worse."

"You know it's not Blair's fault, don't you?" Ellen said.

"No, but he could have—"

"You know what your father was like."

"I know how controlling he was," Tag admitted.

"He never let Blair have an inch," Ellen said. "Never gave him control. Never let him get involved in the money side of things."

"But Blair surely knew—"

"Adam refused to let him look at the books." Ellen shrugged. "He kept it all to himself. Thought he could deal with it all himself."

"Sounds about right." Tag rubbed the weed between her finger and thumb, then let it drop to the ground. "He never did trust any of us to do it as well as he thought he could."

"Right up to the day he died, Adam kept those accounts books under lock and key," Ellen said. "As far as he was concerned, he was still paying everyone's wages, so there wasn't a problem."

"Blair didn't think to ask to see the figures?"

"He tried." Ellen sat on the wall. "We all tried so hard to make Adam hand some responsibility over to us. But he always insisted everything was okay and that nothing needed to change."

"Stubborn bugger." Tag sat next to her.

"That's putting it mildly."

"I can see us having to lay people off, you know," Tag said, "if things don't pick up." The thought turned her heart to lead. How could she even begin to tell Freddie all this? Freddie relied on her, didn't she? Slowly and surely, Tag was gaining her trust, allowing Freddie to have faith in her ability to do the right thing for both her and Skye. Freddie would hate her, would blame her for everything, when none of it was her fault. All this had happened way before she'd come back, hadn't it? But would Freddie see it that way? She'd lash out at the first person available, and Tag knew who that person would be.

"I thought you might say that," Ellen said. She glanced up as she heard a door slam inside the house. "He's still crashing about in there, I hear."

"Crashing about isn't going to make the profits better," Tag said. Raised voices floated into the garden.

"Now he's having a go at Magnus." Ellen sighed. "Great."

"Like it's Magnus's fault?" Tag shot a look towards the back door. "Want me to go sort them out?"

"No." Ellen gave a resigned shrug. "Magnus can give as good as he gets," she said. "He'll argue back, then bugger off up to his room."

"They argue a lot?"

"They don't argue as such," Ellen said. "Just more like father and son bickering."

"About?"

"The usual." Ellen raised her eyes to the sky. "School and working hard and—"

"The sort of stuff parents and kids row about all over the world, huh?"

Ellen nodded. "Yeah, but I'm the one always stuck in the middle."

"Magnus is a good kid," Tag said. "If he was my son, I'd be very proud of him."

"He is," Ellen replied, "and I'm extremely proud of him, but…"

"But?"

"Well, he spends a lot of his time daydreaming," Ellen said, "and it really rubs his father up the wrong way."

"Nothing wrong with a bit of daydreaming."

"No, but Blair wants him to be more involved in the mill," Ellen said.

"And Magnus doesn't. I know. He told me."

"He's spoken to you?"

"We had a chat up on the mountain."

"Well I wish he'd talk to us," Ellen said. "I think that's what seems to annoy his father the most."

"He's barely fourteen though," Tag replied. "Show me a fourteen-year-old who wants to be working in a dusty old mill."

"Yes, but as Blair likes to point out," Ellen said, "at fourteen he was already putting in the hours up there."

"Because we were a one-parent family," Tag said, "and we'd just lost our mother, and—"

Another slammed door made Tag stop talking.

"There you go." Ellen followed Tag's gaze to the door. "Just like I said. They both just go round in circles."

"You want me to have a word with Magnus?" Tag offered. "I don't mind."

"Can't hurt, can it?" Ellen said. "He does like you."

"Does he?"

"Oh, he thinks you're the coolest thing ever."

"Because I am." Tag struck a pose.

The back door opened. Magnus's worried face peeked out from behind it.

"You need to come," he shouted to Ellen. His face was blanched. "Dad's collapsed in the kitchen. I can't wake him up."

CHAPTER SEVENTEEN

Her brother was sleeping when Tag finally found herself alone with him. She sat at his bedside and watched as his chest rose and fell in a slow, deep rhythm. Worry brimmed in her eyes. She pulled her gaze from his face and concentrated on a tumbler of water on the table next to him, afraid that just one more look at his pale face would make the tears spill over. Blair, normally fit and strong, looked so much smaller and more vulnerable now. It was nearly killing her. His face had a grey hue to it, so unlike his normal, healthy-looking complexion, made ruddy from hours out in the fields.

Tag looked back at him. Her big brother.

They'd shared a room when they were children. Back then, he'd always been the one to fall asleep first. Now, listening to him breathe, Tag remembered how she'd lie in bed, looking at the bunched-up blankets that were her brother, and listen to the sound of him sleeping across the other side of the room before sleep overcame her too. Tag sighed. She'd always been envious that he was able to drop off to sleep straight away. Blair had always had the uncanny ability of lying so still that it made him appear as if he was just a part of the room, and not the big lump of her sleeping brother.

Sleep envy aside, she used to find it comforting, certainly in the immediate years after their mother died, to know that there was someone else that would take care of her. She would often lie in the darkness, wondering what Blair was dreaming about. She'd always ask him the next morning over breakfast if he'd had any dreams, and he'd regale her with tales of fighting dragons and sailing on the seven seas.

His dreams were always epic—far more exciting than hers, anyway—and Tag was never sure if he was fibbing or not. She didn't care either way. If Blair had a vivid imagination and chose to make up his dreams just to entertain her, it really didn't matter. All that mattered to Tag back then was that her brother was occupying her mind, filling it with stories of heroes on horseback, pirates on treasure islands, and spacemen in rockets.

Anything so that she didn't have to think about her own grief.

Each morning brought about a new escapade, something new to think about, which was just as well, as the previous day's tale would have been exhausted in Tag's mind by morning. She was only too grateful to have a whole new adventure to think about. Each time her mother tried to creep back into her thoughts, and the awful memory of what had happened, Blair's tales would come in and take over, and the sadness would be replaced with adventure.

Watching him now, Tag tried to remember just why she'd left him all those years before. How could she have been so selfish? Blair had been right before; she hadn't been the only one who'd lost a mother. The guilt overwhelmed her. Without thinking, she pulled out her frayed photo of her, Adam, Blair, and Magnus from her wallet and stared at it. Magnus was so young. Skye's age. Didn't every child deserve to have as much love around them as possible? To be swamped with the unconditional love of their family?

Blair stirred, turning his head slightly, impelling Tag to hastily stuff her photo back and rise to her feet to help him. She didn't want him to see the sorrow and regret the picture provoked each time she looked at it, didn't need his sympathy. She sat back down when he settled once more and rested her elbows on the side of his bed, then resumed watching the rise and fall of his chest.

"If you're thinking you'll have to stay on for my funeral too, I've got good news for you," Blair murmured, peering at her through sleepy eyes. "Doctors say I'm not going to croak it just yet."

"Good." Tag carried on cradling her head, her eyes still on him. His quip made relief wash over her. He was awake. At last. Now all she had to do was hold it together in front of him.

Finally Blair opened his eyes fully. "I assume all these wires are necessary?" he asked. He waved a hand at them.

"They're monitoring your heartbeat, apparently." Tag sat up. She'd sat and watched that monitor for hours, listening to the steady beep, hoping and praying it kept going. She locked her arms out in front of her and straightened her back. "So, yes, they're necessary." Her brusqueness masked her tangible relief.

"Mm." Blair closed his eyes again. "What photo were you looking at just now?" He spoke without opening his eyes.

"Just an old one I had in my wallet." The same photo she'd taken out and looked at over and over during her years away. The only photo she had left of them all.

"If you want a newer one of him," Blair murmured, "I can let you have one."

"Of who?"

"Dad." He caught her eye. "That's who it's of, isn't it?"

Tag pulled it from her wallet again and handed it to Blair. Memories flooded back.

"The harvest festival up at the mill." Blair nodded. "I remember that. End of September and we were all in shorts and T-shirts still." He gazed down at the face of his father. "By the next April, you were gone." He handed it back to her.

"You look young in it." Tag looked down at the photo. "Almost handsome." She made big eyes at him.

"Fewer grey hairs, that's for sure." He sank back into his bed.

"Ellen said you've collapsed before," Tag said slowly. "Few months back?" She put her photo carefully away.

"Yup."

"You didn't think to see a doctor, then?"

"Nope."

"Because?"

"Because I was busy at the mill. Because I didn't want to worry Dad. Because I didn't want to worry Ellen." He rolled his head away. "Because of any number of reasons. I don't know."

"You were arguing with Magnus," Tag said.

"Magnus." Blair's eyes flew open. "Oh God, I remember now."

"He's fine." Tag raised her hand to quieten him.

"He'll have been so worried." Blair's face was fixed with pain. "He'll think it's his fault when it really wasn't."

"He's fine, honest," Tag reassured him. "He's back home. Ellen thought it best. I'm going over to fetch him in a minute, so you can see for yourself he's okay later."

"Thanks."

"So what were you squabbling about?"

Blair sighed. "It was a tiff, that's all," he said, "like the thousands of other tiffs a father has with his teenage son."

"If I contributed towards it…" Tag began. She hesitated. "Well, I didn't mean to."

"You didn't."

"I just thought—"

"It was nothing to do with what you said if that's what you're thinking," Blair said. "Anyway, what you said before was probably right. I should have been more assertive with Dad rather than letting myself be fobbed off by him all the time." He turned his head on the pillow and looked at her. "But our tiff didn't cause this. I probably just didn't have enough to eat today, that's all."

"Even so." Tag inspected her fingers. "I don't want you going the same way as Dad."

"Dad worked too hard," Blair said simply. "Dad worked too hard for too long, ate unhealthily, and drank too much. That's what did for him."

"But why did he always have to work so much after Mum died?" Tag asked. "Just when I needed him the most?"

Blair's face hardened. "And me?" he asked. "Don't you think I needed him as well?"

"You were older."

"I was nineteen!" Blair's voice rose. "I didn't see Dad from the minute I got up until the minute I went to bed, but did you hear me complaining?"

Tag dropped her eyes.

"I needed him just as much as you did," Blair continued, "but I also knew that he needed to work longer hours just to keep everything going." He set his jaw. "But unlike you, I didn't take it personally. I didn't decide to bugger off at the first opportunity just to punish him."

"I didn't want to punish him—"

"All these years you thought Dad didn't love you?" Blair asked. "Yet you never bothered to find out exactly why he did what he did? No. You just chose to believe what you wanted because it suited you to."

"That's unfair," Tag argued. "Dad just switched off. Closed down."

"It's called grief."

"For all those years?" Tag contested. "When we needed him to be there for us?"

"I don't know, Tag," Blair said, exasperated. "Throwing himself into work after Mum died was how he coped, just like it was how he coped again when you left. It's what he did."

An awkward silence settled over them. The beep of Blair's heart monitor, sounding faster than it had done just five minutes before, echoed round the room. Tag focused on a point by her feet, ashamed. Blair didn't need this right now. He'd just come round and she was arguing with him already. Her head pounded. Just how selfish did she have to be?

Tag cleared her throat. "No," she finally said, "it was more than just that. I think he resented me."

"It was his way of managing." A flicker of a sad smile crossed Blair's face. "If only you'd talked to him," Blair continued, "and he'd talked to you, hey? Maybe we wouldn't be like this now."

A shadow of sadness fell across Tag's soul. "I thought for years he didn't love me. Maybe I chose to assume he didn't care because it made my decision to leave that much easier." She laughed hollowly. "However fucked up that might sound." She shuffled back in her chair. "If I thought he didn't care, then it meant I could leave Balfour without any guilt or regrets, couldn't I?"

"And if you'd heard the way he cried himself to sleep for weeks after you left," Blair said, "then you'd know just how much he *did* care."

"I really messed up, didn't I?" Tag said.

"Show me an eighteen-year-old who hasn't messed up at some point." Blair shrugged. "The question is," he said, settling himself back down in his bed, "are you mature enough now to put some wrongs right again?"

❖

Magnus was propped up on his bed in his room, tucked away at the back of the cottage, when Tag entered his room after knocking and being granted entry. He had a large painting folder on his knees, a chewed pencil poking out from the corner of his mouth, and a quizzical expression on his face. He pulled the pencil from his mouth and tapped it on the paper on his knees.

"Trying to suss the shading on this." He pulled a darker pencil from a tin by his bed and started drawing again. "How's Dad?"

"The same." Tag sat on the corner of his bed. "I'm heading back there later." She peered at his pad. "What're you drawing?"

"Remember the snowboarding? It's the cluster of rocks we sat on after our second run down," Magnus said. "I thought it'd make a neat sketch."

"The one with the view across to Swanne?"

Magnus nodded but didn't reply.

"Can I look?"

"If you want." He didn't look up. Instead, he bowed his head further over the paper. His pencil glided effortlessly over the paper, sometimes harder, sometimes lighter.

Tag shuffled further up his bed and looked over his shoulder. He had drawn the most beautiful sketch of the vista that Tag remembered seeing when they'd rested after one of their runs down the slopes, when they'd both admired the view across to the next village. Magnus had pointed out a small loch, Tag remembered, with a jetty leading into it, and a cluster of cottages further along the shoreline. She glanced down at the drawing. He'd drawn it exactly how they'd seen it as they'd peered down through the trees. Right down to the tiniest detail. Tag blinked. It was beautiful. Such was the intricacy of his drawing, she felt as though she was back up on the pile of rocks now, but seeing the view in black and white instead of colour.

"You've got a better memory than I have." She shook her head. "That's why I have to take my camera everywhere with me. I'd never remember all the things I'd seen otherwise."

"Images sit in my head," Magnus said, "and they sit there until they're begging me to put them down on paper." His face coloured.

"Who needs a camera, hey?" Tag joked.

"They kinda bug me, you know?" Magnus said shyly. "Until I can get them out. So that's why I come up here and draw—to get the images out." He pressed his pencil hard onto the paper. "That makes me sound like a total weirdo," he added, "but I know what I mean."

"It just means you have an eye for a good picture," Tag said, "that's all." She patted his leg. "Got any more pictures I can see?"

"You want to?"

"I do, yes."

Magnus tossed his pencil down and reached over to a cupboard next to his bed. He opened it and pulled out a sheaf of tatty papers.

"Some are quite old." He dropped them down next to Tag. "But there's some there from the other week too."

She picked up a handful and sifted through them. Her eyes widened in awe at each one. There were sketches of everything: landscapes, buildings, farm animals. Snapshots of everyday life down in the town. She pulled out one that particularly caught her eye, an intricate drawing of a Regency building, complete with fancy columns, elegant wrought-iron balconies, and bow windows. Each brick in the building had been drawn individually. Each tile on the roof had been painstakingly replicated, and each window's frame was symmetrically correct. Every tiny detail of the house had been drawn to perfection, just as every detail of the trees had been drawn to perfection in his mountain sketch.

"Your attention to detail is awesome." Tag couldn't take her eyes off the drawing. "Where is this?" She held the paper up.

"Edinburgh," Magnus replied. "We went for the day about a year ago with Granddad. That house stood out and I thought about it all day." He shrugged. "So when we came home in the evening, I drew it."

"From a photo?"

"From here." Magnus tapped his hairline with his pencil.

"You remembered it all?"

"Yup."

"Every last window?"

"Yup."

"That's amazing." Tag looked down at it again. "Have your parents seen it?"

"Nope." Magnus stuffed his pencil into his mouth. He reached out and took the sheaf of papers from her, then hastily crammed them all back into the cupboard.

"You should show it to them," Tag said, "they'd want to see it. They'd want to see all of them."

"Nah." Magnus snapped the cupboard door shut. "If it's not to do with the mill, then Dad doesn't want to know. What's the point?"

The seeds of an idea germinated in Tag's brain. "You think you could draw the mill?"

"I can draw anything." He grinned round his pencil. "What specifically?"

"Anything," Tag replied. "The waterwheel, the bakery."

"Sure."

"And then show your dad?"

"Why?" Magnus looked suspiciously at her.

"I think it'd cheer him up." An advertising slogan crept into Tag's subconscious. A sketch. A logo. Black and white, professional and classy. "Make him feel better."

"I'll see." Magnus swung his legs over the side of the bed and stood up.

"Is that an *I'll think about it*?" Tag asked.

"Nope. It's an *I'll see*." Magnus walked to the door, discussion over. He locked his arms above his head and yawned loudly. "So are we going back to the hospital, then?" He threw a look back over his shoulder to Tag. "I'm done here."

"Blair's got what?" Tag's face misted with confusion.

"Hypotension." Ellen pulled out a chair for Tag and gestured for her to sit.

"In English?"

"Low blood pressure."

"Is that it?" Relief drenched Tag's previous fears. "No heart attack?"

"No heart attack. Low blood pressure, acute anaemia, and exhaustion."

It was later the same evening. Now, back at the hospital after her chat with Magnus, Tag had arrived just as the doctors were leaving Blair's bedside.

"So you're going to be okay?" Tag sat down next to his bed. She raised her eyebrows to him. "I mean, your heart's fine? Panic over?"

Blair nodded. "Extreme low blood pressure and an iron deficiency," he said. "That's why I kept passing out."

"And they're sure that's all it is?" Tag pressed. "Nothing more?"

"The ECG was clear," Blair said. "Although…"

"Although?" Tag prompted.

"They reckon stress could have brought it on this time." His face pained.

"Bickering with Magnus, more like." Ellen reached across. She took one of his hands, covering it with her own.

"And me," Tag added. Guilt rode hard. "Despite what you say."

"It could have happened anytime." Blair lay back against his pillow.

"And diagnosis?" Tag asked. "Is there any medication you can take?" Her hand wavered. She wanted to reach out and take his hand, or touch his arm, but couldn't bring herself to. Instead, she placed both hands under her legs and sat on them.

"Just iron tablets, apparently." Blair moved in his bed. His hand moved closer to Tag, and she stared at it, willing herself to take it. "And lots of rest."

"And he has to maintain a healthy diet," Ellen added.

"Pulses, grains, plenty of green vegetables. Lots of water," Blair said. "And cut back on the alcohol for a bit." He caught Tag's eye and gave her a look which said a thousand words. At his look, Tag finally grabbed his hand and gave it a squeeze, gratified when she felt Blair squeeze it back.

"I'm glad you're okay," Tag said. She gripped his hand tighter. "I was scared."

"So was I."

"And if it means you have to stay off the beer for a bit, then that's what you'll do." She released Blair's hand as a nurse appeared by his bedside. She stood and moved to one side, not wanting to be in the way. "I'll stay off it too," she added. "Go teetotal with you."

Blair's sceptical eyes locked onto hers.

"Seriously!" Tag crossed her arms. "I can *so* do that." She backed out of Blair's room. "Solidarity, bro." She raised a fist, the sound of Blair's laugh becoming more muffled as she walked away from his bed and headed for the exit.

Outside in the corridor, the exhaustion hit her. Tag felt light-headed. She put her hand against the wall and bent over, staring at her feet until the dizziness passed. Once she no longer felt as though she would faint, she swivelled herself around and fell against the wall. She put her head back, closed her eyes, and blinked back tears that she hadn't even realized were there. Blair was going to be okay. Her stupid, stubborn, hot-headed brother was going to be okay, and she'd never felt so relieved about anything in her life.

Eyeing an exit to a small quadrangle with benches, Tag went outside and sat. The fresh air was a welcome change from the stale stuffiness of the hospital, and Tag squeezed her eyes shut, enjoying the feeling of the sharp wind on her face. The door to the quadrangle opened again and a patient, an elderly man in bottle-green pyjamas and matching fleece dressing gown, shuffled outside and sat on the bench just across from Tag's.

Tag pulled her phone from her pocket and jiggled it in her hands. Freddie would want to know Blair was going to be okay, she was sure of it. They hadn't spoken since the cafe, hadn't texted since Freddie had cancelled their...was it a date?, and now Tag was desperate to hear her voice again. To hear the reassurance and the kindness. Because that was all Tag wanted right now: to be near Freddie and to gain comfort from being in her company. Tag brooded. Maybe a text would be better? Tag stared down at her phone. Less intrusive than calling. After all, she couldn't keep ringing her, could she?

She rattled off a quick text: *Blair's fine. Low blood pressure. Ha! Who'd have thought it would be something so simple? So bloody relieved right now, though. Would love to see you later. I've missed you xxxxx*

Tag looked at it, then deleted the last line about wanting to see her and missing her. Yes, she did. Desperately on both counts. But did Freddie really need to hear that? Tag sent the text before she could change her mind and bundled her phone back into her pocket.

The man across from her coughed, pulled out a packet of cigarettes, and lit one, blowing the smoke up into the air. He tilted his head back, his eyes like slits in ecstasy at his cigarette, and coughed again. Opening an eye wider and seeing Tag looking at him, he waggled his packet of cigarettes at her.

"Can I tempt you?" he asked. "You look like you need one."

"Thanks, but I don't." Tag raised her hand.

"Very wise." The man put the packet back in his dressing-gown pocket. "They've done for me." He spluttered loudly and pulled on his cigarette again, the tip of it glowing bright red in the fading light of the quadrangle. He shuffled back on the bench, his back partially turned to Tag.

The door to the quadrangle opened and Magnus's pale face appeared. Tag waved to him, loving the look on his face when he spotted her. It was the same expression, Tag thought with a pang, he used to have when he was tiny and he'd come looking for her at the mill after nursery. His perplexity and distress at not knowing where she was would change to delight in an instant, the second he saw her. If it got to her then, Tag thought, it got her a hundred more times now.

CHAPTER EIGHTEEN

The sight of Tag's name flashing on and off Freddie's phone impelled her to snatch it up and answer it before having the chance to dust the flour from her hands. Freddie had been baking. She always baked when she was stressed, and the news of Blair's collapse had stressed her more than she could have ever known.

Now, even though it had been an hour since Tag had first texted to tell her Blair was going to be okay, Freddie was still baking. Still stressed. They'd exchanged nonstop messages during that hour, and even though every text mentioned Blair, each one had gradually focused less on him and had moved more towards friendly, warm conversation. Despite all her reservations and promises to herself, Freddie hadn't been able to stop replying. She'd deliberately shut herself away in the kitchen, on the pretext of baking cookies for Skye, and indulged herself, away from the prying eyes of Pete and Skye. She'd enjoyed it too. The thrill of it all. The fizz of excitement each time her phone buzzed, knowing it would be Tag. The same fizz she was experiencing now Tag was calling. Only stronger.

"Hey." Freddie wiped her free hand down her trousers.

"Hey."

Tag's voice was soft. Quiet. A shiver trickled pleasantly down Freddie's spine. She could tell herself a hundred times each phone call and message meant nothing, but she'd be lying to herself. Freddie relished the excitement of knowing Tag wanted to talk to her, that she needed her to know about Blair. That Tag would even think to ring her to tell her. Freddie felt like a teenager all over again; the knowledge that she had someone's undivided attention was electrifying. She'd quite forgotten how exhilarating it was knowing that, across in the next town, Tag was possibly waiting on her every word, just as Freddie was waiting on hers. "I'm so glad you called."

"You are?" Tag sounded pleased. Freddie wiped her hand slower. Maybe that was just her imagination.

"I was thinking about Blair."

"Oh." Tag paused. "Of course."

"And you." God knows, Freddie had thought of nothing else.

"You were thinking about me?" Tag laughed. "That's nice."

"I've been worried about you," Freddie said. She rested a hip against the sink. "Wondering how you're coping up there."

"I've been thinking about you too," Tag said. "Wanting to call you all day. Wanting to get away for five minutes so I could just hear your voice."

Freddie's heart hammered. "Me too." She hesitated. "To hear your voice, I mean." She squeezed her eyes tight shut. Tell her you miss her. Tell her you want to see her. Give in to it.

"Magnus just turned up."

Freddie sensed the pull in Tag's voice.

"I'll let you go," Freddie said, knowing that was the last thing she wanted to do.

"I'm sorry," Tag said. "Kid's all over the place right now. I better go and talk to him."

"Of course." Freddie smiled. Like she'd deny Tag her time with Magnus? "Go to him."

"I'll try and ring you later," Tag offered. "If you want me to, that is?"

Freddie's answer was instant. "I want you to, yes."

Then Tag was gone. Freddie pictured her, comforting Magnus. She wanted to be there too, to see at first-hand Tag's compassion. But it was more than that. She wanted to be there for Tag, to show her she cared. But the wall she'd built for herself was still just that little bit too high to climb over. Too risky. Freddie tapped her phone against her bottom lip, deep in thought. What if she fell? What if what was on the other side of the wall hurt her when she fell?

"You're lurking in here, are you?" Pete appeared in the kitchen. "Leaving the finishing touches of Skye's palace to us." He moved past her and pulled a roll of parcel tape from a drawer. "Can't say I blame you. Who knew building royal residences out of an old box could take so long to finish to madam's satisfaction?" He nodded his head towards Skye, still in the lounge.

"Blair's better." Freddie motioned to her phone. "Tag told me."

"Are they still up there?" Pete asked. "At the hospital?"

"Yes," Freddie replied. "Blair's staying in tonight for more tests just to be sure, apparently."

"You wanna go up there?" Pete flicked his eyes to her, then back to the roll of tape. "I can take you."

"No, it's fine."

"Sure?"

"No." Freddie laughed. "I'm not sure."

"Remember what we talked about the other day?" Pete discreetly peered at his tape. "The world isn't going to stop turning just because Tag called."

"I like it," Freddie confessed. "I get this feeling, here"—she dug her fingers into her midriff—"when my phone buzzes and it's her."

"Shows you're human," Pete said. "Welcome to the world."

"But it's the same feeling I used to get with Charlotte," Freddie said, "and it makes me scared." She picked up her phone and scrolled down through their messages, then held it up to Pete. "I've started putting kisses after my texts. She's putting them after hers."

"Are we going to start analysing text kisses now?"

"I can't stop myself." Freddie placed the phone back down on the table and pushed it away a little. "One kiss after a message signifies friendliness, right? But five? Six? I should stop, but I can't."

"Kisses at the end of a message mean nothing." Pete shrugged. "It's what people do. Tag won't read anything into it. I reckon she's got way more important things to be thinking about than kisses after a text."

"I guess." Freddie stood.

"Go and see them," Pete said. "Rather than sitting down here tying yourself up in knots over texts and kisses and God knows what else."

"I'll think about it."

"You're reading too much into stuff." Pete walked back to the door. "Stop thinking. Just do what your heart's telling you to do." He called from the lounge. "And I reckon it's telling you to go up to see them all."

Freddie walked to the sink. Perhaps Pete was right. She was reading way too much into things. She stared into the plughole. She'd got carried away, that was all, carried away by the attention, as usual. She stopped dead when she heard her phone buzz. It was Tag again. She looked back at it and watched it as it buzzed for a second time, creeping across the top of the kitchen table with each vibration. Unless Freddie stopped replying to every one of Tag's messages, she'd not stop texting her. So that's all she had to do—cut her off and not reply. Walk away.

But she couldn't walk away.

Freddie blinked. She stared back at her phone and fumed with herself. She snatched her phone up and swiped her finger across the screen. She was being stupid, she knew. Analysing replies and how and when to text when all she had to do was read the damn thing. Her heart jumped when she read Tag's message: *Been thinking about you a lot. Really, REALLY want to see you tomorrow. No...NEED to see you. Can you escape? T xxxx*

Freddie closed her eyes.

Damn.

❖

"Dude." Magnus slung an arm around Tag's shoulder. "Wasn't expecting to see you here until later."

"I finished early." Tag twisted round. She fist-bumped him. "How was school?"

It was the next afternoon and Blair was still in hospital, still wired up to incessantly beeping machines because the doctors wanted to make absolutely sure, bearing in mind Adam's death, that Blair wasn't heading the same way.

But everyone's mood was lighter now that the immediate danger to Blair was over, and she and Magnus made plans to catch some air on the mountain on Saturday if the snow cooperated, then hunkered down to discuss a project that Magnus was working on at school and which he wanted Tag to look at for him because he didn't quite understand the question.

"Tag." Blair called her, his voice groggy but stronger. "Listen up." He motioned to her to come closer.

"You want something?" Tag was at his bedside instantly. "Drink? Something to eat?"

He shook his head. "Go back to Four Winds," he said. "Pack your stuff and come stay with us."

"At Glenside?" Tag's stomach twinged. "With you guys?"

"I'm going to be good for nothing for a while…" Blair paused as if revising what he wanted to say. His brows squeezed together. "I'd like you to come and stay for the rest of your time here," he said firmly. "Have you around more."

Magnus's eyes drifted from Tag's to Blair's and back again, as if willing Tag to answer. She could deny him nothing. And maybe this was her second chance.

"If you're sure?" Tag began.

"Positive," Blair said. "You can have the room next to Magnus's."

Magnus gave a quiet fist pump, subtle enough not to be noticed by his father, but seen perfectly well by Tag. She grinned inwardly.

"I better go say my goodbyes to Connie then, hadn't I?" Tag's face was calm. Inside she was jumping.

"Okay, scat." Blair waved a hand. "I'm going to need all the sleep I can now you're coming to stay."

He settled back, and Tag didn't miss the fleeting smile that crossed his face. The first one she'd glimpsed since she'd returned home.

❖

"So how's it going, big man?" Tag put her phone back into her pocket. Despite her previous misgivings, and even though Freddie hadn't replied to her last text telling her she wanted to see her, Tag had just sent another text off to her. Not about Blair or the hospital. Just a run-of-the-mill message telling her she was still at the hospital and hungry. It was contact with her, sustained contact. Where was the harm in that? Tag shifted along the bench as Magnus sat down next to her outside. "Warm enough in there for you?" She jerked her head towards the hospital.

"You will come and stay, won't you?" He looked worried.

"Once we're done here," Tag said, "I'll be straight over to Four Winds to pack up. I promise."

"I'm glad you'll be closer." He avoided eye contact.

"Me too, bud." She lightly punched his leg, laughing when he comically clutched at it.

"Maybe Dad will be less angry with you closer too," Magnus said slowly.

"Angry, how?"

"Angry with me," Magnus replied. "Like, *all* the time."

"And your mum?"

"She's okay." Magnus pulled at his lip. "She tries to make him not shout at me, but it doesn't always work."

"You know why he gets angry with you, don't you?" Tag pulled Magnus's hand away from his lip and patted it.

"Yeah, yeah. Because I don't do what he wants me to."

"Which is?"

"Study and shit."

"Don't say *shit*."

"Study, then," Magnus repeated. "I told you. He wants me to be a replica of him. He wants me to get my exams then go to agricultural college when I'm sixteen."

"And you don't want to?" Tag asked. She pulled her phone from her pocket and looked at it. No reply from Freddie yet.

"And be stuck doing what he does for the rest of my life?" Magnus looked at her. "No fear."

"What does your mum say about college?"

"Not much." Magnus paused. "When I tell him I don't want to end up working at the mill, he says it's like history repeating itself," he said, "and then that's when he gets angry."

"Is that what you were arguing about in the kitchen yesterday?" Tag chose to ignore the stabbing feeling elicited by Magnus's *history repeating itself* comment. "Your mum and I heard you."

Magnus scuffed his foot harder into the grass, leaving a muddy groove in it. "Yup," he finally said. "I brought a letter home from school. He went ape about it. That's when he collapsed."

"What did the letter say?"

"Same old shi—sorry, stuff." Magnus smiled sheepishly. "Just that I wasn't putting enough effort into my work, that I was a daydreamer, that I was lazy. Blah-blah-blah." He brought his hand to his lips and made a mouthing motion with his fingers.

The door to the quadrangle opened. Ellen poked her head out and looked round, nodding when Tag caught her eye. Ellen seemed to take in the pair of them sitting on the bench, and then she pulled back in, closing the door again.

"Do *you* think you're a daydreamer?" Tag asked. "What do you think about at school when you're supposed to be working?"

Magnus shuffled on the bench. "This and that," he said. "I mainly just think about when I can get home and be left alone to do my drawings."

"Or trying to get your score up on Perdition so it can be as awesome as my score, you mean?" Tag suggested.

"Something like that." Magnus grinned. "I'm good at what I do. The drawings, you know?" He threw her a look. "I like doing them."

"Yet you still won't tell them about it?" Tag pressed. "Might save a lot of arguments if you explained stuff to him."

"He'll just say it's a waste of time," Magnus said. "He'll just say being an artist won't help the mill." He picked up a small pebble and inspected it. "Because that's all he ever thinks about these days. The mill."

"Just like your granddad," Tag said.

"I miss Granddad." Magnus frowned. "Sometimes it was good to go see him when things were heavy at home."

"Bet he never told *you* you were a daydreamer, did he?" Tag threaded an arm across Magnus's shoulder and drew him to her. "Granddads never see any wrong in their grandkids." Unlike their own kids, she wanted to add.

"Do you miss him?" Magnus asked.

"I do." Tag nodded. "Very much."

"Why did you go?"

"Oh, for so many reasons." She removed her arm from his shoulder. "Far too many to talk about now. I was stressed and felt under pressure here."

"People stress far too much about stuff." Magnus tipped his head back and yawned. "I mean, please! You stressed about Granddad when you lived here, Dad worries that I'm going to end up a waster. Sonny's always moaning 'cos Izzy MacIntyre won't even look at him. Freddie up at the cafe constantly stresses about her kid. Tim up there goes on about how he can't afford another car." He grimaced. "Seriously. You guys just all need to chill."

"Freddie worries about Skye?" Her image washed over her.

"Is that the kid's name?" Magnus yawned again. "Yeah, constantly. I hear Mum telling Dad. She's terrified something might happen to her. I think she's had problems before, you know, when her girlfriend left her," he said matter-of-factly. "And I've told Sonny that he needs to tell Izzy he likes her. But he won't and it does my head in."

"Right." Skye was vulnerable. Tag got that. But the thought that Freddie worried about her all the time nearly broke her heart. A wave of fierce protection washed over her. She wanted to be there for Freddie—and for Skye. She didn't want Freddie to have to shoulder all her worries—about Skye, about the mill—alone. If Tag could show her she was responsible, then maybe she and Freddie could have something? Tag drummed her fingers on her thigh. She was moving out of Four Winds and back to Glenside. That had a sense of permanency. Blair needed her. The mill needed her. Tag stole a look to Magnus. He featured in her plans too. But what about the Branson contract back in Liverpool? Could Anna do without her? Her drumming got faster as a plan gathered speed in her head. Anna would have to do without her for now; her family needed her here. Tag wasn't expected back for another couple of weeks still yet. She could extend that further, couldn't she?

"Seriously." Magnus's voice filtered through her thoughts. "I don't get why Sonny stresses over Izzy. You have to go with your gut instinct, right? If you like someone, you tell them. Life's too short to be holding back."

"Magnus"—she slapped his leg—"you've really helped."

"I have?" Magnus looked bemused. "Cool."

"And you're right." Tag picked up her phone. "Life *is* too short to stress about anything. Full stop."

❖

Freddie glanced into the lounge. Buckingham Palace was finally finished. She looked at the clock on the wall. Five thirty. The hospital was fifteen minutes away.

She dialled Tag's number. Tag answered on the second ring.

"How's it going?"

"Hey." The pleasure in Tag's voice was evident. "I was just going to ring you."

"Were you?" Freddie asked. "Well I was just ringing…" She frowned. Why was she ringing? "To see how Blair is." Sounded plausible enough.

"Well, he's still wired up to an ECG," Tag said, "and having a few more tests. Just to make sure there's nothing else causing the low blood pressure."

"I bet you haven't eaten or drunk much all day, have you?" Freddie asked. "I mean, you, Ellen, and Magnus."

"We've hardly left Blair's side since he came in." The pull in Tag's voice was heartbreaking. "It's been a rough few days."

Freddie shot a look to the lounge again. Skye was fine. In fact, Skye was more than fine. Skye was now wearing a crown made of cardboard, the word *Heinz* just about visible above her left eye. Pete was sorting through a pile of DVDs, evidently choosing one for her. Should Freddie go? Or should she just leave them to it?

Freddie closed her eyes. Fuck it.

"I'm coming over," she said.

"When I said I really wanted to see you in my text before," Tag said, "I didn't mean I was expecting you to—"

"I know."

"You don't have to come all the way up here if it's—"

"I know I don't have to." Freddie was already walking from the kitchen. "But I'm sure a bit of moral support won't go amiss right now."

"Well, if you're sure?"

"Never been surer." Freddie stood in the lounge door and motioned to Pete. "I'll bring sandwiches and a flask of coffee over," she said to Tag. "I'm sure you'll all feel better for it."

She rested the phone in the crook of her neck while she pulled her coat from a hook in the hallway, her heart already pounding.

"Besides," she said, shrugging her coat on, "hospital food tastes like shit."

❖

"Who was that?" Magnus asked when Tag had finished her call.

"Freddie." She handed him her phone.

"Freddie from the cafe that I was talking about before?"

"The very same."

"What did she want?" Magnus asked.

"Nosy."

"Just asking."

"She was ringing to see how your dad was."

"Nice of her."

"Yeah." Because that's what Freddie was: nice. "Want to practise Perdition now?" Tag asked. Freddie had finally called. She was coming over. It would be safe to relinquish her phone for five minutes. Magnus wouldn't look at her texts, would he?

"For real?" Magnus gripped her phone. "You rock."

"I know." Tag stood. "Straight to the games though," she said. "No snooping at my messages."

"Yeah, right." Magnus looked up at her and rolled his eyes. "Like you wouldn't do the same?"

"You're smart," Tag said, walking away from him.

"Like my auntie," he called out to her. "Love you, O favourite aunt of mine," he added in a silly voice.

Tag stopped in her tracks and turned to look at him. Magnus already had his head bowed over her phone, his fingers a blur across the screen.

"Yeah, just like your auntie." She made to go. "Love you too," she murmured, walking away again.

CHAPTER NINETEEN

Hospitals, Freddie thought as she stood in the foyer, were designed purely to confuse. She ran her eye over the coloured signs directing visitors to each department: Physiotherapy. Obstetrics. Maternity. Nope, she was pretty sure Blair was in Cardiology. Definitely not in Maternity. But where *was* the cardiology department? She looked up. Blue sign. Follow signs for Dermatology, then turn left at Vascular. Helpful.

Freddie wandered down from the foyer. The rest of her earlier conversation with Tag followed her down the corridor.

"You don't have to come. It's fine." Tag had sounded half-hearted. Freddie could tell.

"I want to, though. Seriously."

"Blair will be pleased to see you...We all will."

Was it necessary for her to come and visit? Would Blair think it strange that she would want to come and see him? Freddie walked on. She was being friendly, that was all. And others at the mill were asking after him, so it was only right she should come up and say hi, then report back. It was no biggie.

"Freddie!"

Rapid footsteps behind her made Freddie swing round.

"I thought it was you." Magnus was out of breath. "I saw you go past. I was outside." He flipped a hand over his shoulder. "Are you going to see Dad?"

"If I can ever find his ward, yes." Freddie rolled her eyes.

"I know what you mean." Magnus stuffed his hands into his hoodie pocket. "Took us forever to find it the first time earlier."

"I think it's a deliberate ploy by the NHS to keep us all fit." Freddie smiled.

"Sorry?"

"Never mind."

"Auntie T says this place is like something out of Rise of the Borthen," Magnus said. "All these labyrinths."

"Rise of the what?"

"Borthen. It's a game." Magnus looked around him. "Me and her play it on my Xbox at home sometimes."

"I see."

"You're not a gamer, right?" Magnus laughed.

"Never caught on with me."

"Auntie T's got every game that's ever been made," Magnus said. "She's awesome. She's got all the Rise ones. That's four. Then she's got Vendetta, Identity Thieves. The whole collection of Bonded by War." Magnus counted them off on his fingers. "Then there's all the ones she's got on her phone."

"That sure is a lot." Freddie studied him while he explained the finer details of Vendetta. She'd never really spoken to him much before, just to pass the time of day up at the cafe. But now, standing straight in front of him, she could see for the first time hints of Adam in him. She'd always known he looked like Blair, but never quite how much like his granddad he was too.

Mostly, though, she saw touches of Tag in his face. They had the same azure eyes, and while his hair was more like Blair's, there were subtle nuances in his expressions that instantly brought Tag to her. His mannerisms were the same as hers, and they talked in a similar way. Just like Tag, Magnus kept his eyes firmly on Freddie's all the while he spoke, like she was the most important person in the world and she had his undivided attention.

"Are you heading down there now?" Magnus pulled Tag's phone from his back pocket. "Take this to her? It's hers, but she let me play Perdition on it. I'm coming down in a mo, but I need to go pee first."

"Right." Freddie took Tag's phone and glanced down at it. "I'll make sure she gets it."

"You rock." Magnus turned round and ran off. "Catch you later."

Sure I rock, but not as much as Auntie T does apparently, Freddie thought with a smile. She continued down the corridor and turned left at Dermatology, then found her feet slowing at the Vascular sign. Magnus adored Tag. Of course he did. She was a natural with him, just like she was a natural with Skye, so why wouldn't he? Tag's leaving hadn't affected Magnus at all; they'd slipped back into their auntie-nephew routine, it seemed, without him harbouring any grudges towards her. Freddie spotted the door to Blair's room. Such was the forgiveness of children, she thought, that Magnus might just be the one person to allow Tag to finally shake off her demons.

With a quick nod to a passing porter, she pushed through a set of double doors and hastened to Blair's room.

Tag worried. She fussed, she sighed, she fidgeted. But Blair was better. That mattered more than any aching backs sitting in hard chairs, or nagging boredom while they waited to hear Blair's prognosis.

It had now been over twenty-four hours since he'd collapsed, and despite Blair constantly telling her he felt absolutely fine, Tag was dubious as she watched him now. His dark face was telling her he was anything but fine.

"What are you thinking?" Tag asked.

"Just that I'm knackered." Blair caught her eye and held it. "Tired of the mill. Tired of trying."

Tag perched on the edge of his bed. "Then it's decided," she said.

"What's decided?" Ellen spoke next to her.

"I'm going to stay," Tag continued. "You're both already putting me up at Glenside, so I'm going to stay on and work with you and come up with a plan for how we're going to get through all this."

"And your other life?" Blair asked. "Your life in England?"

"Not important." Never had Tag felt it as strongly as she did right then. "What's important is you and making sure you're okay."

Blair nodded.

"As important as making sure all those guys up at the mill aren't left high and dry," Tag added. "None of this is their fault. None of this is *our* fault. So we're all going to work together to get it sorted." Freddie needed to hear that too. More than any of them.

"How will you know what to do?" he asked. "The top field needs a plough." Blair raised his eyes to the light in the ceiling. "I need to talk to Gordon Matthews about servicing the Deere, I still need to meet with the bank manager to transfer Dad's bank accounts, and we need to do an audit of the gift-shop takings before the auditors come next week." Tag followed his gaze over to Ellen. "How can I stay here, knowing all that needs doing?"

"Easily," Tag said. "Because you leave all that to us."

"You know what sort of service the tractor needs?" Blair asked. "I doubt that."

"No," Tag came back. "But Gordon does."

"The auditors can be delayed," Ellen said, "as can ploughing the top field."

"You're here to rest." Tag pulled some fluff from his pyjamas. "And not to worry."

"But how can I—?"

Tag shushed him. "I can phone the bank. Gordon knows what's happened, so he's going to collect the tractor himself," she said. "So I'd say we're pretty much—" Her words died on her lips.

Freddie had appeared in the doorway. Tag watched as she glanced at them uncertainly from just inside.

"We're pretty much what?" Blair asked.

"Sorted." Tag's eyes remained on Freddie. She waved. Freddie waved back and came over. Tag breathed in slowly, hoping that the slow drag in of air would calm her crashing heart. No such luck.

Act normal.

"Hi." A fixed smile. Friendly, but not over the top. Perfect.

Freddie caught her eye. "Hi." She made a show of fussing over Blair. "Hello, you. I hear you've been in the wars." Freddie's friendliness enveloped everyone. "Passing out in the kitchen, indeed! You should take more water with it."

Freddie drew them all to her, Tag noted with a shimmer of pleasure. The atmosphere changed in a heartbeat as all eyes were on Freddie. Tag glanced round at the smiles and laughter, any thoughts of tractors and audits already forgotten. It was, Tag thought as she couldn't take her eyes off her, what she now knew to be the instant Freddie effect.

"You know me, Freds." Blair beamed up at her. "Never could hold my beer." More laughter.

Ellen hugged Freddie. "I'm so pleased you came. Did you drive up? How's Skye? Did you get a park okay? It's really good of you to…"

Ellen's voice faded from Tag's awareness. Instead she watched, spellbound. Freddie had Blair and Ellen eating out of her hand. They adored her. Tag sat on the corner of Blair's bed, occasionally catching Freddie's attention, agreeing with something she'd said, then joining in the laughing and joking. Frequently her eyes would drift to Freddie's, hold them for the briefest of seconds, then look away again. Then they'd repeat the whole process over again.

"And you're okay?"

Tag blinked. Freddie was talking to her.

"I'm good. Yeah." She nodded.

"Good."

Snap out of it. "You want to go get a drink?" Tag eventually asked. "There's a canteen down the corridor."

"Hey, don't you be stealing my visitor." Blair frowned. "Freddie's only just got here."

"No, a drink sounds good." Freddie stood. "I'll come straight back up and see you afterwards." She delved into her bag. "You can eat this while I'm gone," she said to Blair. She dropped a cellophane packet onto his bed. "And all this." Apples and bananas tumbled from her bag and landed on his bed.

"You're the best." Blair picked up a sandwich.

"I know." She grinned, eliciting one back from him. "I'll see you later."

"So, we're just going to get a drink." Tag addressed Ellen and Blair. Her face flamed. Of course they knew what she and Freddie were doing.

"You go get that drink." Ellen's mouth twitched.

"I won't be long." Tag tucked a corner of Blair's sheet in.

"You take all the time you need." Blair lifted his sandwich.

Even as Tag walked from his bed, she could feel Ellen's and Blair's eyes boring into her back. There would be questions later. She just knew it.

❖

The small hospital canteen was heaving when Tag and Freddie arrived. Evening visiting was just starting on the wards, and it seemed as though every visitor was grabbing a quick bite to eat before heading down to their respective patients.

The queue was long. Tag and Freddie stood in silence. They shuffled slowly down the line.

"Have you eaten yet?" Freddie spoke first.

Tag shook her head. "Not yet," she said. "I've not been hungry all day." She moved another step along. "Not since he first came in, if I'm honest."

"Well, I'm going to eat," Freddie said. "So you should too."

"Nah." Tag screwed up her nose. "I couldn't face anything."

They ordered a coffee each, and a plate of fries for Freddie. Extra large. Tag's stomach growled at the smell; seemed she was hungry after all. Finding no free tables, they plumped for a booth, tucked away in the corner of the canteen, and sat. The coffee, Tag thought as she took a sip, didn't remotely resemble coffee. But at least it was hot and sweet.

"Before I forget"—Freddie twisted round on her seat and retrieved Tag's phone from her bag—"I saw Magnus in the corridor before. He asked me to give this back to you."

"He's been trying to improve on some game on here." Tag put it into her coat pocket. "I let him borrow it."

"He told me." Freddie forked up a fry. "He also told me that you had the biggest collection of games of anyone he ever knew."

"He exaggerates."

"He's dotty about you, you know that?" Freddie said. "Couldn't stop talking about you."

Tag was absurdly pleased. "I think he's cool too."

"He told me he thinks you're awesome." Freddie stabbed up a clump of fries.

"I think he likes the novelty of having an auntie," Tag said philosophically, "after years of not having one around."

"He called you *Auntie T* at least three times."

Tag put her head in her hands. "I wish he wouldn't call me that." She groaned. "Makes me sound like I'm eighty or something."

"Well I think it's cute," Freddie said.

Cute? Tag blinked.

"Fry?" Freddie pushed the plate towards Tag.

"Maybe just one." Tag took two. Suddenly she was starving.

"It shows Magnus really likes you." Freddie pulled her plate back.

"I know." Tag brooded at her cup. "It's nice being back with him." She reached over and took another fry. "We used to hang out together all the time when he was little," she added.

"You were the cool auntie even back then?"

"Something like that." Tag licked her fingers. "We'd watch cartoons together. Muck around together." She stared at the table. "I'd take him to the park. Jeez, could that boy talk!" Tag laughed. "I'd be knackered by the end of the day. Not from the playing. Just from all his chattering."

"Another one?" Freddie motioned to her plate. Tag took another three fries. "The joys of being an auntie, hey?" Freddie said.

"Yeah."

"Good practice for when you're a mum though?"

Tag's answer was interrupted by a young nurse in scrubs, standing, tray in hand, at their table.

"Can I perch?" He nodded to the end of Tag's bench.

Tag shuffled along her bench and twisted out. "Have the whole bench." She stood. "Give yourself more room."

"You sure?"

"Means I'll be closer to her to steal her fries." Tag grinned and motioned towards Freddie. Any excuse to get closer to Freddie. Tag slid herself in next to her and immediately skimmed a fry from her plate.

The nurse slipped into the booth without a response and immediately plugged himself into his iPod while he hastily crammed back his sandwich and flicked through a magazine. Freddie and Tag sat in silence, the tinny thumping of the iPod faintly audible through the nurse's headphones.

Tag looked down at their thighs, just touching. To Freddie's hand as she picked a loose thread from her front and dusted it away, all in a split second. The nurse had his head bowed over his magazine, zoned out. Tag could so easily take Freddie's hand right now. Put her own hand on her thigh. Touch her. Let the warmth from her hand seep into Freddie's skin. Let her know how she felt. Let her feel her wanting. It would be so damned easy. And yet…

"He looks okay." Finally Freddie spoke.

Tag placed her hands in her lap.

"Who?"

"Blair."

Of course. Blair.

"Better than he did." Tag nodded. Silence returned. The tinny music continued. "Me staying will help." Tag sensed a flicker of something spark from Freddie to her, just as she hoped it would.

"You're staying?" Freddie looked at her. "In Balfour?"

"Mm-hmm." Tag nodded. "At Glenside."

Freddie's look intensified.

"How long?"

"As long as it takes," Tag replied truthfully. "I owe it to Blair." *And to you,* she wanted to add. *To prove to you I can be trusted.* "I'm going to put everything I have into getting the business back on its feet again."

"I want to help you," Freddie said immediately. "I want to be with you in this. Tell me what I need to do."

Just be around. Tag gazed at her. *Just be with me.*

"I need to work out a plan," Tag said, her eyes still on Freddie. "Knowing you'll help me means a lot."

"I know everyone's relying on you," Freddie said, "but you really don't need to be doing this on your own." She hesitated. "I'm glad you told me."

"That I'm going to try and save the business?"

"Yes," Freddie said, "and that you're staying too." She looked at Tag. "I like having you around. Skye does too."

"How is she?"

"She's been working on her masterpiece." Freddie laughed. "Buckingham Palace made from boxes." She pulled out her phone. "She wanted me to take these and show you." Freddie frowned as she searched her phone, then held it up.

Tag peered down at the phone, still in Freddie's hand, her brow creased. Trying to shield the screen from the harsh overhead lights, she cupped one hand behind the hand Freddie was using to hold it, while the other hovered over the screen, blotting out the yellow fluorescent light.

There was Skye, standing proudly next to her pile of boxes, thumbs up.

"Sweet, huh?" Freddie said. "It's nearly finished. Just one or two final touches required."

Tag tried to concentrate on the picture, but Freddie's hair kept brushing against her cheek as she pressed her head closer to hers in order to see the screen more clearly. Their hands touching, combined with her close proximity as Freddie continued to lean ever closer to her, created a dizzying atmosphere. She was so close she could smell Freddie's skin, a sharp tang of oranges and lemons, presumably from a recent shower that was so intoxicating it caused Tag's breath to catch in her throat.

Finally, Freddie pulled the phone away. Tag turned her head to face her, meeting eyes that were fixed on hers, looking back with as much longing and aching and confusion as Tag felt. They studied one another in silence, neither taking their eyes from the other, neither breaking the spell.

The nurse opposite them coughed, disrupting the moment. Tag was in turmoil. How was she supposed to ignore her feelings for Freddie when she was sitting next to her looking at her the way she just had? How was she expected to not act on what she was feeling when every time she saw Freddie, she just wanted her more and more? Tag had tried to keep things simple, for both her sake and Freddie's. Somehow, she thought as she remembered the warmth of Freddie's skin next to hers, she had gone past simple long ago.

"Skye really likes you." Freddie's voice was soft. Gentle. Tag thought she could listen to her speaking all day. "Talks about you a lot." Even the sound of her voice right now was making Tag lose all rational thought. Liquid, velvety, sensuous, like it could wrap itself round Tag and float with her up into the sky.

"I like her," Tag said. "She's a credit to you." She captured her gaze. "And lovely, like you."

Their arms brushed against one another's, and Tag unconsciously let her fingers link briefly with Freddie's. When Freddie didn't pull her hand away, Tag brushed her thumb across her palm with a feather-light touch, savouring the softness of her skin against hers. She carried on stroking her, sensing Freddie's breath quicken slightly as she did so, then reluctantly allowed her hand to fall away as the nurse opposite them snapped his head up from his magazine and waved to another nurse across the canteen, motioning for her to join him.

It had been the briefest of touches, but it had spoken volumes. Tag looked down at her hands. To Freddie's. She didn't need to look at her face to know what Freddie was feeling; her ragged breathing told Tag everything she needed to know.

CHAPTER TWENTY

Large snowflakes were tumbling down like fat goose feathers by the time Freddie arrived up at the mill the next morning. An overnight forecast for light snow had increased to a blizzard, and yet again Balfour was blanketed under a thick carpet of white, the town shivering in the unnerving silence that always accompanied a heavy snowfall. Pure white snow clashed with the purple-and-yellow bruised sky, casting an eerie glow around the town. Muffled footsteps hurried to and from shops. Snowploughs churned powder to slush. But still the snow fell on.

Freddie's car had made it as far as the clock tower in the town square, then refused to even attempt the short, but sharp, climb up to the mill. Swaddling up against the snow, she'd set off the rest of the way on foot, arriving half an hour later. Her face, ruddy and moist from her breath behind her woollen scarf, stung from the cold, and not for the first time that morning she wondered just what the point of opening the cafe would be that day.

"You look how I feel."

Tim's voice made Freddie snap her head up in surprise. He stood, hands buried deep inside the pockets of his padded jacket, and stamped his snow boots hard on the ground in a vain attempt to stay warm.

"I didn't see you there." Freddie put her middle finger into her mouth and pulled a glove off with her teeth. She fumbled in her bag for the keys to the cafe. "You been there long?" she asked, her mouth still full of glove.

"Nah," Tim said. "Long enough to need a hot drink, though." He stepped in through the door. "Remind me why we're opening on a day like today, again."

"Because a light dusting of snow shouldn't stop us?" Freddie said unconvincingly. "Everything else in the town's open. Post office, school, grocery store." She flicked the light switch on, immediately bathing the cafe in a warmer glow. "So what excuse did we have?" She didn't add, *Because if we don't open then we lose even more money, and then have to close down.* Freddie looked around the cafe. It wouldn't come to that, would it?

"Because it'd have to be one hell of an emergency for anyone to want to come up here and buy bread," Tim said, "and it'd have to be a desperate person who'd want to struggle all the way up here just for a coffee."

Freddie nodded, only half listening. Her previous afternoon with Tag kept returning to her. How they'd held hands. Unthinking, she rubbed her thumb over her skin, remembering how Tag's warm skin had felt on hers. She'd come so close to letting her in, despite all her previous reservations, when Tag had told her she was staying on in Balfour. Staying to keep the business going. Tag cared about the business as much as Freddie did, didn't she? She must do if she was prepared to stay and fight for it. Freddie gazed around her. Well, it was a fight they'd face together. She and Tag. She was damned if she was going to let anyone close her cafe down, undo everything she'd worked so hard for all these years. She'd get it up and running again even if she had to go out and drag customers in off the street herself.

"Coffee?" Tim's question was a welcome distraction. "Might as well get one in before the rush starts." He laughed to himself at his joke.

"Cheers." Freddie looked around the empty cafe again. The usual nagging worry returned. It was going to be a long day.

❖

By the time Tag and Magnus had made the most of the fresh snow and had come back down from a Saturday morning's snowboarding on the Ben, the snow had started to disappear from the centre of

Balfour. Whatever the local farmers' snowploughs hadn't shifted had soon been melted by the succession of cars traversing the town on their way to and from the neighbouring villages. Balfour, it seemed, was getting back to normal again.

Magnus had been delivered safely back to Glenside just as Blair returned from hospital. She and Magnus had waited, a shared sense of nervous excitement at his return, standing side by side against the bonnet of Tag's car as Blair's truck bumped and crunched up the gravel path that led to the cottage. Blair's grey face peered at them from the passenger seat. He looked weary, Tag thought. Weary and anxious. Still. Her heart ached for him. Tag didn't know what she expected. That her brother would bound out of the car, looking ten years younger? She pulled herself from the bonnet and hurried to the truck.

"The warrior returns." She opened the passenger door and held out an arm to help Blair from his seat. He took it gratefully, hauling himself down from the high cab.

"I like the welcoming party." Blair gave Magnus, still standing by Tag's car, the thumbs up. "I should be ill more often."

"Or not," Ellen said. She came round to his side of the truck. "Okay. Inside." She bundled Blair to the front door, rolling her eyes as he mock-grumbled at her.

Tag followed them in, Ellen clucking round Blair like a mother hen, instructing him to sit in the front room and wait for her to bring him coffee. It was at times like this, Tag thought, that Ellen became a mother to two children, not one.

"So how is it?" Tag sank down on the sofa next to him. "Really?"

"Better." Blair pulled a footstool out, gently swatting away Tag's hand as she went to help him. He put his feet up on it and rested his head back. "At least I don't feel like I'm going to hit the floor every five minutes," he said. "I'm on a course of iron tablets that the doctors say will have me well enough to get back onto the land in a few days."

"So soon?" Tag tucked her legs up under her on the sofa.

"Yuh-huh." Blair made himself more comfortable. "About time too. Another day in that place and I think I'd have gone nuts." He glanced at Tag. "So how was the snowboarding with Magnus this morning?"

"It was good. Did I do the right thing? Taking him?" Tag asked. "Or would you have preferred me to sit over him until he did his homework, which he *insisted* didn't have to be handed in until next week?"

"No, you did the right thing," Blair said.

Relief.

"I'm really grateful you took him out with you, to be honest," he added. "He'd rather be hanging out with you than anyone else."

And a brownie point from Blair too. Win-win.

"Well, he's shit-hot at snowboarding," Tag said. "Left me in his wake on more than one occasion again."

"He's pretty fearless," Blair agreed. "But then I guess you are when you're only thirteen, right?"

"Has all this made you more fearful?"

"Nah. Life makes me fearful." He laughed hollowly.

"And the mill?"

"You got it."

"We'll get through this, Blair," Tag said. "I promise."

"And if we don't?"

Tag rested her head against the back of the sofa. "The one thing Dad was adamant about was that the mill stayed in the Grainger name," she said. "I owe it to him to try my best to honour that."

"We both do."

"I told Freddie yesterday, by the way." A fierce snapshot of her and Freddie holding hands in the canteen dizzied Tag's senses. It still made her ache. The way she and Freddie had sat while looking at the photo of Skye, the chemistry between them, so intense it gave Tag goosebumps now just to think about it.

"What did Freddie say?" Blair asked.

"She was upset."

"Understandable, in her circumstances."

"I guess. I know she loves the cafe," Tag said. "She called it her little empire once."

An overwhelming desire to see Freddie tumbled over Tag as she pictured her now up at the cafe, the blue apron she always chose to wear wrapped round her. What time was it? Tag glanced at her watch and smiled. It was four thirty. Right now Freddie would be sitting at one of the tables, drinking her last cup of coffee of the day. Despite how quiet it might or might not be the next day, she'd be thinking ahead to the menu. You had to, she'd told Tag once, otherwise you might just as well give up. Guilt pinched at Tag. Right now, Tag knew, and despite everything, Freddie would still be mulling recipes over in her head, lost in her own thoughts. It was a well-worn routine that Tag now knew. That's what made Freddie special. Adorable. And she'd still be worried, Tag was sure of it. Freddie was right, at the hospital: they did all rely on Tag. So she needed to go to her, right now, and reinforce to her that everything was going to be okay. She owed her that at least.

Tag tapped a rhythm with her finger on the arm of the sofa. She needed to tell Freddie of her plan too. The damn good plan that had come to her while she'd lain in bed that night, unable to sleep, thanks to her persistent thoughts of Freddie that had ticker-taped through her mind the whole night. Tag needed to prove to Freddie that she was trustworthy and honourable. Now, more than before, Freddie needed to know Tag would always look out for her.

"You're tired," Tag said to Blair. "So I'm going to leave you in peace."

Blair didn't argue.

Tag unfurled her legs from under her. The pull to go and see Freddie to reassure her that everything was going to be okay was too strong. She stood and looked down at her brother. "You good? Need anything?"

Blair shook his head.

"Blair?"

He looked up.

"I meant everything I said in the hospital," she said. "So let me get us out of this mess and get the mill up and running again, just like it used to."

"How?" Blair blinked wearily. "Where do we even start?"

"We'll talk some more about it tonight." Tag walked out the door. She pulled her phone from her pocket and pointed it at him. "For now, rest." She automatically dialled the number she wanted. Last call dialled. Last call received. No need to look it up any more. The panic when Freddie didn't immediately answer drifted to relief when she finally answered on the sixth ring.

"It's me." Tag's heart crashed against her ribs. "Can I come up and see you?"

CHAPTER TWENTY-ONE

Just as Tag had anticipated, when she arrived up at the cafe, Freddie was bowed over her notebook, coffee cup by her side. The sight warmed Tag. Familiarity. Routine. Her hand on the cafe's door handle, Tag watched her through the door's small windows, wondering how someone in a flour-spattered apron could look so endearing. Freddie, completely unaware that Tag was watching her, continued to scribble in her notebook, a look of concentration on her face.

Finally, Tag entered.

Freddie glanced at the clock on the wall. "Seven minutes." She smiled. "You're getting quicker. I timed you." Her face flushed so adorably, it was all Tag could do to not go straight to her and pull her into her arms. Instead, Tag hung back.

"I'm jotting down some ideas for this place." Freddie tapped her notebook by way of explanation. "I couldn't sleep last night, so I put my mind to work."

"Me neither." Tag caught her eye. "Sleep, I mean."

A shared memory of the hospital canteen flitted between them. Realizing she was still standing by the doorway, Tag walked to Freddie's table and slid herself onto the chair opposite her.

"I wanted to talk to you about yesterday." Tag's voice was small. She cleared her throat. "About how we left things."

Freddie lifted her eyes to Tag's but didn't respond. Tag took her silence as a spur to carry on.

"I think we could be good together." Was she talking about the business now? She had no idea. "It could work."

"Do you want it?" Freddie asked slowly.

"I do." Tag's heart thrummed. Was Freddie reading between the lines? Freddie's expression remained impassive, but her eyes, Tag noted, blazed.

"In the canteen. Last night." Tag wanted to reach across the table, but something held her back. "I wanted to…"

"I know. Me too."

"You've no idea how much."

Tag watched as Freddie looked down at her notepad, then back to Tag. Her expression had changed, as though just looking at her notes had jolted Freddie back to the here and now, taken her out of whatever cloud she'd just been in.

"I'm scared." Freddie's voice was almost a whisper. "Scared of what might happen."

Tag was confused. Was she talking about her future at the cafe? Or a future with Tag?

"This place is my life." Freddie frowned. "It's all I've ever known and all I probably will ever know."

"Forget anything you've ever heard about me or thought about me," Tag said. "I want to help. I want us to be a team. You and me." Freddie would be formidable, Tag knew. She knew the place inside out; if there was anyone who could help get them out of the mess that they were in, then Freddie could.

"I need this job. *Skye* needs me to have this job." Freddie's voice grew emphatic. "That's why I'm so fiercely loyal to the place."

Tag's heart fell heavy. Freddie was putting up a wall, brick by brick, in front of her very eyes. Tag wanted to talk about *them*. Freddie didn't. Freddie, it seemed, wanted to talk about anything but them. The wall was still impenetrable. Well, she could talk business.

"Look, it was circumstances that got us into this mess in the first place," Tag said. "The bypass. The poor summers. Okay, Dad didn't help by ignoring our problems, but if we can work out a way to pull customers back, then I think we have a fighting chance."

Now Freddie looked so lost. As though everything hinged on Tag's words and, depending on what she now said, Freddie would either be in floods of tears or running from her. A rush of protection washed over Tag.

"I know I can help." Tag was on a roll. If she stopped now, then what? Freddie would never hear all the things Tag had spent over twenty-four hours thinking about saying to her. "I don't want to let Magnus down any more. Or Blair. I think I've let everyone down enough already," she said. "But no more."

"How are you going to fix things?" Freddie asked.

"I have a plan." Tag grinned. "And like I just told Blair, you'll have to wait to hear about it for a while."

"A plan?" Freddie asked.

"A bloody good one."

"I'm glad." Freddie visibly relaxed.

"So are we good?" Tag held up her hands. "No more worrying?" A smile touched her lips.

Freddie studied her. "We're good," she said, nodding. She took her empty cup to the sink, and started to hum a tune that Tag couldn't recognize, mostly thanks to the fact that Freddie occasionally veered off-key at the higher notes, before settling back down to normal for the chorus.

Not that Tag cared. She was transfixed by Freddie, humming her out-of-tune song. Her heart—which friends had always joked was made entirely from flint, quite incapable of ever being broken by anyone—was now shattering into a thousand shards, mainly because she'd gained Freddie's trust. Freddie believed in her, and Tag had never been so relieved. That's what Freddie did to her. That's what *wanting* Freddie did to her.

"So, what have you done today?" Freddie glanced over her shoulder at her as she rinsed the cup.

"Snowboarding," she said. "With Magnus."

"You cool dude." Freddie grinned.

"Not so cool when I kept falling over."

Freddie faced away again. Tag's gaze returned to Freddie's body.

"How many times?" Freddie stole another look to her. Tag instantly looked away and studied the menu in front of her. Had she been caught looking?

"Hmm?"

"Today. Snowboarding." Guess not. "Falling. How many times?"
"Once or twice."

"Are you sure you're not exaggerating the truth there?"

Tag met Freddie's eyes. A mischievousness danced across them.

"Couple of times, that's all. I swear." A rush of pleasure hit Tag
as Freddie met her grin with the loveliest look on her face Tag thought
she'd ever seen. They were okay again. Back to how they were. "Ask
Magnus."

"I will." Freddie wiped her hands down her apron. She pulled
the grip from her hair, letting it tumble around her shoulders. "He'll
tell me the truth."

"He'll tell you that he took me out at least five times on the way
down," Tag said. "Don't believe him. The kid exaggerates."

Freddie sat opposite Tag again.

"I'm glad you came up here," she said. "I wanted to call you all
day, but…"

But, what? Tag studied her face, searching for clues. She'd been
too scared? Just like Tag had been scared?

"You want my help," Freddie continued, "and I'm glad of it. I
really do want to work with you to get this sorted. I like the idea of
me and you being a team."

"Me too." The expression on Freddie's face was just too much.
"We'll come up with something between us all, I'm sure."

"Thanks. I mean that." Freddie paused. "Now are you going to
tell me what your plan is?"

Tag considered her answer. "I reckon the whole place needs an
overhaul," she eventually said. "A rethink."

"Mm." Freddie scanned around her. She looked at the walls, the
paintings. "You mean like a rebranding?"

Tag's antennae sprang up. "Just like a rebranding, yes." A
thought wormed its way in. "A redevelopment. New advertising, new
features. Inject new life into the place."

"Except…"

"Except?"

"If the mill's already in debt," Freddie said, "how do we afford it?"

"We do it ourselves." Tag sat back. "We do the redesign ourselves.
I thought Magnus could do some drawings," she continued. "I'm

going to photograph this place and Magnus can put his own swing on them via his sketches." She stood up and started walking around the cafe.

"A joint Grainger effort?" Freddie smiled at the pacing Tag.

"That's exactly it. It's brilliant. Blair will be stoked that Magnus is getting involved, while at the same time seeing what an awesome artist his son is." Tag stopped in front of a painting on the wall. She reached up and straightened it. "It couldn't be any more perfect."

Tag's mind whirred. Slogans, photos, drawings swam in front of her eyes. Catchphrases. Dates. Information. Statistics. Magnus would be perfect for it. She'd photograph aspects of the mill—everyday scenes, machinery, smiling faces. Then Magnus would do the most exquisite pencil drawing of each, in Magnus's own unique way. They'd use those on flyers, advertising hoardings, the website.

"I want to get some advertising out on the bypass too," Tag continued. "Remind people we're still here, and that they don't need to get their coffee from some grotty bypass cafe."

"Maybe we could put out an advert on local radio?" Freddie offered. "Tell people if they want a taste of the real Scotland, they need to come to us. We could throw in a free refill offer with every cup of tea or coffee too."

"Freddie Metcalfe, you're a genuis." Tag rushed to her and pulled a startled Freddie into a hug. She held her, long enough for her to appreciate her softness, every curve of her body, then reluctantly released her, too afraid of what she might do if she held her too long.

Tag spun round, eyes skimming the cafe. Scenes came to her. She'd need photos of the bakery, the gristmill. The waterwheel and the watermill. A panorama of the land behind the watermill, to show customers just how far their wheat had travelled. Her insides danced. This was just what she needed: a free rein to prove to Blair just what she could do. No, to prove to *herself* just what she could do. This project would pull everyone together: her, Blair, Magnus, Freddie. They'd make an awesome team. She and Blair and Magnus would work as Graingers, and Tag could prove to her father that the mill, finally, meant something to her.

❖

"You want to do what?" Disbelief dripped from Blair.

"Change stuff." Tag spoke firmly.

"Change *stuff*?"

"Change brings in new customers," Tag explained, "while at the same time bringing back the old ones that have forgotten all about us, thanks to the bypass."

"Enlighten me."

"Okay." Tag shoved away from the sink and picked up her bag which was hanging on the back of the kitchen door. She pulled out her iPad and set it down on the kitchen table. "So?" She glanced back to Blair.

"So…what?"

"So now we have to focus on getting back the customers that we lost when the bypass was built," Tag said, "along with some new ones who don't already know about us."

"You've said. Twice. And how do you propose we do that?" Blair ran his hands over his face.

"I had some ideas." Tag placed her iPad in front of him. "Look."

Blair stared at the iPad screen, the light from it bouncing off his glasses as he bent closer to inspect the document Tag had brought up.

"Rebranding?" He slid his glasses up onto the top of his head. "You don't know what you're talking about."

"Thanks for the vote of confidence." Tag tapped the screen with her pen. "Just look at these case studies I've worked on down in England over the last few years, and then tell me you don't think it's a good idea. Look at how much their profits rose after we'd helped them to rebrand."

Without a word, Blair pulled his glasses back down and leaned forward in his chair. His eyes scanned the screen. He pursed his lips in concentration as he scrolled down the page, occasionally raising an eyebrow or giving a soft tut of disapproval.

"She knows what she's talking about, Blair," Ellen chastised. "Just go with it, will you?"

He took his glasses off and placed them on the table next to him, then looked evenly at Tag. Eventually he spoke. "You have a lot of Scottish mills in Liverpool, do you? Are you an expert on them, all of a sudden?"

Not the reaction Tag wanted.

"No, but I have experience in advertising, don't I?" She tried not to be irritated. Her brother was stubborn at the best of times. Question his capabilities, and his stubbornness increased hundredfold. "So quit acting like a big kid."

"Me the big kid?" Anger flashed across Blair's face. "Can I remind you that—"

"That she's trying to help," Ellen butted in. "For God's sake, Blair. Take some help when it's offered to you."

"Deveraux Enterprises has many fingers in many pies." Tag crossed her arms over her chest. Time to hit Blair with some facts. "Brand development, corporate communications, digital marketing, image management."

"And? This is a small, family-run flour mill, Tag. Not some massive corporate business."

"I know that. What I'm saying is that Deveraux Enterprises also does advertising, which happens to be my speciality."

"Anyone can advertise," Blair said dismissively. "Few flyers posted around town."

"I'm talking about getting people's attention." Stubbornness and flippancy from Blair. Not a good combination. Tag snubbed his obvious attempts at trivializing her. "A total rebrand of the mill."

"Total rebrand?" Blair sat back.

"That's what I said."

"For what purpose?"

"To remind the people of Balfour and beyond what we stand for," Tag said, "what we can offer them, and how long we've been established, stuff like that." She scrolled down her iPad. "Then maybe we can start to see some light again at the end of the tunnel."

"And how do you propose we do that?" Blair asked.

"I spoke to Freddie about it last night," Tag said.

"You spoke to Freddie about this?" Blair repeated incredulously. "Before speaking to me?"

"We bounced ideas off one another." Tag ignored him. "Freddie came up with really good stuff."

"There's that word *stuff* again." Blair crossed his arms. "Not very professional, is it?"

Tag had heard enough. "Okay," she said, not rising to the bait, "shall I tell you what *is* professional?"

"Hit me."

"Trust me, Blair. I'm tempted." Tag slid a finger down her iPad. "You have to focus on the things that make Balfour Watermill special. Different from all the other tourist attractions around here."

"Everyone round here knows what we stand for."

"Which is?"

"That we're a family company," Blair offered.

"That we're organic?" Tag asked. "Do they know that? Or that we have a zero carbon footprint? People want to know that. They want to know what they're eating, and that the flour they use has only travelled as far as out there in the fields. Not hundreds of miles."

"Is that on the flyers?" Blair tossed a look to Ellen, who shrugged.

"Are you on the tourist trail?" Tag asked. "Do you have leaflets down in the tourist information centre?"

"Of course we are," Blair said, "and of course we do." He frowned. "We're not complete amateurs, you know."

"We need to let people know that we have the best cafe for miles around," Tag continued. She thought of Freddie. Her willingness to unite with Tag for the good of the business. Freddie's enthusiasm for the project, as fiery as her own, as intoxicating as a drug. Thoughts of Freddie, pacing the cafe with her the previous night, so full of ideas—so full of *life*—spurred her on. Doing all this for her and Skye, as well as for Blair, fired up Tag more than any project in England had ever done. "We can put billboards up on the bypass reminding drivers that we're a hundred times better than anything they'd get anywhere on the bypass. We need to get that message out there, that there's been a mill here for generations. That we're organic. That we're environmentally friendly. That we're traditional." Tag punched each point out, remembering how she and Freddie had see-sawed ideas between them until darkness had fallen.

"You've really done your homework on this, haven't you?" Ellen said.

"Because it matters," Tag said. "We have something unique here. Tradition. You don't get that in a service station." She pulled her iPad towards her. "Remember the old threshing machine in the mill?" she asked. "Maybe we can get that up and running again."

Blair watched as Tag pulled up website after website to show him.

"We could apply for a grant to turn the mill into a living museum." Energy surged through her as she peppered Blair with ideas. "We can have a stall at the farmers' market over in Swanne, selling our bread." She beamed at him. "Don't you see? The possibilities are endless, Blair."

"I don't know." Blair sounded weary. "It all seems like such a lot to have to think about. I mean, where do we even start?"

"We start with some new advertising and work from there. The rest will follow." Tag snapped her iPad off. "Here's what I'm going to do," she said. "I'm going to go take some photos of the place." She stood up. "On Monday, so at least it'll be closed. No one to disturb me." Tag pulled her coat from the back of her chair. "And then when I get back later, I'll tell you the next stage of my plan," she said. "Somehow, this is the one I think you'll like the most."

CHAPTER TWENTY-TWO

The text that was waiting for Tag the next morning couldn't have been a nicer one to wake up to.

Come over. Talk some more about plans. I want to show you an advert I've seen. Really excited about this. F xxxxx

Freddie wanted to hang out. What was previously going to be a very run-of-the-mill Sunday had suddenly got a whole lot better.

Tag settled back into her pillows and held her phone up above her head, typing out her reply. *Love to. Midday okay?* A thought burrowed. It was Sunday. She could take Freddie out for lunch, couldn't she? It wouldn't be a date. Tag frowned. No, not a date, a business meeting. She grinned to herself. Much better. And Skye? Her grin widened; what could be better than Sunday lunch out with Freddie and Skye? Right then, Tag couldn't think of a single thing she'd rather be doing. She tapped out an extra part onto the end of her text: *Shall we take Skye to lunch at The Cherry Tree in Swanne? xxxxx*

Tag dropped her arms back to her side, feeling stupidly happy, and rolled over, tunnelling further down under her duvet. Freddie's text came straight back: *No lunch for Skye. She's ill in bed. Tummy. I'm afraid we'll have to stay in xxxxx*

The thought touched Tag far more than she ever thought possible. She imagined Skye, tucked up in bed, little white face poking out above her duvet. Tag's insides melted. Although Skye was probably giving out orders to Freddie, Tag couldn't help the rush of protective feelings that accompanied her thoughts. She imagined Freddie too. She was a good mother, a loving mother. Caring and attentive. Skye was her life, and that thought alone warmed Tag.

Tag pulled the duvet up around her ears. A sudden thought struck her. Hearing someone move around outside her door, Tag called out, "Ellen? That you?"

Ellen appeared in her doorway.

"What do you give as a present to a five-year-old with tummy ache?" Tag propped herself up onto one elbow.

"I assume we're talking about Skye here?"

"Mm," Tag replied. "I thought I'd take her a small present to cheer her up."

"You're going over?" Ellen raised an eyebrow and sat down on the edge of Tag's bed.

"We're discussing the mill." Tag shrugged under her bedding. "Freddie's texting me directions to her cottage later."

"So it's a business meeting?" Ellen's lips twitched.

"Totally."

"Well, don't take sweets if Skye has tummy ache," Ellen offered. "If you want to make an impression with Freddie"—she batted away Tag's protests with a swish of her hand—"then definitely not sweets." She thought for a moment. "Anything pink." Ellen stood. "All girls love pink."

"Ew, not me." Tag fell back into bed. "But thanks anyway."

Freddie, presents, and Skye. Tag hugged herself under her duvet. Could her day possibly get any better?

Tag had chosen her favourite long-sleeved T-shirt for her first-ever visit to Freddie's cottage. She'd fussed forever over a mountain of clothes, tipped untidily onto her bed, finally plumping for a top that was fitted sufficiently to show off her curves, whilst at the same time demure enough to not give Freddie the impression that she'd chosen it specifically to impress her. Which, of course, she had.

After checking her appearance in the mirror twice, dithering over whether her jeans were too tight, Tag finally left the house, offering a middle finger to Ellen's wolf whistles as she went. Making a quick stop at Balfour's one and only newsagents, where she hastily bought a present for Skye on her way up to Lyster, Tag arrived at Freddie's house at exactly a minute after midday. Impressive. And if there was one thing Tag was keen to do, it was to impress Freddie.

"Great timing." Freddie opened the door to her, standing to one side as Tag came in. Her expression, Tag noted as she brushed past her, was a mixture of nervousness and anticipation. Cute. "I've just made coffee."

The warmth inside Freddie's cottage, after the bitter cold of outside, was welcome. A comforting aroma of warm house and fresh coffee tantalized Tag's senses as she stood in the hallway. Nerves flapped at her insides, as the realization finally hit her that she was in Freddie's personal domain at last. She followed Freddie into the front room where Buckingham Palace was moving across the floor towards her.

"I see you finished it, then," Tag said, nodding towards the boxes.

"I can thank Pete for that." Freddie bent her head towards the boxes. "Skye, come out and say hello to Tag again, please."

Skye's familiar honey curls poked out from the box, then shot back inside again. Tag glanced at Freddie, feeling relieved when Skye appeared from round the back of the boxes and walked, more confidently than she had the last time she met her, over to her.

"Hello." Skye looked up at her from under her hairline.

"Hey, Skye." Tag crouched so she was eye level with her. "Are you feeling better now?"

"I was sick at five o'clock this morning, six o'clock, and then again just before *Tom and Jerry*." Skye counted them off on her fingers. "But I haven't been sick again since then."

"And breakfast stayed down," Freddie said, "so I think we can safely say we're over the worst of it." She glanced at Tag. "I hope you don't mind her being here," she said, lowering her voice. "Pete offered to take her out once we knew she was okay, but she was desperate to stay."

Tag straightened. If only Freddie knew. Everything Tag wanted was in the room with her right now: Freddie looking cutely embarrassed, Skye looking both adorable and psyched in equal measures that Tag was there. Tag didn't think she'd ever felt more welcome or at home. It was heartbreakingly touching.

"Stop stressing." Tag touched Freddie's shoulder. She allowed her fingers to travel down her arm, then linger close to Freddie's hand, a pulse travelling through her as Freddie linked her fingers with hers, before letting her hand drop again. "I'm stoked that Skye's here. I was worried about her. I've missed her." The truth crashed around her. She had. She'd missed her more than she'd realized. It had been a week since they'd all been to the park, and there hadn't been a day since that Tag hadn't thought of their day out, or thought of Skye. She turned to Skye, feeling ridiculously happy. "I have to say, Skye, that's an *awesome* T-shirt you're wearing."

Skye visibly grew taller. "It's my best," she said proudly.

"Well, I think it looks amazing on you," Tag said. "And I totally *love* the sailing boat. Have you ever been on one?"

"A sailing boat?" Skye tilted her head and plunged into deep thought. "No, I don't think I have."

"I went on a sailing boat once," Tag said. "We only went round Brook's Bay for five minutes and I was seasick." She held her hand over her mouth, widened her eyes and puffed her cheeks out. Both Skye and Freddie laughed.

"Let me take your jacket." Freddie held her hand out for it, still laughing. "I'll hang it up for you in the hall."

Tag unbuttoned her jacket and shrugged it off, gratified at the shift in Freddie's expression when she saw her top. She handed her the jacket, their fingers brushing for a second, neither taking their eyes from the another's. Freddie draped her jacket over her arm. Her lips twisted to one side as she chewed at her bottom lip.

"Nice top." Freddie nodded. She raised an appreciative brow.

"You think?" Tag looked down her front.

"I think." Freddie's eyes were still on her. "I *definitely* think."

"Thank you." Tag looked straight at her. "It's my best."

"You brought her another present?" Freddie sat down on the floor of the lounge next to Tag, kicking her legs out in front of her. "That's very sweet of you."

"You have to have a present when you're poorly." Tag scrambled to her feet. "Isn't that right, Skye?"

A hand shot out from inside one of the boxes on the floor, swiftly followed by a thumbs up sign. Skye crawled out on all fours and stood, politely expectant, next to Freddie.

"Although, you're not strictly poorly any more, are you?" Freddie teased, reaching up and grabbing her round the waist. Skye doubled over and dissolved into a fit of giggles.

"Don't be mean." Tag sauntered over and handed a plastic bag to Skye. "I hope these make you feel even better." She sank back down next to Freddie on the floor.

"Whoa." Skye's eyes widened as she opened the bag. "Thank you." Tag adored the exuberance and sheer childish joy that poured from her as she widened the opening further and peered inside. She flipped the bag upside down, her jaw hanging open in delight as dozens of small plastic soldiers fell out and bounced around the floor, scattering by her feet. Some were crouching, some were running, some were crawling on their bellies. Most of them, though, were standing to attention, waiting for Skye to place them inside her palace so they could guard the Queen.

"Soldiers?" Freddie picked one up. She inspected it, turning it around between her fingers. "That's so damn cute," she murmured, her voice sending shivers down Tag.

"Every kid loves soldiers, don't they?" Tag cut her glance away, watching as Skye started lining them up in a neat parade on the rug. "Besides, you can't have a palace without soldiers."

"Well, most girls prefer dolls apparently," Freddie said, "but fortunately Skye has never been a doll girl." She placed her hand on Tag's thigh, mouthing a "thank you" to her as Skye began the important task of setting her platoon to work, a look of determined concentration on her face as she did so. Tag looked from Freddie's hand, so at home on her leg, then back to Freddie. She closed her hand over it, pulling it into her own.

"You're welcome," Tag mouthed back to her.

"Woody's not a doll," Skye announced loudly, not looking up. "Bethany Davies from my class said Woody was a doll, but he's not. He's from *Toy Story*."

Tag reluctantly released Freddie's hand and clambered over to Skye. "Woody's most definitely not a doll," she confirmed. "You ask Bethany Davies from your class how many dolls wear a gun holster and a Stetson."

Skye's eyes widened again as she nodded solemnly.

Lunch, once Skye's soldiers were settled into their task, and it had been confirmed beyond any more doubt that Woody wasn't a doll, could finally get under way. After making sure Skye was sitting in front of the TV to await her food, Tag joined Freddie in the kitchen, where she found her preparing to make sandwiches.

"I think you might be even more of a hit with my daughter than you were last week, if that's possible," Freddie said, pulling slices of bread from their packaging. "Anyone who gives soldiers as presents is beyond awesome to her."

"I like to do it," Tag said truthfully. "The look on her face is worth it all." She captured Freddie's eye and held it. Freddie's actions slowed.

"Can I have the crusts off?" A small voice sounded down by Tag's hip, breaking the gaze. "When you cut my sandwiches for me." Skye stood up on tiptoe and stared at the buttered slices of bread, practically balancing herself off the edge of the counter with her chin. "Please?" she beseeched.

"Crusts make your hair curly, you know," Tag said.

Skye bounced back on her heels. She held her hands out to the side of her, then pointed with both index fingers to her untidy mop of curls.

"Fair point." Tag turned her attention to the sandwiches.

A silence returned to the kitchen.

"When we've eaten, I'll show you these adverts I was talking about." Freddie joined Tag at the counter. "For the mill."

The mill. Tag smiled to herself. That's why she was here, wasn't it? In the warm comfort of toy soldiers and sandwiches, she'd quite forgotten.

"I'm going up there tomorrow," Tag said. She placed cheese and slivers of tomato in Skye's sandwich. "Thought I'd take some photos while the place is shut."

"The ones you'll give Magnus to recreate?" Freddie asked.

Tag nodded. "Old machinery, the waterwheel. Stuff like that will be perfect." She squared Skye's sandwiches. "Then I thought a meeting up at the cafe one day next week with everyone would be a good idea."

"Can I have my water in my Spider-Man mug as well, please?" Skye joined Tag at her side again.

Tag put down her knife, then straightened her back and saluted smartly. "Anything else, ma'am?" She grinned widely, making Skye giggle.

"I don't think so." Skye replied, holding her hands up to accept the plate of sandwiches that Tag handed her. She turned and walked carefully back to the lounge, plate held carefully in both hands. "She did squares," she whispered to Freddie as she passed her in the doorway. "Charlotte never did squares, even though I always asked for them."

Freddie stopped dead. Skye had mentioned Charlotte again, but this time, the sound of her name wasn't like a knife to her heart. She looked across to Tag, busy slicing more bread, then back to Skye, eating her sandwiches. Skye occasionally glanced back to Tag, laughing through a mouthful of bread each time Tag pulled a silly face at her. Tag was so lovely with Skye, her attention constantly on her, asking her if she was okay or wanted more. And Skye had her undivided attention too, laughing with her, pulling faces back at her. It had been too long, Freddie thought, since she'd heard Skye laugh as much. Tag had that effect on her. Skye was enraptured by her, over the moon because Tag was there making faces at her and because she'd done her sandwiches just as she liked. Tag hadn't questioned it, or mocked it, like Charlotte would have done. She'd just done the one thing that would make Skye happy. That meant more to Freddie than anything—to see Skye happy again after so many months.

And yet, was she being fair on Skye by letting her get close to Tag?

"Why do kids always want their crusts taken off?" Tag sounded behind her, shushing her thoughts away. "Magnus was the same when he was Skye's age. What have they got against crusts anyway?"

"You tell me," Freddie said. "But thank you for doing her sandwiches just the way she wanted."

"Anytime."

"Tag can sit next to me," Skye called out from the lounge.

"Okay," Freddie replied, walking from the kitchen.

"'Cos she made squares," came the reply.

CHAPTER TWENTY-THREE

A soft wind was buffeting around the base of the watermill as Tag approached it the next afternoon. It was Monday, and she'd set off from Glenside with her camera and notepad, and a renewed sense of excitement at the thought of a whole afternoon of photography. She slowed her steps and glanced up at the top windows, remembering vividly a time from her past when she'd looked out from those very same panes. Memories danced in front of her eyes as her past came back to meet her.

Tag retrieved a key from her pocket. She unlocked the heavy door and swung it back. She stepped inside, immediately being plunged into gloom, the only rays of light coming from the doorway and the slits of windows running up each wall. Tag stood, blinking to allow her eyes to adjust to the half-light.

Finally when she could see better, Tag circled the floor. She gazed up at the walls, to the domed roof. She ran her hands over the rough walls, feeling every bump and groove of the centuries-old stone, savouring the coolness of it. Her mind's eye set up photo scenes. She occasionally glanced up at the slits in the walls, choosing the right angle for each photo, judging where best to stand where the natural light outside would show the building at its finest.

Tag strode across to the other side of the mill, her footsteps echoing around her in the cavernous building. She turned back and looked at the old thresher. That would make the perfect picture. Tag pulled her camera from its case and rattled off one, two, then three photos in quick succession. Then another ten of the grist wheels and sack hoist. She moved to her left and fired off another twelve photos. She was pleased; the light was perfect, the low sunshine from outside bouncing off the honey-coloured walls just inside the door. It looked comfortable and warm—just how Tag wanted it to look.

She walked up the wooden steps to the next floor. Wooden storage boxes lined the walls. Tag's eyes drifted over the details stamped in dark ink on the sides: BALFOUR 1901. PROPERTY G.H. GRAINGER ESQ. 1912. Tag dipped her head and peered. G.H. Grainger? A great-grandfather? She shrugged and photographed it anyway, figuring it would look good in her portfolio whether she eventually used it or not. When she'd finished, Tag ran her eyes over the images on her camera screen.

The light from outside caught her eye and she sauntered across the wooden floorboards to the window. She rested her hands on the sill and stared out, then twisted away and ran up the next three flights, two steps at a time. The view from the very top of the watermill never ceased to amaze her. Four floors up, it yawned out across the fields which were now bathed in sunshine.

Tag noted the landmarks. There was Blair's tractor, parked up in a ploughed rut, lurching slightly to the left. Over to the other side was a half-ploughed field, its furrows speckled with the last remains of the snow. There were trailers covered in tarpaulin, and fields with the first hints of green shoots coming up. She could see bare hedgerows shivering against the chill, and tall, naked trees on the horizon. Tag stood, spellbound, as she gazed out around at land as far as she could see. Grainger land. *Her* land.

A noise on the ground below her pulled her attention back to the room. A door scraping against its frame, followed by footsteps. Tag hurried to the top step and peered over the rail. Tom? It was his day off, surely? The footsteps crescendoed, hastening up the stairs. Tag lurched further over the rail, her eyes finally meeting Freddie's, staring up at her from two floors down. Their eyes locked, her surprise and instant desire igniting sparks in Freddie's gaze. Tag's pulse quickened. Freddie's hair was illuminated by a shaft of sunlight, the rays enhancing the natural highlights in her hair. Her eyes, wide and expectant, sparkled. She was beautiful. Tag drew her breath in. So beautiful.

She gathered herself. "I thought we had burglars there for a second," she called down at Freddie, her voice even, despite her wildly beating heart.

Freddie's hand clasped her chest. "So did I. Bloody hell, Tag. You just scared the life out of me."

"I'm taking photos." Tag lifted her camera from around her neck, by way of explanation. "I told you yesterday."

"Did you?" Freddie still gripped her chest.

Tag nodded, willing Freddie to come to her.

"You left the door wide open." Freddie still stared up at her. "I thought someone had broken in."

Why was Freddie stalling for time? Finally, unable to bear it any longer, Tag went down to her. "Why are you here? We're closed today." She cursed herself. Too harsh. Nerves did that to her.

"I'm going to clean the cafe through."

"You clean on your day off?" Tag looked at her like it was the weirdest thing she's ever heard. She laughed in a vain attempt to quell her fluttering stomach.

"Someone has to."

Fair point.

"I'm sorry I scared you," Tag said sheepishly. "I just thought I'd make the most of the mill being empty." She sat on one of the wooden steps. "It's nice in here, isn't it?" she said. "Peaceful, without the stones making a racket."

Freddie rested her arms on the stair rail. "I come in here sometimes before I leave work, just to think and have a chat with Tom." She looked around her. "There's something strangely lulling about hearing the river running by just outside, don't you think? I love the constancy of it all."

"Me too," Tag said. "No matter where you are, what you're doing, or what you're thinking, that river will always be running. Always feeding the mill. It's weird, but comforting at the same time." Her nerves refused to go. Tag swallowed. Something felt different. A shift in their chemistry, as though they were both gliding together towards…something. But what? She couldn't decipher it, couldn't find the answer in the eyes that continued to look back at her.

"So how are the photos looking?" Freddie asked. If Tag felt nervous, Freddie looked ten times more so.

"Good. Yeah." Tag touched her camera. "I'd forgotten just how nice the view is from the top of here. Plenty of things to get inspiration from."

"You didn't come up here the other week when you were talking to Tom?"

"No, we stayed down on the ground floor," Tag said. "I haven't been up this high for at least ten years." Olivia Leigh had to be ten years ago now, right? "I definitely remember coming up here when I was around sixteen with someone, but nothing after then." Tag dropped her eyes. She held back a smile at the memory of Olivia Leigh.

"That's a very knowing look." Freddie dipped her head to try and catch Tag's eye.

"Maybe."

"Let me guess." Freddie rested her chin on her arm. "You used to bring girls up here? Impress them with your knowledge of wheat?"

"Something like that." Tag chuckled. "But not girls, plural. Just the one."

"Go on, then," Freddie said. "Spill."

"How's Skye?" She was changing the subject. Whatever. "Over her tummy bug?"

"All over it now." Freddie smiled. "She went to school this morning. Couldn't wait to tell Bethany Davies about her new soldiers."

Tag's heart swelled.

"So, spill about your past up here," Freddie persisted.

"It was a long time ago."

"Chicken."

"It was!" Tag protested. "I can barely remember now."

"Fibber." Freddie watched her squirm. "You're a chicken and a fibber, Tag Grainger."

"She was called Olivia."

"Very posh."

"She was." Tag tucked her hair behind her ear. "Her mother was aghast when she found out she was sleeping with the little lesbian from the bakery."

Freddie laughed loudly. Her eyes sparkled. "I'll bet she was."

"I didn't care." Tag feigned indifference. "Anyway, let's just say her darling Olivia wasn't so posh when she was with me."

"Really?" Freddie asked slowly.

"Really."

"I'll bet."

The atmosphere intensified. The air grew thick, warm. All Tag could hear was the tidal pulsing of blood in her ears as Freddie nestled her chin on her hands and studied Tag, her eyes never leaving hers.

"Anyway." Tag burned inside. "It was all a long time ago now." She stood and held her hand out to Freddie, her hand steady, despite the tension that had enveloped them. "Come and have a look upstairs. I'll show you what I've been photographing." She squeezed Freddie's hand when it found its way into hers, finding instant comfort from the feel of it. "And we can look out of the window and bitch about posh exes and their ghastly mothers."

Tag hunched her shoulders tighter against the chill wind that whistled around the top floor of the watermill. She stood to one side of the floor, watching as Freddie moved around the room, her hands waving animatedly as she told Tag of two ideas she'd had.

"So we give tourists a tour of the watermill and grists," Freddie said, "they go into the cafe and shop afterwards and spend lots of money. Win-win, as far as I can see."

"Okay, but how do we make sure they go into the cafe afterwards as well?" Tag asked. Freddie's enthusiasm, she thought with a thrill, was compelling. She paced, her face alive and excited, occasionally pulling her hair from her brow, burying her hands in it as she thought hard about a certain idea or philosophy about the cafe that she felt she needed to explain better.

"We arrange it with the coach company that they arrive around late morning," Freddie said, "and don't leave until around two p.m. By the time they've had their tour and a look around, taken photos from the top of the watermill, and blah-blah-blah—"

"They'll be hungry?"

"Exactly." Freddie raised her hands, palms up. "Now, in order to make sure those lovely people on the coach don't just all turn up with their own sandwiches, we offer the coach company a special deal on a set menu which they charge to the customer as part of the tour."

"And if we offered them all a ten-percent discount in the shop too," Tag said, "that'd encourage them to go and buy something before or after they've had lunch."

"If you think your average coach takes, what, knocking on eighty people?" Freddie calculated. "And each one paying a set price for a two-course lunch…"

"And we can take at least two coach parties a day in the cafe—"

"At a push."

"If we stagger the Mill tours—"

"And open the cafe seven days a week instead of its current six—"

"In addition to the few that'll still just pop in and out…"

"You do the maths." Freddie's voice was triumphant, her eyes gleaming.

"You're a genius."

"Tell me something I don't already know." There was that look again. Longer this time.

Tag felt herself falling. Her head swam with a dizzying cocktail of Freddie's company, her proximity, her body, her warmth, her enthusiasm. They were all conspiring together to weaken Tag, to break down her defences, and to render her helpless in Freddie's company.

She squeezed her eyes shut. Closed Freddie out.

Focus.

"What else?" Tag asked. She needed to concentrate. The business needed her to listen to what Freddie had to say. "You said you'd had two ideas."

"Bread-making courses," Freddie said simply. "I was reading about a mill on the Welsh border that does them."

"People would pay to come make bread?"

"Works very well at this mill, from what I was reading."

"Who'd run it?" Tag frowned. "Can't see Tom being a great teacher."

"I would," Freddie said. "I'd love to have a go at it."

It was perfect. The students would love Freddie; she was patient, charming, funny. "You'd be ideal." Tag spoke her thoughts. "They'd love you."

"Who wouldn't?" Freddie comically dusted down her front. "I'm perfect."

You are. Tag watched her as Freddie laughed.

"I guess then people would take what they'd baked home with them," Tag said, still watching Freddie, "along with a small certificate or a gift or something."

"Like, say, an apron with our brand-spanking-new logo on it?"

"Tell your friends!" Tag spread her arms out wide. *"You too can own this awesome apron if you book with Graingers."* She giggled. *"Roll up! Roll up!"*

"It's got success written all over it." Freddie laughed out loud.

"The apron does?" Tag raised her eyebrows.

"You're silly." Freddie dropped her gaze.

An embarrassed quiet descended.

"Blair's home, by the way," Tag said, purely to break the silence. "I meant to tell you yesterday."

"I saw Ellen in town earlier," Freddie said. "So I knew." She looked at her from the corner of her eye. "That's why I didn't ask." She faltered. "I didn't want you to think I wasn't bothered."

"Don't be daft." Tag looked fleetingly to her, then back out of the window. "I know you care," she said. "Anyway, he's fine. Very chatty. Reckons he'll be back out there soon enough." She lifted her chin towards the fields.

"How do you feel about that?" Freddie asked.

"Scared for him," Tag said truthfully. "Scared that things will return to how they were before I came up here."

"That Blair will shoulder everything alone?"

Tag nodded. "Want to hear a confession?" She threw a look to Freddie. "In some ways, I'm glad this happened."

"Blair?"

"Mm." Tag picked at a flake of paint on the sill. "Because it's given me the wake-up call I needed. It's given us *all* a wake-up call."

"Blair, because perhaps now he can let go a little?" Freddie offered. "And you, because?"

"Because I'm needed and wanted," Tag said simply. "I've felt like I'm part of the family again just lately. I've missed that." *And because I was lonely before I met you.* The truth stung with such ferocity, the words snagged in Tag's throat. Loneliness wasn't something she would have ever admitted to in the past. Loneliness happened to other people, not her. Old people were lonely. Unemployed people. Not successful advertising executives with swanky apartments in—

Tag bridled that train of thought. What gave her the right to think she was so superior? That loneliness couldn't ever affect her?

"I've been lonely." The declaration was out before Tag could stop it. "In Liverpool, I mean. I don't have that kind of family unity down there." Her shoulders sagged. "I have a smattering of friends who are all so busy with their own lives that they can't see that I'm unhappy." Tag bit at the skin inside her bottom lip. "And I'm quickly coming to think that I don't belong there any more."

"You think you could belong—"

"Here?"

"Mm."

"I thought coming back here would be horrendous," Tag said.

"And now?"

"It feels like I've never been away," Tag admitted. "I like that feeling. I guess it kind of surprises me that I do."

"Because it's home?"

"Possibly." Tag frowned. "It's like it's woken up something I'd forgotten about years ago."

"I think perhaps we humans are good at blocking certain things out."

"I guess. But I didn't realize just how much I'd missed Blair and Magnus." Tag drew her eyes heavenwards. "God knows, even how much I missed this place, however fucked up that sounds."

"Family ties are like that, aren't they?" Freddie smiled kindly. "They ping you back like bungee ropes."

"I just wish I'd come back sooner." She looked at Freddie. "While Dad was still alive."

"But you're here now."

"Yes, and that's why I don't want to go back to Liverpool." Tag's eyes sought Freddie's. Because she didn't want to leave Freddie either. Because she'd made squares for Skye. Because she'd felt so comfortable the day before, surrounded by warmth and love, that the very thought of going back to her previous existence chilled her. "Every time I think about it, it makes me feel sick."

"But your life's down there," Freddie said simply. She paused. "Won't your boss mind you staying here?"

"You mean Anna?"

"Yes, Anna." Tag sensed that her name pricked. "Doesn't she need you to go back eventually?" Freddie asked.

"Nothing and no one is as important as staying here," Tag replied. *No one is as important as you.* "I like having a family again." Tag shrugged. "I like waking up every day, knowing I'm going to see them." She kept her eyes on Freddie. "I like knowing I'm going to see you and Skye."

Freddie didn't answer.

"It makes me realize how empty my life is in England." Tag twisted away and stared out of the window. "And that makes me mad at myself for wasting all those years when I could have had what I've got now."

"Which is?"

"Security," Tag replied. "And love."

She gazed down through the smears on the window to Blair's tractor. Soon, she knew, he'd be in it again. Preparing the land and thinking ahead to next year, despite their money worries. Because that's what you had to do. You had to always look forward, never back. Always look to the future. What future did Tag have? Liverpool returned to her thoughts. Anna's face, Stefan's, even. Who were they? Tag wondered. What exactly were they to her? Her apartment, too, wrestled its way into her conscience. Empty and cold. Would Anna have even gone over there to check it over? Tag doubted it. It would be just as she'd left it, she thought with a heavy heart. Characterless and soul-destroyingly sterile.

"You're crying." Freddie's voice sounded beside her.

"Nah." Tag wiped at her eyes. "Maybe just a bit." She felt foolish, wishing the tears would stop. "I don't even know what I'm crying about." She gave a rueful laugh.

Freddie stepped closer to Tag and threaded an arm across her shoulder, drawing her to her. She wrapped both arms around Tag and let her bury her head into her shoulder.

"Sorry." Tag mumbled into Freddie's coat. "I'm making a habit of crying on your shoulder." She pulled back, her eyes searching Freddie's. The look on her face, eyes dark, quickened Tag's breath.

She leaned in cautiously to meet Freddie's mouth. A fleeting worry flashed through her mind as she bent her head to kiss her that she might have misunderstood the situation and this wasn't what Freddie wanted. Her hesitation intensified when Freddie didn't kiss her back at first, but immediately turned to relief when Freddie finally moved her lips over hers. Exploring, teasing.

The feeling of Freddie's lips tasting her own sent a pulse down Tag. She fisted her hands in Freddie's shirt and pulled her closer, kissing her more deeply. Her lips slid urgently over Freddie's, wanting more and more of her with each kiss. She tentatively slipped her tongue against Freddie's, unsure at first, but then more forcefully when Freddie didn't protest. Freddie moaned as she traced the tip of her tongue along Tag's bottom lip. Tag angled her hips forward into Freddie's. They melted into one another, their bodies locked together, their kisses becoming more urgent as days of shared pent-up longing were finally released.

Without warning, Freddie pulled away. She stalked away from Tag, covering her face with her hands, her back turned from her.

"*Shit!*" Freddie's head sank further into her hands. "I'm sorry," she mumbled from behind her fingers. "I shouldn't have done that."

"Why?" Tag half laughed, confused. "Was it really that bad?" She stared at Freddie's back, willing her to turn around and face her. She didn't. Instead, Freddie walked further from her.

"I don't get it." Tag reached out to her. "I thought that was what you wanted." Her insides froze to ice as Freddie twisted away and headed back towards the staircase.

"I have to go." Freddie's face was dark and pained. "It was a mistake. I'm sorry."

Tag's lips still tingled from their kiss. She could still taste her on her tongue and still feel her against her. Didn't Freddie feel it too?

How could she not? "I don't understand." She watched, helpless, as Freddie hastened to the stairs. "Why was it a mistake?"

"Just forget everything." Freddie's footsteps receded. "I can't do this."

Forget everything? A wave of sudden clarity forced Tag to lunge over the rail. Charlotte. Freddie was still thinking about Charlotte.

"How can you tell me to just forget what happened? Freddie!" Tag slammed her hands on the wood and shouted down to her. "Freddie, I'm not Charlotte! And the sooner you realize that, the better."

CHAPTER TWENTY-FOUR

Freddie stumbled from the watermill, tears stinging her eyes. Tag's cries rang in her ears as she hauled the heavy oak door open, letting it swing closed behind her with an angry thud. The thud, Freddie thought as her hands flailed for her car keys, mirrored her leaden heart, its hefty, dull clang sounding the death knell for any hope she might have ever had of having some sort of relationship with Tag. Thanks to her stupidity. Thanks to her fleeing at the first real sign that their friendship had taken a different direction.

Freddie banged her fist on the steering wheel. Had that really been what she'd wanted? A relationship with Tag? She stared back up to the watermill. To a door that never opened. All the time she and Tag had been consigned to the odd bit of hand-holding, Freddie had felt okay. She'd enjoyed it. The flirting, the texts. The longing looks. But now? The situation had shifted towards something Freddie didn't think she'd be able to cope with.

She looked towards the door again. Tag was still in there. Should she go back in and tell Tag her thoughts? What was Tag doing right now? Was she sitting on the stairs, thinking about how wonderful it had felt to kiss her, just as Freddie was now? How, if she closed her eyes, she could still feel her? Taste her?

Freddie's brain ached with conflicting thoughts. Tag wasn't the girl she'd heard gossip about over the years and wasn't who she'd expected her to be. She wasn't selfish or unreliable when it came to her own family. Tag loved her family and loved being a part of a family—both her own and Freddie's. She'd seen it in her eyes the day before, when she'd cuddled up to Skye on the sofa. Had seen it in her expression when it had been time to go, and had seen it in her brimmed tears just now in the watermill.

But yet, everything still always came back to Skye and her needs. She needed a loving, stable environment where she could feel safe. Freddie gave her that. Being with Tag could ultimately subject Skye to more heartbreak, and that was something Freddie would never, could never risk. Despite everything Tag was telling her, at some point Tag would have to return to England, to her old life. She'd still only be a part-time presence in her life, dropping by each time she came back to visit. It just wasn't enough. Skye needed more than that; they both needed more than that.

Freddie fired her engine. This was why she had to be strong. For Skye. Skye was the most important thing in all of this, not her, not Tag. She released the handbrake. And for Skye's sake, she and Tag should go back to how they should have been from the start. Employer and employee. It was far simpler that way. This was why she had to ignore her feelings for Tag and try and move on. This, Freddie thought as she pulled from the car park with one, final glance to the watermill's door, was why she'd forget Tag's kiss had ever happened.

The roads were quiet in Balfour after six p.m., Tag realized. Quieter than Liverpool, anyway. Where did everyone go? Back to their homes? Back to their families? To the pub to drown their sorrows?

Tag bunched her fists in her coat pockets. Pools of orange from the streetlights shimmered and rippled in the puddles as she ambled down the road, her mind foggy with thoughts of what had just happened. What *had* just happened? How had it happened? Tag angrily kicked a pine cone into the gutter and watched as it rolled three times before finally coming to a halt, then walked on.

She missed Freddie. Missed Skye.

Why couldn't Freddie see that?

What was the name of that girl she'd hooked up with when she was nineteen? Just after she'd moved to England? Tag stared down at the pavement as it disappeared under her feet as she strode down the road. Izzy? No, not Izzy. Lizzy? Nope. Lisa? Tag frowned. Mia. Tag dug her hands further into her pockets. That was it. Mia.

Mia had had a niece, Tag remembered, who used to hang around them a lot. She used to be deeply irritating, although perhaps not as irritating as Mia eventually turned out to be. Tag smiled down at the pavement. But Tag had been nineteen then, hadn't she? Mia's niece had just been an annoyance to her back then. A small person who got under her feet and pestered her to sit and watch cartoons with her when all she wanted to do was make out with Mia.

But that was then. She was twenty-seven now, not nineteen. Older, wiser. Okay, maybe not wiser. But more mature, that was for sure.

The wind billowed up around Tag's ears. She hunkered her shoulders up higher and walked on. The roads were deserted. Balfour was a lonely place after dark when you were on your own. Tag shivered, but not from the cold.

She loved Freddie. There, she'd admitted it to herself. She loved her.

But Freddie had shrugged her away, hadn't she? Rejected her. Tag's stomach clenched. Waves of sadness and despair swept over her. She loved Freddie, but Freddie didn't love her. That was the reality of it. Simple as.

Tag blinked and pictured Freddie back at home now with Skye. What would they be doing? Watching TV? Having dinner? Tag so wanted to be with them right now, wished she could rewind the clock and go back to the previous afternoon when she'd sat with Skye watching children's TV. Freddie had lit the fire to make the room cosier. Not that Tag had thought she could possibly feel more comfortable than she had. She'd sat next to Skye, recognizing the smell of warmth and talcum powder that was so unique to children, and one which she'd recalled from when Magnus was Skye's age. Skye had had crumbs down her fleece, Tag remembered, from her sandwich. A few in her hair too. How did kids always manage that? But then, Freddie had managed to get flour in her hair, so...

Tag's heart pricked.

But it was all pointless now, wasn't it? Remembering how it had been. Freddie had made a mistake; those were her exact words.

Tag crossed the road. In hindsight, perhaps she should be relieved that Freddie had snubbed her. After all, how could Tag commit to her? Wasn't that what they both wanted? One hundred percent commitment? Could Tag give her that? No, despite her pain, perhaps Freddie had done the right thing after all. Perhaps it would be better all round if Tag disappeared back to Liverpool, as soon as Blair was better and the mill was back on its feet, and found herself someone who didn't have the baggage Freddie did. Maybe then she could forget all about her. She'd be sorry to leave Freddie, sure. Hurt too. But when the hurt passed and Tag had moved on, she'd thank Freddie for rejecting her and putting her straight.

The road petered out. Tag was at the end of Balfour high street. The Horse and Wagon pub whispered to her in the wind, coaxing her in. She looked at the pub door and heard the muffled thump of music and numerous voices coming from inside. Seemed she'd been right after all. Most of Balfour really did want to drown their sorrows tonight.

❖

Freddie sat staring blankly at the TV. The programme, some dire comedy that had so far failed to raise even the slightest of laughs, was still on in the background. Not that she was taking any notice of it.

It was getting late. All was quiet upstairs, but Freddie knew if she went up to bed now, she'd just lie there, churning things over and over in her mind until she'd have to get up again and come downstairs. Besides, she didn't want to wake Pete, because that would unleash a whole cascade of questions about what was causing her insomnia, and then Freddie would have to admit she'd let her guard down and kissed Tag and…

She hauled herself up from the sofa and padded across the lounge in the half-light. Light flickering from the TV screen cast eerie shapes across the wall. She snapped the kettle on, then sat at the kitchen table and dwelt on what had happened that afternoon. How could she have been so weak? So stupid? Freddie plunged her head into her hands and scratched at her hair in irritation. The one thing she'd been so careful not to do, and what had happened? Tag had cried because of the mill and Freddie had let her resolve weaken too easily.

She'd been so damn good at keeping her guard up for this long too. She had Charlotte to thank for that. But to think one look from Tag had sent her defences tumbling was infuriating. Freddie had let Tag get to her when she'd promised herself that all the time she was Skye's guardian, she'd never let anyone get too close. She hadn't bargained on Tag coming into her life, though.

With the kettle bubbling angrily behind her, Freddie picked up her phone. She dreaded what she might see on her screen. Had Tag texted? Had she rung and left her a phone full of questions? Freddie had left her phone out in the kitchen the whole evening deliberately. If she couldn't see it or hear it, she couldn't answer it. And if she didn't have to speak to Tag, then she didn't exist, and their kiss had never happened, and her hurting and confusion would go away. There was that reverse psychology shit again. She was getting good at that.

Freddie put the phone down and sighed. It was just a fucking phone. An inanimate object, incapable of reading her innermost thoughts, nothing more.

The kettle boiled.

But *had* Tag called? She snatched the phone up and pressed the screen.

No, she hadn't. Good.

Freddie puffed her cheeks out, not knowing whether to be happy or sad. Flashbacks of her kiss with Tag up at the watermill still hustled in her mind. Stronger and more intense with each blink of her eyes. If she closed her eyes, she could still taste Tag. She unconsciously licked her lips. The memory of how it had felt to finally kiss her sent a pulse down through her body. Freddie felt herself swaying and snapped her eyes open. She'd been so stupid. Kissing Tag had been everything she'd thought it would be—better, even—but it just couldn't happen again.

A cloud of steam billowed from the boiled kettle. It swirled around Freddie before lifting to the ceiling and disappearing. Sleep or no sleep, she should get to bed now, or questions would be asked, she just knew.

Freddie gripped her phone tighter. She needed to make sure nothing like what had happened that afternoon ever happened again, and that meant staying away from Tag until she finally returned to England.

It would be easy, she was sure of it. Skye would be upset, sure, but Freddie would stay home more. She'd give her so much attention Skye wouldn't have time to think about Tag, and then nor would she. Freddie quickly fired off a text to Tim, knowing he'd still be up.

Not coming in tomorrow. Feeling ill. Will you be okay on your own?

She pulled herself away from the counter and busied herself making a chamomile tea. She looked back over her shoulder when she heard her phone hum its way across the kitchen table.

Tim. Short and sweet: *No worries. Get well soon x*

Freddie took a sip from her tea, grimacing at the heat. She added cold water from the tap at the sink. Better. She picked her phone up again and scrolled down until she found all her and Tag's texts. Reassuring herself that she really was doing the right thing, she deleted one after the other. Each one disappeared into the darkness of the room until no more reminders of Tag were left. This was absolutely the right thing to do. She walked from the kitchen, switching lights off as she went, and headed up to bed.

Suddenly she had never felt so alone.

❖

Tag's key scraped in the front door. She knew she was making a racket, the sound of her footsteps heavy in the hallway, the clatter of her boots being kicked off. She threw her bag noisily down to the floor and flung her coat towards the rack. It missed its mark and slithered down the wall.

"Fuck." Would nothing go right? She shuffled across the wooden hall floor and into the kitchen, opening the fridge door, extracted a beer, then slammed the fridge shut. She opened the beer bottle with a satisfying hiss.

"That you, Tag?" Blair called out from the lounge. "Only one person could ever make that much noise entering a house."

"If it's not, you're being burgled."

"They'd have to bring it in before they could take it out. Most expensive thing we've got in this place is the TV, and that's over five years old."

"Good job us Graingers aren't materialistic then." Tag flopped down on the sofa next to him.

"You missed dinner," Blair said.

"Not hungry." Tag drank back her beer.

"And, hello? What happened to *Solidarity, bro*?" Blair signalled to her beer.

Tag didn't answer.

"What? No pithy comeback?"

"Nope."

"So how did it go?"

"How did what go?"

Blair moved in his chair. "Your photo-taking session at the mill?"

"Oh. That." Tag had totally forgotten. "Fine."

Freddie hadn't contacted her. She'd pushed her off when she was kissing her, had fled from the watermill, and Tag hadn't heard another word from her. Just like that. Hours had passed. Hours wandering in the rain, checking her fucking phone every five minutes. And still no word.

"Just fine?"

"Just fine." Tag chugged back some beer. "Jeez, Blair."

"Right." Blair picked up the TV remote and absent-mindedly flicked up and down the channels. "Tetchy, aren't we?"

"Nope."

"And Freddie?"

Freddie? Tag glared at him. What about Freddie I-made-a-mistake Metcalfe? She seethed. Any rationale gathered up while she'd plodded the rainy streets of Balfour about what Freddie had done had blown away like dust. Her hurt at being practically thrown off her had changed into anger and embarrassment. Had she read the signals wrong? Nope, Freddie had given her enough hints to know she was definitely interested, hadn't she? Tag had thought Freddie was different from Anna, but now it seemed she wanted to be as big a head-fuck as she was. She should have known better.

Why had Freddie done it? Given out signals then fled from her, even when Tag had reassured her she wasn't like Charlotte? Tag tapped her fingers on her knee. All reasoning disappeared, so all Tag had to cling to was self-preservation. That would get her through the knowledge that Freddie didn't want her.

"What about Freddie?" Tag stared at the label on her bottle.

"Did you see her?" Blair sighed. "Talk your plans through with her?"

"Why would I have seen her?" She was being childish as well as awkward, she knew.

"Because you disappeared up to the mill over six hours ago," Blair said, "and because the only time you're not here these days is when you're with her."

"She didn't need to be there. She knows what I wanted from her." Tag stewed. Oh yes, Freddie knew exactly what she wanted—both at the mill and outside. "It's up to her now."

"Freddie will come up trumps." Blair settled back on the sofa. "She always knows what's best."

But best for whom?

CHAPTER TWENTY-FIVE

"Mm." Great. Tag had managed to forget Freddie for five minutes and now here was Ellen talking about her, ten to the dozen. Tag slumped in her chair.

Two days had passed. How could those two days have dragged so much, though? Despite being caught up in a maelstrom of meetings at Glenside, afternoons in the mountains with Magnus photographing landscapes for the mill advertisements, and phone calls to printers, Tag had never felt so alone. She'd successfully avoided going anywhere near the mill too. Not that it mattered. Freddie, according to Ellen, had called in sick both days since the incident in the watermill. No one had seen her on the school run, no one had heard from her. It was as though she'd retreated back into her safety bolt so she didn't have to think about, or bump into, Tag. That suited Tag just fine. She'd been hoping for some sort of acknowledgement that their kiss had actually happened. But as the hours and days stretched ever longer, and the silence from Freddie became even more deafening, it was clear that Freddie was doing everything she could to avoid her. She wanted to be like that? Fine. She wanted to pretend it never happened? That suited Tag just fine too. If only her heart would comply.

"Our regulars already adore Freddie enough as it is." Ellen watched Tag carefully. "I think new customers would love to have bread-making classes with her."

That was so damn cute. Tag shook her head. Enough.

"Freddie is the lynchpin that holds this place together," Blair said. "I seriously don't know what we'd do without her, do you?"

A meeting with the Freddie fan club. Just what Tag needed. She ran her hands through her hair.

"We could throw in a free lunch with the cost of the courses," Tag said. Subtle ignoring. Always good. "Maybe give them a recipe pack, a bag of free flour, and a Watermill apron." That had been Freddie's idea. They'd laughed about it and mucked about a bit.

Then kissed.

They'd kissed, and then Freddie had run off and now wouldn't even speak to her, and—

"I like it." Ellen was talking. Were they still even there? "Something they can go home with and tell their friends about."

Blair wrote it down. At least he was taking it seriously.

"Redesigning too," Tag said. That had also been Freddie's idea. She sighed. Focus. "The place needs a fresh new look."

"If you think so."

"I do." Tag paused. It was time to hit Blair and Ellen with her master plan. "And I think Magnus could help us with it."

"Magnus?" Ellen and Blair said in unison.

"I thought about it the other day," Tag said. "You know he can draw, right?"

Ellen looked confused.

"I swear to God! Do you lot ever even actually talk to one another?" Tag threw up her hands. "This is why he's been coming out with me and photographing things. The kid's got an artistic eye."

"I don't understand," Blair said.

"Magnus is the most awesome artist I've ever met," Tag said. "You've never seen his pictures?"

"His school stuff, yeah," Ellen said. "I know his art teacher is very impressed with his work."

"And I know he likes scribbling stuff down," Blair began, "but—"

"Scribbling doesn't do it justice," Tag said. "Sit." She pointed to a chair each. "Believe me, what Magnus can do is far better than just scribbling. Let me explain." Tag described the drawings she'd seen, the amazing detail of Magnus's sketches.

"Edinburgh?" Blair's brows knitted in confusion. "That was over a year ago."

"The one and only time we ever took him," Ellen added.

"Okay, well," Tag said, "he drew a picture of some fancy house he saw, and trust me. It has to be seen to be believed."

"It's good?" Blair asked.

"It's more than good." Tag nodded solemnly. "It's the sort of drawing you'd expect a forty-year-old artist to do, not a thirteen-year-old."

"He would have been twelve when he did it," Ellen said slowly. "We went for my thirtieth, remember?"

"That makes it all the more amazing, then," Tag said. "Magnus could totally do the artwork for the advertising banner for the bypass. Maybe he could do some prints of the mill too. Sell them in the gift shop. Trust me, people would love it."

"I don't know, Tag," Blair said, sighing. "I've been thinking. Advertising? Rebranding? Prints? Bread-making classes? It all seems like such a mountain to climb at the moment."

"But one we can all climb together, surely?" They just had to. Anyway, how could she let everyone down now? After all her promises? She'd vowed she'd give it everything she had to get the mill back on its feet again. And despite everything, she still owed it to Freddie, even though Freddie wanted to avoid her. That was Freddie's choice. She just wanted to be friends? Fine. But there was no way Tag was going to let her down. Freddie'd been let down enough in her life. Well, no more.

"Dude, you told them about my drawings!" Magnus flung himself down on his bed. "I said don't say anything, didn't I?"

"Is it such a big deal?" Tag sat on the edge of Magnus's bed. "I think you could totally be just what they need right now."

"Dad thinks I'm nuts," Magnus said.

"No, he doesn't."

"He thinks I should be getting myself ready for life on the farm," Magnus said, "not drawing pictures. If he thinks I spend all my time in my room drawing pictures, he's going to go mental. Why do you think I always downplay what my art teacher tells me at school? Being good at art means jack to Dad."

"I already told him you really like drawing," Tag said gently, "and he didn't go mental."

"Seriously?" Magnus looked dubious.

"Seriously."

Tag sensed him soften.

Magnus sighed. "I like keeping my stuff to myself, you know?" he said. "It's like, it's the only thing I have for myself. I like that no one else knows about it."

"Except me."

"Except you," Magnus agreed. "But you're cool, so it's okay."

"Thanks," Tag said, "I'm honoured."

"You should be," Magnus said. "Not even Sonny knows how much I love drawing, and Sonny knows *everything* about me."

"You've no idea how much this is helping us," Tag said. She hesitated. "Your dad's really pleased you're doing this."

Magnus slunk her a shy look. "You think?"

"I know."

His face reddened.

"He thought you could sketch us some pictures of the mill itself," Tag said. "Use the photos I took the other day up at the watermill." A flashback caught her unawares, as vivid as one of her photographs. Freddie, inches from her. Tag wrung her hands and stared down at the rug on Magnus's floor, desperately trying to get her breath back under control. No text since Freddie had fled from the watermill, and no reply to Tag's texts. No presence up at the cafe for two days. But today Freddie was there; Tag had made a point of finding out from Ellen. Yet she still hadn't called.

"I could totally draw the watermill," Magnus said casually. "Probably do it from memory, to be honest."

"You're awesome." Tag high-fived him.

"I know."

Decision made, Tag stepped to the door and yanked it open. Blair appeared at the top of the stairs.

"Have you spoken to him?" Blair asked.

"I have." Tag stood aside to let him pass. "Now it's up to you to talk to him some more." She rubbed Blair's arm. "Talking is always good, you know."

She shut the door behind her.

"All right, kiddo?" She heard Blair's low voice rumble from behind the door. "Your auntie tells me you've something here that I'd like to see. I think you could really help us…"

Tag felt happy as she walked away from Magnus's room. Perhaps one problem was on its way to being sorted. Now, if she could just work through some of her own, beginning with the dilemma that was Freddie.

CHAPTER TWENTY-SIX

"Dad would be spinning in his grave at the thought of making so many changes, you know that?" Blair said.

"I think Dad would be only too pleased that the Graingers were working together to get this place back up on its feet," Tag corrected, "especially after everything." She paused. "I think he'd be happy with what else I'm going to do too."

Blair looked at her.

"I'm going back to England." Tag rose from her chair.

"You're kidding, right?" Blair's face fell.

"My time here is up." Tag shrugged. Wasn't that the truth? Her time with Freddie, apparently, was up too. "You don't need me so much here now that our plans are being put into motion. Anna's asked me to help deliver a contract in Liverpool. My salary will be doubled." And if Freddie didn't want her in her life? Well, maybe putting some distance between them would make the hurt go away.

"So you're running out on us again?" Blair's eyes followed her as she paced around the room.

Tag whirled round. "I'm going down there to make some wrongs right."

"And the mill?" Blair's face was white with fury. "Magnus? Me?"

"That's why I'm going back there." Tag's voice rose an octave. "Don't you see? I need to go back there for you all: you, Magnus, Freddie." Especially for Freddie. Give her the space she so evidently needed.

"How will disappearing when we all need you possibly help us?" Blair asked. "You're not doing it for us, you're doing it for yourself. Just like all those years ago."

"Except this time I'll be coming back." Tag held her hand silencing Blair. "I feel like I've started to get the mill back on the straight and narrow."

"You have," Blair said. "Magnus has drawn up some amazing flyers, we've got advertisements going out next week, bookings coming in thick and fast. We've been given permission to put a sign up on the bypass—"

"Which I can work on, via Skype, with Magnus while I'm in Liverpool. I can go back to England with a clearer conscience than when I arrived." Tag smiled. "And while I'm there, I'm going to transfer my savings and get it wired to your bank."

"For me?"

"For everyone," Tag corrected. "My savings will pay off our debts, and help pay for all this awesome new advertising Magnus will be working on."

"Tag, you—"

Tag walked away from his protestations. "And my new salary from the Branson deal? Three-quarters of it's yours. That'll keep the mill afloat. Pay off bills. Help pay staff salaries." Tag could live on a quarter salary. Sure, she'd have to stay on in her apartment that Anna helped pay for and let Anna call the shots, but…

"But you won't be here to see it all work out." Blair stood. "You're telling me you'd go back to Liverpool and work for Anna so you can help us up here? You'd leave Magnus and Freddie and Skye behind, work in a job you hate, for a boss you hate even more, just so we can keep the mill running?"

"That's exactly what I'm telling you." Blair's angry words to her, on the first day she'd come back to Balfour, dripped into her head. "Because we all have to make sacrifices for our family, don't we?"

"You don't have to do this."

"I do." Tag's mind was made up. "It's only a four-month contract. Plenty enough time to pay off our debts up here and start again." Suddenly everything was so much clearer. "And I *will* come back. Once this contract is up, I'll be on the first flight back to Scotland.

Then I'm going to buy my own place in Balfour and be a part of this family again." That felt good, saying it out loud.

"You're really serious about this?" Blair couldn't keep the smile from his face. She knew he could see it in her face that this time, she truly meant it.

"Really." Tag lifted her head higher. "I want to prove to you, to Magnus...to Freddie...that I'm going to stick around." It was decided. "After all the hurt I've caused you, I think I owe you that at least, don't I?"

❖

"When you pick me up tonight," Skye said, "can we sing 'Head, Shoulders, Knees, and Toes' again?"

"Hmm?" Freddie turned round. "Yes, okay. If you want." She dug at the grit in her eyes as tiredness snapped at her. Sleepless nights tossing and turning, replaying kisses in watermills, did that to you.

"From the beginning?" Skye hurried beside her. "With all the hands?"

Freddie and Skye both half ran to the school gates. They were late, but it had all been Freddie's fault for oversleeping. When she'd finally awoken, Skye was already up, trying to make herself breakfast. Freddie had stumbled, foggy brained, to a scene of destruction in the kitchen: milk and cereal splattered across the counter. Something else she'd have to sort out when she got back.

"Can we?" Skye's footsteps sounded beside Freddie.

Did ignoring a problem make it go away? Or pretending something never happened? She wasn't being fair on Tag, she knew. Even though the kiss had been everything she knew it would be— more, possibly—Freddie knew it couldn't happen again. And if that meant ignoring Tag, then so be it.

"Freddie," Skye pressed.

"From the beginning, yes." Freddie handed Skye her school rucksack. "And all the hands, yes. Of course."

"Yes!" Skye took her rucksack and hooked it carefully over each shoulder. "See you later"—she reached up on her toes and kissed Freddie on her cheek—"alligator."

"In a while"—Freddie kissed her back—"croco—"

"—dile." Skye giggled and ran to the school door. She yanked it open, sketched a wave, and disappeared.

Freddie stared at the closed door. She always missed Skye the very second she disappeared in through the door. She knew, of course, that Skye didn't give her a moment's thought once they'd parted—too busy spinning Bethany Davies a tale, or breathlessly telling her teacher about Paddington's or Fudge's latest escapade.

Freddie hitched up her bag. She wondered if Skye had been talking about Tag to anyone at school. She'd already had to explain at least three times why Tag hadn't been round lately. She sighed. No point in worrying about that now. Freddie turned to go, the day stretching out in front of her until it was time to pick Skye up again. She ambled away from the school gates, already thinking ahead to dinner. Perhaps they'd have pasta. Skye's favourite. She'd be pleased; Freddie pictured the look on her face when she told her later when she picked her up.

This was Freddie's life: school run-cafe-school run-home-dinner. Not kissing Tag on the fourth floor of a watermill on a Monday afternoon. She dug her hands into her pockets and screwed up her fists inside, then marched purposefully back to her car. That wasn't her; she was a mother to a little girl who needed her more than she needed anyone else in the world.

And the sooner Freddie got that into her head, the sooner she could stop hurting.

❖

Freddie brooded in the dim light of her lounge. The wildlife programme that was playing on the TV in the background could have been about anything. Occasionally a kaleidoscope of colours from the TV screen caught her eye, or a loud burst of music pulled her attention to it, but other than that, she remained slumped, impassively, and allowed the darkness to surround her.

Skye was in bed, finally. She'd asked about *her* again just that afternoon. Tag was fun, she'd told her; Tag told her funny stories and gave her presents. She missed Tag because she pulled faces at her when Freddie wasn't looking, then acted like she hadn't when she finally succeeded in making Skye dissolve into giggles, so Freddie wondered what was going on. Tag chased her round the garden until Skye got hiccups. She pretended to be a monster, making Skye double over with mock fear. Tag, Skye told Freddie, made her insides go all squishy when she did her special monster growl that Skye pretended she didn't like, but secretly really loved. Tag was the distraction that made Skye forget Charlotte ever existed—and that's just what Freddie was afraid of.

Freddie itched with irritation at her own stubborn stupidity. She jabbed at the buttons on the remote. Her pique reached its zenith. She'd not spoken to nor heard from Tag in days. Freddie tossed the remote to one side; she hunkered down further into her sofa and exhaled slow and long. But then, she didn't blame her. Freddie had made it crystal clear by her actions up at the watermill that kissing her had been a mistake. Despite Skye's protestations that she wanted to see Tag, invite her over for tea, or go to the park again, Freddie had stayed firm. Skye would thank her one day, she just knew. Skye would understand that Freddie always, without exception, had her interests at heart. And if it meant the pain Freddie was feeling now was worth it eventually, then so be it. The emptiness, the anger at her situation, and the pain—all worth it if it meant Skye was protected.

Freddie rolled her head as she heard the doorbell ring. A light coughing sounded just outside the lounge window, by the front door. Female. Nervous. Freddie knew she wouldn't have to look outside to see who it was.

She clambered to her feet and made for the front door. Nerves, taut as wires, teased her as she opened the door and faced Tag.

"Hi." The all-too-familiar butterflies flitted about her as she stared into Tag's eyes.

"Yeah, hi." Tag made minimal eye contact back. Was she as nervous as Freddie was? "Can I come in?"

"Sure." Freddie pulled the door open wider.

"I'm sorry to come round so late." Tag addressed Freddie over her shoulder. Freddie's nerves clicked up another notch. Tag was being so formal. So cold. "I thought I'd better come and see you in person, rather than you hearing it from someone else."

They walked to the lounge in silence. Tag sank down into a chair, her hands clenched in her lap.

"I came to say goodbye." Tag cleared her throat. "I'm leaving Balfour."

Nausea hit Freddie's throat. Goodbye?

An advert on the TV, with loud music and cheering, flared into life. Annoying, but nevertheless a welcome distraction to her queasiness. She stared at it while she formulated a lucid answer to Tag. "Back to Liverpool?" she finally asked.

Tag nodded. "I've been offered a contract to work on."

"At Deveraux's?"

"Four months. Good money."

"Too good to turn down, hey?" Freddie's heart was breaking at the prospect, but she couldn't let Tag see. Couldn't let her inside her head. Couldn't allow her to read her thoughts.

Freddie had had six months of getting used to being single, and then Adam Grainger had died and started something which Freddie couldn't stop. If Adam was still alive, there would have been no Tag in her life. No Tag to infiltrate her every thought or to make Freddie jump every time her phone sang or the door to the cafe swung open. No Tag to make Freddie wake up each morning, hoping she'd drop by the cafe just because she was passing. And now she was going again, and Freddie knew it was all down to her and her damn morals. Freddie felt wounded, cut up by her own principles, and yet even though Tag was sitting here, telling her she was leaving, she *still* couldn't bring herself to tell her how she felt.

"Something like that." Tag smiled. There was none of her normal light, Freddie noticed, behind the smile.

"So your work here's done?" Tag had fulfilled her obligations and was heading home. Wasn't that how it was always going to be?

"No." Tag shook her head. "I've barely even started." She took a deep breath. "I'm going because I think it's the right thing to do for everyone." She leaned forward in her chair. "Balfour and the mill? They'll never be far from my mind. Everything I'll do while I'm back in England will be for the business. I'll plough my way through this contract I have to work on because it's what'll pay my wages. Then I'll work like holy hell each evening on advertising for the mill.

Grabbing favours where I can. Ringing contacts. Trying to get grants. Making things happen."

Freddie stared at her.

"I've never wanted anything more," Tag continued. "I've never wanted to work so damned hard in all my life. Because this time it matters. This time it means something. For the first time in my life, my life *means* something because I have a goal." Her eyes sought Freddie's. "Because that goal is you."

Freddie's head swam. The room closed in around her. Tag's words echoed off the walls. *That goal is you.* Tag wanted her as much as Freddie wanted Tag.

Go to her. Tell her how you feel, before it's too late.

"When will you go?" Freddie hated herself right at that moment.

"In the morning," Tag replied. "First train out."

"It's a shame you won't get a chance to say goodbye to Skye." Freddie spoke robotically. "She'll miss you."

"I'll miss her." Tag's voice broke. "And you."

Freddie nodded. *Answer her. Tell her.*

Silence consumed them.

"I love you," Tag said simply. "And I know you don't feel the same way about me, but I'm hoping if I can prove to you that I mean every word I say, you'll feel the same one day." She clenched her fists. "If it takes four months, four years, I'll wait. I'll wait as long as it takes until you can finally trust me and know that I'll never, *ever* let you or Skye down."

The walls squeezed the breath from Freddie. "I…" she began.

"Kissing you in the watermill the other day was everything I dreamed it would be." Tag gave her entire focus to Freddie, consuming her. "I'm just sorry you didn't feel the same way."

Freddie's throat closed. Why couldn't she answer?

"Will you at least think about us while I'm away?" Tag pleaded. "Think about how good we could be together? You, me, and Skye?"

"You know everything I do is for that little girl upstairs, don't you?" Finally Freddie's words would come, even though it wasn't the answer Tag wanted. "She's been through so much in her short life."

"I know." Tag stood. There was nothing more to say. "I'll be in regular contact with Blair while I'm away." Her voice sounded choked. "Anything you want to ask about the rebranding, or whatever, ask him and he can ask me."

Tag stood awkwardly in the middle of the lounge. She looked so lost, so vulnerable. All Freddie had to do was tell her she loved her too, and that she'd miss her every second of every day, and she could let Tag leave with at least a small pinprick of hope. But Freddie couldn't even do that for her. The nausea returned.

Instead of telling Tag what she needed to hear, Freddie simply walked her back to the front door.

"I'm doing this for you," Tag repeated. She sounded distraught. "Giving you space, because I think that's what you want."

"I know." And if Freddie had to force a smile on her face every day Tag was away and pretend she was okay, then that's what she'd do. Because that's what she'd always had to do. "And it *is* what I want."

Finally, Freddie went to her and enveloped her in her arms. "I'm sorry," she said. "I'm so sorry." She buried her head into her hair, breathed in. Savoured her. The feel of her. How good she felt in her arms. Reluctantly, slowly, Freddie stepped away and opened the door.

Then Tag was gone. Just like that.

It was only when her front door was firmly shut and she could hear Tag's footsteps receding back down the path that Freddie finally gave in to her tears.

CHAPTER TWENTY-SEVEN

How could three months feel like three years? Tag stirred her coffee, her fourth that morning, and stared at the screen of her laptop. It was only the coffee that was keeping her going—certainly not the logos for the Branson project which she'd been working through all morning, seeking inspiring tag lines but finding none. Inspiration for anything Deveraux-based, she figured, had been thin on the ground since her return to Liverpool.

Tag sighed. It was no good though; her concentration wasn't going to stretch to another photo of Oliver Branson grinning back at her. Certainly not until she'd finished this coffee, anyway. She snapped the lid of her laptop down and flung herself back in her chair, raking her hands through her hair.

She glanced out of the window. Sun-buttered petunias on her balcony—Tag's attempt at creating some sort of flower garden for her fourth-floor apartment—bobbed their heads in the light May breeze. Tag stared out, breathing in slowly, picturing the changing landscape of Balfour. The lower mountains would be green and lush now, but there would still be snow up on the Ben, she was sure of it. Perhaps not enough for Magnus to snowboard on, though. Just a light smattering on the tops, giving the town one last reminder of winter.

"You're not back until June?" Magnus had been quiet when Tag had told him. He'd hung back in his room, picking at the corner of his phone cover, avoiding eye contact with her. "It's going to seem like forever."

"For me too, bud." Tag had sat on his bed, hating every second of it. "But we can talk every night. The time will fly by."

But it hadn't, for Tag. Hours had turned into days, then into weeks. Tag's mind never stopped turning, never stopped thinking about the mill, about Blair, about Magnus.

Or about Freddie.

She'd thrown herself into work for the mill in a vain attempt to make her brain stop thinking about Freddie, and while inspiration was nonexistent for Oliver Branson, it was overflowing for the mill. Grants had been secured, an engineer had been employed to overhaul the old threshing machine, adverts and banners had been printed, and the press now knew more about Graingers than they'd known in over a hundred years.

It was working. Her plan was working. Reports from Blair told her that her sacrifice had been worth it. Visitor numbers were up, historians were enthusing about the heritage of the watermill, and the bread-making courses were taking off. In short, the mill was well on its way to being a hive of industry once more. Back to how it had been when Tag had been a child. Sure, there was a long way to go yet, but things were definitely going in the right direction. She should have been delighted; her father, she thought over the weeks, would have been proud of her.

And yet her emptiness remained.

The rap on her door snapped her from her thoughts. Pushing the laptop away from her, Tag stood and went to the door.

"I'm hoping you're Tag Grainger." A woman stared back at her, a large brown parcel in her arms.

"You hoped right."

"Found this in the lobby addressed to you." The woman bundled the parcel towards Tag. "Thought I'd bring it up, considering I'm only down the corridor from you."

Tag took the parcel and frowned.

"Number forty-two?" The woman jerked her head to her left.

"Right. Okay." Tag looked at her. Nope, still didn't recognize her. "Well, thanks. Appreciate it."

Tag closed the door. She turned the parcel over and grinned when she saw the return address. Ripping the parcel open, Oliver Branson now well and truly forgotten, Tag caught the contents before they tumbled to the floor. In amongst the photos, flyers, complimentary letters from both past customers and new about the new-look cafe, and offers from coach companies for tours, was a small pile of the previous week's newspapers.

Tag sank to her knees and spread the papers out on the floor in front of her. There were Balfour's local paper, three from the adjoining towns, plus a few from much further afield, stretching from Glasgow to Aberdeen. There were the county's weekly paper, plus three magazines, all from the local area too. Tag picked up Balfour's local newspaper, flicking through until she found what she was looking for. Page five. Tag nodded in approval. Not bad. The headline jumped out at Tag:

> LOCAL FLOUR MILL TELLS CUSTOMERS:
> WE'RE STILL OPEN FOR BUSINESS!

She read on:

> Balfour's last remaining working watermill wants to let their customers know they're very much still open for business, despite the recent opening of the Lyster bypass. Graingers' Watermill and Bakery, run by the brother-and-sister team, Blair and Tag Grainger, have been milling flour for over 150 years.

Tag's eye ran over the words. Brother and sister team? Tag smiled. Nice.

> And now they're proud to shout it out. Their banner, advertising the mill's cafe, gift shop, plus historic watermill, went up on the bypass yesterday, and Blair Grainger, thirty-two, said he couldn't be happier.

Tag looked at the photo. There was Blair, standing next to a huge, bright banner at the side of the road, looking lean and tanned, with a teapot in one hand and a plate of biscuits in the other. "A teapot?" Tag groaned. "Lame, Blair." She chuckled under her breath and reached for her mobile. Blair answered after two rings.

"So what's with the teapot, bro?" she asked.

Blair groaned. "Photographer's idea. Trust me, not mine."

"Looking good, though." Tag flicked through the next paper in her pile. The same picture, slightly different headline, faced her.

"It's been mad." Tag could hear Blair moving about. "The banner went up a week ago and we've been inundated since."

"Awesome." Tag was delighted. "So it really is all working, then? Everything you've been telling me is true?"

"Everything," Blair confirmed. "The ads you've been working on, the coach tours, the bread courses." He paused. "Freddie's been amazing with those, by the way."

Tag's heart squeezed. "Has she?" Her voice was quiet.

"Kind of thrown herself into everything," Blair said slowly.

"Good, good." Tag nodded, afraid to say any more.

"There's a photo in one of the magazines I think you'll like," Blair said. "Of Freddie. Of us all. Just wish you could have been there too." Tag heard him breathing quietly down the phone. "After all, without your input, none of this would have been possible."

"It's all about teamwork, Blair," Tag said, her voice breaking. "Always has been."

Her mind was racing. There was a picture of Freddie? Her eyes fell to the magazines.

She wanted to see her.

She didn't want to see her.

"Just look at the photo of Freddie, Tag," Blair said gently. "You'll like it."

He got it. He *so* got it.

Tag smiled.

"We'll Skype later, yeah?" Blair said. "Magnus wants to see you."

"Sure. Look forward to it."

The call ended. Tag looked back to the magazines, knowing that inside one, she'd be able to do what she hadn't done for nearly four months: look into Freddie's eyes. She swallowed. How could the prospect of looking at a photo make her heart pound so ferociously? Her hands feeling strangely clammy, Tag picked up one of the magazines, briskly thumbing through until she found the right page.

As she opened up the double-page spread, her breath caught. In colour, staring back at the camera, was Freddie. She was standing with Blair, Ellen, and Tom, outside the heavy oak doors to the watermill.

The watermill.

Tag looked away, back out to her flowers. She hadn't allowed herself to think about Freddie, or their kiss in the watermill that day. Each time her brain drifted back to her, to remember her voice, her eyes, the outline of her mouth, Tag would snap the TV on, or turn some music up until it was loud enough to send Freddie away from her again. She wouldn't allow herself to wallow. She couldn't. Every memory of her, every conversation they'd had, every touch was too painful. Tag had decided the day she returned to Liverpool that forgetting about Freddie, at least for the time she was away from her, was the only way she'd make it through the four months.

But with Freddie so close to her again, Tag couldn't look away. She stared into the eyes that looked back at her, consumed every tiny detail of her face. Loved how she looked in a simple turquoise T-shirt that perfectly complemented her auburn hair and showed off slightly tanned, taut arms. She looked stunning. Classic. Beautiful. Tag hadn't seen her in that T-shirt before. Of course she hadn't; last time she'd seen Freddie they'd still been in winter clothes. Tag pulled her glance away again. It had been such a long time.

The flowers bobbed. Tag wiped away a tear. She hadn't cried—well, not much—since she'd left. Not in the last three weeks or so, anyway. It was curious, she thought, as she twisted the ball of her hand into her eye, that the one thing that had set her off again, after such a long time, was Freddie's turquoise T-shirt.

The AC was on in Freddie's car for the first time that year. The cool air tickled her skin as she pulled out of her parking spot in the car park of the college where she'd just been meeting with the college's course directors. It had been a successful meeting: another twenty places secured on her bread-making afternoon, to be held in July. A good mixture of people too. Freddie slid her sunglasses up her nose. It had been a good day all round, really, and she should be happy. If only she could shake the unhappiness that had kept her shackled since Tag had left.

Tag might have left Balfour, but she had never left Freddie's heart. As hard as she'd tried, memories of Tag repeatedly flooded her mind: their very first conversation, when Tag had grumbled about her bill; when Tag had cried on her shoulder at the park. When they'd kissed, and Freddie had been overwhelmed by an explosion of fireworks.

Tag's presence was everywhere. Blair talked about her endlessly; Magnus gave Freddie in-depth analyses of games played with her online; customers repeatedly asked her who was to thank for the resurgence in the cafe.

Freddie swung her car out onto the main road.

"Blair's sister," she'd tell customers. "Blair's younger sister has turned this whole business around." Saying her name out loud was too painful.

Tag, Freddie now thought as she sped up, had kept her promise on two things. She'd put her heart and soul into saving the business, just as she said she would. Her money, sent home each week to Blair, had paid for enough advertising, meetings, favours, and lunches out with prospective investors to see the business well into Christmas. But more importantly, she'd given Freddie the space she'd needed. Since Tag had left, she'd heard nothing from her. No texts, no phone calls, nothing.

She had been true to her word.

Freddie slipped into the flowing traffic of the bypass heading around the town centre and hit the accelerator, pushing her sunglasses up onto the top of her head as the sun slid behind a large band of clouds. But it had been more than just Tag proving she'd been true to her word. She'd proven things on so many other different levels too, adding more layers to her character than Freddie had ever noticed before. Tag loved her family. That was a given. But she also loved the mill and loved Balfour. Giving up her time and money had been so much more than just trying to win back her family's respect and affection. Freddie knew that now. She glanced in her rearview mirror and pulled out into the fast lane. Tag genuinely wanted to be a part of the business again—the same business she'd hated as a teenager. But people grew up, and it seemed as though Tag had finally understood that.

Her campaign had been awesome. Better than Blair or Freddie could have ever imagined. It wasn't a temporary fix, either; Tag had proved she was in it for the long run. She was dedicated to her family, to the business, to Balfour.

To Freddie. To Skye.

Freddie's thoughts turned to Skye. She'd sometimes asked about Tag, of course, after she'd gone. Still did now. But something about Skye was different. Less concerning than when Charlotte had left. All Freddie's worries had stemmed from Skye, but Freddie now realized, her worries had been groundless. Skye was okay. In fact, for a five-year-old, she'd been positively philosophical about Tag going.

"But this is Tag's home, isn't it?" she'd said recently during another conversation about Tag. "Melissa's cat went missing for ages once, but it still came home. They do. Home's…well, home, isn't it?" Skye had thought very hard about that particular point. "It's where everyone loves you. You can't stay away from somewhere where everyone loves you."

Freddie had been astounded.

"And it's not like Charlotte," Skye had said firmly. "She never said she was coming back. I don't think Charlotte loved us really, but Tag does. That's why she's coming back. Because she loves us."

So instead of the anticipated endless questions and tears from Skye about where Tag had gone, Skye simply hadn't crumbled when Tag had left. She'd been fine. Her world hadn't ended, because she knew, with absolute conviction, that Tag would come back one day.

If only Freddie had been as positive as Skye.

The thought struck her, as she sped down the bypass, that it had been her, rather than Skye, who had asked endless questions and had cried herself to sleep through missing Tag. It had been Freddie, not Skye, who had lost out, and who was desperate for Tag to come back to Balfour. Ultimately, it was Freddie, not Skye, who had crumbled.

The huge advertising hoarding passed Freddie in sea of colours, grabbing her attention as she pressed on down the bypass. Freddie grinned. There it was, at last. *Their* advert: hers and Tag's. The one they'd thought up together the night before they'd kissed. The advert had happened, just as Tag promised it would. It had taken time, money, and a lot of phone calls to the Highways Agency to allow it to be placed on the bypass, but it had happened.

And now Tag wasn't around to see her hard work come to fruition. She couldn't share with Freddie the results of their teamwork. Couldn't enjoy the feeling of knowing they'd both made something happen for the good of the business.

And it had all been Freddie's fault for ever doubting her. Freddie shook her head. She hadn't believed in Tag, even when Skye had, and now she was paying the consequences.

The clouds parted and the sun beamed down again, coating everything in a warm glow. Freddie frowned. The clouds had gone. Everything was suddenly so much clearer. More beautiful. Warm. Suddenly everything made sense; it was as though the clouds parting had given Freddie clarity for the first time in months. She'd been so stupid. So selfish. Freddie pulled back into the fast lane, gripping her steering wheel tighter, her heart racing.

"You idiot," she muttered under her breath. "You absolute idiot."

CHAPTER TWENTY-EIGHT

Tag moved her laptop from her knees and let her head drop back against the sofa. Magnus had Skyped. Again. This time on the pretext of asking Tag how Valmour was supposed to steal diamonds from Argo without getting killed in one of the Xbox games Tag had bought him before she left. Tag had talked him through it, stage by stage. She'd laughed with him, ribbed him for his ineptitude, and missed him more than she'd ever missed him before. She loved hearing from him, hearing how things were progressing up at the mill. She looked forward to every call, gratified that all her hard work for the business was clearly paying off, but each one was agony because it just made her miss home all over again. Magnus had changed too, she was convinced of it. In just a few months. Of course, he hadn't, but Tag's pining process made her brain think that he'd grown some more each time, as if just to prove how long it had been since she'd seen him in the flesh.

What time was it now? Tag grabbed a folder. Inside was her work from Anna for the weekend. It was seven p.m. on a Friday evening and where was she? Holed up in her sterile apartment with a weekend's worth of prints to go through because she had nothing else to do and no one else to see. She looked around her. The apartment was too big. She rattled round it, feeling more and more swallowed up by it each day. What she wanted, of course, was a cute little cottage. Something the right size just for her. Tag sighed. Preferably by a loch, near a mountain, so she could still snowboard with Magnus. A cottage with Blair and Magnus in the next village, and Freddie and Skye just down the road.

Tag snatched the folder up. No thinking about Freddie and Skye. That was the rule. She flicked through the folder, seeing words but seeing nothing. She tossed it to one side and sprang up from the sofa. A drink. That's what was needed. Tag looked at the empty beer bottles lined up in the kitchen. One more wouldn't hurt, would it? She slouched to the kitchen and pulled a fresh bottle from the refrigerator, then listened to the satisfying hiss as she flicked the lid.

Tag glanced at her mobile as she heard it ring. It would be Anna, checking up on her to make sure she'd have everything ready for Monday's presentation. She mouthed an obscenity at it and then drank back her beer. It was the little things that pleased her.

Tag jabbed at the *on* button on her TV. It coughed into life and a quiz show immediately brightened the room. Questions and answers ebbed and flowed as Tag fell back onto the sofa, beer bottle propped on her knee.

The medical name for a shoulder blade…

"Scapula." Tag tossed her answer at the TV.

Clavicle.

You're saying clavicle?

"It's scapula." Tag said aloud.

Yes, Brian.

"It's scapula, you idiot." Tag took a drink from her bottle.

You're saying clavicle. The answer, I'm afraid, is scapula.

"Fuckwit." Tag snapped the TV off.

Only the buzz of the intercom prevented Tag from hurling the remote at the TV. Anna? Surely not. She was at Mason's, wining and dining the Pritchard brothers with Stefan. Tag frowned and ignored the second buzz. The third buzz, however, finally pulled her from the sofa. Cursing, she snatched up the intercom phone. Her planned rebuke died on her lips as she heard the quiet voice at the other end.

Freddie.

❖

Tag was aware that she'd stopped breathing. She rested her head against the wall, the cool of the bricks settling her.

"Are you going to let me in?" Freddie's voice was shaky.

Tag pressed the button without answering. She waited to hear it catch, then replaced the intercom phone in its cradle. The few minutes it took Freddie to come in through the main front door and up to the fourth floor of the apartment block felt like forever. The rap on the door was expected but still made Tag's heart hammer in her chest when she heard it.

The Freddie she answered the door to wasn't the same Freddie she'd left. She looked tired and defeated. Grey smudges shadowed her eyes, caused, Tag guessed, by weeks of lack of sleep. She knew, because her own lack of sleep had done the same to her. Eyes that when she'd first met her seemed to have sunshine in them were now dead. But despite all that, she was still Freddie. The unpretentious disposition was still there. So, too, the beautiful hair and the upturned mouth that made her look like she was always smiling.

"How did you…?" Tag finally found her voice as Freddie came into her apartment.

"Blair gave me your address." Freddie stood awkwardly in the middle of the room.

Tag couldn't take her eyes from her. She was here. She was real. Months of yearning intensified as Tag stood, just feet from Freddie, desperate to touch her. To hold her.

"Blair?" Nerves hit Tag. "Is he okay? Is it Magnus?" She'd only spoken to them hours before. How could they…

"They're fine." Freddie stood in Tag's lounge.

"And Skye? Is she okay? Was she at school today?" The words tumbled out.

"She's fine too." A smile spread across Freddie's face at the mention of Skye's name. "Asks about you all the time."

"Does she?" Tag looked up. "What does she say?"

"She knows you're away working," Freddie said. She gazed around at the spartan lounge. Tag knew what she saw. No pictures, no posters, nothing. Just plain blank walls. "She keeps asking when you're coming to the park with us again."

"What do you tell her?" The thought of Skye asking about her was too much. Tag's voice caught. "A drink. I haven't even offered you a drink." Concentrate on the practicalities. She walked to the kitchen, holding a hand out to Freddie, motioning her to follow. "Do you tell her I miss her?" Tag asked over her shoulder. "Because I do."

"I do tell her, yes." Freddie stressed to Tag's retreating back. "Every day."

"She knows it? Knows I think about her all the time?" Tag turned to face her.

"She knows." Freddie's breath was shallow. "She's fine and…" She took a step closer. "Oh, Tag, I've been so stupid." She took Tag's hand and pulled it to her chest. "I'm so sorry it took so long for me to realize what was staring me in the face all along." Slowly, shakily, she brought Tag's hand to her lips. "I was scared. I needed time."

Tag's breath caught. Had she heard right? "You're here now," she whispered "That's all that matters." And nothing ever had meant so much to Tag.

"I was hiding behind Skye." Freddie looked pained. "Using her as an excuse because I was terrified of falling in love again."

Tag's insides jumped. "In love?"

"I'm in love with you, Tag," Freddie said. "I knew it from the start but I tried to ignore it." She gazed at Tag. "I tried really hard to stay away from you, but I can't do it any more."

Freddie was in love with her? Tag felt light-headed.

"I needed to know Skye wasn't just a novelty to you," Freddie continued. "That none of it was. That you cared about us, the business, being in Balfour."

"I do!" Tag pleaded with her. Surely Freddie hadn't come all the way down here to rake over all her insecurities again? To tell Tag that she loved her but it still wasn't enough?

"I know that now," Freddie said. "It took driving past the advert on the bypass for me to finally see the light."

"The advert?"

"It doesn't matter." Freddie smiled. "All that matters now is that you and I have a future. Together." She hesitated. "If that's what you still want?"

Freddie's worried face was just too much. "You've no idea how long I've waited for you to say that." Tag pulled her closer, hesitating briefly in case Freddie didn't want this. When Freddie didn't move, Tag dipped her head, brushing feather-light kisses across Freddie's neck. She smiled against her skin as she heard Freddie's breath quicken.

"Don't stop," Freddie whispered.

"Are you sure?" Tag asked. "Are you sure this is what you want?" Tag's protestations died on her lips as Freddie cupped her face, pulling her to her again. This time she knew she wasn't going to let her go. Freddie kissed her hard, her body pressed tight against Tag's, making her lose all rational thought.

Freddie moaned from deep in her throat as she felt Tag's warm tongue sweep across hers, impelling her to kiss her with even more passion. This was what she wanted, what she needed. This was everything she'd dreamed of doing again since their kiss up at the watermill. Still cupping her face, Freddie pushed Tag back against the kitchen counter, helping Tag as she pulled herself up onto it. Her body throbbed as Tag wrapped her legs tight around Freddie's waist, her heels digging into her as she urged Freddie closer and closer, desperate to feel her body against her own.

Their kisses were hard and urgent. Weeks of mutual longing spilled over as their lips moved frantically against one another's, Freddie moaning against Tag's lips as Tag kissed her deeper and deeper. Finally, they pulled apart. They leaned their foreheads against one another's, their ragged breath warm against one another's mouths. Freddie traced a finger down Tag's thigh, drawing circles on her jeans, while she waited for her heart to slow down again.

"You were saying?" Freddie smiled against Tag's lips. She draped her arms over her shoulders, linking them behind Tag's neck. She kissed her slowly this time, passion replaced with an intense and slow concentration, letting her lips move so lazily over Tag's, the muscles in her stomach tensed and fluttered.

"Nothing," Tag breathed, when Freddie finally stopped. "Nothing at all."

❖

"I don't know what I'm going to tell Anna." Tag thought out loud.

"Mm?" Freddie rested her head against Tag's chest.

"That I'm leaving again," Tag said. "In the middle of a contract this time, though."

"I'm sure she'll cope," Freddie murmured. She lifted her head. "Anyway, you'll be too busy when you get back to worry about what Anna thinks or doesn't think."

"Blair told me the other night the bakery classes are a sell out," Tag said.

"Thanks to you," Freddie said. "You"—she captured Tag's mouth in a long, slow kiss—"are one very clever girl."

"You and Blair are the ones that got people to sign up."

"You're the one who came up with the idea in the first place."

"So we're both as clever as one another." Tag drew her finger lightly over Freddie's cheek. "I'll settle for that."

"I love you, Tag." Freddie gazed into her eyes. "So much."

"I love you too." Tag grazed her lips gently across Freddie's.

Freddie wriggled herself free from Tag's arms as her phone buzzed in her jeans pocket.

"I have someone here who wants to talk to you." Pete's voice sounded before Freddie could speak. She switched the phone to her other ear and propped herself up on one elbow.

"Freddie?" Skye's voiced echoed down the phone. "Are you in England?" To Skye, it could have been the other side of the world.

"I am." Freddie caught Tag's eye and smiled.

"Pete did me pasta for tea. Is Tag there?"

"She's here somewhere." Freddie writhed as Tag dug her fingers into her ribs. "Wait." She handed the phone to Tag.

"Hi, sweetheart."

"Hi, Tag." Skye's voice was breathy. "I had pasta for tea. What did you have?"

"Oh, nothing as exciting as pasta." Tag laughed. Beer, mostly.

"When are you coming home?" Skye asked.

"Soon." Tag's eyes searched Freddie's. "I promise you." She held the phone away as the squeals rang out.

Freddie took the phone from Tag. "We'll be back soon, okay?" Freddie smiled as she heard Skye's reply. "Yes, she'll be with me. I promise." She met Tag's smiling eyes. "Yes, cross my heart."

After a few prolonged goodnights, Freddie finished the call. She figured she'd let Skye tell Pete in her own inimitable fashion.

Freddie nestled back into the crook of Tag's arm.

"She's happy, huh?" Tag said. She smiled as she felt Freddie nod against her. "Freddie?"

"Yuh-huh?"

"What time did you say there was a train back to Scotland tomorrow?"

"There's a direct one at ten forty a.m. from Lime Street." Freddie's voice was muffled. "Why?"

"Perfect." Tag untangled herself from Freddie, ignoring her protests as she stood. She held out a hand to her and hauled her to her feet. Freddie understood the look in Tag's eyes as she pulled her to her.

They hastened to Tag's bedroom, Freddie kicking the door shut behind them. Tag barely had time to turn around before Freddie had bunched her hands into her hoodie and dragged her to her with such ferocity, Tag nearly stumbled. Their kiss, unlike the delicate, soft kiss they'd just been sharing on the sofa, was fierce. Tag twisted her hands into Freddie's hair as she captured her mouth, releasing a muffled groan.

They parted, both breathing hard, Tag aroused by the dark passion in Freddie's eyes. Inch by inch, she unzipped Freddie's top, kissing each new bit of skin that was exposed. Tag moved her hands under the fabric and pushed it from Freddie's shoulders. Freddie's top crumpled to the floor behind her. She tipped her head back, offering Tag her neck, her breath checking a little when Tag drew her lips, then her tongue, gently across her skin.

Tag pushed Freddie gently down onto the bed. She stood, losing her own top in one swift pull over her head, then returned to Freddie. She straddled Freddie's hips, leaning over her so her hands were planted either side of her head, and traced her lips across her skin, trailing a line of kisses down her body. Her control was impeccable, concentrating on every inch of Freddie's skin, wanting to take her time over each little part of her body.

The lightest of touches from Tag's tongue just below Freddie's ribs made her jerk a little, eliciting grins from them both. Tag concentrated even harder on that area, loving how it made Freddie squirm beneath her.

"Too much?" Tag raised her head, a playful smile on her lips. "Want me to stop?"

"Stop now and you die." Freddie's head fell back against her pillow. "If I don't first."

"What time did you say there was a train out of here in the morning?" Tag whispered, still kissing across her skin.

"I told you," Freddie gasped. "Ten forty a.m."

"Then I'd better not waste a second," Tag said, "had I?"

EPILOGUE

Tag Grainger lightly ran her fingers over the bobbled wood of the door frame and nodded wistfully. Olive green. Perfect. Her eye fell to the small crack in the bottom corner of one of the door's windows. Still there. Still a reminder. Should she replace the pane? Tag smiled. Maybe. Maybe not.

She stepped aside to allow a small group of middle-aged women to pass her, thoughts of cracked panes leaving her head as quickly as they'd entered.

"Are you coming in?" One of the women held the door open. "Or were you just leaving?"

"Coming in." Tag put her hand on the door. "I'm not leaving." *Never leaving.* She followed them into the cafe, the unmistakable odour of fresh coffee and baking enveloping her, comforting her.

Her eyes immediately sought out the counter at the far end of the cafe, lighting up when she saw Freddie. Tag hastened to her.

"Hey."

"Hey."

They gazed at one another.

"You left without saying goodbye this morning." Tag leaned on the counter and threaded her fingers in Freddie's.

"You were sleeping." Freddie squeezed her fingers, making Tag grin. "I didn't want to wake you."

"Tonight's dinner is prepared," Tag said. "Skye's bike is mended, and the guinea pig is lying on a fresh bed of hay."

"You've been busy."

"And she'll be even busier this afternoon." Blair sidled up to Tag at the counter and circled his arm around her shoulders. "Another holiday company wants to come and talk to us about doing some more guided tours."

"I'm on it."

"And Magnus said would you like to hang out for a while at ours later tonight?" Blair laughed. "Something about an assassin he's trying to outwit." He looked at Freddie. "If you can spare her for a few hours?"

"I think so." Freddie leaned her head to one side and looked at Tag, a grin spreading across her face. "After all, we have forever together now, don't we?"

Tag smiled. "Forever," she agreed.

About the Author

KE Payne was born in Bath, the English city, not the tub, and after leaving school, she worked for the British government for fifteen years, which probably sounds a lot more exciting than it really was.

Fed up with spending her days moving paperwork around her desk and making models of the Taj Mahal out of paperclips, she packed it all in to go to university in Bristol and graduated as a mature student in 2006 with a degree in linguistics and history.

After graduating, she worked at a university in the Midlands for a while, again moving all that paperwork around, before finally leaving to embark on her dream career as a writer.

She moved to the idyllic English countryside in 2007 where she now lives and works happily surrounded by dogs and guinea pigs.

Books Available from Bold Strokes Books

Because of You by Julie Cannon. What would you do for the woman you were forced to leave behind? (978-1-62639-199-4)

The Job by Jove Belle. Sera always dreamed that she would one day reunite with Tor. She just didn't think it would involve terrorists, firearms, and hostages. (978-1-62639-200-7)

Making Time by C.J. Harte. Two women going in different directions meet after fifteen years and struggle to reconnect in spite of the past that separated them. (978-1-62639-201-4)

Once The Clouds Have Gone by KE Payne. Overwhelmed by the dark clouds of her past, Tag Grainger is lost until the intriguing and spirited Freddie Metcalfe unexpectedly forces her to reevaluate her life. (978-1-62639-202-1)

The Acquittal by Anne Laughlin. Chicago private investigator Josie Harper searches for the real killer of a woman whose lover has been acquitted of the crime. (978-1-62639-203-8)

An American Queer: The Amazon Trail by Lee Lynch. Lee Lynch's heartening and heart-rending history of gay life from the turbulence of the late 1900s to the triumphs of the early 2000s are recorded in this selection of her columns. (978-1-62639-204-5)

Stick McLaughlin: The Prohibition Years by CF Frizzell. Corruption in 1918 cost Stick her lover, her freedom, and her identity, but a very special flapper and the family bond of her own gang could help win them back—even if it means outwitting the Boston Mob. (978-1-62639-205-2)

Edge of Awareness by C.A. Popovich. When Maria, a woman in the middle of her third divorce, meets Dana, an out lesbian, awareness of her feelings bring up reservations about the teachings of her church. (978-1-62639-188-8)

Taken by Storm by Kim Baldwin. Lives depend on two women when a train derails high in the remote Alps, but an unforgiving mountain, avalanches, crevasses, and other perils stand between them and safety. (978-1-62639-189-5)

The Common Thread by Jaime Maddox. Dr. Nicole Coussart's life is falling apart, but fortunately, DEA Attorney Rae Rhodes is there to pick up the pieces and help Nic put them back together. (978-1-62639-190-1)

Jolt by Kris Bryant. Mystery writer Bethany Lange wasn't prepared for the twisting emotions that left her breathless the moment she laid eyes on folk singer sensation Ali Hart. (978-1-62639-191-8)

Searching For Forever by Emily Smith. Dr. Natalie Jenner's life has always been about saving others, until young paramedic Charlie Thompson comes along and shows her maybe she's the one who needs saving. (978-1-62639-186-4)

A Queer Sort of Justice: Prison Tales Across Time by Rebecca S. Buck. When liberty is only a memory, and all seems lost, what freedoms and hopes can be found within us? (978-1-62639-195-6E)

Blue Water Dreams by Dena Hankins. Lania Marchiol keeps her wary sailor's gaze trained on the horizon until Oly Rassmussen, a wickedly handsome trans man, sends her trusty compass spinning off course. (978-1-62639-192-5)

Rest Home Runaways by Clifford Henderson. Baby boomer Morgan Ronzio's troubled marriage is the least of her worries when she gets the call that her addled, eighty-six-year-old, half-blind dad has escaped the rest home. (978-1-62639-169-7)

Charm City by Mason Dixon. Raq Overstreet's loyalty to her drug kingpin boss is put to the test when she begins to fall for Bathsheba Morris, the undercover cop assigned to bring him down. (978-1-62639-198-7)

Let the Lover Be by Sheree Greer. Kiana Lewis, a functional alcoholic on the verge of destruction, finally faces the demons of her past while finding love and earning redemption in New Orleans. (978-1-62639-077-5)

Blindsided by Karis Walsh. Blindsided by love, guide dog trainer Lenae McIntyre and media personality Cara Bradley learn to trust what they see with their hearts. (978-1-62639-078-2)

About Face by VK Powell. Forensic artist Macy Sheridan and Detective Leigh Monroe work on a case that has troubled them both for years, but they're hampered by the past and their unlikely yet undeniable attraction. (978-1-62639-079-9)

Blackstone by Shea Godfrey. For Darry and Jessa, their chance at a life of freedom is stolen by the arrival of war and an ancient prophecy that just might destroy their love. (978-1-62639-080-5)

Out of This World by Maggie Morton. Iris decided to cross an ocean to get over her ex. But instead, she ends up traveling much farther, all the way to another world. Once there, only a mysterious, sexy, and magical woman can help her return home. (978-1-62639-083-6)

Kiss The Girl by Melissa Brayden. Sleeping with the enemy has never been so complicated. Brooklyn Campbell and Jessica Lennox face off in love and advertising in fast-paced New York City. (978-1-62639-071-3)

Taking Fire: A First Responders Novel by Radclyffe. Hunted by extremists and under siege by nature's most virulent weapons, Navy medic Max de Milles and Red Cross worker Rachel Winslow join forces to survive and discover something far more lasting. (978-1-62639-072-0)

First Tango in Paris by Shelley Thrasher. When French law student Eva Laroche meets American call girl Brigitte Green in 1970s Paris, they have no idea how their pasts and futures will intersect. (978-1-62639-073-7)

The War Within by Yolanda Wallace. Army nurse Meredith Moser went to Vietnam in 1967 looking to help those in need; she didn't expect to meet the love of her life along the way. (978-1-62639-074-4)

Escapades by MJ Williamz. Two women, afraid to love again, must overcome their fears to find the happiness that awaits them. (978-1-62639-182-6)

Desire at Dawn by Fiona Zedde. For Kylie, love had always come armed with sharp teeth and claws. But with the human, Olivia, she bares her vampire heart for the very first time, sharing passion, lust, and a tenderness she'd never dared dream of before. (978-1-62639-064-5)

Visions by Larkin Rose. Sometimes the mysteries of love reveal themselves when you least expect it. Other times they hide behind a black satin mask. Can Paige unveil her masked stranger this time? (978-1-62639-065-2)

All In by Nell Stark. Internet poker champion Annie Navarro loses everything when the Feds shut down online gambling, and she turns to experienced casino host Vesper Blake for advice—but can Nova convince Vesper to take a gamble on romance? (978-1-62639-066-9)

Vermilion Justice by Sheri Lewis Wohl. What's a vampire to do when Dracula is no longer just a character in a novel? (978-1-62639-067-6)

Switchblade by Carsen Taite. Lines were meant to be crossed. Third in the Luca Bennett Bounty Hunter Series. (978-1-62639-058-4)

Nightingale by Andrea Bramhall. Culture, faith, and duty conspire to tear two young lovers apart, yet fate seems to have different plans for them both. (978-1-62639-059-1)

No Boundaries by Donna K. Ford. A chance meeting and a nightmare from the past threaten more than Andi Massey's solitude as she and Gwen Palmer struggle to understand the complexity of love without boundaries. (978-1-62639-060-7)

Timeless by Rachel Spangler. When Stevie Geller returns to her hometown, will she do things differently the second time around or will she be in such a hurry to leave her past that she misses out on a better future? (978-1-62639-050-8)

Second to None by L.T. Marie. Can a physical therapist and a custom motorcycle designer conquer their pasts and build a future with one another? (978-1-62639-051-5)

Seneca Falls by Jesse Thoma. Together, two women discover love truly can conquer all evil. (978-1-62639-052-2)

A Kingdom Lost by Barbara Ann Wright. Without knowing each other's fates, Princess Katya and her consort Starbride seek to reclaim their kingdom from the magic-wielding madman who seized the throne and is murdering their people. (978-1-62639-053-9)

Season of the Wolf by Robin Summers. Two women running from their pasts are thrust together by an unimaginable evil. Can they overcome the horrors that haunt them in time to save each other? (978-1-62639-043-0)

The Heat of Angels by Lisa Girolami. Fires burn in more than one place in Los Angeles. (978-1-62639-042-3)

Desperate Measures by P. J. Trebelhorn. Homicide detective Kay Griffith and contractor Brenda Jansen meet amidst turmoil neither of them is aware of until murder suspect Tommy Rayne makes his move to exact revenge on Kay. (978-1-62639-044-7)

The Magic Hunt by L.L. Raand. With her Pack being hunted by human extremists and beset by enemies masquerading as friends, can Sylvan protect them and her mate, or will she succumb to the feral rage that threatens to turn her rogue, destroying them all? A Midnight Hunters novel. (978-1-62639-045-4)